all our
summers

holly chamberlin

KENSINGTON BOOKS
www.kensingtonbooks.com

KENSINGTON BOOKS are published by

Kensington Publishing Corp.
119 West 40th Street
New York, NY 10018

All Kensington titles, imprints, and distributed lines are available at special quantity discounts for bulk purchases for sales promotion, premiums, fund-raising, educational, or institutional use.

Special book excerpts or customized printings can also be created to fit specific needs. For details, write or phone the office of the Kensington Sales Manager: Kensington Publishing Corp., 119 West 40th Street, New York, NY 10018. Attn. Sales Department. Phone: 1-800-221-2647.

Kensington and the K logo Reg. U.S. Pat. & TM Off.

ISBN-13: 978-1-4967-1923-2 (ebook)
ISBN-10: 1-4967-1923-9 (ebook)

ISBN-13: 978-1-4967-1922-5
ISBN-10: 1-4967-1922-0
First Kensington Trade Paperback Printing: July 2020

10 9 8 7 6 5 4 3 2 1

Printed in the United States of America

As always, for Stephen
And this time, also for Veronica Donner

Acknowledgments

Thanks once again to the best editor I could ever hope to have, John Scognamiglio.

Thanks also to Kathryn and GG for bringing light into my life, all the way from Nebraska.

This book is in memory of Joe Riillo, friend and musician extraordinaire, taken from us too soon.

For age is opportunity no less
Than youth itself, though in another dress,
And as the evening twilight fades away
The sky is filled with stars, invisible by day.

—Henry Wadsworth Longfellow

Chapter 1

It was a beautiful, early summer day in the town of Yorktide, Maine. The temperature was politely hovering around seventy-five, the humidity was low, and the pink and white peonies were in magnificent bloom.

Summer was Bonnie Ascher Elgort's favorite time of the year. It didn't matter that she was spending the day at Ferndean House, her family's homestead, dusting and polishing furniture, vacuuming rugs and draperies, keeping an eye out for spiders, and checking for burned-out lightbulbs. The windows were open and the cooing of a pair of mourning doves filled the air. Life was good.

Bonnie leaned over the deep kitchen sink to scrub at a mark on the backsplash. The motion caused an ache in her shoulder. At sixty-two, Bonnie was heavier than she had ever been. She knew she had lost about half an inch in height; she could see how her shoulders were slightly hunched. It didn't bother her; she still felt strong, and that was what mattered. Her medium-brown hair had dulled a bit over time, and since her husband Ken's illness and death it had become threaded with gray. This didn't trouble Bonnie. She had been told by friends that she had a youthful air about her, though she wasn't really sure what that meant or if it was important. Probably not.

What really mattered in life was on the inside. Unlike her sister,

Carol, Bonnie had never been particularly interested in clothes. It had been years since she had worn a pretty dress and carried a fancy bag, and that had been at the wedding of a friend's grandson. And, of course, there had been Ken's funeral a year ago come September. As the grieving widow, form had required her to make a certain appearance and she had, in the only skirt, blouse, and jacket that still fit her. Shoes had been a problem. Her daughter, Julie, had taken her to one of the outlets in Kittery, where after a grueling hour or two they had finally found a pair of tan low-heeled pumps. Bonnie had not worn them since the funeral. Maybe she would wear them to her granddaughter's high school graduation in a few years.

Bonnie moved from the kitchen into the dining room, where she ran a dustcloth over the carved bits of the massive oak sideboard that held pride of place. It was one of Bonnie's favorite pieces in the house. No one was quite sure who had brought it to Ferndean or when, but the sideboard had been there as long as Bonnie could remember. Truth be told, almost every single piece of heavy furniture, every knickknack no matter how cracked or otherwise damaged, every painting darkened with age and lack of professional care, every plate and saucer decorated with a pattern long out of fashion, held special meaning for Bonnie.

Which was why it had not been difficult for her to come to a decision about her future. She would sell the cottage in Yorktide in which she and Ken had lived for all of their married lives and move permanently into her family home. Ferndean House had been left equally to Bonnie and Carol by their parents, Shirley and Ronald Ascher, but Carol lived in New York City and had done since she was nineteen. Ferndean meant nothing to Carol Ascher. It meant the world to Bonnie. It was a member of the family. It was alive.

Ferndean House, located at 23 Wolf Lane, was situated on twenty acres of land that boasted a good-size pond (a stop-off for migrating birds in autumn and home to peepers in early spring); monumental oak, pine, and maple trees; and a profusion of native ferns, high and lowbush blueberry bushes, and flowering shrubs such as azalea and rhododendron. The house itself was about three thousand square feet with two floors of rooms and an attic that had

formerly served as servants' quarters. There was a big stone fireplace in the living room; a charming front porch that ran the entire
length of the house; a back deck that had been added at some
point in the 1940s; a large flower and kitchen garden; and the puz-
zling remains of a stone structure set at one end of the large lawn
that stretched behind the house.

Ferndean had been built by Carol and Bonnie's great-grandfather
for his much younger third wife. He had named the structure after
the house in *Jane Eyre* where Jane and the blind and crippled Mr.
Rochester were reunited. The novel—only recently published—
had been his wife's favorite; indeed, it was Bonnie's favorite novel,
too. Marcus and Rosemary's wedding portrait, taken in June of
1848, still hung in Ferndean's living room, in what Bonnie had
been told was its original frame.

After Shirley Ascher's death some thirty years earlier, Bonnie
and her sister, in a rare instance of accord, had decided to rent the
big house during part of the summer season. It would be a good
source of income, most of which would go toward the upkeep of
the old place. What was left over was pure profit; that profit bene-
fited Bonnie and her family enormously, but Carol, who didn't
need an additional source of income, routinely put her share back
into the fund kept for the maintenance of the building and
grounds.

Taking up full-time residency at Ferndean House would elimi-
nate the income from seasonal renters, but Bonnie wasn't concerned. She would have cash from the sale of the cottage. Besides,
she was not an extravagant person. Her needs were small, and she
was used to living on a tight budget. All would be well going forward.

It would have to be well, Bonnie thought as she left the dining
room, because she thoroughly believed that she was entitled to full
possession of Ferndean. She was the one who had cared for Shirley
Ascher in her dying years. She was the one who had helped to raise
Carol's troubled daughter, Nicola. She was the one who had handled the management and maintenance of the family homestead
for the past thirty years.

Who had changed Shirley Ascher's soiled sheets, prepared her meals, and taken charge of administering her medicines? Who had attended Nicola's school events from the time she came to live with her aunt in Yorktide? Who had cleaned up when Ferndean's pipes had burst? Who had mowed the lawn, planted the flowers, harvested the herbs and vegetables? Who had repainted the kitchen and bathrooms every ten years? Who had dealt with the summer tenants—finding them, vetting them, cleaning up after them?

Bonnie fondly patted the curved wooden banister of the grand staircase that led to the second floor. Yes, after all these years as full-time caretaker of her family homestead, Bonnie Ascher Elgort was entitled to be Mistress of Ferndean. It was something she had been dreaming about for a long time, pushing aside Carol's claim to the house and reigning supreme. But Ken had always held her back from making waves with her sister. Ken, the calm and reasonable husband, the broker of peace, the man who had wholeheartedly accepted Carol's troubled child into his home. And Carol Ascher hadn't even had enough respect for such a wonderful man to attend his funeral.

But now that Ken was gone, there was no one to keep Bonnie from achieving her dream. That the dream was largely fueled by ancient sibling rivalry didn't make it any less desirable. On the contrary, ancient sibling rivalry gave Bonnie's dream its incredible power.

In the living room now, Bonnie straightened the framed photos that were grouped on a table draped with a yellowed lace cloth. The entire family was represented, from Marcus and Rosemary to Bonnie's granddaughter, Sophie. Bonnie was especially fond of her parents' wedding portrait. Both looked so young and so solemn! And here was a photograph of Bonnie and Carol taken when they were quite young, three and six, Bonnie guessed. The girls were wearing bulky snow suits; behind them, Ferndean House, laced with snow, rose in its classic New England majesty. The image was a bittersweet reminder of the happy, almost idyllic childhood the sisters had shared at Ferndean, long before Carol had abandoned her home and her family for fame and fortune in New York City.

The distinct sound of a key in the front door caused Bonnie to turn from the table of photographs. It was probably Nicola, Bonnie thought, though her niece usually knocked before entering when she saw her aunt's car in the drive.

"Hello!" Bonnie called out as she made her way to the door. She felt a smile come to her face. She always felt like smiling when Nicola was around.

The door creaked loudly as it opened inward and a woman's figure stepped inside. The dustcloth Bonnie had been holding fell to the floor. She felt her stomach drop along with it. Her right hand went to her heart.

"What are *you* doing here?" she gasped.

Chapter 2

New York City
Two weeks earlier

The past few days had been unseasonably warm; heat seemed to rise visibly from the concrete sidewalks and to shimmer in waves above the busy streets. Even though she would be comfortably seated in an air-conditioned, chauffeur-driven town car, Carol was glad she didn't have to commute from her home on the Upper West Side to her office in Chelsea and back again.

The reason that Carol Ascher was able to avoid the steamy streets of Manhattan was because a month earlier she had sold her business—Ascher Interior Design—to her long-time, dedicated, and very talented junior partner. There was no doubt in Carol's mind that the company she had birthed and raised would find as much success in the future as it had found in the past. Still, there were several moments each day when Carol effectively forgot that she was no longer at the helm. When she realized with a start that she was no longer needed. When she found herself worrying about things for which she was no longer required to worry.

Carol passed through the hallway that led from her bedroom at one end of the apartment. As was her habit, she glanced at her image in the Art Deco mirror that hung over a black lacquer occasional table just outside the living room. She was pleased with what she saw. She hated that awful term sometimes used to describe a woman who appeared younger than her biological age. Well-preserved. Like a bit of dinosaur bone at the Museum of Natural History. What Carol was, in fact, was well taken care of. She got regular therapeutic massages; attended Pilates and yoga classes; had her hair professionally cut and colored every five weeks; and took her vitamin, calcium, blood pressure, and cholesterol pills as recommended by her doctor. At sixty-five, she was as tall and straight as she had been at nineteen, when she first arrived in New York City.

Even as a child Carol Ascher had instinctively known that appearances were important. As an adult, her wardrobe was highly curated; she favored a small handful of well-established designers. Her jewelry collection was comprised of basics from some of the big houses—Bulgari, Van Cleef & Arpels, Tiffany & Co.—as well as unique creations by several contemporary independent designers. She owned a Hermès bag that had cost more than she guessed her sister, Bonnie, had spent on bags, shoes, and coats in her lifetime. She owned a vintage Cartier diamond ring that had cost almost as much as the four years of Nicola's college tuition.

Like most responsible parents, Carol intended to leave the bulk of her estate to her child. But given the kind of woman Nicola had become since moving in with her aunt and uncle ten years earlier, Carol highly doubted that she would get any pleasure from the Hermès bag, the Cartier ring, or the Chanel suits. The paintings and sculptures she might admire. But maybe not. In many ways, Nicola Ascher had become a stranger to her mother.

With that in mind, Carol had begun to consider that it might be worth leaving a few of the precious or particularly meaningful items originally intended for Nicola to someone who would truly enjoy them. It was at this point that she met an impediment. She had no godchild. She was not close to the children of her acquaintances or colleagues. As for the other members of her family, well, with the possible exception of her seventy-year-old cousin, Judith, there was no one who appreciated good design and craftsmanship like she did.

Carol was bothered when she realized this. It was human nature to want to leave a legacy, to pass along a skill, a passion, a treasured object to a person you cared about. There was, of course, her former junior partner, now owner of Ascher Interior Design. But the truth was that Carol and Ana had never been close outside of the office. Carol had wanted it that way.

From the living room, Carol passed into the library. It was her favorite room in the apartment, light and airy in spite of the thousands of books, the carefully selected objets d'art, and the grand piano that had once belonged to one of the most prestigious of Old New York families. This morning, however, only one item was of interest to Carol. She picked up a card that sat on the three-legged, marble-topped table by one of the windows. The card was a note from a client and her husband, expressing gratitude for Carol's having made a generous donation to the research foundation seeking a cure for the childhood illness that had recently taken their seven-year-old son.

The boy's death had hit Carol hard. Very hard, even though she had met little Jonathan only once. Jonathan had been a charmer. Bright, socially adept, physically beautiful. His death—untimely, unfair, ghastly—had brought home to Carol with the force of a thunderclap the fact of her relative isolation in the world. Forget about who would cherish her possessions after her death. The more important question was: Who would mourn her?

Because this vital question had been haunting her for weeks, Carol had finally decided it was time to make peace with her family. That might be easier said than done. Carol had not heard from Nicola since a phone call Christmas morning. Nicola's tone had been markedly cold. And there had been a sharp decline in Bonnie's correspondence since Ken's death the previous September. Carol had not been able to attend the funeral; she had been in India on business. Maybe she should have visited her sister upon her return to the States.

But she hadn't.

Well, Carol thought, returning the card of thanks to the marble-topped table, she was going home now. To Yorktide. Better late than never.

Still, she had yet to put her apartment on the market, though she knew Realtors would eagerly line up for the chance to sell the home of famous interior designer Carol Ascher, a perfectly appointed, nine-room apartment with views of Central Park.

The reason for her procrastination was both simple and not so simple. Nicola's bedroom. Everything in the room was exactly as it had been the day Nicola had gone to live with her aunt in Maine. To dismantle the room would be in some way dismantling the most precious part of Carol's past. Nicola's childhood.

Carol straightened her already-straight shoulders and briskly banished the mood of melancholy that was suddenly threatening to overwhelm her. She would sell the apartment as soon as possible. A person was more important than four walls and a jumbled assortment of dolls, board games, and sparkly headbands.

Nothing would stand in the way of her homecoming, Carol thought as she strode from the library to her home office, not even her family's possible—probable?—refusal to see her if they were given advance warning. To that end, Carol had decided to show up in Yorktide unannounced, where Ferndean House, the family homestead, awaited. Carol still had a key. And the house was currently empty; for some unfathomable reason, Bonnie hadn't booked summer renters yet. But that was perfect; the sooner Carol could get started with major renovations on the old place the better. For all she knew parts of the building were structurally unsound, in spite of her brother-in-law's assurance that Ferndean continued to pass inspections.

Carol sat at her desk and opened her laptop. She was fully aware that taking your enemy by surprise might be considered a power play.

Enemy? Carol frowned. That was the wrong word. Adversary? That was a bit harsh, too. Well, whatever the term, Carol expected some resistance to the idea of her occupying Ferndean House. Bonnie could be contrary where Carol was concerned, but that didn't really worry her. Once Bonnie heard her sister's more than generous offer for her share of the Victorian wreck that had been left to the Ascher girls, she would happily sign on the dotted line.

Successful, wealthy, universally admired businessperson that she was, Carol Ascher was sure of it.

Chapter 3

Gilbert Way was one of the least attractive streets in Yorktide. It was on the very outskirts of the town, a generally forgotten area occupied by the poorest of the community. Nicola Ascher's apartment was on the third floor of what had once been a rooming house. The original wooden building had been re-covered with vinyl siding. The small front porch felt loosely attached to the structure. Her apartment, one of seven in the building, was reached by two sets of steep, narrow wooden stairs that smelled suspiciously of mold. The landing outside her apartment was grim. The floors were badly in need of refinishing; her neighbor was in the habit of piling all of his shoes and boots in a heap next to his door; and every so often there was a vague smell of rotting food emanating, it seemed, from the walls themselves.

All of the tenants at number 35 were young and either just starting out in their careers or not much concerned with a career at all. Most were living alone. The guy in the apartment just above Nicola's liked to throw weeknight parties that involved insanely loud techno-pop. After a third incident, Nicola had approached him and asked that the next time he gave a party he be aware that some of his neighbors had to get up early for work. That had done the trick. For a while.

Nicola would not easily forget the first time her aunt and uncle had seen the apartment on Gilbert Way. They had not been happy about their beloved niece living in such a rough and tumble place. When Ken died the previous September, Bonnie had suggested that Nicola move back into the cottage. Though grateful, and sympathetic of her aunt's sudden loneliness, Nicola had declined. She needed to maintain a degree of independence. She was, after all, twenty-five years old.

She had done her best to make the apartment attractive, but she was no interior designer like her mother. She had been happy enough to decorate the tiny apartment with hand-me-downs, a few posters she had had since college, and a selection of framed photos of her family. There was a photo of her aunt Bonnie and her uncle Ken taken at last year's Fourth of July party at Ferndean House. There was a portrait of her cousin Julie, Julie's husband, Scott, and their daughter, Sophie, taken at the mall one Christmas season when Sophie was a toddler. There was a photo of her aunt's cousin Judith taken at Nicola's high school graduation. There were no photos of her mother.

Nicola walked from the tiny kitchen area to the tiny living area, glancing as she did at the antique silvered mirror that hung on the wall. The mirror had been a great flea market find. The image reflected back at Nicola wasn't clear, but it didn't need to be. Nicola knew well enough what she looked like. Her eyes were not her mother's famously steely gray ones. Presumably she had inherited her brown eyes from her nameless and faceless father. Her hair was light brown; she often cut it herself. Given the nature of her job as a social worker at Pine Hill Residence for the Elderly—and her own preference—she regularly wore clothes that were serviceable rather than attractive. When she thought about the last year she had lived in New York—which she rarely did—she was always surprised to recall her near obsession with the latest fad in clothing and bags and shoes. She knew now that her interest hadn't really been in those popular items but in the popular kids who were the first to wear them. What a waste of time and money! Then again, she had only been a child.

Like her mother—and presumably her father, that unknown sperm donor—Nicola was tall and slim. She wasn't what her aunt

Bonnie would call a man magnet, but she did attract a fair amount of male attention, most of which she deflected almost unconsciously. Rarely was her interest aroused and when it was, it didn't last for long. In fact, Nicola had been in only one long-term romantic relationship. She wasn't a virgin. But she wasn't experienced, either. She had never dreamed about marrying. Falling in love—maybe. That was probably inevitable. Like death and taxes, things you just couldn't escape, but hopefully more pleasant than either.

Nicola Ascher got along well with just about everybody. There were members of her circle of coworkers, former classmates, and neighbors with whom she was friendly, even, at times, briefly confidential. But as for an intimate friend, there was no one. And that was okay. Nicola genuinely liked people. It was one of the reasons she had gone into social work. She just didn't need one particular person to be at her side—literally or virtually—at all times.

In short, she wasn't unhappy. Still, for the past few months she had felt that there was something *else* she could be doing, another way in which she could be helping others and leading a productive life. The answer, Nicola thought, might be the Peace Corps. And she had decided she would like to be stationed in Ukraine. She couldn't explain her preference other than the fact that she felt instinctually drawn to the culture and history of Eastern Europe. The more she read, the more interested she became.

Her aunt Bonnie had frowned at this. "It could be terribly dangerous," she said.

"The Peace Corps educates you about the region you're being posted to," Nicola had told her. "There can be risks, but people need help."

"But you're needed here," Bonnie had pointed out, her distress evident. "You do such important work at Pine Hill. And . . . and I need you. We all do, Julie and Sophie, too, especially now that Ken is gone and Scott . . . Well, with the troubles in the marriage."

"I'm aware of how my absence might affect my family," Nicola had replied carefully. "But I can't feel guilty for wanting to move on and do something for the greater good. You'll be fine, Aunt Bonnie. I know you will. Besides, I'll be back in two years and we'll be in touch as often as possible, I promise."

Assuming, of course, that Nicola went through with the notion. In truth, while the idea of service attracted her, sometimes she wondered if her motives for wanting to help others were entirely pure. Everyone knew that when you helped another person you often felt good about yourself as a result. That was selfish, but not the bad kind of selfish. But what if she was so insistent on being of service to others as a sort of rebuke to her mother, that supremely self-centered woman who had abandoned her own child in her moment of crisis? Could Nicola have some sort of saint complex, the need to prove to the world that she was better, more self-sacrificing than the average person? Was she ever smug about her intention of joining the Peace Corps?

No. She didn't think that she was. She hoped that she wasn't. And if she did ever act obnoxiously, who would tell her the truth? She hoped that someone would, though her aunt Bonnie did tend to coddle her, and Julie never said a critical word to anyone, no matter how justified. Judith. Judith would call her on bad behavior, Nicola thought. It was something she managed to do with the people she cared about without alienating them in the process.

Nicola's cell phone chirped; it was the tone she had chosen for Bonnie.

"Hi," she said. "What's up?"

"Your mother has come home."

"Who?" Nicola replied senselessly. "Wait. What do you mean? Yorktide isn't my mother's home."

"Tell that to her." Her aunt's voice cracked as if she was struggling not to cry. "She's moved into Ferndean House. Nicola, you have to help me. I don't know what to do."

Chapter 4

The Millers' house on Thames Road was small, not much larger than the cottage in which Julie had grown up, but it had always suited her just fine. She and Scott had managed to buy it only a few years into their marriage. They had scrimped and saved to come up with a decent down payment. Julie would never forget the day they closed on the house. Next to her wedding and the birth of her daughter, it was the most momentous occasion of her life.

Now, almost eighteen years later, on this early summer afternoon, Julie Miller found herself wandering from the living room to the kitchen, from upstairs to downstairs, noting her surroundings with something akin to surprise. It was almost as if she was in a stranger's home. Or, as if Julie was the stranger in her own home. She felt disoriented.

Julie Miller, the forty-two-year old daughter of Bonnie and Ken Elgort, was about five feet three inches tall. She had dark brown hair, which she wore in a bob. If she could, she would live in jeans, sweatshirts, and sneakers, but for work she made the concession of dressing like the responsible adult she was paid to be. Still, managing a group of five-year-olds for several hours a day required low heels, fabrics that could be sponged clean or tossed in the washing machine, and absolutely no dangling jewelry. Aside from a watch, the only other bit of jewelry Julie regularly wore was her wedding ring, a plain gold band.

Julie was not pretty; her personality, her intelligence, and her good heart were her strong points. Early in her relationship with Scott she had wondered what he could possibly see in her, the ugly duckling to his swan. But she had gotten past that insecurity, convinced by his words and actions that he was in love with her precisely because she was who she was.

These days Julie wasn't convinced of anything other than that her life was a mess.

The summer months stretched out painfully empty before her. True, there was the three-session workshop headed by the principal of Yorktide's grammar school, to which she had committed ages ago. Still, time seemed Julie's enemy. In past summers, she had taken part-time jobs, waiting tables at one of the big family-style restaurants along Route 1 or working as a sales assistant at a seasonal shop in Ogunquit, but this year she had made no effort to look for employment. It was irresponsible. But Julie felt stuck.

Julie *was* stuck.

And she was lonely. She and Aggie, her best friend, were not in a good place at the moment. They had known each other since kindergarten and had gone through grammar, middle, and high school together. Aggie had attended a college in New Hampshire while Julie had earned her degree at the University of Maine, but they had remained close. Julie had been Aggie's maid of honor and Aggie had been hers. When Aggie's first child was born prematurely, Julie had stationed herself at the hospital both day and night until little Colleen was ready to go home.

But then something nasty and vile had come between them. Julie's husband, Scott, had cheated on her, not with Aggie, but Aggie had known about the infidelity—at least she had heard rumors—and had failed to tell Julie. That act of betrayal had destroyed a relationship that had been born close to forty years before.

No job. No best friend. And certainly no summer getaways. Should Scott, for some unfathomable reason, suggest a camping trip in Acadia National Park or even a weekend in Booth Bay, Julie would have no choice but to refuse. The entire town of Yorktide would be waiting eagerly to witness the results of the vacation. Had the couple reconciled, or was Julie Miller still refusing to forgive and forget her husband's transgression?

At least fifteen-year-old Sophie had an exciting summer to look forward to, Julie thought, as she continued her slow ramble through the house. Sophie had gotten a job as a counselor at a local day camp. It paid very little, but it kept her busy three days of the week. How good she was with the children, Julie didn't know; probably not very. Sophie had never shown any great interest in children. The real draw of the job for Sophie was the opportunity to hang out with other teens, several of whom lived in neighboring towns. Julie had heard her daughter mention a few names she didn't recognize as Sophie's classmates, all of whom Sophie had known since first grade. There was a Tom, or maybe it was Tim. He was a few years older than Sophie. And some girl named Stacy. Maybe another boy; Julie couldn't recall and when she remembered to ask Sophie about her fellow counselors, Sophie was typically uncommunicative. "They're fine." "They're okay."

Julie never pressed. Sophie was a good kid and besides, if she had a problem with one of her coworkers she would come to her mother. Or she would go to her grandmother or to Nicola. Sophie was fine.

It was her mother who was not fine.

Julie was depressed and it showed. She had forgotten about her last hair appointment and hadn't bothered to make another. She had gained weight. She was still gaining weight. She felt sluggish but had no energy to do anything about it. She hadn't been for a hike in weeks. The last time she had been on her bike had been back in the spring. The bike was propped against a wall of the garage. The tires needed air.

There was more. The house was getting out of control. Julie wandered over to the foot of the stairs that led to the second floor and picked up a crumpled T-shirt draped over the banister. It was Sophie's and it was dirty. When had Julie last done laundry? When had she last dusted the blinds or vacuumed the rugs?

She dropped the T-shirt back onto the banister. The laundry would get done when it got done.

Julie made her way into the kitchen. Several photographs of Sophie were stuck to the fridge with magnets in the shape of oranges, apples, and bananas. In the most recent photo, Sophie was proudly modeling the new coat her grandmother and her cousin, Judith, had chipped in to buy her for Christmas.

Sophie had her father's build, tall and slim. She wore her dark brown hair long, as did most of the girls at Yorktide High. She had her mother's eyes, which were wide set, very blue, and surrounded by long, thick lashes. When Sophie was thirteen, a boy at school had told her that her eyes were beautiful. That afternoon she had spent almost forty minutes and all of her allowance in the makeup aisle of Hannaford's pharmacy department, choosing eye shadows and pencils and liners. Julie had talked to her about not allowing a boy's opinion—good or bad—to influence her decisions, and about how real beauty was found in nature and not in artifice. Sophie had seemed to listen but had stuck with the heavy makeup for a while until, Julie supposed, she simply got tired of spending so much time layering it on and scraping it off. The half-empty tubes and used brushes were still piled in the top drawer of Sophie's dresser.

Still, Sophie was undoubtedly vain. Of course, it was possible that what Julie saw as vanity was in fact simply a realistic appreciation of the self. And, Sophie had never displayed any signs of the anxiety and depression that had plagued her mother at various times in her life. That was a very good thing.

The ringing of the landline brought Julie back from her musings. She recognized the number on the phone. It was one of her neighbors. She debated letting the call go to voice mail. Then, on the fifth ring, she picked up the receiver. She didn't know why she did.

"Hi, Janet," she said flatly.

"Did you hear the news?" Janet asked, her voice squeaky with excitement. "Your aunt Carol is back!"

"What do you mean?" Julie asked wearily. There was absolutely no privacy in a small town. It was a big part of why she was suffering so badly in the wake of Scott's betrayal.

"I mean, she's here in Yorktide. Rumor has it she's staying at Ferndean House instead of one of the big hotels she usually stays at."

"She's probably just on vacation," Julie said. She didn't really care one way or the other.

"Maybe," Janet admitted. "But don't you think it strange that she's at the Ascher family homestead? I mean—"

"I have to go," Julie said abruptly. "Goodbye."

Only after she had hung up did the news begin to sink in. If it was true that Carol Ascher was staying at Ferndean . . . But so what if she was? It didn't necessarily mean that Bonnie's plans to sell the cottage and move into Ferndean were in any danger. Unless . . .

Julie reached again for the receiver. As she punched in her mother's number, she realized that for a few moments at least, Janet's news had served to turn her attention away from her own emotional pain.

That was interesting.

Chapter 5

"You looked stressed," Judith said. "Sit. Relax."

Bonnie's cousin, Judith, was the only child of Shirley Ascher's sister Mary and her husband, Matthew. She wasn't much older than Bonnie, but she often acted like a mother-figure. Though Bonnie might never have said so, she appreciated the fact that Judith was strong and wise.

Nicola took her aunt's arm and led her to the kitchen table. "Judith is right. I'll make some tea."

"I don't want any tea," Bonnie said, sinking into a seat.

"Julie came and went in a hurry," Judith noted.

Bonnie restrained a sigh. Julie had stopped by earlier, but finding her mother with Nicola and Judith she had rapidly taken off again.

"She looks so sad," Nicola said, taking the third seat at the table.

"She has reason to be," Bonnie murmured.

Truth be told, from the very start of her daughter's relationship with Scott, Bonnie had been doubtful about the long-term success of the pair. It was an unpalatable fact that often in relationships where the man was markedly more attractive than the woman things would go wrong. And if Scott wasn't exactly vain, he was not unaware of his physical appeal. If only Julie had fallen in love with an average-looking guy with a manageable interest in sex. But no one could dictate matters of the heart. More was the pity.

But while Bonnie was angry with Scott for messing up so badly, she still loved him. He had always been respectful of her and of Ken; in a way, with his parents gone to Florida many years ago, he had come to treat the Elgorts as his parents. And he was a good father to Sophie, if a bit lenient in ways Bonnie thought he shouldn't be. But that was the Millers' business, not hers.

What bothered Bonnie most about the situation was the fact that her daughter was being forced to heal in the full glare of the publicity surrounding Scott's actions. Not that Julie was healing; she seemed to be suffering more keenly as time went on. It was all so unfair, but then again, no one had ever promised that life would be fair.

Bonnie turned to Judith. "Did you know my sister was planning to show up unannounced?" she asked.

"Of course not. I haven't spoken to Carol in ages. And if I had known she was intending to resurface in Yorktide, I would have told you immediately."

"Why did you allow her into Ferndean?" Nicola demanded.

"The house is half hers," Judith pointed out.

Bonnie nodded. "Judith is right. I couldn't exactly push her off the porch or slam the door in her face."

Nicola folded her arms across her chest. "Well, I don't want to see her."

Judith sighed. "Don't be ridiculous."

"Why should I want anything to do with her? She threw me out when I was only fifteen!"

"That's not what happened and you know it," Judith said sternly.

Bonnie frowned. That was debatable. "There's more," she said. "Though she says she doesn't want the town to know yet, she's intending on making Yorktide her home again. She wants to buy me out of my share of Ferndean."

"She can't do that!" Nicola cried.

Judith whistled. "So, what are her terms, exactly?"

"She didn't give me details. I . . ." Bonnie swallowed hard. "I ran off before she could. I was just so shocked."

"You need a lawyer." Nicola reached for her cell phone. "I know someone who might be able to help."

Judith put her hand on Nicola's. "I suggest we all calm down. There's no need for panic. We need to hear what else Carol has to say."

"What's the point?" Bonnie sighed resignedly. "Carol always spoils things for me."

Judith raised an eyebrow but said nothing.

"We won't let her spoil this for you," Nicola said firmly.

Bonnie wished she could believe her niece. But since Carol Ascher had abandoned her family when her younger sister was only sixteen, Bonnie had become increasingly aware that Carol got whatever Carol wanted, no matter who or what stood in the way. She was a force of nature; she always had been. Way back when they were children, Bonnie had been happily in thrall to Carol, awed by her, entertained by her. And, she had thought, loved by her.

But then . . .

"Aunt Bonnie?" Nicola was frowning worriedly. "Are you okay? You look—gray."

"I'm making that tea," Judith said, rising from her seat. "And if you happen to have a bottle of brandy, a bit of that wouldn't go amiss, either."

Chapter 6

Growing up, friends had envied Carol Ascher living at Ferndean, but she had never shared their enthusiasm. Something about the proportions of the big, old house were unpleasing to her eye. The windows, with a few exceptions, were too small, and the slope of the floors, grown worse over time, made her feel slightly queasy. Add to that the fact that Carol's personal tastes had always been very different from those of her mother and the other Ascher women who had gone before. She found the flocked wallpaper in the hallways fussy, the muddy brown paint in the living room depressing, and the hugely hideous sideboard in the dining room an eyesore.

Carol wandered into the den and over to the room's one window. She touched the heavy draperies and cringed. They were dreadfully ugly. Carol remembered when her mother had bought them; she had hated them from the start. The draperies would go into the trash; the room would benefit from as much natural light as its one window would allow. And the rug would go, too. It was threadbare.

Having had enough of the gloomy den, Carol returned to the living room. Knickknacks and doodads and tacky souvenirs of the seaside covered every surface. Nothing in the room worked harmoniously, at least not for someone with Carol's aesthetic sensibility.

Colors clashed, textures argued with one another, and furniture from various periods clamored for attention.

But the décor could be dealt with later. At the moment, the most interesting matter for Carol to consider was Bonnie's reaction to finding her sibling on the doorstep. Carol had anticipated Bonnie's being surprised, but she had not imagined that she would literally run off after only a brief conversation. Carol lowered herself gingerly onto a small love seat. The cushion was rock hard but at least it supported her.

It seemed that reuniting with her family was going to be more of a challenge than Carol had anticipated. She would need to convince them that she was in earnest about wanting to become part of their lives again. But so much time had passed. And Carol herself had been the architect of the family's existing emotional structure. Carol Ascher versus Bonnie and the others.

There was a reason for this. There had been a period in Carol's life, after a major surgery, when she had become addicted to prescription opioids. That addiction had been a major factor in her decision to send her daughter away from home to live with her aunt and uncle in Maine.

No one in Carol's family or among her acquaintances had ever known about the addiction; in order to keep fast her dark secret, Carol had grown more reserved, self-sufficient, even isolated over time, and though the addiction had been conquered years ago, the habit of secrecy had survived its death.

Now, Carol knew that she had been too much alone for too long.

And she was tired. She was sixty-five and while that was not aged by contemporary standards, she had been on the go for so many years that sometimes she felt as if she were seventy-five. Or eighty.

And there was no one in New York to stay for. She had friends, but they were not close friends. It was the way she had always been, a casual connector. But now she was seeing the end of her life—even if it turned out to be fifteen or so years away—and it didn't feel quite so good being solitary and self-sufficient.

And there was the death of that poor little boy. It had hit her so hard.

The solution seemed easy. She would settle at Ferndean, secure in the knowledge that her family was living close by. She could see them whenever she wanted.

Assuming they wanted to see her.

Suddenly, Carol felt afraid. A picture of Nicola's empty bedroom back at the New York apartment flashed before her mind's eye.

So much in her life had been lost. And what had been gained?

Carol got up and headed for the kitchen. She wasn't hungry, but she would find something to eat among the groceries she had brought in earlier. She would need to keep up her strength.

Chapter 7

Nicola sat curled up in the one armchair she owned. It wasn't very comfortable, but she didn't really mind. She had bought it at a secondhand shop; it had been cheap and relatively clean. She was trying to read a jaunty popular mystery, but her mind would not let go of the crisis suddenly facing her family. The audacity of her mother, to show up out of the blue and announce what was basically a coup d'état!

Well, sort of.

How she missed her uncle Ken! Nicola sighed and let the mystery novel drop to the floor. She wished he were still around to tell her mother to go away and leave them alone. People listened to Ken.

But Carol Ascher never listened to anyone. She did what she wanted when she wanted. Which was probably the reason she had chosen to have a child in the way that she had. Entirely on her own terms, terms she had attempted to explain to Nicola when Nicola was five.

There was no daddy in the house because her father was an anonymous man who had donated his sperm so that she could be born. A simple story that meant absolutely nothing. For a while, Nicola had thought her father's name was Andyomous. That was what her mother had said, wasn't it?

Growing up, Nicola had never given all that much thought to

her anonymous sperm donor father. Lots of her New York friends' parents were divorced, and missing—or too many—parents were almost the norm. For some, it was even a point of honor to be the child of an "interesting" home, not one of those deadly boring two-parent, heterosexual households that had been done to death and badly by just about everyone who was no one. There were even a few other kids at Nicola's school whose fathers were anonymous sperm donors. No big deal.

Still.

At the age of ten, Nicola told a new girl at school that her father was in hiding, the hereditary prince of a country she was under strict orders never to name in case the information somehow led to his discovery.

At the age of twelve, Nicola told a cute boy she met at summer camp that her mother had shown her the résumé her biological father had submitted to the agency that had arranged for her conception. He was a brilliant scientist. He had three doctorates and spoke seven languages. He was also a descendant of George Washington.

When she moved to Maine at the age of fifteen, Nicola finally found herself with a very satisfactory, flesh-and-blood father figure. Pretty much all thoughts of her biological father vanished. She was happy to consider Ken her dad.

Only when Ken died did Nicola begin, for the first time in her life, to experience a sense of curiosity about her biological father, the real man, not a figure of her fantasy. The fact that she knew nothing about him—What month was he born? Who was his favorite artist? Did he have brothers and sisters?—suddenly felt almost unbearably frustrating. For the first time in her life she felt rootless. Not entirely, but enough to cause distress.

Nicola leaned her head against the back of the chair and sighed. Still, as much as she craved a sense of rootedness, she had no desire to search for the anonymous sperm donor. First, the search was likely to be fruitless. Second, what if she did manage to find him? She could never approach him; if he had wanted to claim his child, he would have been a "known donor." No, a sense of her real place in the world would have to be found elsewhere. If it could be found anywhere.

One thing was for sure. A sense of security and purpose could have nothing to do with the reemergence of her mother in Yorktide.

Nicola knew that for a fact.

Chapter 8

Julie was heating frozen dinners. It was not the healthiest choice she might have made for her family, but she found that she didn't much care if she served them heavily salted processed food loaded with fats and cholesterol. Only weeks earlier she would have been washing fresh greens and slicing lean meat.

But that was in another lifetime.

As she waited for the microwave to bring the meals to life, Julie's thoughts drifted to the strange situation in which her mother currently found herself. One thing was clear. Bonnie didn't deserve Carol's high-handed treatment, especially after all that she had done for the family, starting with the death of Julie's grandfather.

Ronald Ascher had passed out behind the wheel of his car; later, the doctors told the family that he had died of cardiac arrest. His death came as a terrible shock. Ronald and Shirley had had plans to spend a night in Portland, a rare treat. Ronald had been in the middle of several house projects, including the reconstruction of part of Ferndean's front porch. And he had recently joined the newly formed Men's Charitable Association at church.

Carol had paid for the wake, funeral, and burial. Bonnie had handled the details and carried the bulk of her mother's emotional burden. Carol arrived in Yorktide two days before the services and left two days afterward. Duty done.

Not long after Ronald's passing, Shirley fell gravely ill. It was a virulent cancer. Carol sent money but left the day-to-day care and decision making to her sister. For the last month of Julie's grandmother's life, Bonnie lived with her mother at Ferndean, while Ken stayed at the cottage with Julie. Bonnie Ascher had never complained, not once.

Years later, Bonnie had taken in her sister's daughter. Again, she had never complained.

The timer on the microwave went off and Julie removed the ready-made meals. If anyone deserved Ferndean House, she thought, it was Bonnie Ascher Elgort.

"What's for dinner? I'm starved."

It was Sophie. She was wearing a pair of jeans that left little to the imagination. Ordinarily, Julie would have said something on the order of, How can you breathe in those things? but now she said nothing.

Julie brought their meals to the table. They were still in their aluminum servers.

Sophie wrinkled her nose. "Since when do we eat this stuff?"

"Since now." Scott walked into the room. "Thank your mother for making the effort."

Sophie said nothing but plopped into her usual seat. Julie knew that by scolding Sophie, Scott was trying to show his respect for his wife. She didn't care.

"Nicola told me her mother wants to buy Grandma out of her share of Ferndean," Sophie announced, her fork poised dubiously over her food. "Nicola is so pissed."

"Don't use that word," Scott said.

His daughter ignored him. "What's the big deal if Carol wants to live there?"

"It's a long story," Julie said wearily. "The short of it is that Grandma deserves the house."

Scott cleared his throat. "Maybe you shouldn't get involved if Bonnie and Carol are going to start tussling," he said. "You have enough to worry about. Not worry about," he added hastily. "I just mean, you have—"

"Don't tell me what I should and should not do," Julie said quietly. She poked her fork into the food on her plate but didn't lift it to her mouth.

"I wasn't. I just thought that . . ."

Julie kept her eyes glued to her plate. "Well, don't. Don't just think."

The sound of a utensil clanging against the table made Julie jump.

"I'm done," Sophie announced.

"You've hardly touched your dinner," Scott said.

"I said, I'm done. I can't eat with you two . . ." Sophie shook her head. "Never mind."

"It's okay," Julie said. "You can go."

Sophie got up and left the kitchen. The pounding of feet on the stairs made it clear that she was headed for her room.

"We need to talk," Scott said quietly.

"Not now." Julie pushed her chair back. It scraped against the floor. She picked up Sophie's plate and took it over to the trash bin. She heard Scott get up from the table.

Julie was alone.

She had known when she met Scott that he had a reputation as a player, but she hadn't minded at first; Scott was cute and funny and kindhearted. It was only after they had been dating for several months and Julie realized that she might be falling in love did she fear that Scott's past behavior might interfere with their becoming a real couple. So, she had worked up the courage to confront him with her concerns. He swore he hadn't cheated on her since they had been dating. He swore that he hadn't even wanted to, not since he had realized he was in love with her. "Things are different with you," he told her. "Better."

Julie believed him. Their relationship grew stronger. Everyone could see that they were devoted to each other. Yorktide began to think that Scott Miller was a reformed man.

But he wasn't. Not yet. He told Julie about his one-night stand before anyone else in Yorktide could. Maybe he wanted to spare Julie as much pain as he could by preparing her for any public scrutiny that was to come. He swore he would never again cheat on Julie. Julie, touched and impressed by his honesty, forgave him.

Miraculously, no one ever found out about Scott's indiscretion. If they had, they would have talked. Such is the nature of a small town.

A few months later, Scott asked Julie to marry him. He couldn't afford an engagement ring, but Julie didn't care. She happily accepted his proposal. She forgot about his one slip. Almost.

Scott cried at their wedding ceremony. The reception was a lot of fun. The band played on past the time they were scheduled to quit. Anyone who was still standing at five the following morning went to a popular local diner for breakfast. Yorktide talked about the party for weeks afterward.

Julie had been very happy in her marriage. The reality of Scott's infidelity hit her hard. Unhelpful people said: "You knew what Scott was like when you married him. How can you be so surprised now?" But Julie was surprised. And hurt. And angry. But not angry enough, at least, not with the person who deserved her anger.

Julie blamed herself for Scott's affair. At least, she considered herself a motivating factor in Scott's decision to cheat.

Still, she didn't want a divorce. A divorce would be financially devastating; they would have to sell the house and she would have to move in again with her mother, either in the cottage in which Julie had grown up, or, if Carol could be made to disappear, at Ferndean House. Her mother probably wouldn't mind, but Julie would. She would feel like even more of a failure than she did now.

And what would a divorce do to Sophie? She was already suffering. Could her parents splitting up really be helpful? Would Sophie choose to live with her mother and grandmother, or with her father? Sophie was mad at her father, but she was still Daddy's Little Girl, and there was no doubt that if she went to live with Scott he would spoil her rotten in an effort to make up for the chaos he had caused. That wouldn't be good for Sophie in the end, but Sophie would only be focused on how fun life was at Dad's, with a lenient curfew and him catering to her every whim.

Julie put her hand to her head. What a mess. She still loved Scott. She did. She wanted to grow old by his side. She wanted them to be like her parents had been, an utterly devoted couple. There had to be a way through this . . .

But Julie was afraid to go to couple's counseling. There was no doubt in her mind that the counselor would see her fatal flaws immediately. "You had just cause to cheat," the counselor would say to Scott. "Just look at her."

How Julie reconciled this belief with the fact that Scott Miller had a long history of being unfaithful in relationships, she didn't bother to question.

Maybe, Julie thought now, it was the decision not to have another baby that had precipitated the decline of the marriage. Originally, Scott and Julie had wanted two or three children. But after Sophie's birth, Julie went through a terrible postpartum depression that manifested itself in an overwhelming loss of energy, a sense of hopelessness, and debilitating feelings of worthlessness and shame. Her doctor had put her on an antidepressant and had referred Julie to a therapist who specialized in women's health issues. Eventually, Julie returned.

It was Scott who brought up the idea of keeping their family the way it was. "One child is perfect," he had said to his wife. "You've given us a beautiful daughter and we're so very lucky."

Julie had been worried, fearful she was letting him down, but also relieved.

Maybe he had been lying about being lucky.

Julie picked up a knife to scrape what remained of her meal and of Scott's into the trash. Instead, she used the knife as a fork to eat the leftovers, cold and unappetizing as they were. There was a box of donuts in the fridge. Julie ate them, too. Sophie would probably complain the next morning when she wanted one for breakfast.

Julie couldn't bring herself to care.

Chapter 9

Bonnie couldn't seem to put down the sponge. Her mind was racing and while wiping away invisible spots of grease from the stovetop and nonexistent smudges from the handle of the fridge was serving to occupy her time, it was not blocking the memory of a family dinner that had taken place back in February. All but Sophie had been present.

When they had gathered at Bonnie's kitchen table around a meal of roast chicken, green beans, and mashed potatoes, she had announced her plan of selling the cottage and taking sole possession of the family homestead.

"What do you mean by sole possession?" Judith had asked with a frown.

"I mean that I want to live there on my own. No renters. And I don't want any more help from Carol."

Julie had not been optimistic; she thought the plan economically foolish and said so plainly.

Nicola was thoroughly supportive of her aunt's desire, but certain that her mother would ruin Bonnie's plans for a peaceful future at Ferndean. "She'll never grant you sole residence," she said darkly. "My mother only cares about herself."

Judith agreed with Julie. "You'd be crazy to try to handle Ferndean on your own," she said. "Things are tough enough for you as it is, now that Ken is gone."

"Maybe there's a way," Scott had ventured. "Maybe you could talk to Carol and—"

Nicola had interrupted. "My mother didn't even care enough about us to come back to Yorktide for Uncle Ken's funeral. She doesn't deserve Ferndean. End of story."

"I'm glad someone here is on my side!" Bonnie remembered saying, squeezing Nicola's hand in gratitude.

"It's not a matter of taking sides," her cousin had pointed out in her maddeningly reasonable manner. "It's a matter of being realistic about the situation. And to be fair, Nicola, your mother was in India, not exactly a hop, skip, and a jump away."

To be fair.

The conversation had continued.

"It's just that it's about time I'm Mistress of Ferndean."

Judith had raised an eyebrow. "That's a bit grandiose. Mistress of Ferndean? This isn't a nineteenth-century novel. This is twenty-first century life. On a budget. Without a staff."

"I know that," Bonnie said irritably.

"Then what's your deep-down reason for wanting to live at Ferndean on your own?" Judith had pressed.

"Do you feel too sad in the cottage without Dad?" Julie asked.

"No," Bonnie had said truthfully. "Ken loved the cottage; everywhere I look I see examples of how he took such good care of our home."

Scott shook his head. "So, why do you want to sell it?"

Bonnie didn't want to say the words out loud.

Because of the almost lifelong rivalry between the Ascher sisters.

Because Bonnie felt she had been neglected and taken advantage of for too long.

"Why should I have to ask Carol for permission to move into Ferndean House?" she finally blurted.

"To keep things civil, for one," Judith had pointed out. "That and the fact that she is legally co-owner of the house and property."

"It's not like Aunt Bonnie would be doing anything underhanded," Nicola had protested.

"Exactly. I'm just going to move in and write to Carol to tell her what I've done."

"I don't claim to know Carol better than you do," Judith had said with a laugh, "but I do know her well enough to guess that she won't be thrilled with the news of a fait accompli."

Bonnie put down the sponge and dried her hands on a dishtowel. How naïve she had been! She had felt so sure that she could accomplish her goal! But she should have remembered that Carol Ascher always got what she wanted.

Case in point: the summer a traveling carnival had come to Yorktide. Thirteen-year-old Carol had been mad to attend but at the last minute, Mr. and Mrs. Ascher were called out to assist an elderly couple from their church. "We'll go to the carnival tomorrow night," Shirley Ascher promised.

"We'll go tonight," Carol said when their parents had gone.

Ten-year-old Bonnie had protested. She had seen a television show about a carnival and it had frightened her. There was loud, strange music at fairgrounds, and unsuspecting children wandered into those big peaked tents to see a six-legged donkey or a two-headed cat and they never came out again. Bonnie would only go to the carnival with her parents.

"Oh, don't be silly," Carol said. "It'll be so much fun."

Unable to say no to her sister, Bonnie found herself tagging along through a wilderness of powerful smells (popcorn and frying sausage) and troubling sights and sounds (women in beards and tinny music that hurt her ears). Malachi the Marvelous Mind Reader knew her every thought. The fortune-teller's wizened monkey ran across her shoes.

For months afterward, Bonnie had nightmares of disembodied clown faces and leering strong men and animals with too many heads. Had Carol gotten in trouble for disobeying their mother? It was unlikely.

Bonnie sat heavily at the kitchen table. For a moment, she felt absolutely and utterly lost. For the first time in her life she was on her own, forced to consider only herself when planning meals, to consult only her own desires when choosing what movie to see at the local cinema, to make the sort of decisions she had always made with a partner. The change was enormous and exhausting.

What would the rest of her life look like? What would Ken want her life to look like? Happy. Peaceful. Secure.

She should probably go back to work.

But maybe not just yet. Not until the matter of Ferndean House was settled. Until it was, her life was stalled.

Bonnie drew back her shoulders. There was no other way. She had to confront her sister, not wait around for Carol to drop another bombshell. And this time, she would not run away from the confrontation, no matter how ugly it got.

Bonnie went to her landline phone and dialed the familiar number, the one that had not changed in almost forty years.

After five rings, Carol answered. "Hello?" she said.

"It's your sister," Bonnie announced, her voice trembling. "We have to talk. About Ferndean."

Chapter 10

If only it were her cousin Judith who was coming by to discuss the future of Ferndean. Judith was the only member of her family from whom Carol did not anticipate trouble; they had always gotten along just fine.

Judith, now seventy years old, was five feet nine inches tall. Her hair was silver—Carol knew some women in New York who paid good money for that exact shade—and she wore it shoulder length. Her taste in clothing was similar to Carol's. She favored clean, classic lines in a palette of neutrals, reserving color for accessories like scarves and bags.

The resemblance between Judith and Bonnie was almost nonexistent, but Judith's resemblance to Carol was fairly pronounced. They both had what used to be called an aristocratic nose, long and narrow. They both had rather almond-shaped eyes of a peculiarly steely gray, and both had long, delicate fingers. All in all, Carol and Judith could easily be mistaken for sisters rather than cousins.

But they weren't sisters.

The doorbell rang. Carol noted that Bonnie did not use her key.

Her sister stood rigidly on the front porch. Her expression was grim.

"Come in," Carol said, gesturing with a sweep of her arm.

Bonnie marched into the house and came to an abrupt halt in the foyer.

"Beautiful weather," Carol commented. "Why don't we sit in the living room?"

Bonnie took a seat in the armchair that had been their mother's favorite. Carol perched on the arm of the couch directly across from her sister.

"Can I get you something to drink?" she asked. "Tea? Coffee?"

Bonnie shook her head. "You should probably know that Nicola is thinking of joining the Peace Corps."

Carol was caught off guard. Bonnie had delivered that bit of information with a certain smugness, almost as if she was happy to be wounding her sister with the news that Nicola was leaving Yorktide just when Carol had returned.

"Is she," Carol said flatly.

"She's hoping for a posting in Ukraine," Bonnie went on. "She's interested in all things Eastern European. I have no idea why."

"It's funny how things happen," Carol said.

Or not so funny. Because Nicola's father was not an anonymous sperm donor. His name was Alex Peters. His grandparents had come to the United States from Ukraine, changing their last name from Petrenko. Alex had been baptized Olexsandr, after his maternal grandfather, but in college he had changed it to Alexander. Was Nicola's interest in Ukraine a tell-tale sign of her father's heritage coming to light? It was said that blood will out. As would secrets, Carol thought. No matter how hard you tried to keep them hidden.

"You can't ask her to stay," Bonnie said. "It wouldn't be fair."

Carol bristled. "I have no intention of asking Nicola to abandon her plans."

"Good. You can't stop her from doing what she wants to do. Nobody stopped you from leaving Yorktide all those years ago."

"I'd have found a way to get out no matter the obstacles. As will Nicola, if she's my daughter."

Bonnie frowned and said nothing.

"About Ferndean," Carol went on. "After all, that's what you came here today to talk about. As I mentioned the other day before you hurried off, I want to buy you out. I've decided to give up my life in New York and retire here, where I belong."

"You haven't lived in Yorktide since you were nineteen," Bonnie cried, her face growing red. "How can you possibly know you'd be happy here? You weren't happy here as a child. If you had been, you would never have left. Or, you'd have gone away for a while, sowed your wild oats, and come back to us. But you didn't."

"I'm here now," Carol pointed out. "Better late than never."

"I don't believe that's always true. Anyway, what makes you think you can just show up and be welcomed with open arms? Are you so used to getting your way that you assumed you could remake our world—mine and Nicola's—here in Yorktide, at Ferndean, to your specifications?"

Carol let that remark go. It was indeed close to what she had assumed, but there was no need to admit that aloud. "Why are you so bothered by my coming home?" she asked.

Bonnie suddenly leaned forward. "Because . . . Because I want to live at Ferndean House. I believe I have a right to it. After all those years of . . ." Bonnie hesitated; there were tears shining in her eyes. "Of devotion," she went on. "It should rightfully be mine."

So that was it, Carol thought. Never in a million years had she imagined Bonnie wanting sole possession of Ferndean House. Why hadn't she?

"I wholeheartedly agree that you worked long and hard for the sake of the family home, as well as for Mom and Dad," Carol said carefully. "And for me. But it doesn't necessarily follow that you should be gifted Ferndean."

"Why didn't you come to Ken's funeral?" Bonnie demanded, her hands gripping the arms of the chair.

Carol knew this was a question Bonnie had been burning to ask.

"I told you back when Ken died," she said calmly. "I was in India on business, sourcing fabrics. I couldn't get a flight that would get me to back to the States in time for the service. I sent you a card and flowers. What else could I have done?"

Bonnie didn't reply immediately.

Carol sighed. "Be honest, Bonnie. You didn't really miss me at the funeral. How could you have?"

"I did miss you," Bonnie insisted. "I needed my sister at my side. I had Judith and Nicola and Julie and Scott and friends and neighbors and Ken's family, but not my sister. The one person who—"

"Who what?" Carol asked.

"Nothing," Bonnie said fiercely. "Nothing." Abruptly, she got up from the chair. "This is not over," she said. "The matter of Ferndean."

Carol remained perched on the arm of the couch as once again her sister ran off. What was it Bonnie had been about to say? "The one person who mattered." Could that have been it? But why? How could Carol have mattered above all others at that moment of crisis in Bonnie's life? Surely, Bonnie's daughter and her niece, and possibly even her cousin, were closer to her than her virtually estranged sister?

But maybe that was it, Carol realized with an uncomfortable sense of shame. Carol was Bonnie's sister. She had known Bonnie from almost the first moment of Bonnie's life. Carol Ascher was the only other person alive who remembered what their childhood had been like in Ferndean House; she was the only other person who remembered Shirley and Ronald Ascher as Mom and Dad. The sibling relationship was a primary one. That was a fact.

Suddenly, Carol felt terribly weary. It was a kind of weariness that had been coming upon her in the past few months. She had meant to see her doctor before heading north to Maine, but she hadn't. She wasn't sure why. Anyway, she was probably just run-down; selling her business had taken an unexpected emotional toll. That was all.

She rose from the arm of the couch. She decided to lie down, to allow her body and her mind to relax so that she would be ready for the next encounter with her sister.

Because there would be another one.

Chapter 11

Nicola had gone to her aunt's house, where she found Julie and Bonnie at the kitchen table, drinking coffee. Her cousin looked haggard and unkempt. She barely replied to Nicola's greeting. But Nicola persisted.

"How is Sophie doing at her job?" she asked.

"Fine," Julie said.

"Does she get along with her fellow counselors?" Nicola pressed.

Julie shrugged. "I guess."

Nicola shared a glance of concern with her aunt. She had always liked Scott, thought him a decent guy, and to find that he was just like the majority of men—shallow, careless, prone to putting their sexual needs and desires above all other concerns . . . It had taken Nicola weeks before she could hear Scott's name without experiencing a rush of anger and moral self-righteousness.

More difficult had been figuring out how to deal with Julie, what to say to her, how to act. Nicola had asked her aunt for guidance.

"Julie doesn't want advice from any of us at the moment," Bonnie had said. "What she needs is for us to simply be there, to listen, to give her a hug."

So, with some effort, Nicola had put her anger with Scott out of sight; certainly it would do Julie no good to witness it. And, Nicola had a generous heart. She knew no one was perfect; certainly she wasn't. Besides, sustaining negative emotions was exhausting; it made you feel sick; it made you look ugly. All you needed to do was to look in the mirror when you were feeling angry and you would see the negative emotions made visible.

"Have you seen your mother yet?"

Julie's question took Nicola by surprise. She hadn't expected her cousin to be at all concerned with what was going on in the family.

"No," she said.

"I'm sure she wants to see you," Julie went on mildly.

Bonnie's face went red. "Since when have you taken Carol's side?" she demanded of her daughter.

Julie took a sip of her coffee before answering. "I haven't," she said. "I'm not on anybody's side."

"I just don't see what's in it for me," Nicola said. So much for having a generous heart, but since when had her mother considered her daughter's needs and desires? Not in a very long time, if ever.

"I don't think that Nicola should feel compelled to see her mother if she doesn't want to," Bonnie stated.

But Julie was no longer engaged in the conversation. She took her coffee cup and wandered into the backyard.

Nicola took her aunt's hand. "Don't worry about me," she said. "How did it go with my mother?"

"I told her I thought I had a right to Ferndean."

"You do."

"Carol doesn't think so. She said my hard work for the family doesn't necessarily translate to my having the right to live there as I please."

Nicola felt her blood boil. "How dare she," she muttered.

"I told her you're thinking about joining the Peace Corps. I told her she couldn't stop you."

"Why would she want to stop me? I'm sure it doesn't matter to her what I do with my life."

"It matters to me."

Nicola reached for her aunt's hand. "I'll never abandon you, Aunt Bonnie," she swore.

"I know. And I'll always be here for you."

"Together forever," Nicola said, her voice husky with emotion. "Like family should be."

Chapter 12

Julie stared down at the trash container. It was full. The bag needed to be tied up and brought to the garbage can out back. It was already starting to smell.

Julie closed the lid of the container. She would get to it later.

She wandered out of the kitchen and found herself in her office. The only place to sit was her desk chair. The armchair in which she used to spend hours reading was buried beneath piles of old newspapers and dirty clothing. Julie sat at her desk. When was the last time she had done any real work at it?

She couldn't remember.

Her aunt probably never suffered depressions and anxiety and self-loathing, she thought. Not a woman like Carol Ascher.

Unlike Nicola, Julie had no reason to refuse to see her aunt; still, she was glad she hadn't yet encountered her. Bonnie Elgort's glamorous, big-city sister would understandably want nothing to do with the mousy, pitiful wreck Julie Miller had become. Julie had grown up with her mother telling stories about Aunt Carol that rarely portrayed her in a good light. For the most part, Julie had listened without comment, though secretly she had often wished she could play a small part in her aunt's exotic world of travel and beauty. It was only when Nicola had been sent to live in Maine that

Julie's opinion of her aunt took a nosedive from which it had not fully recovered.

Julie sighed. The office was depressing. It made her think of how little she had accomplished since . . . since she had learned of Scott's affair. She got up from the desk chair and went into the den, where she lay down on the old plaid sofa. She wanted to sleep. It was as close to oblivion as she could get. As Julie shifted into a more comfortable position, she caught sight of the basketball trophy Scott had won in high school. MVP. He was so proud of that achievement. Julie had always been touched by his pride. Every week, for all the years of their marriage, she had polished the trophy until it shone. Now the sight of it on the shelf over the old stereo brought back every painful and humiliating moment of the past months.

The first sign that something might be wrong had come on Julie's birthday back in March. Scott had given her a funny card. That was odd. Normally, he gave her a sentimental card. They had gone out to dinner at their favorite Italian place, but Scott had been distracted and distant. Every few minutes he had glanced around the dining room, as if he was expecting someone. When they got home, Scott made an excuse for not coming straight to bed. When Julie fell asleep around midnight, Scott still had not come up to their bedroom.

The distracted and distant behavior continued for another week before Julie felt sure that something was going on. Scott had a history of infidelity. Could it be that he had reverted to his old ways? Julie felt sick even considering this possibility. A wife was supposed to believe in her husband. To trust him unconditionally. Love was patient and kind.

But love also rejoiced in the truth.

So, Julie began a search for evidence.

There were no shirts stained with lipstick stuffed in a drawer. No matchbooks from local hotels hidden in a pocket. No torn hotel receipts at the bottom of the trash.

But Scott continued to live an almost parallel life to that of his wife, so Julie turned to her dearest friend. Agnes Sexton lived with her husband, Prescott, and two small children on a small but thriving dairy farm on the outskirts of Yorktide. Prescott had inherited the farm from his uncle and ran it with an unprecedented efficiency and business savvy. Aggie, for her part, kept the domestic ship afloat, no small task.

Julie would never forget that day at Sexton Farm, the day her world began to fall apart.

"I think something's going on with Scott," she said when the two women had taken seats at the kitchen table, a pot of coffee and a plate of freshly baked muffins before them. "I mean, I think he might be having an affair."

"Why?" Aggie asked, stirring her coffee. "Have you found evidence?"

"No," Julie admitted. "But he's been acting differently. There have been a whole bunch of little things. Like every Friday night Scott brings home two large pizzas, but last Friday and the week before he showed up empty-handed. He laughed it off, saying that work had been insanely busy and he just spaced."

"Mmmm," Aggie said.

Julie shook her head. "Why do you keep stirring that coffee?"

Aggie put her spoon on the table. "The thing is," she began, "a few weeks ago I ran into Katie Essex. She mentioned that she had heard from a reliable source that Scott was spending time with someone not his wife. Honestly, I completely dismissed it as being one of Katie's nasty little lies. You know what a troublemaker she can be. Besides, she couldn't even name the woman Scott was supposedly seeing, or her so-called reliable source."

"Why didn't you tell me?" Julie had demanded, her hands tightening on her coffee cup.

"Because there was nothing to tell," Agnes said fiercely. "Just a nasty rumor. Scott loves you. He adores you. It can't be true."

A roaring began in Julie's head. Her best friend in the world had betrayed her. "I can't believe this is happening," she said thickly. She rose abruptly from the table, grabbed her bag from the back of the chair, and strode toward the kitchen door.

"Julie, wait," Aggie cried, pushing back her own chair and rising. "I'm so sorry. Look, maybe there's nothing at all to the rumor.

Maybe Scott's acting differently because like he said he's under stress at work."

Julie whirled around. "Why are you defending him?"

"I'm not!" Aggie protested. "It's just—"

But Julie was already out the door. Since then, she had ignored her friend's texts, e-mails, and phone calls. Aggie was sorry. She was full of remorse.

Julie didn't care.

Julie sat up on the sofa and rubbed her eyes with the palms of her hands.

She had spent the hours after her visit to Aggie in an agony of indecision. Maybe, she thought, she should just stop worrying. After all, lots of men had affairs and after a while their marriages went on much as they had before. Didn't they? Or was that a lie, meant to convince a betrayed wife that if she just waited a bit like a good girl all would be well?

It was several days before Julie was able to confront Scott directly. She had made sure that Sophie would not be home by suggesting she spend the night at her friend Anabel's house, if it was all right with Anabel's mother. It was.

She made dinner as usual. She and Scott took their customary seats at the kitchen table. "I love this dish," Scott said with a smile, ladling a heaping portion of the chicken casserole onto his plate.

Julie let him eat for a few minutes. She herself had no appetite. Finally, she could stay silent no longer.

"There's no easy way for me to ask this question," she said. "Are you having an affair?"

Scott put his fork onto his plate. He looked directly at Julie when he spoke. "Yes," he said, not at all defiantly. "But I've decided to end it. Now. Tonight. I'll call her. I'll send a text if you'd rather I not talk to her."

This was the second memorable moment that would come to define the collapse of Julie's happy world.

"Who is she?" she asked. Her voice was steady.

Scott hesitated. "Laci Fox," he murmured after a moment.

Julie's stomach lurched. Laci Fox was a notorious flirt and had been known to sleep with married men as often as not. How could

Scott have betrayed her with such a person? It was despicable. It was tired and clichéd.

"Who else knows?" Julie asked. What she meant was, had Scott bragged to his friends at work about the affair? She had never known him to be a braggart, but maybe she had never really known anything about the man she had been calling her husband for almost twenty years.

"No one," he said.

"Don't be ridiculous! Aggie heard a rumor weeks ago. By now everyone in Yorktide must know you and Laci Fox have been carrying on."

Scott flinched. "I'm sorry," he said. "It's all I know what to say right now."

"Why did you do it?" Julie asked. She wondered if it was a stupid question.

"I . . ." Scott shook his head. "I can't say."

Julie knew what Scott meant. He no longer loved his wife. He was unhappy. His marriage was an inconvenience. His promise to end the affair was an empty one.

The third nail in the proverbial coffin. From that moment, Julie Miller turned against herself. She didn't entirely let Scott off the hook, but she now included herself among the guilty.

"I see," she said. "Well, I guess that's it then."

Scott blanched. "What do you mean, that's it? Julie, our marriage isn't over; please don't say that, don't even think it."

Julie had no response to her husband's plea, if that was what it was and not just a bunch of words that had spilled out of his mouth in a moment of panic. The silence between them stretched out. The casserole left in the pan began to congeal. Julie's throat felt dry as dust, but she couldn't seem to pick up her glass of water.

"I'll sleep on the couch," Scott said after a time. He sounded defeated.

"You can tonight," Julie told him. "But tomorrow, when Sophie is home, you'll sleep in our bed with me. I don't want her to know anything is wrong. She might not have heard the rumors." But she would soon enough. Nothing stayed secret for long in a small town like Yorktide. Especially not something as titillating as a marital scandal.

Scott put his hands to his head. "What have I done?"

"I don't know," Julie had replied. "I really don't."

"Julie? Julie, are you home?"

Julie jumped off the sofa. It was Scott. She wanted to run away. But where could she go? She lived here. Scott lived here. They each had the right to be exactly where they were. Until one or the other decided to leave.

"There you are. Didn't you hear me calling?" He was standing in the door to the den.

She wanted to grab his beloved trophy and hurl it at his head. But that would be stupid. She was always thinking stupid things.

"I heard," Julie said, lowering her eyes and walking swiftly past him.

Chapter 13

"Darn!" Bonnie cried. She hurried to the sink and ran the cold water over her thumb and forefinger. That stupid old toaster!

No. That stupid old woman, allowing herself to be distracted by an accumulation of depressing thoughts, a litany of all that had been going wrong in her world.

Ken's illness and death. Scott's affair. Poor Julie's terrible reaction to her husband's betrayal.

"I wish I could just hide or go away or . . ." Julie had told her mother the day after Scott had admitted to cheating.

Bonnie had been alarmed. "But you can't do either," she said firmly. "You have a child. Julie, we'll get through this together. As a family."

"Scott was my family."

Bonnie had reached out and drawn Julie to her.

"I wish Dad was here," Julie sobbed against her mother's shoulder.

"So do I," Bonnie had whispered. "Every moment of every day."

And that was still true, Bonnie thought. Especially now that Carol was back in Yorktide to steal Ferndean away from her sister.

Bonnie turned off the water and dried her hand. No real harm done. She didn't want toast anyway.

The landline rang. It was Judith.

"What's going on?" she asked. "Any word from Carol?"

"No," Bonnie said. "I feel so hopeless. What can I do? What are my rights? Should I get a lawyer after all?"

"All is not lost," Judith said firmly. "Besides, Carol will be bored with Yorktide in a few weeks' time. Be patient, then approach her again."

Bonnie sighed. "I wish Ken were here."

"But he's not. This is a matter for the sisters to handle."

"Maybe you could help," Bonnie suggested, a tiny flicker of hope dawning. "You've always got along so well with Carol. She respects you. She'd listen to you."

"Honestly," Judith said after a moment, "I'm reluctant to get involved. And I refuse to take sides, though I do feel that you have a far stronger claim to Ferndean. Fairness and all that."

"Please, Judith. You know how Carol is, she's a bulldozer. I've never been able to stand up to her."

Judith sighed. "I suppose we could meet at my house. I could act as mediator. Not that I've ever done that sort of thing before."

"I really need your help," Bonnie pleaded. "Promise?"

After another moment, Judith promised and hung up.

Bonnie rubbed her forehead. Judith had agreed to try to broker an agreement between the sisters. That was good. Now, Carol would have to agree to a negotiation.

And that might take a miracle.

Chapter 14

Carol couldn't recall ever having been in this neighborhood of Yorktide. It had a run-down feel that was so markedly at variance with the area surrounding Ferndean, Carol almost felt as if she must have taken a wrong turn and wound up in another county entirely.

But there was the sign for Gilbert Way, the street on which Nicola currently made her home. Carol slowed down and began to look for number 35.

Not a day of the last ten years had gone by that Carol had not thought of her daughter with longing. But Nicola probably wouldn't believe that. Carol couldn't blame her if she didn't. By the time Carol had broken the habit of abusing opioids, Nicola was already in college and Carol had felt—she had believed—that it was too late to ask her daughter to return home. Nicola had her own life. Why would she suddenly want to leave it behind to reconcile with the woman who had rejected her?

It had been a mistake; Carol knew that now. She should have tried. Why hadn't she? Fear of rejection. She knew that now, too.

Number 35. Carol parked and got out of her car. The building was poorly kept. It bothered Carol that her child was living in such an ugly and possibly unsafe place.

The front door opened. Nicola stepped out of the building. Carol felt her heart begin to race; it was an uncomfortable feeling.

Nicola was plainly dressed in chinos and a T-shirt, and her hair was pulled into a neat ponytail. It suddenly occurred to Carol that her daughter might be on her way to work and that this surprise visit might be a big inconvenience. Why hadn't she thought of that before now?

As Nicola came down the front stairs, Carol thought she saw the image of Nicola's father superimposed on his daughter. Alex Peters. Not Anonymous Donor. She felt almost faint.

"Nicola," she called when her daughter had reached the sidewalk.

Nicola looked up, saw her mother, and came to a halt. "What are you doing here?" she demanded.

"I wanted to see you," Carol said, walking closer. "You haven't been answering my calls. Can we go up to your apartment?"

"No," Nicola said firmly. "If you have to talk, we'll go to the diner down the block. I don't have much time. I'm due at work at ten."

Nicola walked quickly. Carol hurried alongside. They were soon at the diner.

Inside, they were shown to a booth. They took a seat across from each other.

"You know it's wrong to ambush someone who doesn't want to see you," Nicola said angrily.

Carol smiled nervously. "Desperate times call for desperate measures."

"It's rude."

"You're right," Carol said. "I won't do it again."

"Please don't."

The waitress, dressed in a uniform almost identical to the one Carol had worn in her waitressing days back in the 1970s, arrived to take their orders.

"A cup of coffee," Carol said.

"A cup of decaf."

"When did we last see one another?" Carol asked when the waitress had gone off.

Nicola shook her head. "Don't you remember?"

"Of course, I do. Asking was a conversation opener." And not a very good one, Carol thought. She cast around for something else to say and found that her mind was suddenly blank.

And Nicola, it was clear, was not going to make this any easier.

Finally, Carol cleared her throat. "I know you must be wondering why I came back to Yorktide," she began. "The truth is I came back for you. And for Bonnie."

"Don't you mean you came back for Ferndean?" Nicola snapped.

"Well, that too, but primarily for my family. I miss you."

Nicola leaned back and folded her arms across her chest. "If you expect me to believe that, you must think I'm pretty stupid."

"No," Carol protested. "I don't think anything of the kind. I—"

"That summer I refused to visit you in New York," Nicola said, "you didn't even try to argue with me. Why?"

Carol folded her hands in her lap. "You were eighteen," she said. "Legally an adult. You had the right to make your own decisions." She lowered her voice. "Look, why are you suddenly so angry with me? What have I done to deserve this . . . this mood of aggressive dislike."

"It's not sudden," Nicola snapped. "And it's not aggressive. It's . . . Never mind."

"Is it to do with my not coming back for Ken's funeral?" Carol asked.

"I said, never mind." Nicola shook her head. "No, wait. I *do* have something to say. I *am* angry with you. You showed no respect for me, for your sister, or for my uncle, the only father figure I'd ever known. You could have come to Yorktide when you got back from India, but you didn't even do that. You left us to mourn on our own."

Carol took a breath. "I thought that was what you needed," she said carefully, "to be left on your own, you and Bonnie, with your grief."

That was not strictly true.

"Well, it wasn't what we needed," Nicola snapped. "But it doesn't matter now, does it?"

Nicola slid out of the booth. Carol reached for her wallet, but Nicola tossed two dollar bills onto the table. "I can pay for my own coffee," she said. "I've got to get to work. Don't come to my home again."

Nicola stalked off.

Shaken, Carol made her way back to Ferndean.

Marcus and Rosemary Ascher's wedding portrait hung where it had for as long as Carol could remember. She stood looking at it now, for the thousandth time in her life.

The wedding had taken place in 1848, just eight years after Queen Victoria had married Albert, and Rosemary had followed the fashion set by Victoria for wearing a white wedding dress. On her head was a half crown of flowers—Carol wondered if they were orange blossoms, like the ones Victoria had worn—and a long lace veil. The bride's waist was impossibly tiny.

Ferndean House had been built as a gesture of love, a gift from husband to wife. A grand gesture, if not exactly a perfect one.

Carol turned from the portrait and sank onto one of the ancient couches. A spring poked into her behind. She moved a few inches to the right. There was a strange depression in the cushion. Carol didn't bother to move again.

Love. She had been in love only once in her life and it had not ended well.

In her late thirties, Carol had met a man named Martin Gehrig. She had fallen hard. It was magical. But after almost a year together Martin left her. It had come as a shock to Carol. He said she was too self-centered to love him in the way he needed to be loved. He was right.

Carol had always known she was a person for whom intimate attachment wasn't a high priority. She had always been the one to end her casual affairs before the man could get needy and annoying. Even as a child she had been more concerned with being admired than liked, envied than appreciated. Still, Carol had been crushed. Her ego was shaken, her heart was broken, her entire sense of who she was in the world was rattled.

Martin married less than six months after the breakup.

Mourning the loss of her relationship, Carol hit upon the idea of having a baby. It would be the perfect way to show Martin that she was not an entirely self-centered person. And it was perfectly normal for a woman to want a child. Her biological clock was ticking. No one would question her motives. There was, however, the problem of a father.

The answer to that sticky question was Alex Peters.

Carol and Alex had met several years before when he hired her to design and furnish his apartment on the Upper West Side of Manhattan. Before long, it was clear that Alex was in love with Carol. But Alex was content to be what Carol wanted him to be—a friend and nothing more. He was chivalrous, a gentleman. He was handsome, intelligent, kind, and cultured. He tolerated Carol's selfish desires. He was happy to be in her life.

Yes, Alex Peters would make the perfect father. As long as he agreed to create the child via IVF and to absent himself from that point on. Carol did not want to marry Alex, nor did she want to raise the child with him. She did not understand the enormity of what she was asking from her friend. But she asked anyway.

Alex agreed. He did, however, request that he be sent regular updates on the child's progress. He would soon be gone from New York. He had just been chosen to head up his company's Buenos Aires headquarters.

Lawyers hammered out the agreement. About a year later, a baby was born.

Carol was not a terribly sentimental person, but she did have enough of a sense of gratitude to name the child after two members of Alex's family, his grandfather Nikolas and his grandmother Kateryna. Hence Nicola Kathryn Ascher.

Over the years, Carol had occasionally felt a pang of guilt when she thought of how she had used Alex's devotion against him. But what was done was done. It was too late to change course. She convinced herself of this.

Suddenly, Carol got up from the couch and walked over to the wedding portrait of her ancestors. It was time for a change. It was time the photograph came down. Carol reached up to lift the frame from its hook, but the look in Rosemary's eyes stopped her cold. She had not known Rosemary Ascher, of course, but family legend had it that she was as formidable in character as she was lovely in appearance.

All right. The photograph of the lovers would stay. And no matter what, Carol would not leave Yorktide without winning back her daughter, if not her sister.

Rosemary seemed to approve.

Chapter 15

Carol Ascher claimed to have come back to Yorktide for her family. What a joke!

Nicola kicked off her sneakers and let her hair out of its elastic. She was tired. Work had been more challenging than usual. And all day her mother's surprise visit had preyed on her mind. How dare her mother ambush her!

Still, Nicola was glad she had had the opportunity to tell her mother how angry she was that Carol hadn't moved heaven and earth to be at Ken's funeral. Carol's failure to support her family at that traumatic moment was one more bit of evidence to prove her fundamentally self-centered character.

Unlike Bonnie and Ken. They were the two most unselfish and loving people Nicola had ever known. Not that coming to live with them ten years ago had been smooth sailing right away.

At first, Nicola had kept in frantic contact with her friends from school; she called them friends because that was easier than trying to figure out just what they really meant to her. But after only two weeks, they told her they were bored with her complaints about how deadly dull life was in Yorktide. Allie said, "So just leave. Come back to New York. You're not a prisoner." Ben said, "If it's so boring, make trouble." After another few weeks Caitlyn stopped replying and the other two blocked her texts. By the time Nicola's birthday rolled around that November, Ben, Allie, and Caitlyn were entirely absent.

By then, Nicola had realized that a few kids at her new school were okay. She was enjoying most of her classes. Christmas in Yorktide and the neighboring towns was like something out of a picture book, even better than Christmas in Manhattan, and that was saying something. By the turn of the new year, Nicola was being greeted in town as if she had been born in Yorktide. She knew most of the people she met by sight if not by name.

Time passed. Aunt Bonnie was kind. Uncle Ken was funny. She got along with her cousin, Julie, and Julie's husband, Scott. Sophie, five, was cute. Nicola made friends, loved living near the beach, and was finally able to have a dog, something her mother had never allowed. Uncle Ken took her to the local animal shelter, where Nicola had picked out a three-year-old mixed breed with a damaged ear. No one knew his name; Nicola called him Lucky. Like her, he had accidentally found a home in which he was happy.

Nicola graduated high school with better grades than she had ever gotten back in New York, and went on to the University of Southern Maine. After that she earned a master's in gerontological social work and took a position at the local nursing home. Lucky eventually died and Nicola had yet to adopt another dog. For a long time, she felt the pain of his loss too greatly. One day, when she had a real home of her own, she would adopt another neglected pup, maybe two.

Carol had come to visit a few times that first year. Visit number one was a disaster; Nicola was still furious with her mother for abandoning her.

The second visit was marginally less fraught.

By her mother's third visit, Nicola felt perfectly in charge of her emotions. But she was not sorry to see her mother drive away after two days.

Nicola padded into the miniscule kitchen and opened the fridge.

There wasn't much to eat; there never was. She closed the door. She wasn't hungry anyway. Her mother had taken away her appetite.

Suddenly, alone in her awful little apartment, Nicola began to sob. Carol Ascher should have been at the funeral of the only father figure Nicola had ever known.

Nicola had needed her.

Chapter 16

Julie sighed and rubbed her eyes with the palms of her hands. She had sworn to herself that she would work on the mess that was her office that morning. But she had failed to keep that promise. She had failed even to attempt to keep that promise. If a person could be so disloyal to her own self, how could she possibly be of service to anyone else?

It was almost noon. Another morning down, another afternoon to go. And after that, she could go back to bed without guilt. Without too much guilt.

Now she stood in the kitchen, unsure of what to do next. Assuming she had the energy to do anything. Vaguely, Julie noted that the pan in which she had roasted a chicken two days earlier was still soaking in the sink. Maybe she would get to it later. Along with the watering of the three small plants on the windowsill. One was almost dead. But maybe it could be revived. If she got around to watering it. There was always so much to accomplish. Sometimes lately Julie wondered how she had ever managed to do all that she had done and to do it so well before . . . Before Scott had had the affair.

But she had been different then.

Suddenly, Sophie came loping into the room and stopped short when she saw her mother. "Oh," she said. "You're here."

Where else would I be, Julie thought. *This is my home.* At least, it had been her home. Now, it felt alien. Or maybe she was the alien. The one who had been denied the respect she had been promised so solemnly before God and man.

Sophie went to the fridge, opened the door, and stared into its depths. Julie wondered when the fridge had last been cleaned. Did it matter?

"Have you spoken to your father today?" she asked.

"No."

"Sophie—"

Her daughter slammed shut the door of the fridge and whirled around to face Julie. "What?" she demanded. "I hate what he did to me. What am I supposed to say to him? Am I supposed to pretend nothing happened when my entire life has been ruined because he acted like a jerk?"

My entire life has been ruined. Julie didn't want pity from her child, but she did want at least an acknowledgment that *she* had been hurt and betrayed. But maybe Sophie was just reacting like a normal self-centered teen to an event that had rattled the status quo. Or maybe she was proving to be more like her father than otherwise. A self-centered person from start to finish. Julie literally shivered at the unworthy thought.

"You need to forgive your father," she said firmly.

Sophie shrugged. "Why? *You* don't forgive him."

"I do." Julie was aware that she was lying.

Sophie laughed bitterly. "That's what you say, but you don't mean it. You don't even talk to him. You just . . . Why don't you just scream at him or something?"

Julie flinched. Why was she incapable of hiding her despair? Why did she have to be observed, judged, despised for her weakness? Was she in fact courting the observation, hoping for pity? These were questions the answers to which she was not prepared to explore.

"Forgiveness," she said woodenly, "is the key to healing."

Sophie rolled her eyes. "Where did you read that? In a fortune cookie?"

"Has your father tried to talk to you about what happened?" Julie asked, ignoring her daughter's smart remark. "Has he told you his side of the story?"

"Why do you want to know?" Sophie asked with a frown. "You're trying to turn me against Dad, aren't you?"

"He's the guilty one," Julie snapped, "not me! He's the one you said ruined your life."

"I know what Dad did was wrong! You don't have to keep reminding me."

"Sorry." Was she sorry? "I just meant that maybe he . . ."

"I'm out of here."

There was no point in trying to stop Sophie from leaving. Julie realized that nothing she could say or do would help her daughter at that moment.

The front door slammed. Julie jumped.

How had it come to pass that her life seemed all about people walking away?

The memory of a slamming door.

Days had gone by after Julie had told her mother about Scott's affair and still she hadn't said a word to Sophie.

Then, one afternoon when Julie was alone in the kitchen, the front door had slammed.

A moment later Sophie had come stomping into the kitchen and tossed her backpack onto the table. Her face was flushed.

"I know what's been going on," she declared loudly. "Why didn't you tell me? Why did I have to hear about my father's affair at school?"

Julie felt herself blush. "Nothing is—I mean, there's nothing—"

"Don't lie to me, Mom. Dad's been sleeping on the couch."

"I didn't ask him to." It was a stupid response.

"It doesn't matter. And there have been other signs. Like you two are hardly talking, and you didn't watch *This Is Us* together the other night. Did you really think I didn't know something was wrong?" Sophie put her hands to her head and groaned. "I was so stupid not to have figured out what it was! I thought you had just had a fight. But an affair? I can't believe bitchy Cora Brunner had to tell me my own father was sleeping with the town whore!"

"Don't use that word."

Julie's command was a knee-jerk response. She had always been a feminist, supportive of other women's choices, giving the benefit of the doubt to women who slept with the husbands of other women because who knew the motives that had informed their actions? Now, she felt befuddled. What was she supposed to think of a person like Laci Fox? Was she allowed to hate her, to call her names? No. She didn't want to do either. She wanted to love and forgive because she was a good person. But she didn't have it in her right then to love or to forgive. Not Laci. Not Scott. Not herself.

Sophie laughed harshly. "Why shouldn't I? I'm sure it's what you've been calling Laci Fox when you and Agnes talk about what happened."

"Aggie and I don't talk about it," Julie said flatly.

"Why not?"

"Never mind," Julie said. "It's not your business."

"Oh, really? I'm only your daughter! Does Grandma know? What about Judith? And Nicola? Did everybody but me know?"

Julie didn't need to answer that question.

"This is unbelievable! What am I supposed to do now? Why is Dad even still here? Don't you have any self-respect? Why haven't you thrown him out?"

"It's not that simple," Julie had begun. And it wasn't. But she couldn't expect a fifteen-year-old to understand a tenth of what was involved in a marriage crisis.

"I'm going to—I don't know what I'm going to do. I'll be at Grandma's. Somewhere. Anywhere but here."

Before Julie could beg her not to leave, Sophie was gone, slamming the front door behind her. Again.

Julie remembered feeling an odd sense of relief at that moment. She had been so intent on keeping up appearances. Now she could abandon all pretense that her marriage was fine, that she hadn't done something or failed to do something that had caused her husband to turn away from her.

But maybe it was not something she had done or not *done*. Maybe the problem lay with who she *was*. Rather, who she was not. A sufficiently interesting, beautiful, and devoted wife.

She had sent Scott a text message. *Sophie knows.*

A few minutes later, he responded. *I'll talk to her when I get home.*

Good luck, Julie had thought. Her husband was going to need it.

Chapter 17

If Carol could just show up at Ferndean, Bonnie thought, so could she. Bonnie had no particular goal in mind. She just wanted to walk through the doors of what by all rights should be her home.

Her beloved Ferndean. It stood proudly, a symbol of continuity, of family, of tradition. She used the old knocker instead of the bell to announce her presence. It was in the shape of an anchor.

"I'll be home soon," Bonnie whispered to the house, her hand lingering on the knocker. "Don't you worry."

The door opened. Carol was wearing a gray linen tunic and matching linen pants.

"I wasn't expecting you," she said.

Bonnie held herself taller. "I have a right to come and go as I please. I am half owner. And," Bonnie went on, "you probably haven't even noticed we have a vegetable and herb garden that needs tending. That's always been my responsibility."

Carol didn't reply but stepped back. Bonnie followed her inside.

"The washing machine isn't working," Carol said. "I've talked to the repair service. It would be a lot more cost-effective to buy a new one."

Bonnie frowned. Ken might have been able to fix the washing machine. Scott was handy, but Bonnie was hesitant to ask him for help. She didn't doubt that he would comply with her request—

out of guilt, if not out of goodwill—but how, exactly, was she supposed to approach Scott when his wife was barely speaking to him and his daughter professed to hate her father? Ken would know what to say to Scott. But Ken wasn't here to fix that problem, either.

Suddenly, Bonnie was overcome with doubt. Maybe Judith had a point. Maybe she was being foolish, thinking she could manage Ferndean all on her own.

"So, do I have your consent to go ahead and buy a new washing machine?" Carol asked. She sounded impatient.

Bonnie nodded. Her consent. What did that really mean at this point?

Silently, she followed her sister into the living room.

"Look at this lampshade," Carol said, stopping short and poking at the shade on a small marble lamp that had been in the Ascher family for generations. "It's literally in shreds."

"It can be fixed," Bonnie said quickly.

"It should be thrown out. This place is like a shrine to the whole lot of Ascher ancestors. You've changed nothing since Mom died, have you? The furniture is almost all broken down. The rugs are threadbare. The kitchen and bathrooms are badly in need of an upgrade. How did you ever manage to rent this as a getaway?"

"All that matters is that we did rent the house," Bonnie said stubbornly. "Ken and I never had trouble finding tenants."

"Still, why not spruce the place up, make it feel lighter and airier, more modern," Carol said.

"It's a Victorian era house."

"But it doesn't have to feel that way," Carol pointed out, "at least not entirely. Why do you need to cling to the past so tenaciously?"

"Why do you treat the past so cavalierly," Bonnie snapped back, "like it's something you can just smash up and throw away?"

Carol sighed. "Just because something is old doesn't automatically confer value upon it. The past was not necessarily a better place. Some old stuff is horrible now because it was horrible then, back when it was made. Bad taste is as old as civilization."

Bonnie felt as if she had received a physical wound. "Are you saying that Ferndean House is in bad taste?" she demanded.

"Some of it is." Carol pointed. "Like that pique assiette vase. That sort of thing was never in fashion, not with people in the know."

"It's a recognized form of folk art," Bonnie argued. "It's not meant to be in or out of fashion. And if you ever tried it you'd see just how fun it can be."

"Shard arts are not my thing." A cell phone beeped. "I've got to take this," Carol said, already walking out of the room. "I'll only be a moment."

Bonnie realized that she felt a bit light-headed. She leaned against the back of the worn maroon velvet couch. Again, she wondered if Judith was right. Was she crazy thinking she could manage the family's legacy all on her own, without the help of Carol's superior intellect and business acumen?

Shirley and Ronald Ascher had been so proud of Carol's success; they had eagerly followed news of her career and never missed an opportunity to boast about every new development, from a feature in *Architectural Digest* or *The New York Times*, to an award for best small apartment redo or innovative vacation house design, or whatever someone like Carol Ascher got awards for doing.

Her parents' unrestrained pride had taken its toll on Bonnie. In fact, it wasn't long after Shirley Ascher fell ill that Bonnie began to question her motives for taking on the role of uncomplaining caregiver. Were they entirely pure? Or was she seeking approval, a pat on the head—even the reward of full ownership of Ferndean one day? Carol Ascher might be rich and famous, but Bonnie Ascher Elgort could administer medicines and cook tempting meals for a dying woman. Who was more valuable?

Then, Shirley Ascher had died and Bonnie learned that her mother hadn't changed her will in favor of her younger daughter. Ferndean still went to both Carol and Bonnie.

Thirty some odd years later, the insult still stung.

Carol returned from her call.

"Thank God Mom and Dad weren't alive to witness you abandon your daughter," Bonnie blurted. "They would have been horrified."

Carol crossed her arms over her chest. "I protest your choice of the term *abandon*," she said. There was an unmistakable tremor in her voice. "You know that's not what it was. But you would have liked seeing Mom and Dad turn against me, wouldn't you? Little Miss Goody Two-Shoes. You like to think of yourself as beyond reproach."

"I most certainly do not," Bonnie protested. "I've made plenty of mistakes and I've never pretended otherwise. Look, the bottom line is that I don't want you here, at Ferndean or in Yorktide."

"I'm sorry you feel that way," Carol replied. "But everyone has a right to her opinion."

Bonnie opened her mouth to make a smart reply—something stinging and memorable—but no words came out. She wasn't used to argument and confrontation, let alone to name-calling. She felt the first pricking of tears and panicked. She would not cry in front of her sister. Instead, Bonnie turned and hurried toward the front door. In a moment, she was climbing into her car.

Her hands were trembling when she started the engine and pulled out of the drive. She couldn't go far. Tears were blurring her vision. She pulled off the road only yards from Ferndean and leaned against the headrest.

Carol had come too close to the truth. Bonnie knew that by setting up Carol as the Bad Sister, she had of necessity set herself up as the Good Sister. You couldn't have darkness without light; it made no sense. When the truth was that neither sister was all bad nor all good. Few people were entirely one or the other. That was right, wasn't it?

Bonnie sighed. She had lied when she told Carol that she didn't want her in Yorktide. Sort of. Once, Bonnie had wanted Carol to come home. She had wanted that badly. But not now.

Not now.

Chapter 18

Carol was wandering around Ferndean House. She was also stewing.

The incident with her sister that morning had unsettled her. Why was Bonnie so intent on keeping alive an absurd and imagined rivalry? It was maddening.

And when Bonnie had accused her sister of rejecting the past as valueless! Ridiculous. If Bonnie only knew that Carol had kept Nicola's childhood bedroom exactly as it had been. . . .

Not that she ever needed to know.

Carol sighed. She hadn't expected to be welcomed with open arms and rejoicing, but neither had she expected such animosity. She didn't think she deserved it.

An old, tooled leather box on a side table caught Carol's attention. She hadn't noticed it before. Then again, the house was stuffed with items; who knew where they had come from or what long-dead family member had brought them here. She should probably do a detailed inventory. The thought made Carol feel tired.

Still, she mustered the energy to make her way to the attic. She hadn't been up there since before she left Yorktide in 1974. The attic contained even more "stuff" than it had back then—more bits of broken furniture, more cardboard storage boxes, more old clothing piled high on random surfaces. Otherwise, it was just as she remembered it. Low ceiling. Tiny windows. Barely finished walls. And to think that once upon a time people, servants, had made their lives up here! The thought was depressing.

Carol had turned to leave the attic when she spotted a plastic storage bin with her name written on its lid in big letters. She hesitated. Was she really interested in the contents?

And then she was prying the lid off the bin and confronting evidence of her earliest days. Watercolor paintings. Crayon drawings. Most of these, done on paper, were crumbling. There were a few small canvasses that were still intact. And there were sketchbooks. Endless sketchbooks.

Carol put her hand to her heart. She wasn't sure what she was feeling in that moment. A strange tenderness for the little girl who had been? A sense of age and of ending? A sense of loss?

One thing she was sure of. For as far back as she could remember, she had been interested in art and design. After the age of four she was rarely without a sketchpad. She made scrapbooks of images she cut from magazines. Whatever caught her fancy—a beautiful dress, a contemporary building, a picture of a famous old painting, an exotic bloom. She taught herself to sew her own clothes so that she could stand out from every other teenaged girl in Yorktide.

And she did stand out.

After high school, Carol enrolled in Yorktide Community College. Back then, it didn't have the good art program it eventually became known for. Frustrated, Carol quit after a year. But her education continued when she arrived in New York in late summer 1974. The city itself was her university. For the first time, she met people who had immigrated to the United States from countries other than Canada; people who had never lived in anything but apartment buildings; people who didn't own cars or have a driver's license because public transportation met their needs; people who worshipped in mosques or synagogues rather than churches.

And the museums! Carol would visit the Metropolitan Museum of Art once or twice a week (the museum was free in those days). She spent countless hours gazing at the living room of the Francis W.

Little House, Minnesota 1912–1914, designed by Frank Lloyd Wright. The Metropolitan had saved the Prairie School-style house when it was due to be demolished.

The first show Carol saw at the Costume Institute was The Glory of Russian Costume; it was seared in her memory. When the MMA mounted the world-famous show of treasures from the tomb of King Tutankhamun, Carol was one of those who visited several times.

She adored the Brooklyn Museum and its twenty-three period rooms. She developed a particular attachment to the famous Moorish Smoking Room from the Worsham-Rockefeller House, built circa 1864–1865 and remodeled circa 1881. It was the work of a professional interior designer, a role that was born in the mid-1870s. Learning this bit of information had made Carol realize that she was hoping to enter a field even older than she had supposed when she was a girl growing up in a small town in southern Maine.

And she read voraciously. The New York Public Library and The Strand became like second and third homes. Books. Magazines. Whatever she could get her hands on.

She was entranced by the architecture of Manhattan. The Art Deco skyscrapers like the Empire State Building and the Chrysler Building; the remaining Fifth Avenue Gilded Age mansions that had been built for the likes of the Vanderbilts, Fricks, and Carnegies; the magnificent churches and temples—Saint Patrick's Cathedral (Gothic and English Gothic Revival), St. Bartholomew's Church (Romanesque and Byzantine Revival); Central Synagogue (Moorish Revival).

Still, there was benefit to a formal education, so she took what courses she could afford at the Fashion Institute of Technology and Parsons School of Design. It was a dream to attend Parsons, the first school in the United States ever to offer programs in fashion design, as well as interior design and advertising.

Suddenly, Carol came crashing back to the present. How long had she been standing in the attic of her childhood home, in a trance of reminiscing?

She put the lid back on the plastic storage box that contained the relics of her past. She wasn't sentimental like her sister.

Well, not as sentimental as her sister, Carol thought as she turned out the light and made her way downstairs. The truth was that she felt terribly lonely for New York. It had been her home for a long time, far longer than Yorktide had been. Maybe Yorktide could never be home again.

But Yorktide was where Nicola lived. It was where Bonnie lived. And that meant everything. It had to.

Chapter 19

Nicola sat behind the wheel of her car outside the woodland park where Sophie's day camp met. She had arranged to pick up her cousin for a little excursion.

Suddenly, her attention was caught by the sight of a tall, skinny guy loping through the gate. He was wearing a counselor's T-shirt; there was a gold chain around his neck. A moment later he was leaning over a much younger girl, also wearing the T-shirt of a counselor. Her back was against the fence; if she wasn't trapped she was still cornered. Nicola frowned. She didn't like the looks of the guy. He fairly oozed bad news.

Sophie came running through the gate just then and all thoughts of the creepy guy and the girl he had cornered fled from Nicola's mind. Her cousin threw herself into the car. "Where are we going?" she asked. "I hope it's someplace good."

Nicola smiled. "How about that new place on the pier at the end of Burberry Lane?"

The idea was amenable to Sophie. When they had secured a table with a perfect view of bobbing boats and swooping seagulls, Sophie ordered the most expensive cold, frothy drink on the menu. Nicola made do with a plain iced coffee.

Suddenly, Sophie let out a moan. "First Grandpa had to die," she said, "and then my parents' marriage is falling apart! My life sucks."

Nicola choked on her drink. "I don't think you should assume that your parents' marriage is falling apart," she said carefully.

"Why not?" Sophie demanded. "They're always fighting. That is, when Mom isn't sulking. Before I knew what was going on, I was annoyed. I mean, how am I supposed to grow up to be a normal person if my parents are acting crazy? Now that I know what's behind the whole thing, I'm angry. Why is this happening to me?"

Sophie's self-centered reaction to her family's situation was entirely normal. As was any sense of disgust she might be feeling. The last thing a fifteen-year-old needed, smack in the middle of figuring out her own sexuality, was to learn that a parent was guilty of a sexual transgression. An affair threw in her face the fact that her parents were people who took their clothes off and did stuff to each other.

"I'm sorry," Nicola said finally. "I know it must be really difficult."

"It is! I mean, why are adults always so pissed off? Grandma and Great-Aunt Carol bicker like they're in middle school. Get over it! I am so glad I don't have a sister!"

"I don't think all sisters bicker like they do," Nicola said. She remembered something she had read in a college course on social anthropology. She thought it was Margaret Mead who had said that the sister relationship was the most competitive relationship in a family, but that when the sisters became adults, the relationship was the strongest.

So much for social anthropology.

"Anyway," she went on, "I've heard they got along just fine when they were young. It was Carol's going away to New York that changed things."

"How?" Sophie asked.

"I'm not sure, exactly," Nicola admitted. "But Bonnie's led me to believe that nothing was ever the same between them again."

"Maybe Grandma was jealous that her sister got out of Yorktide and she didn't. It's so boring here."

"I don't think it was that. Bonnie was happy in Yorktide. She still is. I think it had more to do with the fact that Bonnie felt abandoned when Carol left. They were never close again."

"I want to get out of Yorktide, too," Sophie announced. "I think your mother was smart."

"So was Bonnie," Nicola argued. "Each sister did what she wanted to do." And that, Nicola thought, was the point. No one could rightly blame Carol Ascher for living her life. As much as some people may want to. "Do you really mean it, about getting out of Yorktide?"

Sophie nodded. "I do. This town is just too small. I mean, if I stay here I'll never get away from being the kid whose parents' marriage was ruined by her idiot father who had an affair with the town tramp. Everyone knows everything about you or they think they do, which is worse. How can I ever be me—whoever that is!— if I stay here?"

Nicola didn't know what to say. Sophie had a point.

"Is that why you want to join the Peace Corps, to get away from Yorktide?" Sophie suddenly asked.

Nicola laughed. "No! I like it here. I'm thinking about joining the Peace Corps to challenge myself. I believe I'll come home to Yorktide after my service a better, stronger person." If, Nicola thought, she ever left in the first place.

"If I were going away I'd go to, I don't know, Aruba maybe. Someplace warm!" Sophie suddenly snapped her fingers. "Hey, maybe your mother could help me if I decide to move to New York!"

Nicola felt a stab of jealousy. Would her mother lend a helping hand to Sophie in a way she hadn't been able—or willing to—for her own daughter? "New York is hardly much warmer than Yorktide," she said lamely.

"Yeah, but it's a lot bigger and there's way more stuff to do!"

"Well, I can't argue with you there," Nicola said. Museums on Saturday afternoon. Ice skating in Central Park. The Bronx Zoo. Dinners in Chinatown. Broadway theaters. Yes, her childhood had been filled with exciting activity, and she did not forget it and she was not unappreciative. Maybe one day she could tell her mother that.

Suddenly, Sophie sighed. "Anyway, it's not like I'm going away soon. I have to at least finish high school. And—"

"And what?" Nicola asked. Sophie's expression had turned sober.

"Nothing. Well, just that Mom probably would miss me if I left home."

"So would your father," Nicola said. "We all would."

"Yeah, I guess I'd miss you guys, too."

Nicola took a sip of her iced coffee. She had often wondered if her mother had ever missed her once she was living in Maine. She must have. Carol Ascher was not a monster. Nicola had seen the stricken look on her mother's face at the diner the other day when she had stormed off. To show up at Nicola's apartment, uninvited and unwanted, must mean that her mother had been desperate to see her.

But Nicola didn't want to think about that.

"How's the job going?" she asked.

"It's fun," Sophie said, "except for the kids. Well, a few of them are okay, but mostly they're annoying."

"And the other counselors?" Nicola asked, remembering that nasty-looking guy she had seen earlier.

"They're okay." Sophie shrugged.

"Come on," Nicola said, getting up from her seat. "I'll drop you home."

"Thanks, Nicola," Sophie said, after she had slurped the remainder of her drink. "For listening."

Nicola smiled. "My pleasure."

Chapter 20

Scott had gone to work and Sophie to her job at the day camp. Julie was alone in the house. She was sitting at the kitchen table with the remains of three breakfasts. There was a blob of grape jelly on the butter dish. That would have been Sophie. She could be very messy at the table and never cleaned up after herself. That was Julie's job.

Scott had taken his empty bowl and coffee mug to the sink. It was beyond his domestic abilities to put them into the dishwasher. That was Julie's job, too.

Julie sighed and folded her hands on the table. She was still wearing her wedding ring. She had sworn she would wear the ring Scott had given her until the day she died. She thought of her mother, who was still wearing her wedding band. Ken Elgort's death didn't erase the fact of his marriage to Bonnie; Bonnie Elgort was as devoted to her husband now as she had been when he was alive. Julie respected that devotion. It was what she had always wanted in her own marriage.

The ring. The visible token of her commitment to Scott. A commitment that had been mocked.

Suddenly, Julie decided that she would take the ring off. It was a symbol of what had never really been. From the start her marriage had been a myth she had convinced herself was true in order to be like every other married woman in Yorktide. Safe. Content. Loved.

Julie tugged at the band of gold. It wouldn't budge. The flesh of her finger looked puffy above and below the band. She tugged again with no luck. She went to the sink and ran cold water over her hand in the hopes that her finger might shrink enough for the ring to move. That didn't work. She soaped her finger. Still, no luck. Short of having the band severed by a jeweler it was staying where it was. On her fat finger.

No doubt about it. The ring was now a sign of how trapped she had become in her troubled self, a prisoner in her own body, a slave to a mind she could not control.

Scott wasn't overweight. Scott wasn't a victim of crippling self-doubt and self-loathing.

But he was a liar and a cheat. Two things Julie was not.

Not long after Julie had confronted Scott about the affair, she had gone in search of his wedding band. The idea that he might have lost or sold it was plaguing her.

The ring lived in Scott's sock drawer; he only put it on for special occasions, like Sophie's baptism and Ken's funeral. And there it still was, in the original box from the jeweler, next to the underwear and socks, some of which were so threadbare they should be thrown away. Julie had stared at the socks. Why should she continue to perform the myriad little services she had always performed for her husband, like replacing his socks when they were worn, presoaking the most stained of his work clothes, and making sure he took his daily vitamin?

Because she was still his wife. She had not asked Scott to make her doubt the validity and importance of her role in his life. But he had.

Julie had left the worn socks where they were.

Slowly, Julie rose and brought the dirty breakfast things to the sink. She turned to open the dishwasher and stopped. Shoulders hunched, she made her way upstairs to her bedroom. On the way, she remembered that her mother and her aunt were meeting that morning at Judith's house with the express purpose of coming to a fair and amicable agreement regarding Ferndean House. Julie highly doubted that such a thing was possible given the fact that each sister wanted all or nothing. Well, maybe Judith could work a miracle.

Julie highly doubted that, too.

Chapter 21

Bonnie and Carol arrived at the same moment. Bonnie didn't know how to take this. Was it mere coincidence, or had Carol planned to upstage her sister's entrance? But that was silly. She needed to calm down and keep a clear head if she was to emerge victorious from this meeting.

Each sister got out of her car. Carol looked as if she was dressed for a board meeting of a big corporation. She was wearing a tailored lightweight suit and pumps with heels. Her face was made up, and as Bonnie got closer to her sister she realized that Carol was wearing a scent. It smelled expensive.

Bonnie was now acutely aware of her own casual appearance. The cotton pants she had on could pass for pajama bottoms, and the blouse had to be at least ten years old. It was clean but faded. Bonnie had never minded that before. The sandals on her feet had also seen better days.

Carol nodded at her sister just as Judith opened the door and waved to them.

"I don't think I've ever been to your home before," Carol noted as they came up the walk and passed through the front door, on which was hung a wreath of dried herbs.

"You haven't. Welcome."

Bonnie liked Judith's home. It was very cozy. It had been built in the bungalow style and was decorated with all of Judith's favorite things: seashells, rough gemstones, fluffy pillows, books, milk glass items, more books. The furniture had accumulated over the years, largely culled from flea markets and antique shops. The walls were covered with artwork—paintings by local artists; posters from museum exhibits; embroidered samplers Judith had inherited from her mother.

Bonnie noted that in deference to Carol's dislike of dogs, Judith had let Cocoa and Puff into the yard, where they were happily romping with each other and their pile of outdoor toys.

"I've made coffee and tea, and there are scones and muffins," Judith said as the women took seats at the table in the sunny kitchen. "I don't think important conversations should take place on an empty stomach."

Carol accepted a cup of black coffee. Bonnie poured a cup of tea and added her customary milk and two sugars. Neither sister took a scone or muffin. Judith put one of each on her plate and began to eat with relish. "So," she said between mouthfuls, "we're here to see if we can come to some sort of agreement about the future of the family homestead. Yes?"

"Yes," Carol said briskly.

Bonnie nodded.

"As I understand it," Judith went on calmly, "Carol, you want to buy Bonnie's share of the house and live there full-time. On your own."

"That's my plan," Carol said.

Your desire, Bonnie corrected silently. *I have to consent and I won't.*

"And, Bonnie," Judith said, "you want to live at Ferndean full-time. Alone."

"Yes, I can't afford to buy Carol's half of the house, even if I sell the cottage. She knows that. It's not fair. I'm the one—"

Judith put her hand in the air. "One step at a time. Carol?"

Carol looked squarely at her sister. "My buying you out of your share of Ferndean is a win-win for you. You get a packet of money and the house stays in the family. You'll no longer be burdened with the care and upkeep, but you'll be able to visit."

Bonnie frowned. "How can I be sure you won't decide to sell Ferndean to some stranger next year or the year after that, just because you've grown tired of Yorktide again? No, I don't trust you."

"Well, at some point the house might have to be sold." Carol's tone was maddeningly reasonable. "Properties are investments. If a disaster strikes that makes it necessary for me to sell the house and the land it sits on, I'll have to do it. I can't promise what it's not in my power to promise."

"Scone? Muffin?"

Judith was holding the plate of baked goods aloft. Bonnie, usually unable to resist bread in any form, shook her head. Of course, Carol wouldn't have anything. She probably never ate carbs. Or only rarely.

"Properties are not investments," Bonnie said, turning back to her sister. "Well, maybe some are, but not Ferndean. It's a home. It's a legacy."

"We're going in circles," Judith murmured.

"And whose fault is that?" Carol asked. "My sister refuses to see reason."

"Your reason is not the same as my reason," Bonnie snapped.

"It's time for old wounds to heal," Carol declared. "It's time for us to be close like we once were, when we were little."

"Why?" Bonnie demanded. "Because you want it? It takes two to reconcile, Carol. And I'm not sure I want to reconcile on your schedule and according to your rules."

"What rules? And what schedule? I'm not in any rush."

Judith laughed. "Sorry. Just that none of us at this table are spring chickens. Our time on this earth is limited."

"Judith has a point. We're not getting any younger," Carol said. "If I lived here in Yorktide, we could help each other as we age."

"I'm not stopping you from moving back to Yorktide," Bonnie cried, her voice high and thin. "Buy yourself a swanky condo on the beach or one of those McMansions in a gated community. I want to live at Ferndean. I believe I have a right to the house. I've been the one taking care of it. Besides, I know Mom and Dad would have wanted me to have Ferndean."

"If they'd wanted you to have the house, they would have changed their wills."

Judith cleared her throat. "Forgive me for pointing out the obvious, but there's no reason both of you can't live comfortably at Ferndean. The house is certainly big enough."

"No," Bonnie said emphatically.

"It wouldn't work," Carol said firmly.

"And what, exactly, is your objection to living under the same roof as you did when you were children? Bonnie, you go first."

Bonnie hesitated. "We're *not* children," she said finally. "Nothing is the same as it was."

Carol nodded. "Bonnie is right."

"Fair enough," Judith murmured.

Carol suddenly turned to face her sister. "If my being at Ken's funeral meant so much to you," she said, "why didn't you postpone it until I was back in the States?"

Judith choked on a bit of scone.

Bonnie was appalled by the callousness of the suggestion. "My husband," she said coldly, "deserved a timely burial. Who do you think you are that you'd matter more to me than Ken?"

"You could have hosted a memorial the following month," Carol pointed out. "I would have been here for that."

"Would you have?" Bonnie laughed a bit wildly. "I don't think so!"

Once again, Judith raised her hand. "Whoa! We're way off topic now. Calm down, the both of you."

Carol rose from her chair. Bonnie noted how her sister held herself, so erect and still; she looked as if she might be royalty. Bonnie felt a shiver of fear.

"I think we're done here," Carol said. "I'm open to another meeting at a time when my sister is ready to take a negotiation seriously."

Judith rose. "I'm sorry we don't seem to have made any progress," she said.

Carol nodded and left the kitchen. A moment later the front door opened and closed.

"Well, that was unproductive," Judith said, sinking back into her chair. "But I think if you're going to get anywhere with your sister you're going to have to give a little, just at first, sort of open the gates as it were."

"If I give an inch she'll take a mile," Bonnie said darkly. "Anyway, what can I give? There's no compromise here, Judith."

Judith sighed. "Maybe not. I just don't know."

"Thank you," Bonnie said feelingly. "It was good of you to try to broker a peace."

A few minutes later, Bonnie slid behind the wheel of her car and started the engine. Her relationship with Judith had always been warm and uncomplicated. There were several reasons why they got along. The biggest one, Bonnie believed, was that they were not sisters.

Bonnie glanced at the dashboard clock. It was only ten thirty, but the morning had been a trying one; she was ready for a nap.

Chapter 22

Carol was surprised her daughter had agreed to meet. After their last meeting, she had been fairly sure Nicola would make it a point to avoid her mother like the plague. Of course, the intention behind Nicola's agreeing to see her mother now might be to lambast her for her bad behavior or to criticize her for her poor decisions.

Because Nicola had made it clear she didn't believe her mother had come back to Yorktide for her family.

"Thanks for meeting me," Carol said, taking a seat across from Nicola in a little coffee shop Judith had recommended. Since when did a mother have to thank her child for agreeing to have coffee with her? Since the mother had unintentionally created a situation of estrangement.

Nicola didn't respond. Nor did she look directly at her mother. For a second, Carol felt almost sick. Did her daughter genuinely dislike her? Then she got a grip on herself.

"Have you heard anything from the Peace Corps?" she asked.

"Not yet," Nicola said shortly. "I heard you and Aunt Bonnie met at Judith's to talk about Ferndean. Bonnie said it didn't go very well."

"No, it didn't." Carol decided to say no more. That matter was between the two Ascher sisters. Carol only hoped that Bonnie hadn't told Nicola about her suggesting that Bonnie should have delayed

Ken's funeral. Yes, she knew of cases where just such a thing had been done, but she should have known it was a choice her sister never would have made.

Nicola leaned forward. "Why are you doing this to her? Why are you persecuting your own sister?"

"I'm not persecuting anyone," Carol protested. She had been right. Nicola had agreed to meet her mother only to take her to task. "I have an equal right to the house."

"Maybe legally, but not morally."

"The money Bonnie would make from a sale of her half of the house would set her up for the rest of her life."

"You can't equate money with time and effort and love," Nicola argued. "Bonnie and Ken put all of those things into Ferndean over the years. That's worth far more than any amount of cash."

Carol restrained a sigh of frustration. "Can we let this subject drop for the moment?"

Nicola sat back again. "Fine. For the moment."

"Thank you. By the way, I haven't seen Julie yet. Has anything changed between her and Scott? Is she feeling any better about herself?"

"I don't think so. All I really know is that the situation is hurting Sophie. Children feel their parents' troubles very keenly."

"I'm aware," Carol said carefully. "So, you and Julie aren't close?"

"I didn't say that," Nicola argued. "It's just that she doesn't talk to me about what she's feeling since she found out about Scott's affair."

"Is she talking to anyone?" Carol asked. "A friend maybe?"

"Why do you care so much about Julie anyway?" Nicola demanded.

"She's my niece," Carol answered.

"You hardly know her," Nicola countered.

"And?" Carol said. "Do you need to know someone intimately before you can feel sympathy for them in a time of need?"

Nicola frowned. "No, sorry." Then she shrugged. "Julie has a best friend, Aggie, but Bonnie thinks they haven't seen each other in a while."

"So, she's pretty much isolated."

"No, she isn't. She has her mother and me and Judith."

"All too close to the situation to be of real help. She needs the perspective of an impartial counselor. I don't suppose Scott would agree to couple's therapy?"

Nicola shook her head. "I have no idea. I haven't said more than two words to him since all this happened. My intuition is . . . Never mind."

"No," Carol pressed. "Tell me."

"Aren't I too close to the situation to be of any help?" Nicola snapped. Then, she shook her head. "Okay, my intuition is that Scott would do whatever it takes to get the marriage back on track. I think it's Julie who's . . ."

"Stalled."

"Yes, that's one way to put it." Suddenly, Nicola pushed back her chair and reached for her floppy canvas bag. "I really have to be going."

"But we—" Carol began.

"Thanks for the coffee."

And Nicola was off, hurrying to the door of the coffee shop.

Carol remained where she was.

Had there been progress between mother and daughter?

No. Not much.

A burning itch on the left side of Carol's neck prompted her to raise her hand, then drop it. One did not scratch the evidence of eczema or psoriasis. Stress. This always happened when she began to feel out of control of a situation. Overwhelmed. Plagued by self-doubt.

Abruptly, Carol rose and left the coffee shop. She did not want to go back to Ferndean.

She wanted to go home. To New York.

Chapter 23

Nicola and Sophie had promised to help Judith set up a trellis in her backyard. Judith had promised them pizza as payment for their time and labor. Nicola would do just about anything for free pizza. Besides, she liked Judith and hoped to grow into the sort of woman her relative was—independent, kind, wise, funny. In short, all things good.

Not like Carol Ascher. Okay, she wasn't an evil person, but she could be so incredibly annoying, saying that family wasn't capable of helping Julie in her current crisis. Julie's family *was* being of help, Nicola was sure of it. At least, she hoped they were.

And another thing. She probably shouldn't find her mother's interest in Julie suspicious, but she did. It wasn't that she was afraid Julie would snatch away what little attention Carol currently paid her daughter. It wasn't that at all.

And she wished her mother hadn't mentioned the Peace Corps. She still couldn't understand why she hadn't taken a step beyond the preliminary research she had done weeks earlier. She was annoyed with herself; it wasn't like her to stop before she had gotten started.

But there was Judith's house. Sophie's bike was leaning against the garage. Scott had bought the bike on Craig's List for a song and had refurbished it beautifully for his daughter. Scott was not a bad guy. It was a shame he had done what he had done.

Nicola joined the others in the backyard. Sophie was wearing the shortest of jean shorts. How did she ride a bike in those things, Nicola wondered? Judith was wearing cropped jeans, espadrilles, and a navy-and-white-striped boatneck T-shirt. She always managed to looked put together, no matter how casual or spontaneous the occasion. Nicola glanced down at her own oversize T-shirt and floppy, knee-length shorts. A fashion icon she would never be.

It didn't take long for the three women to get the trellis in place, after which they sat around the table with the promised pizza and homemade lemonade. Judith was drinking a beer. She was a fan of the local breweries.

"Can I give Cocoa a piece of my pizza?" Sophie asked. The mutt was staring up at Sophie with big brown doggie eyes that could move even the stoniest heart.

"Sure, but you'd better give one to Puff, too. He gets jealous very easily."

"You spoil them," Nicola said with a smile, scratching behind Cocoa's floppy ear as he chewed the last of his snack.

"Guilty as charged."

Having gotten their treats, the dogs trotted off. Judith had adopted the brothers when they were puppies. Now, they were going on ten. Adults they may be, but they often still acted like silly children.

Suddenly, Sophie sighed. "If only Grandpa were alive, Dad never would have had an affair. He would have been too afraid of what Grandpa would think of him."

"Dear girl," Judith said, her tone ever so slightly amused, "sex is far more powerful than the thought of being taken to task by an irate father-in-law. Nothing could have stopped your father from having an affair with that woman, not once he'd entertained the thought."

Sophie groaned dramatically. "I swear, I am never going to have sex ever if all it causes is trouble."

"Sex when you're in love is wonderful," Nicola said automatically. Not that she knew all that much about sex or about love.

Sophie shrugged. "Whatever."

"How is your mother faring?" Judith asked suddenly.

Sophie shrugged. "You know."

"If I knew I wouldn't be asking," Judith pointed out.

"It's got to be tough for her," Nicola said gently.

Sophie suddenly got up from her chair. "I have to go," she said huskily before she turned and began to hurry away.

"Thanks for your help," Judith called to Sophie's retreating back.

Nicola sighed. "When I look at her I can't help but see myself at her age. It worries me. I know we're very different people and the circumstances of our family life—mine then and hers now—are very different. But still, I wish I could make things better for her."

"We're doing what we can," Judith said. "It takes a village, or at least an extended family when times are tough and the parents seem unable to function at their best. And we're that family."

"My mother thinks that you and Bonnie and I are too close to Julie to be of any real help to her."

Judith shrugged. "Well, maybe she's right. But I don't think it hurts to try."

Nicola smiled gratefully at her cousin. "I agree," she said. "Like how you tried to help my mother and aunt at your house the other day."

"Not that I was successful," Judith noted.

"How could you have been? My mother is as stubborn as a mule when it comes to Ferndean. Well, to anything, really. She wants what she wants when she wants it."

"She was always a willful person, as far back as I can remember. That willfulness probably had a lot to do with her success in business."

But what about success in the personal sphere of family and friends? No, Nicola thought. There was no way Carol Ascher had come back to Yorktide for her family, no matter what she claimed. "Do you have any hope at all that my mother will forget about Ferndean and leave us in peace?" she asked.

Judith looked thoughtful for a moment. "I really can't say," she admitted. "I have a feeling there's something more going on with her being back in Yorktide than she's letting on. I suppose we'll just have to wait and see."

"Yes," Nicola said. "I suppose we will. But I'm not happy about it."

"You're not the only one."

Chapter 24

Julie was sitting at the kitchen table. She had eaten half a package of Oreo cookies in less than ten minutes. She was sure there were dark cookie bits in her teeth and knew she should brush them or at least rinse her mouth with water, but she couldn't seem to move.

The day before, Scott had asked Julie if she wanted to go to a new place in town for dinner. "How about it?" he said. "I hear they do a mean mac 'n' cheese, and they've got a nine-dollar burger and fries special."

Why should she say yes? Julie had thought. So they could sit in sulky silence or have an argument in public? So they could pretend that no one was watching their every move? "No," she said.

"But we have to go out at some point," Scott had pressed. "We have to get back to living our lives together."

Did they? Julie had been wondering. What did that mean, anyway? But maybe Scott had no intention of reviving their life together. Maybe by asking her out he was torturing her, mocking her, aware she felt unfit for public scrutiny.

Public scrutiny or not, there were times when Julie felt compelled to leave the house. Only that morning, just as the shops opened, she had driven into town to her favorite bakery for one of their massive cinnamon buns. On her way from the bakery back to her car she had spotted her impeccably dressed aunt walking purposefully along on the opposite side of the street. Julie had put her head down and quickened her pace. It had been a merciful escape.

Julie had eaten the cinnamon bun in the car.

"Julie?"

She looked up, startled. Scott was standing over her. She felt like a small, defenseless animal that had been cornered by a predator.

"I need to talk to you," he said. He sat in the chair across from her and pushed the package of Oreos to the side. "I need you to listen to me, please, Julie."

Julie didn't say yes or no.

"Sometimes," Scott went on, taking her silence for acquiescence, "I feel overwhelmed by you and your mom and Nicola and Judith and now Carol. Part of what's frustrating me is that I feel we're never alone. We're surrounded by all these people watching us and waiting for something to happen and—"

"These people love me," Julie said, finally finding her voice. "They're my family."

"I know that. But we need to find a way to be alone," he pleaded, "just you and me, to work this out."

What did Scott mean by being alone? Sex? Because that was never going to happen again. He would only be thinking of Laci Fox and of how Julie came up short compared to The Other Woman. Wasn't that always the way?

"You're ignoring us, Julie," Scott went on, his voice now low and urgent. "And you're ignoring Sophie. I'm trying with her, I really am, but she's so mad at me. You're her mother. You've got to help her."

"She doesn't need any help," Julie replied automatically. Why had she said that? Of course, Sophie needed help.

Scott shook his head. "Haven't you heard her talk about that guy at her camp, Tim? He's no good, Julie, I can feel it. I've asked around, but nobody seems to know who he is or where he comes from. I'm afraid she's getting involved with him and if she won't even talk to me there's nothing I can do to protect her." Scott sighed. "God, I wish Ken were here. Sometimes I feel so lost without him. In a lot of ways, he was more of a father to me than my own was." Scott swallowed hard. "Julie," he went on, "I know you're depressed. It's obvious, like the last time, after Sophie was born. I'm worried about you. You don't seem to care about riding your bike or hiking or about . . ."

"About what?" Julie said. "My appearance? Well, you're right. I don't. What's the point?"

Scott put his hands to his head. "The point is that . . . I don't know how to put it. The point is that it's wrong. I mean, it's not right that you shouldn't care about yourself."

Julie rose from her chair. "Why don't you run off to Laci's house then?" she snapped. "I'm sure she's skinny and pretty enough for you!"

"That's unfair." Scott dropped his hands and rose from his seat. His expression was grim.

Julie shook her head and walked from the room. *Unfair*, she thought. *Welcome to my world.*

Chapter 25

"Oh, my God, I haven't seen you two side by side in forever!"

Bonnie managed a smile. Carol didn't seem able to, or maybe she just didn't care to.

"So, Carol, what are you doing in Yorktide?"

Gina Collins was a nice woman and there was nothing at all wrong with her greeting two people she had grown up with. Still, Bonnie wished she would go away.

"I'm visiting my family," Carol said. She didn't ask after Gina's family.

Bonnie continued to say nothing.

Gina looked a bit miffed. "Well, nice seeing you," she said before walking off.

"How did things go with Nicola?" Bonnie asked her sister when Gina had gone, moving her coffee spoon from one side of the saucer to the other.

"I'm sure you know that they didn't go well." Carol smiled slightly. "Sometimes I get the feeling you've turned my daughter against me."

"I did no such thing," Bonnie said loudly. Quickly, she glanced around the café. There was only one person other than Bonnie and her sister, and he was wearing ear buds. She doubted he had heard her, or that he cared what two mature women were talking about.

"What happened?" Carol pressed. "We haven't been terribly close in years, but now it's almost as if I disgust her. Is it something to do with Ken's dying? Did it affect her badly?"

Bonnie laughed. "Of course, it affected her badly! He was her father for the last ten years."

"Yes, all right. I know she's angry with me—you all are—for missing Ken's funeral. But it's got to be more than that. Has she had problems in other areas of her life since Ken died? Work? Friends?"

"No, she's been fine," Bonnie insisted.

"Any romance?" Carol asked.

"No."

Carol was quiet for a moment, occupied with stirring her coffee, though she had added neither milk nor sugar.

Bonnie wondered again why she had accepted her sister's suggestion that they meet for coffee this afternoon. She doubted that Carol had undergone a radical change of heart about Ferndean. Indeed, so far Carol hadn't said a word about the house. But she hadn't been particularly harsh or combative, either. That might be a good sign.

Suddenly, Bonnie became aware of the song playing softly on the café's music system: "You and Me Against the World."

"This song was a big hit the summer of '74," she said. "The summer you went away." Bonnie hesitated a moment before going on. "It reminds me of when we were young, the two of us against the world."

"I think it's pretty insipid," Carol replied. "I've always been more interested in art that challenges and provokes."

"I think you should be able to understand lyrics," Bonnie countered. "And I don't want to look at a painting and have no idea what it is I'm supposed to be seeing."

Carol shrugged. "To each her own."

Suddenly, the door to the café opened and in walked Judith. Bonnie waved eagerly at her cousin.

"What have you two been discussing?" Judith asked, joining them. "Wait. Let me guess. Ferndean."

"Art, actually," Carol said.

"We have different tastes," Bonnie said stiffly.

Judith laughed. "No surprise there."

"What Carol finds amusing, I find cruel."

Carol said nothing.

Judith frowned. "Cruel? What are you talking about?"

Bonnie gripped the cup of her now-cold coffee. "The ghost," she said.

"What ghost?" Judith asked.

"I thought it would be fun to scare my kid sister," Carol explained, in an unmistakably weary tone, "so I invented a story about a fifteen-year-old servant girl who had worked for our ancestors."

"It wasn't entirely a fiction," Bonnie cut in. "Carol showed me a photo of Ferndean's staff from around 1860. There was a teenaged servant girl. There's no record of what happened to her."

"Or of her name," Carol went on. "I called her Emily. I told Bonnie that Emily had fallen in love with the son of the local big-wig and that he had seduced her and, finally, as the son of a bigwig would, dumped her. Poor Emily was so heartbroken—and possibly pregnant—that she lost her mind and went rambling off into the winter's night in only her nightgown. By the time she was found the next day, she was delirious and sick. She was brought back to the house and died two days later in her bed in the servants' quarters, now the attic."

"Then," Bonnie went on with a frown, "Carol told me Emily's spirit roamed the halls at night, moaning and sighing over her cruel lover. Can you imagine how the tale affected an eight-year-old? For months, I was petrified to turn the lights off at night. Finally, Mom got me to tell her why I was so upset and set me straight."

Judith whistled. "Carol, you really were a little shit at times, weren't you?"

"It was only a story," Carol protested. "I was an imaginative kid."

"And you didn't get punished for terrorizing me, did you?" Bonnie said.

"It was hardly terrorizing."

"I couldn't go near the attic for years!"

"Well," Judith said, "it's normal for siblings to taunt and tease one another. But not when they're adults, I should think."

Carol took a sip of her coffee.

"I agree," Bonnie said robustly. "Adult siblings should treat each other with respect."

"Our mothers weren't particularly close," Judith noted. "But they were nice to one another."

Carol shrugged. "Weren't they eight years apart? Maybe the age gap kept them from being closer."

"I think that age might have been a factor early on," Judith said. "But it shouldn't have been a problem when the sisters were adults. I think their poor relationship had to do with my mother and father joining that whacky church when I was little. Even though they didn't stick with the church for all that long, they were different people after. Far more liberal than Shirley and Ronald." Judith shrugged. "Then again, that's my mother's explanation for the divide. Who knows what Shirley would have to say about it."

Bonnie wondered. A problematic sister duo that prefigured the troubled relationship between Carol and Bonnie. The sins of the mothers being visited upon the daughters? One thing was pretty certain. The eight-year age difference between Shirley and Mary had made it unlikely they ever dated the same man while growing up.

Suddenly, Judith rose from her chair. "I'm off," she said. "I only stopped in because I saw you two sitting here." With a wave, she was gone.

"I should get going as well," Carol said, rising and adjusting the chain strap of her tiny, quilted leather Chanel bag. Bonnie's bag was a handmade patchwork affair big enough to hold a loaf of bread, a carton of milk, and a library book, along with her wallet, keys, and package of tissues.

Carol walked briskly to the door and out of the café. Bonnie brought the cups and saucers to the counter. She thought about what she had said only a moment earlier, that adult siblings should treat one another with respect. Well, even if Carol couldn't bring herself to follow that simple rule of conduct, Bonnie could. She was the bigger person.

On her way home, she would stop off at Ferndean House and spend some time tending the vegetable garden. And whatever produce was ready to be harvested she would leave on the back deck for her sister. And if Carol didn't appreciate her sister's efforts, well, that was her problem.

Chapter 26

Carol was stretched out on the bed in what had been her parents' bedroom so long ago. She had a headache that strong black tea and three ibuprofen had not been able to budge. Add to that the fact that her eczema outbreak was still going strong, and it could be said that Carol Ascher was not a happy camper.

It was not pleasant having the past, both the good and the bad of it, staring you in the face. And how could it not? She was sleeping in what had been her parents' bedroom (though the bed had long since been replaced). Every morning she ate her breakfast in the kitchen where her mother had fed her family cold cereal in summer and hot oatmeal in winter. Every evening she saw virtually the same serene view from the back deck that her father had enjoyed observing while he smoked his daily pipe.

Earlier, Carol had been surprised to learn that Bonnie was still upset about that silly ghost story she had made up all those years ago. She had thought: One had to move on, let go of the past, get over childhood fears and resentments.

Carol put her hand to her aching head. Easy enough to say when you didn't live in the town where you had been born. Of course, Bonnie couldn't let go of the past. It was the very air she breathed.

Not that it was ever advisable to forget all that had gone before. Certainly, Carol had no desire to forget the wonderful early years of her daughter's life. If she viewed those times now with all the warm fuzziness of nostalgia, so be it.

The tiny curl of dark hair at the nape of Nicola's neck. The way her wee fists would wave when she was excited. The little sighs she would utter as she fell asleep.

Carol breastfed for six months. It wasn't always easy or convenient, but she was glad to do it. She enjoyed bath time with her daughter, soaked clothing and all. She loved going for long walks in the city, Nicola strapped to her chest; she would point things out to her baby daughter, talk to her constantly, know that she was absorbing knowledge faster than her mother could impart it.

Men came and went in Carol's life, but she kept them away from her daughter. She might not have been the perfect mother—she had never believed that she would be—but she had provided a stable home life. Dinner was always at six unless one of Nicola's school activities pushed it forward or backward. There were strict bedtimes, and access to television, video games, and social media was limited and monitored. Reading was emphasized. She taught Nicola the value of a budget.

It was only when Nicola turned fourteen that things began to go wrong.

Suddenly, she was angry at the world. Her school work began to suffer; she started to get into trouble both in and out of school.

One night she was brought home by the police. She had been involved in a fight at an adult nightclub where she should not have been. In truth, she was innocent of taking part in the brawl, other than in cheering on one of the brawlers. Carol and the parents of the other kids involved were able to pull strings and keep their children from being formally charged.

Carol tightened security measures at home, but Nicola managed to work around them. She was smoking and drinking. There was a shoplifting incident.

Carol took Nicola to a therapist. It did not go well.

After being caught cheating on a test, Nicola's exclusive private school threatened to expel her.

Carol told none of this to Alex. At times, she felt guilty about her silence. At times, she desperately wanted to turn to *someone* for help, anyone. But she never did.

Maybe if she hadn't gotten sick things might have turned out differently.

But she had gotten sick. She had been experiencing severe pelvic pain and bleeding for some months before she decided to undergo an abdominal hysterectomy. The surgery was radical. It involved a large incision and a slow and painful recovery. Her doctor predicted six weeks at home before Carol would be ready to go back to work and assume normal activities such as grocery shopping and going to the gym.

But what did doctors know? The pain did not abate like it was supposed to. And before she knew what was happening, Carol found herself addicted to the opioid painkillers she had been prescribed. At the time, she hadn't known that if you took opioids for three or four days, it was likely that a year later you would still be taking them.

After a time, Carol needed access to more drugs than she could get from her doctor. A colleague on a museum committee, a high-society wife addicted to cosmetic surgery, became her supplier.

Managing the addiction, running a competitive business, and trying to parent a wildly unpredictable teenager proved exhausting. After Nicola faked her own assault in a bid to punish her mother, Carol knew she had to take a drastic step to end the nightmare.

Nicola might be sent to live with Bonnie and Ken in Maine. Life in a stable home with her stable aunt and uncle might help straighten Nicola out. Bonnie and Ken had been good parents to their daughter, Julie. And they had taken excellent care of Shirley Ascher in her last years. It could not have been easy, tending to a sick and dying woman who refused to leave her home when she might have been better off in nursing care.

Yes, Bonnie and Ken knew what they were doing. And Carol would pay them for Nicola's upkeep—food, clothing, education, allowance—as well as give them a sum for their pains.

Surprisingly, Bonnie and Ken agreed almost immediately. Almost. Carol wasn't sure who was the holdout; it didn't matter in the end.

Nicola was not happy. "Maine? I'm going to live in Maine? You've got to be kidding me. People wear plaid without irony. No. Way."

But to Maine Nicola had gone. Ten long years ago.

Carol slowly rose to a sitting position, pillows propped behind her back.

Maybe if Bonnie knew the whole truth, she might feel less angry at and resentful of her sister.

Or she might grow even angrier and more resentful.

Which was why Bonnie could never know about her sister's addiction.

Ever.

Chapter 27

"Are you sure you don't need anything for your apartment? Maybe a paper towel dispenser? I don't know why you don't have one. They're convenient and keep the towels from getting dirty before you can use them."

Nicola was trying her best to ignore her aunt's chatter. Her nerves felt frayed. Maybe she should have gone straight to her apartment after work. Instead, she had stopped at the cottage. In so many ways it was still her real home. But sometimes, it was best not to go back there.

"I'm going to Reny's anyway, so really, it would be no problem to pick up whatever you need. Did you ever replace the plastic colander you melted by accident? A nice aluminum one would be better, I think. Or I could—"

"Aunt Bonnie, stop! I said I don't need anything."

Bonnie looked as if she had been slapped.

Nicola shook her head. "I'm sorry. I didn't mean to use that tone of voice. It's just that my mother's being here is really upsetting me. I feel like she's invaded our . . . our sanctuary. It's making me short-tempered and I don't like it. Today at work I came close to snapping at one of the more difficult residents. I've never, ever done that."

Her aunt's expression transformed into a smile and she opened her arms for a hug. "It's all right," she said. "I should have seen that you weren't in the mood to natter on about home goods."

Nicola smiled. "We haven't had a real argument in almost ten years, not since I first came here to Yorktide and was so miserable and resentful."

"This is a trying time," Bonnie said.

"But we can't let my mother come between us."

"We won't," her aunt assured her.

"I know I keep saying this, but I wish Uncle Ken was here."

"Me too. Every moment of every day."

"Will we ever stop missing him?"

"I don't think so," Bonnie said. "But what we feel will change over time."

"Sometimes I have trouble remembering his face," Nicola admitted, her voice trembling. "How can that be? He hasn't even been gone a year. It frightens me. What kind of person does that make me? Uncle Ken was the best father I could have had for ten years of my life."

Bonnie took her niece's hand. "Grief is messy. I don't claim to understand it and maybe that's the point. It can't be understood, just . . . endured."

"I know. I mean, intellectually I know. But going through it I feel as if I know nothing. I was unprepared to feel so . . . vulnerable. Frightened. Sad. Tired. So many things and sometimes all at once."

"We're told to remember all the good times we had with the person who died," Bonnie said musingly. "To embrace those memories. To talk about them freely. We're told not to make a pariah of the dead person."

Nicola managed a smile. "It's a nice idea. Bonnie? Would it be awful of me to ask you to make your infamous spaghetti and meatballs for dinner tonight?"

Her aunt laughed. "Infamous? Sure thing."

Chapter 28

Julie had woken that morning with an inexplicable feeling of generalized optimism. In spite of what she had said to Scott, she knew she had been relatively absent from Sophie's life this summer. Why not seize the opportunity her good mood presented and suggest that they spend some quality time together? Sophie had the day off from camp. And she rarely, if ever, said no to a shopping expedition.

Still, it had taken some doing before Sophie had agreed to accompany her mother to the Reny's in Wells. Briefly, it occurred to Julie that Sophie might be embarrassed to be seen in public with her mother. But that was an unworthy thought. Sophie loved her mother.

No, Julie decided. The embarrassment was her own. She was the one painfully aware of having been branded with a scarlet *S* for "scorned." How was it, she wondered, that some wives who had been cheated on could be so powerfully angry about it, so loud in their condemnation, so eager to spread the word that their husbands were worthless bastards? And others, like Julie, drowned in quiet suffering.

Almost an hour after entering the popular discount store, Julie and Sophie emerged laden with large plastic bags stuffed with bargains.

"Thanks, Mom," Sophie said brightly. "This turned out to be way better than hanging out with Liz. She's been kind of obnoxious since she started seeing that guy. Like getting a boyfriend is a big deal or something. Please. Anyone can do it."

Julie smiled. She had allowed Sophie to spend more than she should have. She knew it was a bribe of sorts; no parent was completely immune to bribing a child in return for good behavior. Or for respect.

"It was fun, wasn't it?" Julie said. "I'm not sure how much I really need a new wallet, but I'm kind of glad I let you talk me into it."

Sophie rolled her eyes before putting on her sunglasses. "Mom, that old thing you've been carrying around is disgusting. The minute we get home you're taking everything out of it and tossing it in the trash."

She was touched by her daughter's concern for her mother's— happiness? Contentment? Whatever the word, Julie was thankful.

"You know what we should do?" Sophie said as they made their way through the parking lot. "We should see the movie about Freddie Mercury. It's playing again in South Portland."

"Since when are you into Queen?" Julie asked. She was genuinely surprised. She had assumed her daughter was only interested in the latest pop trends.

"OMG, Mom, really? Queen is awesome."

"I agree," Julie told her. "I'll check online for the showings." Scott also loved Queen, but Julie wouldn't ask him to come along.

"Hey," Sophie said suddenly, "isn't that what's her name, Sally Alcott over there? Look, getting out of that orange bug. I haven't seen her around in ages. I thought she moved away or something."

Sally Alcott. Julie darted a look in the direction Sophie had indicated. Yes. It was her. Julie hadn't heard her name spoken aloud since before Sophie was born. Scott had been briefly involved with Sally just before he and Julie started to date. Julie had often wondered if Sally was the woman with whom Scott had cheated not long before Scott and Julie got engaged. He had never said and Julie had never asked.

"Mom?"

Julie startled. "Yes. I don't know." She quickened her pace.

What was the likelihood of her running across Sally Alcott now, after all this time? What did it mean? Julie's good mood fled as suddenly as it had appeared. Did Sally know about Scott and Laci Fox? Did Scott still think about Sally? Did he still see her, secretly, behind his wife's back?

"What's the rush?" Sophie complained from behind her mother. "I can't run in flip-flops!"

There was the car. Julie began to shift the shopping bags in her right hand to her left in order to reach into her bag for her keys. And then she stopped in her tracks.

"What's wrong?" Sophie demanded.

What was wrong was that someone had hit Julie's car while she and Sophie were in the store. There was a large dent in the passenger door behind the driver's seat; the paint was badly scraped.

"Oh, my God, someone hit us!" Sophie cried indignantly. "I can't believe he didn't even leave a note. What a jerk!"

A hit and run. An act of disrespect. An attack even. Had the driver known the car was Julie Miller's? Could it have been Laci Fox? Of course not. But why not?

The shopping bags dropped from Julie's hands and she squeezed her eyes shut. She could feel her heart racing dangerously. A sob escaped her lips. She felt Sophie's hand awkwardly patting her shoulder.

"Mom, it's all right, it's just a dent. We'll get it fixed. We have insurance, right?"

But Julie barely heard her daughter's attempt at comfort. All she heard was the sound of mocking laughter in her head.

"Mom, come on, please." Sophie's voice was strained. "People are looking."

Was that true? Julie didn't care. And she very much did care.

"I'm going to call Dad."

Suddenly, Julie opened her eyes. "No!" she said fiercely. "Not your father. I'm fine."

Sophie looked unsure. And afraid. "Maybe you shouldn't be driving," she said.

Julie picked up the bags she had dropped onto the pavement. "I said I'm fine. Get in."

Sophie did. They drove back to the house in silence.

Julie's grip on the steering wheel was tight. Her emotions could not be trusted. They were too precariously balanced one upon another like building blocks piled high by an unsteady toddler. The slightest breath of air could knock all to the ground, resulting in a jumbled mess.

It was only when Julie pulled the car into the driveway that she finally spoke.

"Look," she said quietly, "don't tell your father that I . . . that I was upset. Please."

Sophie nodded; she didn't look at her mother. She got out of the car, grabbed her shopping bags from the back seat, and went into the house.

Only then did Julie follow.

Chapter 29

Bonnie was on her way to Ferndean. She had suggested that Julie come along for the ride; she suspected her daughter didn't want to be alone after the trauma of the accident and she was right.

Still, Julie wasn't keen on coming face-to-face with her aunt; she told her mother she would stay in the car.

Bonnie was bending down to leave the box of miniature garden gnomes she had purchased for the backyard just outside the front door when it opened. Bonnie stood up, almost dropping the box as she did. She had hoped to get away before Carol knew she was there.

"You didn't tell me you were coming by," Carol said.

"I'm just dropping off these garden gnomes," she said, annoyed that her voice was trembling.

"Why do we need garden gnomes?" Carol asked with a frown.

"We don't need them, exactly. I just thought they would look nice. I ordered them months ago, before you—"

"Well, you might as well come in." Carol waved to the car, beckoning Julie to join them.

"She doesn't want to visit," Bonnie said. "She told me so."

But Carol was undeterred. She continued to beckon until Julie emerged from the passenger seat. Of course, Julie had capitulated. No one could withstand Carol Ascher.

Bonnie felt she had no choice but to accept her sister's less-than-gracious hospitality. She brought the box of gnomes inside and placed it on a small table.

"I just made a pot of coffee," Carol said as she made her way to the kitchen.

Was she offering coffee to her guests? Bonnie took a chance. "Thanks," she said, following her sister. "I can come by another time when you're not here to set them up."

"Set what up?" Carol asked.

"The gnomes."

Julie appeared then in the kitchen. Bonnie was acutely aware of her daughter's disheveled appearance.

"Hello, Julie," Carol said. "Would you like a coffee?"

Julie attempted a smile. "Sure. Thanks."

"It's good to finally see you. Though you look distressed. What's wrong?"

"Julie was a victim of a hit and run," Bonnie blurted.

"Just now? Were you hurt?" Carol asked. She put her hand on Julie's arm for a moment.

Bonnie continued to speak for her daughter. "The other day. She wasn't in the car at the time. It was parked in a lot. Whoever it was drove off and didn't leave a note."

"Bad luck, but at least no one was injured," Carol said, as she set three cups on the kitchen island. "Hopefully insurance will cover the cost of repairs."

Julie took a sip of her coffee. "Of course, this would happen to me," she said suddenly, with a pained little laugh. "I'm clearly not one of those people meant for success or happiness."

Carol took a sip of her own coffee. "Self-pity isn't attractive, Julie," she said.

"Don't I have the right to self-pity?" Julie retorted, to her mother's surprise. "Doesn't everyone have that right at some point in her life?"

"Yes," Carol said. "But only for a bit. Other people get tired of a demonstration of self-pity pretty quickly."

Bonnie felt the blood rush to her cheeks. "Don't talk to my daughter that way," she spat.

"What way?" Carol said calmly. "I'm just trying to help. A year from now, nobody is going to have any time or attention to give to Julie and her woes. There will be new scandals to talk about."

"They'll still care," Bonnie insisted. "Yorktide will still care that one of its own was betrayed."

"It was a case of infidelity, mundane, boring, and unfortunately, all too common," Carol said. "Yorktide will soon wonder why Julie hasn't gotten on with her life."

"I don't want Yorktide to be thinking anything about me," Julie said fiercely. "I hate that my life is so public. The shame and humiliation . . . I feel like they'll never go away as long as I live here."

"But leaving Yorktide is out of the question, I suppose?" Carol asked.

"Of course, it is," Bonnie snapped. "This is Julie's home. It's where she's raising her child. She can't just uproot Sophie and drag her off somewhere foreign to start all over again. Of course, that's what you expected of your own daughter, that she start over again with—"

"With her family in a place she'd known since she was a baby," Carol snapped. She turned to her niece. "Are you thinking about leaving Scott?"

"I'm not leaving him," Julie said firmly.

"Okay, so you're committed to staying married to Scott and to staying here in Yorktide. Now what?"

"What do you mean, now what?" Bonnie said.

"Does Julie just let the depression go on without getting some professional help?" Carol asked. "If she hopes that the marriage is salvageable, the longer she's miserable, the more difficult it will be to set things right with Scott."

Bonnie opened her mouth to reply when suddenly, Julie slammed her cup onto the island.

"I just want to be left alone, all right? Look, I'm going to go for a walk. I'll meet you back at the car, Mom."

Neither of the older women tried to stop her from leaving.

Bonnie was furious. "Don't you have any compassion?" she hissed when Julie was gone. "She's depressed, Carol. She can't help herself."

"I do have compassion for someone in her situation," Carol said firmly. "More than you know."

"Her marriage was the most important thing in her life. Scott's betrayal has turned her world upside down. All she wants is to be able to believe in her marriage again."

"That's all well and good," Carol said. "But the marriage vow shouldn't be a manacle. When a person is being damaged by the union, she should be free to get out."

"So, you want Julie and Scott to divorce?" Bonnie demanded.

Carol sighed. "You're putting words into my mouth. All I know is that Julie is my niece and I don't like seeing her so miserable."

Bonnie felt chastened. "All right," she said. "Fair enough."

Carol busied herself fetching a paring knife and an apple. Bonnie cast an eye around the kitchen. Things looked pretty much the same as they had the day Carol Ascher had descended on Yorktide this summer. And Bonnie was relieved to see that the photograph of their parents taken on their honeymoon in Acadia National Park was still on the wall by the old landline. She thought that Carol might have hidden it away in a drawer, her relationship to the past not being one of warmth and affection.

Unlike Bonnie's. She watched as her sister took a dainty bite of a skinless apple slice. To this day, she could recall everything about the morning Carol left Yorktide. She could see it all so clearly in her mind's eye, the stricken look on her mother's face, the way the clouds dispersed just as Carol stepped onto the bus, the loud cheer that erupted from everyone who had come to see Carol Ascher off on her big adventure.

"I remember what you wore the day you left us," Bonnie said suddenly. "It was an orange mini dress with a white Peter Pan collar. I thought you looked so cool. For one crazy minute, I thought of going with you. Not that you would have wanted me to tag along."

"And not that Mom and Dad would have let you," Carol pointed out. She scooped the apple peel into her hand and turned toward the trash bin.

Bonnie stopped herself from telling Carol that the peels should be put in the compost bin.

"Do you remember the dress?" she asked instead.

"No," Carol said.

"Do you remember what you said to me just before you boarded the bus?" Bonnie pressed.

Carol smiled. "I said, 'Don't do anything I wouldn't do and if you insist upon doing it, keep it a secret.'"

"That's not what you said."

"Then it was probably something like it."

"You promised you would come home to Yorktide for Thanksgiving and Christmas." Bonnie swallowed hard. "And for my birthday in January."

"I would never had said something so silly," Carol protested. "Where would I have gotten the money to travel between New York and Maine so frequently? I had less than two hundred dollars to my name when I left Yorktide."

"You said it," Bonnie insisted. "I remember."

Carol sighed. "Well, if I did, it was just something people say to make the people they're leaving behind feel better. I'm sorry you took it so seriously."

"Why should I have thought my sister was lying to me?" Bonnie felt her face flush.

"It was an emotional moment. My intentions were good." Carol rubbed her temples before going on. "Look, I did nothing wrong by leaving Yorktide, and I'm tired of you trying to make me feel that I did."

"You should have come home more often," Bonnie said, "once you had the money."

"Why? Because you wanted me to?"

"Yes. Mom and Dad, too. We all wanted you to."

"Well, I didn't want to. You could have visited *me*."

"You know Ken and I couldn't really afford trips to New York," Bonnie said angrily. "And we didn't have the time to spare. Not with me taking care of Mom after Dad died and raising Julie and Ken's running the shop."

"Why didn't you ask me for help? You could have stayed at my place. I could have paid for your train tickets. I know Ken refused to fly."

"I would never have taken money from you." Other than for Nicola's care, Bonnie amended silently. But that was different.

"Fine. But that was your decision, not mine." Carol shook her head. "Look, this is ridiculous. I think you'd better go now."

Bonnie was out of Ferndean in less than thirty seconds, taking the box of garden gnomes with her. She didn't trust her sister not to throw them away. She felt slightly sick to her stomach. It was very clear to her now that a reconciliation was not possible. Every time she and Carol took a small step toward the old, childhood closeness, something yanked them back. If the relationship continued to degenerate at this pace there would be nothing left of the Ascher sisters by the end of the summer.

And Bonnie would lose Ferndean. She wasn't at all sure she would be able to handle visiting the home she loved with her sister in sole residence, watching her tear down walls and who knew what else, witnessing her making changes just for the sake of change.

Julie was waiting in the car, the windows rolled down.

Bonnie slid behind the wheel.

"We shouldn't have gone in," Julie said flatly.

Bonnie nodded. "I know."

Chapter 30

Garden gnomes? Carol shuddered. Creepy. But Bonnie had taken them away with her. Now there was nothing to spoil the serene view of lawn and trees and shrubbery and blooming flowers, still bright in the dying evening light.

But the lovely scene failed to soothe her. Carol was feeling a bit guilty. Maybe she had been too hard on Julie earlier. That tough love stuff was all well and good with someone who was simply being stubborn or lazy, but it wasn't so effective with someone who was suffering genuine emotional anguish. If only there was something Carol could do or say to lend support to her niece. What that might be she really didn't know.

And that ridiculous argument about Bonnie's not visiting Carol and Carol's not visiting Bonnie! Her sister was infuriating. It was as if for Bonnie, time—at least a strand of it—had come to a halt in the summer of 1974.

Still, what Carol had said about not wanting to visit Yorktide was not entirely true. There had been times when she had longed to be with her family, but something had always stood in the way. Tangible things like deadlines and duties. And intangible things, like fear of being sucked back into a life that wasn't hers to live.

Carol sank into her father's old armchair. She remembered so clearly those final weeks in Yorktide. Her parents had tried to be enthusiastic about their older daughter's adventure, but Carol was launching herself into the unknown and there was little, if any, substantial help or specific advice they could offer. Neither had ever been to New York City. All they knew of the place was what they read in the papers and very little of that at the time was good, certainly not when you were imagining your nineteen-year-old daughter arriving at Port Authority and coming face-to-face with criminals and drug addicts and prostitutes.

And yet, neither of her parents attempted to get Carol to change her mind. Why bother? Carol never changed her mind once it was made up; she just didn't. Shirley's sister had given it her best shot one afternoon, but her efforts were pathetically inadequate.

"Your parents are worried about your safety," Aunt Mary had said.

"Worrying is a waste of time," Carol had countered.

"You don't know anyone in New York."

"I'll introduce myself."

"Bad things happen to young women on their own in a big city."

"Like being kidnapped by white slavers?" Carol's tone was lightly mocking. "I'll be fine."

Aunt Mary had given up after that.

Absent-mindedly, Carol traced a worn spot on the right arm of her father's chair. How the chair had become "his" she didn't know; maybe simply because it was bigger than the others in the living room. That was usually the way. Father got the prominent place and Mother sat at his side. At least, that was how it had been with the Aschers.

That was one of the many reasons Carol had needed to get out. She dreaded falling into the domestic pattern embodied by her parents and everyone else she knew in Yorktide. But as the day of her departure drew near, she had become ever more afraid that she might lose the nerve to leave home. Underneath the excitement and her flippant dismissal of her family's concerns lay an awareness of how little she knew of what awaited her, along with an unexpected surge of fondness for all she was leaving behind. Bonnie was unhappy, her parents were anxious, her friends were jealous and admiring at the same time. Not one of them offered to go to

New York with her. "I'm bored, but I'm not crazy!" one of them said when Carol casually floated the idea of a traveling companion.

"I've never felt the draw of city life," Judith, twenty-four at the time, had admitted to Carol. "But I can recognize it when I see it. I think you're doing the right thing. I think you're doing what you need to be doing."

Carol had appreciated her cousin's words of support. Judith was someone she admired, and not only because she had the courage to be an openly gay woman in a time and place where many others might hesitate to be so honest. Later, in New York, there were times when Judith's example helped Carol to stay the path in spite of obstacles tumbling across her way.

Obstacles and accidents, like the loss of her necklace.

Carol's parents had given it to her on her sixteenth birthday. It was comprised of a thin gold chain from which hung a very small but very bright emerald. She had put it around her neck the morning she was due to leave Yorktide and in an uncharacteristically sentimental moment, promised herself that she would not take it off until she had "made it" in New York. What "made it" meant specifically, Carol didn't bother to define; she would know it when it happened.

But only weeks into Carol's new life in New York City, she realized the necklace was missing. She was at The Atlanta, the residential hotel where she was living, when she noticed its absence; for a moment, she felt hopeful that the necklace might turn up under her narrow bed or in a drawer of the rickety dresser. But a thorough search revealed nothing. Carol knew there was no point in looking elsewhere; if someone had found the necklace she would have kept it. Or maybe it had been crushed underfoot.

Whatever the case, the necklace was gone and suddenly Carol wanted nothing more than to give up on her foolish dream of a glamorous urban life, to settle safely into domesticity and routine back in Yorktide, and to never, ever think about what might have been.

But she didn't run away. And she never told her parents that the necklace was lost.

With a weary sigh, Carol got up from the armchair and went to the kitchen to make a cup of tea. She was not happy to have these memories dredged up. So much of one's past was best left forgotten. But coming back to Yorktide, settling in this old house chockfull of lives lived and lost . . . What had she expected to happen?

Still, the struggle might be worth it if only she could bond with her family so that one day, when her time on this planet was up, there would be someone to genuinely mourn her.

Carol didn't think that too selfish a desire.

Chapter 31

It had been Nicola's idea to get together and yet, she wasn't happy about it.

Why couldn't she just sever ties with her mother? Why this need to engage with the one person for whom she felt such a jumble of complicated emotions?

The stupid mother-child bond! It was enough to make Nicola decide—almost—never to have a child of her own.

Her mother had responded enthusiastically to Nicola's invitation. Why? Nicola had nothing that Carol Ascher might want.

Except love? Affection?

Ridiculous.

Nicola looked up as the bell over the door to the diner tinkled. Her mother was dressed as if they were meeting at The Plaza in New York City. She probably wished that they were.

"Hi," Carol said as she slid into the seat across from Nicola. "I hope I haven't kept you waiting."

Nicola shrugged. "It's fine." In truth, her mother was exactly on time. Nicola picked up the menu.

"Have you had the garden salad here?" her mother asked.

"I'm sure it's just a normal salad," she said testily. "You know, lettuce, tomato, cucumber."

Her mother just smiled.

A waitress came over to take their orders. Carol ordered a BLT. Nicola asked for a bowl of chicken noodle soup.

"I didn't know you eat bacon," Nicola said when the waitress had gone off.

"Why wouldn't I?" her mother countered.

Because . . . Nicola realized she had no clear idea why she had made that comment, except that she had meant it to be uncomplimentary in some way.

"What's Ana up to these days?" she said instead. Her mother's right-hand woman. The good daughter, Nicola thought. The kind of daughter her mother had wanted her to be, though she had never said as much. She hadn't had to.

"Running the business," her mother replied, "no doubt making changes to assure she stays afloat for a good many years to come."

"What does she think about your leaving New York?" Nicola asked. "I bet she was surprised."

"I didn't tell her about my plans to move back to Yorktide."

"Why not?" Nicola asked. "Wouldn't she want to know?"

"Maybe," Carol allowed, "but it's not as if we're close friends. We never spent much time together out of work."

"Who *are* your close friends then?" Nicola asked. "I don't remember people coming to the apartment all those years ago. I don't remember you spending time with other women unless it was at some business function."

"Mostly," Carol said, "I spend my time with myself. I get invitations to dinners and cocktail parties, but I usually don't go. I find them boring. And I've cut back on my committee work. Too many members are only showing up to get out of the house and away from a spouse they've come to despise. People like me get stuck with all the real work."

"What do you mean, people like you?" Nicola snapped. "People with no one to go home to?"

Again, her mother just smiled.

Nicola felt ashamed of her last comment. She, herself, didn't go home to anyone at the end of the day. Not having someone to go home to wasn't a sign of anything negative. It often was a sign of something very positive, like a strong sense of self-worth. "You didn't answer my question about friends," she said. "I know so little about you." And maybe her mother had wanted it that way.

The waitress delivered their lunch. When she had gone, Carol spoke.

"Let's focus on you," she said. "Tell me about *your* friends."

"I don't want to talk about my friends," Nicola snapped. "I want to talk about Ana. I want to know why you lavished so much attention on her, way more than you ever did on me."

"I did not lavish anything on anyone," Carol protested. "I told you, my relationship with Ana is professional and always has been. She's not my daughter."

"And your daughter is different from other people?" Nicola challenged.

Carol Ascher shook her head. "Of course."

Nicola picked up her spoon but realized she had no appetite. "Why didn't you ever think of me as a potential successor to your company?"

"Because I could see from early on you had little interest in design or decorating. You were always far more interested in, well, in people."

Nicola couldn't deny that. As long as the sheets were clean, there was a chair in which to curl up in with a book, and a table on which to set her laptop, she was reasonably content. Still, she was not willing to let her mother off the hook.

"You didn't really come back to Yorktide for me, did you?" she said.

"Didn't I? Look," Carol said with a sigh, "why did you ask me to have lunch with you today? To argue? Or maybe to talk like two women who happen to share the most intimate bond of all. A mother and her daughter."

"A daughter and her mother," Nicola corrected.

Her mother ignored the correction. "I saw Julie," she said. "She came by Ferndean with Bonnie."

"I didn't know," Nicola said.

"I think I was a bit rough on her. I didn't understand just how damaged she is right now."

"I told you she was hurting."

"Yes," Carol said. "You did." She picked up her sandwich and then put it back on the plate. "You're not eating."

Nicola shrugged. "Neither are you."

Suddenly, Nicola felt an icy wave of misery crash over her. This was awful. Painful. She felt sick. "I need to leave," she announced, clambering out of the booth.

"Nicola, wait," her mother began, reaching out to grab her arm.

But Nicola dodged her mother's touch and ran.

Chapter 32

Julie shifted on the wooden bench by the side of Byron's Pond, a fairly isolated spot she had been coming to since girlhood to be alone with her thoughts.

There were ducks floating about in the still water. The tall grasses along the edge of the pond were swaying ever so slightly in the breeze. The sun was warm. Julie wished she could take off the large, loose shirt she was wearing over her T-shirt, but then everyone would see how heavy she had become.

Julie almost smiled. Who was there to see? The ducks?

Scott used to come out to Byron's Pond when he was a kid. He liked to catch frogs, but he always released them so they could go back to their families.

Family mattered to Scott.

It mattered to Julie, too. At least, it used to.

Scott brought his lunch to work, as did most of the men on the construction team. Since the affair had come to light, Julie had occasionally forgotten on purpose to make his lunch the night before. The other day, she had genuinely forgotten to buy the sandwich bread Scott preferred. That morning, when Julie came into the kitchen, Scott was staring forlornly at his open lunch box.

"There's no bread," he said, looking up at his wife.

She had not replied but gone to the coffee machine to pour herself a cup.

"There are no cold cuts, either," Scott went on. "There's nothing for me to take for lunch."

Julie had turned from the coffee machine, cup in hand, and shrugged. "There are some yogurts, I think. And . . . No, Sophie ate the last of the bananas."

"Julie, I—" But Scott had not gone on. He simply turned and left the kitchen and then the house. His lunch box remained on the table.

Fine, Julie had thought. Scott would buy lunch. They could ill afford overpriced sandwiches and soft drinks on a regular basis, but maybe this would teach him to take responsibility for his . . . His what? Wants? Needs?

Julie remembered sinking into a chair at the kitchen table as a terrifying thought struck. Had she been ignoring Scott *all* the years of their marriage, somehow unaware that he was suffering?

It was possible. She could be stupid. It was probable.

Battered by feelings of self-doubt and worthlessness, Julie had fled the house for the peace of Byron's Pond.

Not that her troubled thoughts hadn't followed her there.

Julie sighed. When Carol had first arrived in Yorktide, Julie had felt almost relieved that there was a different crisis on which she could focus—the battle between her mother and evil Aunt Carol, come to steal away the beloved Ferndean. But now, Carol had joined the bandwagon loaded with people trying to force Julie to resolve the situation with Scott.

The problem was, Julie didn't want to engage with Scott in fights or in negotiation. Scott couldn't make her talk to him. No one could. So why didn't they stop trying?

Julie shifted again on the hard, wooden bench. She wished her father was alive. He of all people was the one who might have done something to make it all better. Julie had always been very close to her father. She had so many wonderful memories. The sixth-grade father-daughter dance. His patience while teaching her how to ride a bike. Sitting curled up next to him on the couch, gazing into the crackling fire on cold winter evenings. His walking her down the aisle at her wedding. His joy at the birth of his granddaughter. If Julie's relationship with her father was idyllic in memory it hadn't been far from idyllic in reality.

And one thing Julie did know for sure. Ken Elgort would not have encouraged his daughter in self-pity. He would have agreed with her aunt Carol in this. People got bored with self-pity. They got bored with people who were always depressed. And that meant that one day, maybe sooner rather than later, for all his desire to reconcile, Scott might decide that he was sick and tired of his wife's misery and silence, that he no longer cared about repairing the marriage, that he wanted to leave.

And then what? Would she care? Julie wondered. Was that what she really wanted, to leave the decision-making to Scott, to force him to act so that she didn't have to? How much of her stance toward her husband was based on passive aggression; how many of her feelings and how many of her actions was she really in control of at this point?

Julie was so very tired. She was so very sad.

Her phone chirped. She took it from her pocket. Aggie had sent her a text. It said: *I'm not giving up on our friendship. I can't. I miss you.*

There was a sad face emoji and a pink heart.

Julie did not reply to her friend's text. But she did get in her car and drive to the grocery store. Her family needed bread and cold cuts and bananas.

Chapter 33

Bonnie parked on the street outside her daughter's home. The things Carol had said about self-pity and about Yorktide growing bored with Julie Miller's story kept nagging at her. Carol might have badly underestimated the good nature of most Yorktide residents, but there was no denying that Julie was suffering.

Ordinarily, Bonnie didn't like to stop by without first calling to see if her visit was convenient, but now was not a time for niceties.

Bonnie got out of her car and walked up the drive to the front door. She rang the bell. After a full minute, she rang it again. Still, no one came to the door. As Bonnie was contemplating ringing the bell for a third time, Julie suddenly appeared. Her hair was uncombed. She was wearing sweatpants and a stained T-shirt.

"Oh," she said to her mother. "I was taking a nap."

"May I come in?" Bonnie asked, forcing a smile.

Julie didn't reply but turned and began to walk toward the kitchen. Bonnie followed, after closing the door behind her.

When she reached the threshold of the kitchen, Bonnie came to a halt. Julie had always been a good housekeeper. Maybe not as good as Bonnie herself but better than most. But since Scott's affair had come to light, she seemed to have lost interest in keeping a clean and tidy home. A month earlier, Bonnie had been mildly concerned. Now, she was alarmed.

A quick glance showed Bonnie that there were congealed spills on the stovetop. The floor hadn't been swept that morning or maybe even for days; Bonnie identified stray coffee beans, bits of crushed cucumber, and bread crumbs. An open can of Boston baked beans sat on top of the toaster oven; a spoon jutted from the can. There were unwashed dishes on the counter. How much energy did it require to load the dishwasher? Sophie had to be bothered by the state of her home. But not bothered enough to help out with the chores being left undone. Or maybe she was refusing to help her mother with the domestic chores as a gesture of defiance and anger.

At least, Bonnie thought, the lawn had recently been mowed. From the outside her daughter's home looked presentable. Not that any of the neighbors were ignorant of what had happened in the Miller marriage.

"Why did you stop by?" Julie asked, leaning against the sink.

Was there a note of suspicion in her voice? "I was just in the neighborhood and I . . . No reason."

"Do you want some tea or something?"

The offer wasn't really an offer and Bonnie declined. But as long as she was here, maybe it was best to say what she had been wanting to say for some time now. Bonnie cleared her throat.

"Julie, honey, you seem to have put on a lot of weight these past months. I've heard good things about that diet Bella from my old book group went on last year. She lost fifteen pounds just like that. Well, not just like that but—"

"I thought you always said that appearances don't matter," Julie snapped. "That it's what's on the inside that counts."

"Well, yes, of course," Bonnie said hurriedly, "but . . . I'm just concerned about your health, that's all."

"You think I look bad," Julie stated flatly.

"You don't look your best." Bonnie paused. "And I know you don't feel your best, either."

"I'm fine."

"Julie—"

"Mom! I said I'm fine."

"How is Scott?" Bonnie asked.

"What do you mean, how is he?" Julie said with a laugh.

"I mean, is he well? Is work going all right?"

"I don't know. We're not really talking."

"Don't you think that maybe you should—"

Julie laughed harshly. "Should what?" she demanded. "What do you know of infidelity? You have no idea of how I feel, of what I'm going through!"

"I'm sorry," Bonnie said. She felt very stupid.

Julie rubbed her eyes and took a deep breath. "Look, Mom," she said. "I know you're concerned. But right now, I'm busy so . . ."

Bonnie nodded. "I'll be on my way." She was about to add, "I'm sorry I came," but she didn't.

She got into her car and fastened her seat belt. The fact was that she wasn't sorry she had popped in on Julie, though she was sorry for the tactless way in which she might have spoken.

And for the first time since learning of Scott's affair with that dreadful Laci Fox, Bonnie felt sorry for him. Living with Julie when she was in this state could not be easy. In a way, he could be blamed for his wife's decline, but that didn't make it any easier on him.

"Oh, Ken," Bonnie murmured as she pulled away from the curb. "I need you. We all do."

Chapter 34

Carol sat in Ferndean's gloomy den. She hadn't bothered to turn on a light, making the room even darker and more glum than usual. The atmosphere suited her mood.

Nicola simply couldn't believe that her mother had come back to Yorktide for her family. And all those questions about Carol's relationship with Ana. Had Nicola really felt jealous of Ana? Why hadn't Carol noticed?

Maybe she *should* have considered Nicola as a successor to the business, at least asked her if she was interested in learning the ins and outs of her mother's profession. Instead, she had just assumed that she knew her daughter's mind.

And Nicola's running out of the diner . . . Carol had sat alone in the booth, numb, embarrassed, devastated, until the waitress had come by and with exaggerated delicacy, asked if Carol wanted the check.

At that moment, alone at Ferndean House, Carol doubted the wisdom of every major decision she had made in her personal life. The strange deal with Alex Peters. Shutting Nicola out of the business. Sending Nicola to Maine.

That day. That dreadful day. The day she had sent Nicola away.

Scott and Julie had come to drive Nicola to Maine; Carol hadn't trusted Nicola to travel on her own. Nicola refused to say farewell to her mother. She got into the back seat of her cousin's old white Subaru, crossed her arms over her chest, closed her eyes, and leaned her head against the back of the seat. Carol assumed she remained in the position for the entire journey to Maine.

Carol had returned to the apartment. She felt as if she might crumple to the ground. She couldn't bear to look in Nicola's room, not because of what she would find, but of what she wouldn't find. Her daughter.

That evening she received a call from Bonnie. She was too nervous to answer, so she let the call go to voice mail and later listened to her sister's message. She couldn't read her sister's tone of voice. Was it smug? Cautious?

Nicola is here safe and sound. She doesn't want to talk to anyone right now. I'll try to get her to call you tomorrow or the next day. (PAUSE) I hope you know what you're doing, Carol.

Carol had hoped so, too.

It wasn't until Nicola had been in Yorktide for almost a month that Carol told Alex what she had done. She did not mention her opioid use. Alex was not thrilled with the fact that Carol hadn't even hinted at the major decision she was considering on Nicola's behalf. He said as much. But Carol knew he wouldn't make waves; she knew she could trust him not to interfere. Because Alex Peters loved her.

Night was falling. The den was even darker now; Carol could barely see her hands lying flat on her lap. The dark felt comforting. It hadn't always felt that way. Certainly not during the years of her opioid use. She had remained highly functional and managed to keep her life running smoothly. Work was completed on time and more often than not, acclaimed. Bills were paid. She traveled to Morocco, to France, to Australia. She sat on the board of several arts organizations. When she visited her family in Maine she appeared the usual glamorous, trouble-free Carol Ascher everyone had always admired.

Only when Carol was alone in the dead of night did she feel like a fraud, worthless and ashamed. She knew she was not alone in these feelings, but the very last thing she would ever do was reveal her secret to her family. No, she would continue to suffer as she deserved to suffer, alone, overwhelmed by waves of self-hatred, despairing of ever being free of her demon, of ever being fully forgiven by her child.

Suddenly, Carol had had enough of the dark. Briskly, she got up and turned on every light in the den. On one of the higher shelves along the far wall sat the collected works of Charles Dickens in old, hardbound leather volumes. She remembered her mother buying the set for a dollar at a yard sale. Her family would laugh if they knew that Carol turned to Charles Dickens and his memorably odd characters when she needed a boost of spirits. They knew so little about the real Carol Ascher. Maybe they liked it that way.

And Carol knew so little about her family.

She didn't like it that way.

Chapter 35

Nicola sat heavily on her battered old couch. She felt slightly nauseous. Why was she thinking of that day now? It was almost as if someone or something had put the memory into her field of mental vision and compelled her to examine it afresh.

The day she had left New York and come to Yorktide, Maine.

A turning point in her young life. A momentous occasion, at least in retrospect. At the time—a nightmare.

The first few hours of the journey north, sitting in the back seat of Scott and Julie's car, was largely a blank now; Nicola had been in such a heightened state of emotion she had been almost paralyzed. Had she been playing her music? Probably. Maybe not.

It was only when they had reached Massachusetts and pulled in at a large rest stop that Nicola became alive again. She considered fleeing. The parking area was crowded; she could easily give her cousin the slip, but she had very little cash on her and no credit or debit card. Her mother had seen to that. Supposedly Aunt Bonnie was to control Nicola's finances for the foreseeable future.

The three of them got out of the car. Julie and Scott stretched. Neither seemed concerned that their charge would bolt. Maybe they trusted her. Maybe they just didn't care. But standing there in that busy parking lot, streams of people passing to and from the building that housed the bathrooms, fast-food vendors, and tourist shops, the sun beating down harshly, Nicola realized she felt too weary and defeated to attempt an escape. She would wait until she got to Yorktide, saved up some money, made a plan, and then she would . . .

They began to walk toward the building. Scott asked Nicola what she wanted to eat. Nicola said she wasn't hungry. Julie suggested Nicola have at least a snack. Something about the sympathy in her cousin's eyes, the warmth in her voice penetrated Nicola's emotional armor. She nodded; she couldn't trust herself to speak. Scott went off to the men's room. Nicola followed Julie into the building and onto the line at one of the food vendors. The smell of French fries tempted her. She realized she was famished. She hadn't eaten much of anything for days. When they reached the counter, Julie ordered a burger and fries; Nicola did as well. And a chocolate shake.

Scott met them at a table in the center of the space; he had gotten two slices of sausage pizza and a massive cookie studded with M&M's. Something about the cookie made Nicola smile. It was the first time she had smiled in . . . in a very long time.

They had eaten without speaking much. Scott offered both women a piece of his cookie. A half hour later they got back in the car. The rest of the drive north passed quickly.

And then she was in her new home.

It was only years later that Nicola began to understand how difficult it must have been for Scott and Julie to perform the task of bringing her to Maine. They had been young parents at the time; what had they made of Carol Ascher's decision to send her child away?

No doubt about it, Nicola would be forever grateful to her cousin and to Scott for their friendship. If Scott had messed up with Julie, well, that didn't erase the good things he had done and the sacrifices he had made for Julie's family.

Suddenly, Nicola became aware that night had fallen. She had been lost in memories for hours. She still hadn't eaten dinner and wasn't sure if there was anything other than peanut butter and a can of soup in the house. She wished someone was there to feed her.

She wished . . .

Chapter 36

Julie knew why her mother had come by the other day. To check up on her. Julie had been annoyed but also ashamed at how dirty and messy things had gotten in her home. Once she had found genuine fulfillment in offering herself and her family the gift of a clean and tidy home.

Once.

But her mother's unexpected visit had shaken her into action. At least, into the intention of action.

The first room she decided to tackle was her office. Every surface was covered with papers and books, unwashed coffee mugs, plates, and glasses. First, Julie gathered the latter and brought them to the kitchen. Next, she returned to the office and from underneath the desk, she dragged a cardboard box of miscellaneous papers and dumped the contents onto her work table. There had to be hundreds of photographs in the mix of school reports, clippings, and receipts. Here was a shot of her and Scott taken at their engagement party at Ferndean House. Julie frowned. Here was another of them taken at Christmas a few years before her father died. She turned abruptly from the table.

Julie moved across the room to an old metal filing cabinet she had inherited from the school. The frames inside two of the four drawers had somehow gone missing; in those two drawers Julie kept stacks of articles she had been collecting from magazines and newspapers since before her marriage. It was unlikely she would ever reread any of those articles. Why was she still holding on to them? The papers on the bottom were probably yellowed; some might even have crumbled into dust.

"Anybody home?"

Julie startled. She hadn't heard the front door open. She slid closed the drawer of the filing cabinet. A moment later Nicola stood in the doorway of the office.

"Sorry to just drop in," Nicola said brightly. "But I was in the neighborhood and I thought, why not?"

Julie bristled. In the neighborhood? Had someone sent Nicola as a spy?

"What are you up to?" Nicola asked, glancing around the room.

"Organizing," Julie said tersely.

Nicola went over to the pile of papers and photos on the work table and began to sift through them. "I make it a point to throw something out every day. Getting rid of stuff on a continual basis helps keep my place organized. And my head, for that matter."

Julie said, "Mmm."

"Oh, this is cute!" Nicola held up a class photo that showed Sophie in pigtails and wearing a My Little Pony T-shirt. "What grade was she in?"

"That was kindergarten," Julie said.

Suddenly, Nicola laughed. "Oh, this is embarrassing! This is me, the second summer I was living here. Why I thought men's overalls were a good idea I'll never know. Still, they were comfortable."

Julie remembered those big, baggy overalls Nicola had lived in that summer. Maybe she should get herself a pair. The overalls would mask her ever-increasing figure.

"Where was this taken?" Nicola asked, lifting another photo from the pile. "It says May 1974. That's the year my mother left Yorktide."

Julie peered at the white bordered photo; the colors were slightly faded. "That was Dad's family's backyard," she said. "The Elgorts still had that old swing set when I was little. And that's Judith on the end, and Bonnie next to her. That guy I don't know, or that girl. But those two are, of course, Carol and Ken."

"But he's got his arm around her waist."

Julie shrugged. "Well, they were dating."

Nicola looked up at Julie, her eyes wide. "Wait a minute, my mother dated Uncle Ken?"

"Yes," Julie said matter-of-factly. "I assumed you knew. I found out about it when I was a kid. Not that Bonnie or Carol ever talk about it. I guess you could say it's a secret hiding in plain sight."

Nicola tossed the photo back onto the table. "I can't believe this!" she said, her voice trembling. "Aunt Bonnie and Uncle Ken were made for each other! What could he possibly have seen in my mother?"

"She was beautiful—well, you can see that in the photo—and she was vivacious, the sort of girl every guy wants to date and every girl wants to be friends with. Anyway, that's what I've heard."

"But . . . I can't wrap my head around this!"

"You don't really have to. It was ages ago." Julie glanced at the window, as if expecting to find someone peering in. "Though small towns never forget."

Nicola was silent for a moment; then she said, "I just had the strangest thought. What if my mother thinks that Aunt Bonnie stole Ken from her? Maybe she's trying to steal Ferndean as a way of getting back at her sister."

"Revenge? You don't really think that's what's going on, do you? And why would she wait all these years before acting?"

"I don't know," Nicola admitted. "Revenge is a dish best served cold?"

"I think Carol wants Ferndean for herself because she's a selfish person and always has been. There's nothing more to it than that."

Nicola visibly bristled. "Carol is my mother, you know," she said coldly.

"Sorry," Julie said. "But I thought you felt the same way the rest of us do."

Nicola shook her head. "I do but . . . Never mind. Sorry I snapped."

"Look, did someone send you here today?" Julie asked.

"No! Absolutely not."

Julie studied her cousin's face. Nicola was telling the truth. "Do you want something to drink?" she asked. "I think there's a packet of iced tea mix around somewhere."

"No, that's okay. You're busy. Sorry if I interrupted." Nicola began to hurry toward the door.

"Nicola?" Julie called. "Thanks for stopping by."

"Sure." Nicola waved and was gone.

The articles in the filing cabinet. Two drawers stuffed full of them. Julie stared at the old metal cabinet for a long moment. And then she left the room.

Chapter 37

"What a nice surprise. I wasn't expecting you."

"Am I interrupting anything?" Nicola asked.

"You're never an interruption," Bonnie said warmly.

Nicola had come through the kitchen door rather than the front. Only close family ever did that.

"I don't know why you want to leave this place," Nicola said, taking a seat at the kitchen table. "It's so cozy. I mean, I know you love Ferndean and you have a right to it, but . . . I don't know. All the wrangling with my mother . . . Is it really worth it?"

"I'm fine," Bonnie assured her niece quickly, but she did not answer her question.

"You never told me that Uncle Ken dated my mother before he hooked up with you," Nicola blurted.

Bonnie's eyes widened. "I guess I just assumed you knew," she said. "Your mother never told you?"

"Not a word. I just found out about it at Julie's. There was a photo from 1974, taken at the Elgorts' house, and I asked her about it. What on earth did Ken see in my mother?"

Bonnie hesitated before answering. "There's a lot more to your mother than what you allow yourself to see," she said finally. A lot more than Bonnie had encouraged Nicola to see.

"Like what?" Nicola demanded.

Bonnie sighed and feeling more than a little guilty, she sat down across from Nicola. Absent-mindedly, she began to trace the pattern of roses on the tablecloth. "Carol was different from everyone else in Yorktide," she said. "She had a natural flair for attracting attention. Some people are just like that, effortlessly magnetic. You can love them for it or you can grow to dislike them for it." *That's what happened with me,* Bonnie thought. *I grew to dislike my sister for being who she was.*

"How did the relationship between them end?" Nicola asked.

Bonnie hesitated. Should she tell Nicola the truth, the story Ken had told her, the one that didn't match the public tale? Yes, she thought. Why not?

"Ken ended things and not long afterwards, Carol left Yorktide. I had always liked Ken, and once Carol was gone he noticed me. We started to date after a while and when I was eighteen, we married."

"Mom must have been furious," Nicola said.

"I don't know what she felt," Bonnie said truthfully. "She sent me a note of congratulations from New York. That was just before Ken and I were engaged. She came to my wedding and acted like nothing had ever happened between herself and Ken."

"But she wasn't your maid of honor," Nicola stated.

"No," Bonnie said. "Not given the circumstances." But she had wished it could have been Carol by her side at the altar. How she had wished it!

"I thought I knew all there was to know about this family," Nicola murmured.

Bonnie wondered. Could her niece really be so naïve as to believe anyone ever knew all there was to know about her family? "Well," she said, "it should make no difference to you that your mother dated your uncle for a time."

"I suppose," Nicola said. But she didn't look convinced.

Bonnie rose from her seat. "How about staying for dinner? I could whip up some macaroni and cheese with breadcrumbs on top. Just the way you like it."

"Awesome. You spoil me, Aunt Bonnie."

Bonnie felt her heart swell. "It's always been my pleasure."

"Is there any weeding to be done?" Nicola asked. "I don't know why, but I find weeding therapeutic."

Bonnie smiled. "There's always weeding."

Nicola went off to the backyard and Bonnie began to gather ingredients for dinner. She went about chopping chunks of dried bread for breadcrumbs and grating cheese, all the while aware that without Nicola her life would have been so very different. Less fulfilling. Less happy. But if Bonnie's reservations had prevailed . . .

Because it had been Bonnie, not Ken, who was against their taking in Nicola. The fact that Nicola's father was an anonymous sperm donor had always bothered Bonnie. At the back of her mind lurked the possibility that the man might have been a psychopath or a moral degenerate. Was fifteen-year-old Nicola's wild behavior the incipient sign of something much more dangerous to come? Was it insanity to bring such a potentially damaged person into one's home? Bonnie had never been comfortable with the idea of The Unknown. She couldn't be blamed for that.

To these arguments, Ken had replied: "She's family. We have to do this."

Ten years later, Bonnie knew that her fear of Nicola's revealing herself to be mentally ill had had more to do with her own feelings of moral superiority, a way to feel she had won where Carol had failed.

Bonnie had had her child the "normal" way.

"Ken," she said aloud, as she reached for a mixing bowl. "You were always right about the important things. Why can't I sometimes be right, too?"

Chapter 38

"I've never been here before," Judith noted, with an appreciative glance around the bar of the restaurant Carol had chosen for their outing. "A bit rich for my blood. Thanks for offering to pick up the check."

"No problem," Carol said. And it wasn't. She had been wanting to try The BlueFin since arriving in Yorktide.

Judith was drinking a dry martini, and Carol had ordered a Manhattan. They had chosen an appetizer of a dozen raw oysters. Carol had just enjoyed her first oyster when she became aware of a woman not so discreetly looking at her from across the room.

"Who is that rude woman staring at us?" Carol said quietly.

"I don't know and she's staring at you, not me. Wait a minute," Judith went on. "I do know who she is. Nancy somebody or other. She used to own a gallery in Perkins Cove about twenty years ago."

"You'd think I had a notorious reputation the way some people stare. All I did was leave town."

"For a lot of people, that's notorious enough."

Carol sighed. "I was always an outsider in Yorktide. But now that I want to belong, no one will let me."

Judith raised an eyebrow. "Is being accepted into this community what you really want?" she asked. "What would you do with yourself in Yorktide? Nothing much happens here besides the rising and setting of the sun, the coming and going of the tide. Sure, we have the occasional black bear sighting in someone's garden, and when the corn comes in late there's a minor panic. Otherwise, we enjoy our peace and quiet."

"I plan on getting to know my sister and my daughter again," Carol said promptly.

"But they have lives to lead. You can't expect everyone to be at your beck and call, free to entertain you."

Carol took a sip of her drink. Judith didn't need to know that she hadn't thought through the details of what her new life in Yorktide might entail, the challenges she might face, the obstacles she might encounter. She had acted so quickly after the news of little Jonathan's tragic death. She had felt so desperate and alone.

When Carol answered her cousin's question she did so in a manner intended to cover the fact of her distress. "I'll offer my services as a speaker to the local women's society or the community college," she said. "I could mentor young men and women interested in going into interior design."

Judith nodded. "Fair enough, but what will you do for entertainment?"

"I'm perfectly capable of entertaining myself," Carol replied readily. "It's not like I'm a thirty-year-old needing to be out until all hours drinking and dancing. And if I feel the need for culture, I'll pop down to Boston or New York or up to Montreal or Quebec."

"There's plenty of culture in Maine, you know. There are several good museums and lots of music and theater and galleries. The Ogunquit Playhouse puts on a good show twice a summer. Musicals, mostly. They do a very professional job."

"See? I'll be just fine."

"Have you considered mud season?" Judith said suddenly. "You'll have to buy yourself a pair of wellies or some sturdy waterproof walking shoes."

Carol fought back a grimace. She remembered what mud season was like. She felt damp and chilled just thinking about it. But she had seen a pair of so-ugly-they-were-chic wellies online recently. They would help get her through.

"Mud season only comes once a year," she said. "I'll survive."

And then an idea began to form in Carol's mind. Not a brilliant idea or even a very unusual one, but one so simple she wondered why she hadn't thought of it before. "I'm going to host a family dinner, at Ferndean," she announced. "I haven't seen Sophie yet this summer, or Scott for that matter. A dinner party might be a way to bring everyone together and pave the way for real communication in the future."

Judith frowned. "They won't come. Not all of them, anyway."

"Of course, they will," Carol said, with far more conviction than she felt. "And if they do resist, you'll convince them it's a nice idea."

"I will?" Judith shrugged. "I can try, but I'm not promising anything."

"We won't talk about anything serious or contentious. We'll keep the conversation light. It will simply be a pleasant evening where we can all let our guard down and get to know one another again."

"Are you hallucinating?" Judith asked. "What's in that drink anyway?"

"No, I'm not hallucinating. All right," Carol admitted, "I know it won't be easy to get everyone to Ferndean. Certainly, Bonnie and Nicola won't be thrilled. But that's the whole point. To connect." And it meant so very much to her that she connect.

Judith raised her empty martini glass. "I'll have another drink if anyone's asking."

Carol gestured to the bartender. When she had gone to prepare their drinks, Nancy somebody or other, her companion in tow, approached Carol and Judith. The woman's air was deferential.

"Excuse me," Nancy said. "Aren't you Carol Ascher, the famous interior designer?"

"Yes," Carol said. "I am."

"We love your work," the other woman gushed. "I mean, what we've seen of it in magazines. You wouldn't by any chance . . ."

"What my friend means," Nancy continued, "is that we were wondering if you would be willing to give a talk at the Wilde Gallery. It's in Kennebunkport. We're on the board, you see, and—"

"I'm sorry," Carol said in a tone she had perfected over the years. It was a tone that conveyed regret at having to refuse a request while at the same time leaving no room for argument. "I'm afraid I'm unable to help you. But thank you so very much for asking."

Nancy seemed genuinely surprised at Carol's negative response. Her companion looked flustered. Neither woman seemed to know what to say next.

"Good evening," Carol said, turning back to the bar, where her Manhattan was waiting.

"They're gone," Judith announced a moment later. "Scurried out of here with their tails between their legs. But why did you say no? Surely it wouldn't have been a big deal to make an appearance, sip cheap wine, and answer a few questions?"

"That sort of command performance can be especially draining," Carol explained. "It's far easier to speak to a roomful of professionals than a gathering of admirers. Trust me."

Judith shrugged. "I'll have to. No one's ever asked me to give a talk about anything to anyone."

"Lucky. So, you'll help me make my family party a success?"

"Do I have a choice?" Judith asked. "You're buying me dinner."

Chapter 39

"How are things between you and your dad?" Nicola asked.

Earlier, she had suggested that Sophie might want to go to a showing of the movie classic *All About Eve* at a tiny art theater in South Berwick.

"You'll love it," Nicola had assured her cousin. "I promise."

But Sophie had just shrugged. "I'm not really into old stuff," she said. "But we could go shopping in Kittery."

So, they had gone to the outlets in Kittery and were now having a late lunch in a family-style restaurant. Nicola had ordered a crab roll. Sophie had chosen fish 'n' chips and was now working her way through an ice-cream sundae.

"I want nothing to do with him," Sophie stated, scooping up vanilla ice cream and chocolate sauce. "I wish he would just leave. I don't know why Mom doesn't kick him out. My friend Barry's mother kicked out his father when he cheated on her."

Nicola took a sip of her iced coffee and answered carefully. "It's not that easy. Your parents probably still love each other."

"I don't see how they could!" Sophie declared. "If you love someone you don't cheat on them. And if someone cheats on you, you have to be furious and throw them out."

Nicola smiled. "Is that the law?"

"No, but it should be!"

"Marriage is . . . Each marriage is unique," Nicola said, cringing as she spoke. Words were so often so inadequate. "A betrayal doesn't always mean that love is gone. Look, Sophie, it's complicated. You have to let your parents figure out their relationship, okay? What I mean is, don't write off your dad just yet. Or your mom."

"You're lucky you don't have a father," Sophie declared. "Men are such jerks!"

"Not all men," Nicola pointed out. "Your grandfather wasn't a jerk."

"He was different. He wasn't a man. Oh, you know what I mean! He was Grandpa."

Nicola felt sure that in spite of her young cousin's protestations of anger, she desperately missed her father. And how could she explain to Sophie what she had been feeling since Ken's death, that without any information about her own birth father, she felt rootless? It was better to have an imperfect parent than to have no parent. Maybe.

"I know what you mean," she said finally. "I feel the same way about Uncle Ken, that he was special, apart from other men."

"The father you never had," Sophie said. "Right?"

"Right." Nicola sighed. "Maybe you don't want to hear this, but I'm going to say it anyway. I really believe it would be best for you to forgive your father and allow him to make things up to you rather than to cut him off for good. Okay, maybe you're not quite ready to forgive him, and I get that. But please, Sophie, don't refuse to be open to the idea. Life is too short to—"

"To what?"

Nicola hesitated. She thought of the wall she had put up against her mother. It was a case of the pot calling the kettle black. Do what I say, not what I do. "To be unnecessarily unhappy," she said finally.

Sophie rolled her eyes and ate the last bit of her sundae.

"Okay," Nicola went on hurriedly, "then think of it this way. If someone you cared about an awful lot decided to cut you off because you made one stupid mistake, how would you feel? Would you think it was fair?"

"No," Sophie admitted. "But Dad made a really big stupid mistake."

Nicola sighed. "Well, it's your life," she said. "You'll decide what to do with it."

Sophie suddenly reached across the table for Nicola's hand. "Sorry," she said. "I mean, thanks for trying. And for lunch."

"Sure." Nicola asked for the check and while she waited for Sophie to come back from the ladies' room, she wondered why it was that she felt such a strong need to punish her mother. Maybe Carol Ascher *had* come back to Yorktide for more than just Ferndean.

So, what if she had? Nicola didn't owe her mother anything.

Nicola cringed. What had she just said to Sophie about not writing someone off on the basis of one mistake? Even a big mistake.

If Carol Ascher *had* made a mistake in sending her child to live with relatives. And it wasn't clear that she had.

"Ready to go?" Sophie asked.

Nicola slid out of the booth and followed her cousin and her cousin's four bulging shopping bags out of the restaurant.

Chapter 40

"What am I going to do?" Julie muttered.

She was standing in her bedroom, a pile of discarded clothes on the floor. Trying to find something to wear that wasn't in need of a wash and an iron, and that, more importantly, fit was a complete nightmare. How could she have gained so much weight in so short a period of time?

And there was the fact that Julie hadn't read any of the material Sara Webb had assigned. She had tried; she really had. But her powers of concentration seemed to have abandoned her.

Julie felt a wave of panic rising in her. Maybe she should call in sick, though missing today's workshop would only prolong the inevitable. The next meeting would come around and she would have to face this moment all over again.

It was only with a supreme effort that Julie finally made it out of the house, wearing a pair of loose cotton pants badly in need of a pressing (she had been afraid to use the iron; her hands had been shaking so badly she was sure she would burn herself) and an old Oxford button-down shirt over a logo T-shirt that belonged to Scott. She hadn't wanted to wear her husband's clothes, but the Oxford shirt would not button across her chest and her own T-shirts were all stained or simply too small.

She drove with more deliberation than usual, her hands sweaty on the wheel, her shoulders tense with concentration. It was a bit of a miracle that she arrived at Yorktide's grammar school in one piece. She met no one going into the building and hurried through the corridors to the teachers' lounge/meeting room.

When she opened the door, she saw that her colleagues were already gathered. To a person, they were looking their best. She noted the bright pink blouse on Melanie, the seventh-grade math teacher. Thom, the foreign language teacher, had a new and flattering haircut. There was a diamond ring on the fourth finger of Shelly's left hand. Could she have finally gotten engaged to her longtime girlfriend? Julie had always liked Shelly, an award-winning history teacher, but now she couldn't work up an ounce of good feeling for her.

Sara Webb called the meeting to order. She was an excellent principal, a figure of authority without the thirst for power, fair-minded and open to suggestions. She was not the sort to embarrass one of her staff—especially one hitherto highly efficient and responsible—for an unprecedented lapse.

"No worries," Sara said briskly when Julie was forced to admit she had not read the assigned material. "I would suggest you take the time to read it at some point, though."

Julie simply nodded. She knew it was clear to all in the room that she was not her usual self. Where was the happy and energetic person she had been last summer and the one before that? Where had her enthusiasm gone, her excitement about the coming semester, her eagerness to meet the new crop of little students?

After what seemed like a painful eternity, Sara Webb called the workshop to an end. Julie's colleagues got up from the table and began to chat in smaller groups, some pouring cups of coffee or nibbling on cookies. All Julie wanted was to hurry from the room but before she could make her way past the knot of fellow teachers sharing stories about their summers, Tessa Landry, the art teacher, stopped her. Back in the spring she had become a grandmother for the first time and her world now revolved around her grandson.

"How are you doing, Julie?" Tessa asked, her voice gentle and low. Her obvious kindness touched Julie through the layers of shame and self-recrimination, and brought her to the brink of tears.

"Okay," she said with a small, quick smile.

"If you ever want to go for a stroll on the beach one morning, call me, okay?" Tessa smiled. "I promise not to bore you with pictures of my grandson. Well, I'll try not to."

Julie nodded and Tessa moved off toward the coffee urn. One of the newer faculty, a young woman named Miranda, who had moved to Yorktide only the year before from New Jersey, was suddenly by Julie's side. Julie had never really taken to Miranda, though she wasn't able to put a finger on the source of her dislike.

"Hey!" Miranda said brightly. She was wearing slim-fitting white jeans, wedge sandals that put her a good few inches over Julie, and a silky blue blouse.

"Hi," Julie said.

Miranda tilted her head back and looked Julie over from head to toe. "You look like you've been enjoying the ice cream this summer," she said with a laugh.

The room was suddenly silent. Before Julie could form a reply—and what could it possibly be?—Miranda's expression underwent a radical change from a look of jovial bonhomie to a look of shocked embarrassment.

"Oh," she said, reaching a hand toward Julie's arm but not making contact. "I'm sorry. I didn't mean . . . I didn't think . . ."

Still looking shamefaced, Miranda hurried toward the refreshment table. The others in the room resumed conversations. Julie stood on her own, unable to move. Was she having another form of panic attack, the kind that paralyzed a person, leaving her unable to act on or react to the world around her?

How could she ever go back to work in September in this condition? She had always loved being a teacher and it would break her heart to give up her vocation, but if she wasn't competent to care for the children, what choice did she have? If she couldn't eat sensibly, dress decently, make normal conversation, if she was paralyzed or left shaking uncontrollably by the smallest word said in passing, how could she go on?

The worst of it was that Scott was not responsible for her predicament. Julie was the one responsible for allowing her emotional pain and her mental distress to dominate all of the good in her life. And she was the one who would have to be responsible for righting that situation. But she felt so very helpless.

Suddenly, Julie's right hand twitched. She purposefully flexed her fingers. She could move again. In truth, she had only felt paralyzed for seconds. Maybe no one had noticed her rigid stance. Maybe no one had cared.

Julie hurried from the room. She was tired of being a spectacle.

Chapter 41

"A formal invitation card! Who does she think she is?"

Judith shrugged. "I think it's a nice gesture."

Bonnie tossed the invitation onto her kitchen table. If she were a drama queen like her sister, she would have torn the card to shreds. "Well, I'm not accepting, that's for sure."

"Why not? I'm accepting. I think that for the sake of good karma you should as well. And Nicola and the rest of the family, too."

"Karma?" Bonnie frowned. "I don't believe in that sort of thing."

Judith sighed. "What are you afraid of, Bonnie?"

"Nothing."

"You've met up with Carol several times this summer. What's the big deal about this dinner?"

The big deal, Bonnie thought, was that her sister was acting as if Ferndean were already hers, and it most certainly was not. But saying yes to the invitation would, at the very least, get Bonnie inside Ferndean's four walls again and allow her to see what damage her sister might have done to the house. "All right," she said, grudgingly. "I'll accept. But I'm not happy about it."

"And you'll tell Nicola and Julie and her family to accept as well. Carol hasn't seen Sophie at all this summer."

"Yes," Bonnie said grudgingly. "I can't guarantee they'll listen to me, though."

"They will. Pull rank if you have to."

"I never—"

Judith raised an eyebrow. It was enough to stop Bonnie's false protest. Instead, she sat at the table across from her cousin.

"Julie had a workshop at school this morning," she said, glad to be off the topic of Carol Ascher's dinner party. "She called me when she got home. She was very upset. First, she was unprepared, which is totally unlike her, and then someone said something hurtful to her—she wouldn't tell me what—and she said she literally froze, couldn't move a muscle."

"It sounds nasty. But I'm surprised she talked to you about what happened. That might be a good sign."

Was it a good sign? Bonnie just didn't know. "I can't help but feel that I failed Julie," she admitted. "Why is she so terribly down on herself? I thought I taught my daughter the importance of self-esteem. Maybe I didn't do a very good job. And maybe I failed with Nicola, too. Maybe one day she'll find she's unable to deal with a great injury done to her." Bonnie considered for a moment. "Then again," she went on, "she wasn't devastated by her mother's leaving her and that says something for her inner strength."

"Her mother didn't leave her, Bonnie," Judith said sharply. "Stop adhering to that narrative. It's not true, and the more you cling to it the more damage will be done."

Bonnie's cheeks flushed.

Judith reached across the table and patted Bonnie's arm. "Let's not worry about Nicola right now," she said. "She's fine. Let's focus on you. Bonnie, you're not responsible for your daughter's handling of her life. You were a good mother; you are a good mother. Julie is her own person and she has been since she moved out of your house and started her own family."

Bonnie put her hand to her temple. "It's just that lately, so much of my energy has been directed toward this stupid stalemate with Carol. I haven't paid proper attention to what really matters. My child. And my grandchild, for that matter."

"That might be true," Judith conceded. "But it doesn't make you responsible for Julie's depression. She has a history. I'm not being harsh, just honest. She knows she needs to be on watch for the signs of distress and when they rear their ugly heads, it's her responsibility to call for help."

"Not everyone *can* call for help," Bonnie countered, "not once they start to sink."

Judith sighed. "I know. I'm just trying to lighten the load of guilt you've heaped upon yourself. But maybe it's not my place to do that."

"You're never not a parent," Bonnie said softly. "It's supposed to get easier, but it never really does." *I so wish Ken was here,* she added silently. *But he's not. When am I ever going to get used to that?*

"Yet another reason I'm glad I opted out of parenthood," Judith said as softly as Bonnie had spoken. "I could never be sure I had what it would take."

"I don't think anyone is sure when they start out," Bonnie said. "Ken and I had a baby because that's what married people did. At least, the married people we'd grown up around. You always assumed that one day you would be a parent, so there wasn't a lot of thinking about if you had what it would take to be a good one."

"I grew up around those same people," Judith pointed out. "But given the fact that I knew I wasn't going to be getting married to a man and having a baby the good old-fashioned way, the opportunity to think through the idea of parenthood was pretty much thrust upon me."

"Of course. I never thought of it that way." Bonnie realized that she felt a bit ashamed of her ignorance. Or was it lack of imagination? Neither was a good thing.

"You didn't have to," Judith pointed out. "Be thankful for small favors." She rose from her chair and stretched. "I'll be on my way. I'm going to a lecture at the library."

"What about?" Bonnie asked.

"I'm not sure, exactly. Something to do with the current state of artificial intelligence."

"I didn't know you were interested in that sort of thing," Bonnie noted.

"I'm not. But at my age I'll take any opportunity to keep the mind active. If the lecture forces me to use the old gray matter, good. See you around."

Bonnie continued to sit at the kitchen table after Judith had gone. What she had not admitted to her cousin was that on some level she was annoyed with Julie. Scott had done wrong, but he hadn't killed anyone or bankrupted his family or been caught torturing innocent animals. Yes, Bonnie felt compassion for her daughter, but she also believed that as a parent Julie had an important job to do, one she was not performing.

Back when Julie and Scott had gotten engaged, Bonnie told Ken her worries about their daughter marrying a man with Scott's reputation for playing the field. "If Julie trusts him," Ken had said, "then we should, too." That was Ken all over. Kind. Open-minded. Sometimes too lenient.

Not long after the wedding, Julie had admitted to her mother that Scott had cheated on her once before the engagement. Bonnie had kept that bit of disturbing information from Ken, but maybe she had been wrong to do so. Maybe if Ken had known of Scott's transgression he could have taken him aside for a man-to-man talk and . . .

Bonnie sighed. She felt sure that if her husband was alive now he would be more disappointed in Scott than angry with him. He would have tried to broker a peace between his daughter and her husband; he would not have wanted the marriage to end if it could be saved. And Ken might well have succeeded where Bonnie never could.

Suddenly, Bonnie felt terribly lonely. She looked around the kitchen Ken, his father, and his uncle had built over forty years ago. She wondered if she had really considered what it would mean to sell this place to a stranger, the home in which she and Ken had lived so happily for so long, raising a daughter, hosting meals for family and friends, building snowmen in the front yard each winter, welcoming trick-or-treaters at Halloween with carved jack-o'-lanterns, greeting the first signs of spring with the blooming of the two big forsythia bushes Ken tended so carefully.

Bonnie sighed again, this time more deeply. So much was changing and so quickly. The last thing any of the family needed was this silly dinner party of Carol's. But Bonnie had promised Judith she would be there, and Bonnie tried very hard never to break a promise.

She would be there.

Chapter 42

Carol had dressed as she would for any dinner party, whether one she gave or one she attended, not in her very finest but in silk separates. Her family, however, seemed to have dressed as if for a casual outing to the mall. Bonnie was wearing sweat pants and an oversize T-shirt. Scott was in a pair of heavy jeans and a plaid shirt. Carol had rarely seen him wear anything else.

Julie looked terrible. Her expression was pained. Her hair looked lank and maybe even unwashed. No, things were not going well for Julie.

As for Nicola . . . It saddened Carol to see her daughter wearing absolutely no bit of adornment or color. Tan pants. A gray T-shirt. Beige sneakers. Was she really such a serious person through and through? As a little girl, Nicola had enjoyed wearing lots of jewelry and wild colors. What had happened to her in Maine? Had she grown into her true self or into someone Bonnie had made her, decidedly not-Carol? There were so many questions.

At least Judith showed a sense of style. A navy-blue and Kelly-green scarf tied jauntily around her neck elevated an otherwise basic outfit of navy slacks and a white blouse. A pair of gold hoops in her ears and a chunky gold ring on the middle finger of her right hand added elegance.

As for Sophie, she was dressed as so many of the teen girls Carol had spotted in Yorktide were dressed. In as little material as was commensurate with public decency. Her shorts were too short; her T-shirt cut too low; her flip-flops were dirty. "I wouldn't have recognized you," Carol said, hiding her disapproval of her niece's appearance. "It's been so long."

"And whose fault is that?" Bonnie snapped.

Carol laughed a practiced social laugh. "Entirely mine. May I offer anyone a cocktail?" she asked.

"I'll have a vodka tonic, no fruit, please," Judith said briskly, stepping away from the others who were grouped together awkwardly.

"Ken and I are not big drinkers," Bonnie said. "I mean, he wasn't one. Nor am I."

"You don't have to be a big drinker to enjoy a cocktail on occasion," Carol said mildly. "But there's soda water if you prefer. Scott?"

Scott looked generally embarrassed, but he had nerve enough to ask for a scotch. Carol poured him the drink. Sophie reached for a can of soda. Carol looked to Nicola, who shook her head, then to Julie, who whispered, "No," and then poured her own drink.

"To family," she said brightly.

"To family," Judith echoed.

Scott raised his glass, glanced nervously at his wife, and took a sip. No one else seconded the toast.

"Where are you sleeping?" Bonnie asked suddenly.

"In the master bedroom," Carol replied. "My old bedroom is so small and the closet is insanely shallow. I'd forgotten about that. I don't know how you ever managed to get renters with all the quirks and inconveniences of this old place."

"Location, location, location," Judith said. "If it's close to the water, it's a gold mine."

"Well, that may be, but one of the first things I'm going to do is put in air conditioning, at least in the bedrooms."

"Ferndean doesn't need air conditioning," Bonnie said.

Carol smiled. "Well, I do and as I'm the one who's going to be living here . . ."

Bonnie's face grew red and she turned away.

"A bit less presuming, Carol," Judith advised quietly. "Nothing is set in stone yet."

Carol nodded. Judith was right. It was just that Bonnie made her so angry sometimes.

"Where's the green vase that sits here?" Bonnie was pointing to an occasional table with a white marble top.

"That hideous thing?" Carol said with a laugh. "I put it in the hall closet. I should probably have just thrown it out."

"You can't throw it out!" Bonnie cried. "It belonged to our grandmother!"

"That might be," Carol said, "but it's worth about two dollars at a garage sale."

"It's a priceless heirloom," Bonnie insisted. "It's been in the family for years and years!"

Carol sighed. "Fine, then take it home with you."

"It belongs here, in Ferndean House, where it's always been." Bonnie's voice was now tremulous and Carol was sure her sister was about to burst into tears.

Judith cleared her throat meaningfully. "When do we eat? I for one am starved."

"The food is already on the table," Carol said, gesturing for the others to follow her to the dining room. Once there she began to take the covers off the silver-toned chaffing dishes.

"Did you do all this?" Sophie asked. Carol thought she sounded impressed.

"The caterer provided everything," Carol told her. "I'm afraid I'm out of practice."

She took the seat at the head of the table, where Ronald Ascher used to sit. Bonnie hurried to take Shirley Ascher's seat at the other end of the table. Julie sat at her mother's right side; Sophie sat on Bonnie's left. Scott took the empty chair between Sophie and Carol. To Carol's other side sat Judith and then Nicola, next to her cousin, Julie.

"There's wine on the table," Carol said. "And water. Help yourselves. Bon appetite."

The meal consisted of roast beef with gravy, scalloped potatoes, green beans, rolls, and for dessert, a chocolate torte. Judith patted her stomach before reaching for the potatoes. "Now this is the kind of spread I could get used to," she declared. "Stick to your ribs stuff."

"A bit heavy for summer," Nicola commented, taking one thin slice of beef.

Carol smiled at her daughter. "My appetite has never been affected by the weather," she said. And since when had her daughter's?

"These rolls are awesome," Scott commented. "Aren't they, Julie?"

There were two rolls on Julie's plate and she was busily chewing a piece of a third. She seemed startled by her husband's question—or maybe by his addressing a question to her directly—and hastily swallowed. She did not reply.

Bonnie, Carol noticed, had put a bit of everything on her plate, not too much and not too little. That was Bonnie. A carefully middle-of-the-road person. Not one prone to excess or to its opposite. Carol wondered if her sister would help herself to seconds of anything. Maybe to the cake. Bonnie had had a sweet tooth as a child. Did she still?

The meal progressed. Carol's sense of failure and frustration grew.

Sophie was acting the typically bored teenager, annoyed beyond measure with the dull adults with whom she was forced to spend the evening, bending her head over her phone whenever she thought no one was looking, occasionally sighing but otherwise silent.

Julie was strenuously avoiding looking directly at Scott. For his part, Scott looked miserable, the cheating husband among his wife's female relatives. Carol had nothing personal against him and as he was a guest, she treated him politely, asking if he would like more scalloped potatoes and inquiring as to his job. He said it was fine.

Just when Carol was tempted to do something drastic to inject some life into the party, her sister piped up.

"I ran into Linda Hopkins this morning," Bonnie said. Carol had no idea who this Linda Hopkins was. "It's been a very difficult pregnancy for her. Just last week her husband had to rush her to the emergency room because—"

"We should consider Scott before embarking on a topic like pregnancy woes," Judith interrupted, for which Carol was glad. "His being the only man among women."

"That's how he likes it," Sophie muttered. Though she sat only inches from her father, the essential distance between them seemed a gaping void. Carol was sure she was not the only one to notice this.

Julie picked up her glass of water and gulped down enough to make her sputter and cough.

"Someone tell me what's going on in Yorktide politics," Carol said brightly.

This topic seemed to energize the guests gathered around the table. Even Julie offered a brief remark regarding a proposed change in parking laws. Aside from Carol, who largely listened, only Sophie had nothing to say.

When everyone's knives and forks were silent, Carol rose and began to clear. Bonnie insisted on helping. Carol did not protest. When the empty plates had been stacked on the kitchen counter, Carol shooed her sister back to the dining room while she took the cake from its box and placed it on a footed stand she had found in one of the cabinets. It was a rather attractive cake stand; Carol thought she would keep it, though much of the contents of the kitchen would see its way to the dump. Unless, of course, Bonnie thought it all precious heirlooms and carried it off to her own home.

"I see you still have a sweet tooth," Carol noted when the cake had been cut and Bonnie picked up her fork.

"And?" Bonnie snapped.

"And nothing. I hope you enjoy the dessert."

"I'm sure it will be fine." Bonnie took a bite, then another, and placed her fork on the edge of her plate.

Carol hid a smile. Fine. It didn't bother her one bit if Bonnie felt the need to deprive herself of a delicious dessert in an effort to insult her sister. If that, indeed, was what she was doing. Maybe, Carol thought, she was simply no longer hungry.

Nicola had declined a piece and Carol wondered if by refusing the cake, Nicola, too, was making a statement, refusing her mother's efforts at peace and reconciliation.

When was a piece of cake just a piece of cake?

"This is killer," Judith pronounced, scraping the last of the chocolate from her plate. Sophie nodded and reached for the knife to cut herself another piece.

"Would you cut me another slice, too?" Scott asked his daughter.

Sophie ignored him.

No one said a word about the incident. Carol wondered if Julie had even noticed; she was determinedly chewing, her eyes fixed on her plate.

The evening wound down quickly after the cake had been eaten and coffee drunk. Thanks were murmured and within a very few minutes Julie, Scott, and Sophie were getting into their car; Nicola was opening the passenger side door of her car for Bonnie; and Judith was climbing into her vehicle.

When the last of her family had disappeared down the drive, Carol closed the front door firmly and sighed. What a disaster. She had badly miscalculated the possibility of a successful gathering.

Talk about drama, and not even all that interesting drama. Okay, so Scott had cheated on his wife. That was bad, but there was plenty worse he could have done. And Bonnie had been so hypersensitive, taking offense at every innocent comment Carol made. And Sophie, the troubled teen. Well, that was no fault of her own. As for Nicola and her grim determination not to offer her mother a kind word, let alone a smile . . .

Well, Carol was sensitive to her daughter's situation even if no one else thought her so.

At least Judith had behaved well. Judith had always had a steady nature; maybe it was because she was an only child and hadn't had to contend with an irrational sibling.

Suddenly, Carol's eye caught sight of the hideous green vase on the occasional table. It was back. Someone—Bonnie? Nicola?—had retrieved it from the hall closet and reinstated it where, according to her sister, it belonged.

The nerve, Carol thought, her pulse quickening. This was her home—or soon to be—and it was her right to decide what she did and did not want on display. When had she—Bonnie or Nicola—done it? When Carol had gone to the bathroom? Had everyone witnessed this act of blatant disrespect?

And then the craziness of it all struck her and she laughed out loud. Fine. She would leave the thing where it was. For now.

Carol looked at the mess that remained after the meal, shrugged, and went upstairs to the master bedroom. There was nothing that couldn't wait until morning and she was suddenly very, very tired.

Chapter 43

Nicola couldn't sleep.

Her closet-size bedroom was hot. The fan was running at its highest speed, but the air in the apartment was so close the fan had little effect. She considered moving into the living room, but the couch was the least comfortable surface in the apartment. Better to stay where she was and stew.

The audacity of her mother, hosting a dinner at Ferndean, treating the house like it was already her own! Only Judith seemed to have enjoyed herself, but in a way she was an outsider. She had no personal stake in Ferndean House. It could be argued that Nicola and Julie didn't, either, but it was their mothers who were battling for sole ownership. They were too close to the situation not to feel intimately involved. That both younger women were on Bonnie's side in the war was irrelevant.

Nicola kicked off the sheets. Her stomach grumbled. She should have eaten more at dinner. Pride and a generalized antagonistic attitude had gotten in the way of common sense and politeness. What was wrong with her?

Her mother was what was wrong with her. Her mother being back in Yorktide was forcing Nicola to . . .

Nicola sighed. That was wrong. No one was forcing her to act badly, to choose anger over forgiveness. She had sole responsibility for thinking and acting as she was, which was a little too much like she had been acting in the year before she had been sent to Maine to live with her aunt and uncle. Bad-tempered. Self-focused. Careless.

With another sigh, Nicola sat up and left the miniscule bedroom. There was some leftover Chinese takeout in the fridge.

Nicola sat at her little table and hungrily consumed the cold sesame noodles. And for the first time in a long time, she realized that she felt lonely.

Really lonely.

Chapter 44

Julie was lying in bed, staring at the ceiling. Scott might be on the couch in the living room or in the den or in the garage, which doubled as his workshop. There was a lawn chair in there; it couldn't be comfortable, but Julie didn't care about her husband's comfort.

Not much.

What a trial the evening had been! Julie had felt so uncomfortable in the presence of her aunt, who had been dressed so nicely, even elegantly, though Carol had been nothing but polite to her. To everyone, really.

No, Carol had not been the problem, at least not for Julie.

It had cost her greatly not to look directly at Scott. Ignoring someone wasn't natural. And it had felt childish, but Julie had been powerless to turn in Scott's direction even once, powerless to acknowledge his presence. What sort of example her behavior was setting for Sophie she could only imagine.

A bad example. Sophie had been downright rude to her father. And Bonnie hadn't been a shining example of good behavior, either.

Julie rubbed her forehead. She had such pleasant memories of family meals at Ferndean. What a difference between the past and the present! What an unhappy difference.

Julie stretched her left arm across the bed. No one was there. But she knew that.

She realized that she felt lonely. Relieved, as well, that Scott wasn't breathing beside her.

But lonely.

Chapter 45

Bonnie lay on her side of the bed—she still thought of the right side as hers and the other as belonging to Ken—and stared up into the darkness. The entire evening had been a disaster. She never should have allowed Judith to convince her that a family dinner hosted by Carol Ascher would be a good idea. Carol hadn't even prepared the food herself! Okay, it had been delicious, especially the cake, but still. How lazy did a person have to be?

And that remark Sophie had made, the one about her father preferring the company of women. Bonnie had been on the point of scolding her granddaughter for speaking disrespectfully, but she had caught herself. She might only make a bad situation worse by calling attention to Sophie's rudeness.

Bonnie sighed and glanced into the darkness to her left. If only Ken had been with them. He had been a uniting presence, able to engage the shyest person in a pleasant exchange, to calm the conversational bully, to deter a controversial turn in the talk by introducing a neutral but interesting topic.

And the nerve of Carol to have hidden the green vase! Their mother had loved that vase; it was a treasured piece of family history. Well, Bonnie had solved that little problem, at least for the moment, but if she found that Carol had made the vase disappear again she would simply take it away with her for safekeeping. And when Carol was gone back to New York—and she had to go!—Bonnie would return to vase to its rightful place.

Poor Julie. Bonnie sighed. She had hardly uttered a word the entire evening. And not once had she looked at her husband, who, on the other hand, Bonnie had caught staring rather forlornly at his wife. His attitude had been a mix of embarrassment and shame that had made Bonnie—and no doubt the others, too—very uncomfortable. Well, Scott should be embarrassed and ashamed, but if something didn't change between Scott and Julie soon it would be impossible to be around the two of them together ever again. Julie should . . . But what should Julie do? Forgive her cheating husband? Throw him out?

Bonnie wanted to see Julie smile, to hear her laugh, to watch her spontaneously wrap Sophie in a hug, or to kiss her husband's cheek. But none of that was going to happen until Julie's mood lifted. It was all too close to the depression Julie had suffered after Sophie's birth. But then she had gotten professional help.

At least Judith seemed to have had a good time. But Carol wasn't Judith's sister. And it didn't matter to Judith what happened to Ferndean House, not like it mattered to Bonnie.

Bonnie turned on her left side and put her hand on the empty pillow. "Good night, Ken," she whispered. "I miss you so very much."

Chapter 46

For days after the dinner party she had hosted, Carol had not heard from anyone but Judith. None of the others had written a thank-you note or sent a thank-you e-mail. That wasn't forgetfulness. That was rudeness.

So, when Judith called one morning and suggested that the three cousins meet for coffee that afternoon, Carol's first impulse was to say an emphatic no. But she considered the idea for a moment in relation to her goals—the sole ownership of Ferndean and the reestablishment of a decent relationship with her family—and agreed.

"Good," Judith had said. "And we will not talk about Ferndean. We will simply be three women of a certain age sharing a cup of coffee and chitchat. And hopefully, the air will be somewhat cleared."

"Why are you still doing this?" Carol asked. "Acting as peacemaker. You saw what a disaster my party turned out to be."

"Family harmony," Judith said after a moment. "Contention makes me ill."

So, there they were. Bonnie, Carol, and Judith, sitting around a table in a corner of a coffee shop Judith had chosen. Bonnie was visibly tense. Carol didn't feel very relaxed, either. Judith seemed her even self.

"You've been spotted," Judith stage-whispered when they had been seated only a moment or two with their cups of steaming coffee.

Carol had to control a cry of surprise. The woman who was approaching their table had to be in her late eighties, but she was as keen-eyed and as straight-backed as she had been when she taught math to the Ascher sisters when they were children.

"Mrs. O'Keefe!" Bonnie cried. "It's so good to see you. Won't you have a seat?"

Mrs. O'Keefe shook her head. "Just on my way out," she said in the same clipped way Carol remembered so well. "Just saw the young Ascher girls and didn't want to miss the opportunity to say hello. Haven't seen you two together in forty some odd years. Hello, Judith. Well, time passes, doesn't it? Good day."

She was gone before Carol finally found her voice. "Time doesn't seem to pass for her!" she said. "She's hardly aged. Is there a fountain of youth on her property?"

"Good, clean living," Bonnie said with a firm nod.

"Never a fan," Judith murmured.

"The young Ascher girls. How is it I now feel much older than I did this morning?"

"Well, I certainly don't."

Bonnie's tone struck Carol as smug. "Good for you," she said with a false smile. "Tell me, though, when was the first time you realized that the *world* saw you as old?"

"What are you talking about?" Bonnie demanded. "The world, whoever that is, doesn't see me as old."

"Maybe you just haven't noticed," Carol suggested. "Or maybe you chose to interpret the nice young man's letting you go ahead of him on line at the post office as a gentlemanly gesture rather than as an act of pity performed for an old lady who reminds him of his grandmother."

Judith laughed.

"I'm younger than the both of you," Bonnie pointed out.

Carol nodded. "True. But when was the last time a man flirted with you?"

Bonnie opened her mouth and then closed it. "Well, there was always Ken," she said.

"He wasn't glued to your side twenty-four/seven, was he?" Judith said. "And since when has a wedding ring ever prevented a man from chatting up a woman he finds attractive?"

"It's been a while," Bonnie admitted. "But I didn't care then and I certainly don't care now."

Carol thought the lady protested too much, but she let it go.

"Did you face discrimination in your career as you aged?" Judith asked Carol.

Carol thought for a moment before replying to her cousin's question. "I did lose a few clients over time, but I can't say it was due to my age as much as it was due to people wanting a fresh perspective. I've done quite a range of interiors, but I'm not the only one out there. There's always a new crop of talent coming along, a new social set darling to watch out for. But my business didn't suffer. There are always people—maybe not as many as there used to be—who remain loyal to their tastes and the people who help them achieve the right results."

"What about you, Judith?" Bonnie asked.

Judith shook her head. "When I announced my intention of retiring, Dr. Rowan was stunned. He begged me to stay on as office manager for another year or two, but I was done. I enjoyed my time at the practice, but I'd had enough. Now, every time I run into Dr. Rowan he tells me that as good as my replacement is, he wished he could have found another 'mature' person to take over the job. Worth ethic seems to be lacking in people under thirty-five, if he's to be believed."

"So, what do you do with yourself since you retired?" Carol asked.

"A million things. I don't know how I ever had time to hold down a job! Now I can read as much as I like and take a nap in the middle of the afternoon and spend hours tinkering in my garden. I can stay out late on a weeknight and not have to worry about being bright-eyed and bushy-tailed the next morning."

"Where do you go on these late nights?" Carol asked.

"Depends on the day of the week," Judith replied. "Mondays

it's poker with the girls. We take turns hosting. Every Wednesday I meet up with an old friend for drinks at our favorite pub, and to win at Quiz Night. Which we mostly do. There are movies and lectures at the library and the college, and concerts at the churches. I keep busy."

"So, are you interested in meeting someone special?" Carol asked. It had been a while since Judith had ended a ten-year relationship with her partner, someone who had been found guilty of unspecified bad behavior. Carol assumed it had been cheating, but for all she really knew it could have been passing bad checks.

Judith laughed. "I'd say we're all interested in meeting someone special. Who would want to meet someone ordinary? But I know what you mean and sure, why not? But I'm not going out of my way looking for her!"

"What about your social life?" Carol asked her sister. "Apart from your family."

Bonnie folded her hands in her lap. "Ken and I spent so much of our time together," she said after a moment. "We were each other's best friend. We didn't ever have many other friends, and the ones we did have either moved away or died or there was some silly falling out. It's difficult getting used to Ken's not being here. It's . . ." Bonnie shook her head and took a crumpled white tissue from the pocket of her sweater.

Judith reached over and patted Bonnie's arm. "There, there," she said. "Let it out."

Carol lowered her eyes. The sight of her sister crying made her feel uncomfortable. Helpless. She should never have asked about Bonnie's social life. Contrary to what some people thought of her, she was not heartless, if at times she was unwittingly callous.

"And you?" Judith asked Carol when Bonnie had recovered her composure. "What's your love life been like for these past few decades? I'm assuming there were a few gentlemen callers, even if you did choose the father of your child from a catalog."

Carol was not offended. Judith was refreshingly blunt. "Men come and go," she said lightly. "Rather, they came and went."

"But was there anyone who made a difference?" Judith pursued.

"Yes," Bonnie added. "Did anyone ever love you?"

Carol hid her annoyance at this unpleasant phrasing. She laughed lightly. "I'm afraid I'm taking the secrets of my romantic life to the grave."

"Wise," Judith said, "I wish I had been so smart. There are still a couple of wild stories running about regarding the exploits of my younger years."

Bonnie's eyes widened. "There are? I never heard them."

"People probably wouldn't have told you," Carol said.

"Why not?" Bonnie demanded.

"Carol is implying that you're easily shocked," Judith explained. "You've only had one man in your life. Your sexual experience is limited compared to those of us who have had several partners. Ow!" Judith's eyes were wide as she put her hand to her shoulder. "Sorry. An old injury acting up. That's what I get for being a rough-and-tumble kid."

"I remember the time you landed flat on your back after jumping out of a tree," Carol said.

Judith cringed. "I was seriously lucky that time. I could have been paralyzed."

"You know what?" Carol said. "I just remembered something that happened to Bonnie and me when we were about eight and eleven. We were out on our bikes. Mom had told us not to go beyond the end of the road. She didn't want us coming into contact with the traffic out on the main road."

"I remember this," Bonnie said briskly.

"Maybe I spaced," Carol went on, "but the next thing you know we were well beyond the end of our road when suddenly I heard Bonnie cry out and I turned just in time to see her flying over the handlebars!"

"It all happened so fast," Bonnie said to Judith.

"This being way before anyone wore a helmet or carried a cell phone, I was in a total panic," Carol went on. "I dropped my bike and ran back to Bonnie. There was a cut on her forehead and it was bleeding, which made me feel sick, but I took off my windbreaker and tied it around her head and pretty much dragged her back to the house."

"I think I must have blacked out," Bonnie said. "The next thing I remember was Mom driving me to the hospital."

"I went with them," Carol said. "The cut wasn't bad after all, it didn't even require stitches, but I remember crying for what seemed like hours. I couldn't seem to stop."

"But you didn't get punished for putting my life at risk," Bonnie stated.

"Mom and Dad gave me a stern talking-to," Carol corrected. "And believe me, my conscience punished me enough."

"I think you're misremembering," Bonnie said irritably. "Mom and Dad never scolded you for anything. They let you get away with whatever it was you wanted to do."

"That's simply not true," Carol argued.

Judith cleared her throat. "I feel the need to interject at this juncture. I remember the entire episode. My mother and I were at Ferndean when Carol came staggering in, bearing the bloody body. Sorry. Couldn't resist a little melodrama."

"You were there?" Bonnie asked with a frown.

Carol shook her head. "I don't remember you and Aunt Mary being there at all."

"I was. I'm not surprised neither of you remember. You were both pretty shaken up. Anyway, I distinctly remember Aunt Shirley saying, "I told Bonnie not to go beyond the end of the road!" She scolded Carol, too, for not doing her duty as big sister, but the fact is that both of you were at fault, if it can be said that a kid is at fault in such a situation."

"It could have been so much worse," Carol said musingly.

Bonnie frowned. "I had to wear a cast on my arm!"

"It was a sling to support a sprained wrist," Judith corrected.

"If what Judith said is true," Bonnie said after a moment, a look of contrition on her face that surprised Carol, "neither of us was to blame in the end. We were kids. We were caught up in having a good time. And accidents happen."

"Yes," Carol said. "They do. But you know what? I was the older sibling. I should have been looking out for you. So, if I didn't apologize back then, I'm doing it now."

"Thank you," Bonnie said. "I mean . . . Thanks."

"Another coffee?" Judith suggested.

But Bonnie had an unspecified errand to run and Carol, while rather glad that Judith had arranged the morning's get-together, was eager to leave on a peaceable note.

Imagine running into Mrs. O'Keefe, Carol thought as she turned her car toward Ferndean. She had pretty much forgotten about her former math teacher, as she had pretty much forgotten so much of her childhood in Yorktide. Being here now was like trying to walk through a dense forest without stepping on roots and fallen branches. Memories were everywhere, underfoot, overhead, around every corner.

At the moment, Carol was not sure just how she felt about this. Pleased. Horrified.

Maybe something in between.

Chapter 47

Judith had never been to Nicola's apartment before and though Nicola wanted to make a good impression on her relative, there was little she could do about the sparse furnishings and the rattling of the ill-fitting windows every time someone in the building shut a door.

There was a knock on her own door and Nicola opened it to find Judith, her hand over her heart, and breathing heavily. "Next time," she panted, "you might want to arrange a hydraulic lift to get me up here."

"Sorry," Nicola said. "I should have suggested we meet somewhere else."

Judith stepped inside and waved her hand dismissively. "I'm exaggerating. Anyway, I could use the exercise." She looked around the space, from the tiny kitchen to the Batik cloth hung over the doorway to the miniscule bedroom, from the plastic milk crates containing books and magazines, to the worn couch whose upholstery pattern dated it to the 1970s. "I'd say nice place you've got here, but . . ."

Nicola shrugged. "It's cheap."

Judith lifted the corner of the piece of brightly patterned fabric that Nicola had nailed over the kitchen window as a curtain. "You clearly didn't inherit your mother's decorating skills," she said.

"I know. At least the place is clean."

"Clean goes a long way," Judith admitted.

"Would you like tea?" Nicola asked.

"Sure," Judith said. "As long as it's not Earl Grey. Makes me nauseous."

"It's not a name brand," Nicola explained. "But it's basic black tea and pretty strong."

Judith nodded in approval.

Nicola went about her task. The mismatched mugs were from a local thrift shop; she had bought a box of sugar cookies at Reny's for sixty-five cents. The milk would have to be poured from its plastic container as Nicola had no pitcher. The sugar was in a tea cup with no handle. No one could say that Nicola Ascher was a spendthrift.

When they were seated at the rickety folding table that served as Nicola's dining table and desk, and Judith had piled four sugar cookies next to her mug, Nicola wasted no time in posing the question that had been uppermost in her mind for the past twenty-four hours.

"What was Aunt Bonnie's wedding like?" she asked. "You see, I know that my mother dated Ken before he started to see Bonnie."

"That's never been a secret," Judith replied. "And what do you mean, what was the wedding like? One wedding is pretty much like another when you come down to it. A bunch of people dressed in their finest, toasting to a happy couple—or a couple pretending to be happy—eating mediocre food and drinking lousy champagne."

"But my mother was there," Nicola went on, ignoring Judith's jaded comments. "Did she cause trouble?"

Judith laughed. "Of course not. The thing you shouldn't forget, Nicola, is that your mother had never been in love with Ken. She dated him briefly. They broke up. End of story. Your mother was a model guest at Bonnie's wedding, not the maid of honor, though it's not entirely unheard of in a small town for a boy to date two sisters in turn or a girl to date two brothers. In any generation, the pool of eligible dating partners is pretty small."

"I guess," Nicola said.

"The truth is that once Carol had gone to New York and your aunt got together with your uncle, no one really cared that Carol and Ken had been an item for a time. The only one who continued to care about that relationship was Bonnie."

Nicola frowned. "What do you mean?"

"Ever since Carol left Yorktide," Judith went on, "Bonnie has been comparing herself to her sister, coming up short in one department or declaring a moral victory in another. She can't seem to live and let live. And if recent behavior is anything to go on, time doesn't seem to have lessened her desire for comparison and criticism."

"But I thought Ken broke up with my mother," Nicola said musingly. "Wouldn't that have made a difference to Bonnie? Made her feel, I don't know, secure?"

Judith shrugged. "It probably should have. Anyway, I was never sure who ended that relationship but as it wasn't meant to be, what does it matter?"

"Do you think Uncle Ken ever slept with my mother?" Nicola asked suddenly. "You know, had sex with her."

Judith raised an eyebrow. "I do know what 'sleeping with' means. And how should I know if they had sex? Probably. It's what wild and crazy teens do and remember, it was the nineteen seventies, smack in the middle of the counterculture revolution. Even here in Maine people had heard of so-called free love and boys with long hair and girls who'd burned their bras."

Nicola took a sip of the strong tea. She would have to process what Judith had told her about her aunt Bonnie's constantly comparing herself to Carol. Was that really true, or was it only Judith's take on her cousin's state of mind these past forty years? Suddenly, Nicola experienced a twitchy sense of guilt. She wondered how much of her own harsh attitude toward her mother had been influenced by her aunt's unhappiness. She wondered if Bonnie was aware that her own prejudices toward Carol Ascher might have affected Nicola's attitude toward the woman who had given birth to her.

"Mmmm," Judith said, calling Nicola back to the moment. "Gotta love me a sugar cookie."

Nicola smiled. "How was it for you, dating in Yorktide?" she asked. "I mean, in the sixties and seventies being gay wasn't really considered okay, was it?"

"No," Judith agreed. "But I was lucky. Any girl I was seen hanging out with was euphemistically called my special friend. I never actually came out because I didn't have to. As people left me to myself, I simply didn't care to make a fuss. That sort of attitude didn't make me particularly popular with the politicized gay community—back then or today—but I've always believed to each her own."

"Well, I don't think you're a coward," Nicola said staunchly.

"I should hope not! It takes courage to live in or out, along the sidelines or hiding in plain sight. No one has it easy in this life."

Nicola agreed. No one had it easy. But sometimes, it was hard to remember that. "'To thine own self be true,'" she said. "Isn't that Shakespeare?"

"Everything is Shakespeare." Judith reached for another cookie. "Thank you for coming here today."

"You're welcome," Judith said with a smile. "Now, I could do with another cup of tea. And get these cookies away from me. But not yet."

Nicola rose to put the kettle on the burner.

"By the way," Judith said, "I'm going to be getting rid of a perfectly decent sofa for no reason other than I'm bored with it. Do you want it? Oh, wait, you'll be leaving before long for parts unknown, won't you? Everything you own will have to go into storage or be gotten rid of."

Nicola felt herself blushing. Her family didn't know that her plans to apply for a position in the Peace Corps had stalled. Nicola honestly didn't know why; she was still passionately committed to the idea of service. But something was preventing her from taking the next step on her proposed journey.

"Yes," she said vaguely, bringing the tea kettle to the table. "But at some point, I'll need help furnishing a new place and I'll be happy to take whatever you have to offer."

Judith laughed. "Don't be so sure!"

Chapter 48

Julie was sitting at the kitchen table, a half-empty cup of coffee before her. She had let the coffee grow cold and was debating whether it was worth the effort to get up and bring the cup to the microwave. She was still struggling with this question when Sophie came into the kitchen. Her hair was piled up in a messy bun and dotted with sparkly clips. She was wearing pink sweatpants and a matching sweatshirt. They had cost a small fortune, and Julie remembered that she had told Sophie to return the pieces to the mall. Had that been last month or the month before?

"Mom," Sophie said, "where's that dress you were going to hem for me? I want to wear it later when I meet my friends from camp."

Julie frowned. "What dress?" she asked.

"Uh, the sundress I got at Urban Outfitters? The one that comes to my knees, but it should only come to mid-thigh so you said you'd hem it for me, like, four days ago?"

Julie thought hard. What had she done with the dress? "I'm sorry," she said. "I totally forgot. Can you wear something else?"

"I could," Sophie replied, "but I don't want to. I already planned my whole outfit. If I can't wear the dress I have to start all over again."

Julie sighed. She could probably hem the dress in less than an hour. But the thought of tackling even that relatively simple task seemed too daunting. "I'm sorry," she said again. Did she sound as pathetic as she felt? "I'll do it tomorrow. I promise."

"Why should I believe you?" Sophie cried. "No wonder Dad cheated on you! You're pathetic. You just mope around here all day! I'm embarrassed to have my friends over. I don't want them to see you this way! You used to be so . . . Oh, never mind!"

"So what?" Julie asked. She wasn't sure why she had; did she really want to hear the answer?

Sophie lowered her eyes. "So normal," she said quietly. "Fun even. My friends liked coming here. I was proud that you were my mom."

"And now?" Julie's voice trembled.

"*Grrrrrr!*" Sophie threw her arms in the air and let the palms of her hands slap down against her thighs. "Don't make me say it!"

She turned and stomped from the kitchen.

Julie stared down at the cold coffee. She was angry. She had not been put on this earth to entertain her daughter's friends. She had a right to her misery, just like everyone else did. If Sophie couldn't care about her own mother when she was struggling, then . . .

Then what? Did that make Sophie an ungrateful child? Or only an ordinary one?

Abruptly, Julie rose from her seat, dumped the cold coffee into the sink, and put the cup in the dishwasher.

She had a responsibility to her daughter.

She would hem the dress now. With any luck, it would be ready if Sophie still wanted to wear it later in the day. But she probably wouldn't.

Chapter 49

Bonnie hurried to answer the knock on the door. The last time she and her sister had met and talked about that long-ago bike accident, Bonnie had been left feeling that things between them were a bit less tense. They were a long way—maybe a very long way—from reconciliation, but Bonnie felt somewhat confident that she might be able to convince her sister of the rightness of her cause. To that end, she had finally invited Carol to the cottage.

"Welcome," Bonnie said.

Carol, dressed in a linen sheath dress, smiled and stepped inside. She looked around the front room, which served several purposes—living room, TV room, den—and nodded. "This is a charming home."

Something about the tone of Carol's pronouncement—judgment—hit Bonnie the wrong way.

"You've been here before," she said briskly. "Don't you remember?"

"Of course, I do. And I found it charming then, as well."

"When was it that you were here?" Bonnie challenged. Suddenly, she felt sure her sister was lying. She felt sure that Carol had forgotten the meals they had eaten at the kitchen table in the days between their mother's death and her funeral. She felt sure that Carol had dismissed the memory of the college graduation party

Bonnie and Ken had hosted for Nicola. There had been other occasions, too, but as they had not been grand affairs, no doubt her sister had barely noticed them.

"I've been here many times, Bonnie," Carol replied calmly. "The week before Mom's funeral. Nicola's college graduation party. The first year that Nicola came to live with you and Ken I visited at least three times. I remember being shown her room, the one that had been Julie's. Ken had helped Nicola paint it yellow. Is that enough proof for you that I haven't blocked out all memory of your home?"

"I thought no such thing," Bonnie replied heatedly. She refused to feel embarrassed about her earlier assumptions. A few random memories hardly measured up against a more general history of neglect. "Come through to the kitchen."

The kitchen was small but well laid out. And it was spotless. Bonnie nodded toward the table and Carol took a seat.

"Have you given any more thought to my offer to buy you out of Ferndean?" Carol asked.

Bonnie, standing at the counter, her back to her sister, froze. What had she been thinking? They had achieved no closeness the other day. It had all been in Bonnie's stupidly hopeful imagination.

Bonnie turned, a tray of tea things in hand. "I don't need to give it any more thought," she said firmly. "The answer is still no. I refuse to sell."

"Bonnie, I—"

Bonnie put the tray on the table with a bang. Tea cups that had once belonged to their grandmother rattled dangerously. "You see Ferndean House as just a professional project, something to be torn apart, rebuilt, photographed for a magazine. But it's more than that. Ferndean is a living, breathing part of the Ascher family." *It's a living, breathing part of me*, she added to herself. *And I'm proud of that.*

Carol sighed. "Please, sit down."

Bonnie remained standing.

"Why won't you accept my offer?" Carol went on. "It will be a very generous one, I promise, above current market value. You're just being stubborn saying no."

"I am not," Bonnie cried. With effort, she lowered her voice. "I love Ferndean. I always have. I've been the one to care for it all these years! Do you realize how much time and energy I've put into keeping Ferndean happy and healthy?"

"I probably don't," Carol admitted, "but I take your word for the fact that it was a big job, managing the old pile. But, Bonnie, once the house is mine you can visit. You can have your old room if you like, use it as a little getaway. I'll have some changes made to suit you, maybe put in a nice window seat or build out a bigger closet. And let's face it, the money you'll get by selling the house to me will solve a lot of your problems."

Bonnie bristled. "And what, exactly, are those?"

"Ken can't have left you particularly secure."

"How do you know how Ken did or did not leave me?" Bonnie retorted angrily. "He was an excellent husband. Not that you know anything about husbands, except maybe stealing them from other people."

"I have never, ever stolen a man from a woman. You've never seen the real me, just an image you created of some coldhearted, attention-seeking bitch." Carol paused and when she went on her tone had softened. "We liked each other when we were kids. I remember. We both do. So, when was it that I became someone you chose to hate?"

"When was it that I became someone you chose to lord it over and mock?" Bonnie snapped.

"I have never mocked you," Carol stated. "And why would I lord anything over you?"

Bonnie leaned over her sister in what she realized could be perceived as a menacing way. "Because you've always needed to be better than everyone else!"

"Oh, this is nonsense!" Carol said angrily. "We're talking in circles again and I'm putting a stop to it immediately."

She rose from her seat and reached for her Chanel bag. Bonnie had to take a step back for her sister to move away from the table.

Carol walked from the kitchen with a show of dignity, her step slow and even, and that angered Bonnie even further.

The front door closed. Carol had not let it slam. She was always so eager to prove that she was in control!

Bonnie sank into her usual seat at the table.

When *had* Carol become someone she had chosen to hate?

No. Not hate. Never hate.

So, when had Carol morphed in Bonnie's mind from an admirable if sometimes difficult human being to a person with only bad and selfish intentions? How had Bonnie allowed that transformation to happen?

It seemed likely that the physical distance between the sisters after Carol left Yorktide had contributed to this growing distortion. Physical space could too rapidly be filled with imagined crimes. If Carol had stayed on in Yorktide, things might have been different between them. But Carol, being Carol, could not have stayed on, not without doing irreparable damage to her true self. Even Bonnie could admit that, if grudgingly.

Gingerly, Bonnie touched the rim of one of the old tea cups. She was suddenly overcome with regret about the way she had behaved with her sister just now. But she wasn't sure she had it in her to throw off the attitude of resentment and suspicion that had come to weigh so heavily around her.

She just wasn't sure.

Chapter 50

Judith had persuaded her cousin to meet her at one of her favorite craft breweries in the next town. Carol hated beer, but she needed to vent.

The two women were seated across from each other at a picnic table, one among rows of end-to-end picnic tables that constituted the seating provided for beer lovers. Carol tried to ignore the strong smell of hops or yeast or whatever it was that went into beer and took a sip of water. What sort of place didn't serve wine? Even a cup of coffee would have been appreciated.

"So," Judith said, after a long drink of a beer the color of mud, "what's bugging you?"

"Bonnie. What else? She invited me over for tea and I was stupid enough to think that it was a gesture of friendship, or at least a sign of a thaw, but within two minutes she was on the defensive and then she was attacking me, accusing me of all sorts of bad behavior. I mean, what's that about?"

Judith sighed. "I can't speak for Bonnie, you know that. All I can do is guess that she feels she's in over her head with you. She badly wants something that you also want and in her mind, with the exception of Ken, you always come out the winner."

"That's ridiculous. She hardly knows me! She has no idea what

I've suffered in the years since I last lived here in Yorktide. Believe me, I've had my share of losses."

"Of course, you have. We all have."

Carol shook her head. "Bonnie is truly maddening. Was she always this stubborn and closed-minded, or is it just that I've been away for so long I've forgotten the worst of it?"

"Have you ever heard of the Cain Complex?" Judith asked.

"Is it the title of a book?"

"No, Cain as in Cain and Abel. The Cain Complex is the unconscious desire of an older sibling to kill the younger sibling."

Carol's eyes widened. "Good Lord, I've never wanted to kill Bonnie!"

"Maybe not, but why are you trying to bully her into selling Ferndean to you?"

"I'm not bullying my sister," Carol said after a moment. "That's ridiculous."

"You're a bulldozer, Carol. You always have been and maybe that's been helpful in business, but it's not often, if ever, helpful in relationships."

"I never bulldoze my clients," Carol countered. "I listen carefully to what it is they want in their homes and—"

"And then you lead them to what *you* think they should have. And that's fine. But not with Bonnie."

There was some truth in what her cousin said. But Carol wasn't in the mood to examine her character flaws. "You should be glad you never had a sister," she said. "I know that if Bonnie were a boy—I mean, if I had a brother—we'd be close, certainly closer than Bonnie and I are now."

"You can't know that. And I've never cared either way about having a sibling. I don't know anything other than being an only child. And it's always suited me just fine."

"Not all sisters are so grossly incompatible," Carol murmured. "Look at the Blackwell sisters, or the Grimké sisters. Productive together. Game changers."

Judith raised an eyebrow. "Look at Jackie O and Lee Radziwill. Not such smooth sailing there."

"You haven't answered my question. Has my sister always been this maddening?"

"As maddening as you are to her? Probably. People don't change all that much over time. We might like to think that we do, but we don't. We're all fundamentally who we were when we were little."

Carol frowned. "How very reassuring. Or how very depressing, depending on your point of view."

"Romulus and Remus," Judith said.

"What have they got to do with anything?"

"Romulus killed Remus. They were twins."

"I know who they were. Legendary founders of Rome, suckled by a wolf, blah blah. And I'm still not thinking of killing my sister."

"Good," Judith said. "Because the idea of visiting someone on death row scares me. Are you sure you don't want to try a beer?"

Carol grimaced. "I'm sure."

Chapter 51

"Thanks, Nicola." Sophie took a lick around her ice-cream cone.

Nicola was always charmed by the Nubble Lighthouse in York. Sophie, because she was Sophie, was most interested in Dunne's Ice Cream shop. Before they settled on a bench looking out to sea, Nicola bought her young cousin a Chocolate Extreme cone.

"Did you put on sunscreen before we left?" Nicola asked. The midday sun was beating down brutally.

Sophie gave Nicola a teenaged look. "You sound like my mother. Well, like how my mother used to sound. These days she doesn't seem to notice me."

"I'm sorry," Nicola said.

Sophie shrugged and continued to eat her ice cream. After a while she said, "What was going on before you came to live with Grandma and Grandpa? I mean, all I know is that you were going through a tough time and that your mother sent you here because she thought it was safer or something."

Nicola thought carefully before answering. She did not want to make her past troubles sound in the least bit glamorous. They had not been glamorous. And she had gotten so used to blaming her mother for sending her away she had almost forgotten what must have led her mother to make that drastic decision.

"I went a bit crazy I guess," she said finally. "Not crazy as in in-sane," she added quickly, "just a bit wild. It started when I turned fourteen. Before that I was a pretty average kid. I did okay in school. I was fairly spoiled, though not as badly as some of my classmates. There were two girls I was sort of close to, but I didn't have a best friend. Maybe that was unusual, I don't know. Anyway, it's all a bit foggy now."

"Like, you blocked it out?" Sophie asked.

Nicola squirmed inside. Yes, she had blocked things out. In order to keep the focus on her evil mother.

"I guess so," she admitted. "Anyway, a few of the tough kids in my class started being friendly to me—at least, I thought they were being friendly, but they probably just thought they could get some-thing from me, don't ask me what." Nicola shook her head. This was not going well. "Sorry," she said. "I've never really talked about that time of my life. All you need to know is that I started doing things I never would have dreamed of doing."

"Like what?" Sophie pressed.

"Stupid things," Nicola said firmly. "Dangerous things. Cruel things."

"Was it peer pressure? Adults are always talking about peer pressure."

"At first maybe peer pressure played a part," Nicola conceded. "Every kid wants to fit in, feel important. A lot of adults, too." She paused a moment before going on. "Later," she said, "I think I was frightened and that's why I acted out."

"Frightened of what?" Sophie asked.

Nicola swallowed hard. She had never said these words aloud. Maybe now was the time. Maybe not. But she was going to speak. "Of my mother dying," she said simply. "She'd had this big opera-tion, but she wouldn't let me visit her in the hospital and she never told me details of why she'd needed a radical hysterectomy—like if it was cancer."

Sophie frowned. "Whoa," she said. "That is scary."

"Then," Nicola went on, "when she came home from the hospi-tal she was so sick and weak for so long. She kept me at arm's length and since I'd already started to get into trouble, there was nothing at that point to stop me from getting into more trouble. The next thing I knew I was being shipped off to Maine."

"I totally would have freaked out if my parents sent me away," Sophie said.

"I did. At first. But not long after I moved in with Aunt Bonnie and Uncle Ken, I don't know, I started to get back to the old me. And I started to grow up." Nicola looked closely at Sophie. "Why do you want to know all this now? Is it something to do with what's going on with your parents?"

"No," Sophie said quickly. "I don't know. Maybe."

Nicola took Sophie's hand. "You can talk to me and to your grandmother if you can't get through to your mother or father. We're not going anywhere."

"You are. You're going away for two whole years."

"Well," Nicola said, taking her hand from Sophie's. "I'll still be a part of your life, just not living down the road."

Sophie shrugged. "Yeah, I know. Anyway, I'm fine. My parents' problems aren't my problems."

"You're right," Nicola said. "They're not. But remember this. When you're fifteen, stuff can really seem insurmountable, but things usually aren't insurmountable. When you're a teen, perception is wonky. It wobbles between a kid's view and an adult's view, and when it comes to rest for a split second it usually lands somewhere in between, which is not in the least bit helpful. I don't know how anyone survives being a teen. But the majority of people do survive and manage to forget the bulk of the torturous stuff they went through."

"Really?" Sophie asked, after she had munched the last of her cone. "Or are you just saying that so I don't do something stupid?"

Nicola's eyes widened. "You're not thinking—"

"No! Sheesh. I just meant are you telling me a lie to make me feel better?"

"I wouldn't do that," Nicola said earnestly.

"I believe you. A lot of adults would, though."

"Thanks," Nicola said. She *was* an adult. It wasn't a new realization, but there were times when she felt so much like a teen still, or even a child, like the nights when she couldn't get to sleep because she felt waves of generalized anxiety and all she wanted was to be back in her little room at Bonnie and Ken's house, tucked safely into the narrow bed under the quilt Bonnie had made specially for her sixteenth birthday. It could be a shock to remember that she was a bona fide adult with an education, a career, a home. She paid her own bills and voted and recycled and kept her clothes clean.

But those weren't the only things that made you an adult. Being an adult also meant that you treated others with respect; that you tried your best to forgive hurts and insults; that you exercised empathy and compassion; that you abandoned angry actions based on knee-jerk reactions; that you experienced your emotions without necessarily letting them determine your treatment of others.

"You in there?" Sophie asked with a frown.

Nicola shook her head and laughed. "Yeah, just thinking."

"Well, it must have been about something terrible because you were frowning."

"Not terrible," Nicola corrected. "Just important."

"I'm sorry about your mother being so sick back then," Sophie said suddenly. "I know what it feels like to be worried about your mom. It sucks."

Nicola smiled. "That's one way to put it."

"It's not supposed to be that way. Kids aren't supposed to have to worry about their parents."

"Life is rarely the way it's supposed to be," Nicola said gently. "But it's often pretty good anyway."

Sophie's expression brightened. "I know. Like, I'm totally furious with my dad right now, but the other day he gave me twenty-five dollars for no reason at all. One of the counselors at camp has this awesome red sports car, and he drove me to the outlets in Kittery and I got this fabulous denim miniskirt."

Nicola restrained a frown. Scott's giving his daughter money "for no reason" was of course a bribe to buy back his daughter's affection. Not a great idea. Then again, if buying the skirt brought even a temporary smile to Sophie's face, maybe Scott's gesture hadn't been entirely ill-conceived. But what did Nicola know about raising children? It could never be easy, for anyone.

Including Carol Ascher.

"Cool," Nicola said. "I mean, about the skirt." A silver lining to the dark cloud that had been looming over Sophie's shoulder this summer.

Silver linings were good.

Chapter 52

"Well?" Sophie demanded. "Don't you notice anything different?"

Julie looked up from her desk. "No," she said after a moment. "Sorry."

Sophie rolled her eyes. "My new skirt. Dad gave me the money to buy it. I got it on a super discount in Kittery. Isn't it fabulous?"

Sophie was wearing a denim miniskirt. The word *fabulous* did not come to Julie's mind. "How did you get to Kittery?"

"I got a ride from a friend at camp."

Julie thought for a moment. What were the names of the other counselors? Sophie must have mentioned at least one or two of them. No matter.

"I was with Nicola earlier," Sophie announced, propping herself against the old filing cabinet. "We went to the Nubble and we talked about a lot of stuff. She said my parents' problems aren't my problems. Well, I said it and she agreed."

Sophie's tone was combative. Julie didn't know how to respond. She said nothing.

Suddenly, Sophie stood away from the filing cabinet. "Why don't you just have an affair?" she said angrily. "Maybe it will make you feel better. Then you and Dad will be even and we can get back to being a happy family and you can stop being so . . . so not here!"

Julie's immediate thought was not: That's a bad idea. It was: Who would want to have an affair with an overweight, depressed woman?

Not: I refuse to stoop to revenge.

But: No one would find me attractive.

What sort of person did that make her? Weak? Self-absorbed? As bad a person as Scott?

"Mom?"

"Sorry," Julie said, shaking her head. "Don't be silly. I'm not breaking my marriage vows just to . . . No. That's a very bad idea. Infidelity is wrong."

"Well, do something! I can't take much more of this. It's like living with . . . it's like . . . *Grrr!* I don't know what it's like, but it's awful."

Sophie stomped out of the room. Julie opened the notebook on her desk and picked up a pen. She held the pen poised above the empty page on which she was supposed to be writing her ideas about changes to the school's dress code; the aim was to make the code more inclusive for all.

Ten minutes later, the page remained blank.

Suddenly, a sense of something amiss made Julie look up from the notebook.

Scott was standing in the door to the office.

"Why are you here?" Julie asked. "You should be at work."

"I thought we could have lunch together and maybe talk."

Julie looked back down at the blank page before her. "I'm not hungry."

Scott sighed. "You don't have to eat. We can still sit across the table from each other and have a conversation."

What would Scott say, Julie wondered? That he was sorry? Well, she knew that already. That she wasn't interesting enough for him, or sexy enough for him? She knew that already, too. That he wanted to leave her?

"We can't," she said.

"We can," Scott insisted. "You won't. Julie, look at me, please."

Julie did. She knew the expression on her face, in her eyes, was as blank as the notebook page before her. She could tell from Scott's reaction. He took a step back and then turned around and was gone.

Chapter 53

"What are you doing here?"

Carol smiled and held up a plastic bag. "I brought you tomatoes from the cutest little farm stand out by the Morrison estate."

Bonnie frowned. She hadn't seen her sister since the debacle in this very cottage. She didn't need Carol to bring her produce. She could get her own produce easily enough.

"Thanks," she said. She took the bag.

Carol didn't go away. Did she want an invitation to come inside? Bonnie was not comfortable being rude. She wanted to close the door in her sister's face but could not.

Silently, she stepped back and Carol followed her into the kitchen. Bonnie put the bag of tomatoes on the table. "Do you want something to drink?" she asked stiffly.

Carol shook her head. "No, thanks. But you'll never guess who I ran into at the farm stand. The editor-in-chief of the *Yorktide Chronicle*, Bill Elliott. He must be eight-five if he's a day, but he told me he's in no hurry to retire."

"Bill is a nice man," Bonnie said. The truth was she knew him only by reputation, but she wanted to stake some small claim to her fellow resident of Yorktide.

"He asked what I was doing back in Yorktide. I told him I was spending a quiet summer with my family. And then he suggested he do a feature article about Yorktide's native daughter-made-good and how she finds the Yorktide of today compared to the one of her youth." Carol smiled. "I didn't have the heart to say no."

Bonnie felt the blood rush to her face. That the *Chronicle* was going to publish an article about Carol Ascher was an insult to everyone who had stayed in Yorktide to make a living and raise a family.

Suddenly, something in Bonnie shifted. Or snapped. Or broke.

Until this very moment, she had never confronted her sister about the public falsehood she had labored under so long ago.

Until this very moment, she had never intended to tell Carol that she knew what had really happened between her and Ken.

In those first weeks after Carol had left for New York, people around town had talked ceaselessly about how they had known all along that Carol Ascher was too ambitious for a small-town boy who was set to take over his family's auto repair business, and how it must have broken Ken's heart when Carol left him. Bonnie had bit her tongue, refusing to break Ken's confidence, and had let Yorktide assume that Bonnie was a rebound, when in fact she was nothing of the sort.

She was the Ascher sister Ken loved.

"I know the truth," Bonnie blurted. "I know that Ken dumped you and that he let you tell everyone that you had been the one to end the relationship because he knew you couldn't handle people knowing you'd been rejected."

Carol laughed lightly and began to fiddle with the collar of her blouse. "Poor Ken," she said. "He must have been more devastated than I thought. No, Bonnie, the truth is that I broke up with him. He was too boring and provincial for me. I guess he lied about what really happened to save his male ego."

"Ken was not boring!" Bonnie cried. "And if he was provincial, then so am I."

"Which made you two a better match than Ken and I could ever have been. I could see that we had no future, even if he couldn't. So, I ended things." Carol shrugged and let go of her collar.

Bonnie felt as if she had been slapped. "That's a lie!" she cried.

"I should get going," her sister said. "I'm interviewing a landscape architect this afternoon about rebuilding that old stone maze or whatever it is on the property. I think enough of it remains to get some idea of the original design, but without the actual plans someone will have to bring some creativity to the project. I was thinking maybe a zen garden would be nice, something to bring a sense of worldliness to the estate."

The old stone maze. Since Bonnie's childhood all she had known of it was a jumble of half-submerged stones, some of which seemed to have the remains of carvings made long ago, weather-worn and rubbed almost smooth by hundreds of passing seasons.

Carol was right about there being no surviving plans. And even if the Aschers had been able to locate the plans, there had never been enough money to restore or rebuild the structure.

But Carol had money. And Carol wanted Ferndean.

"Bonnie? I said I'm leaving now."

Bonnie nodded. She was barely aware of her sister walking from the room. She sank into a chair at the table. Her heart was racing and she felt sick to her stomach.

Could Ken have been lying all the years of their marriage? *Could* Carol have ditched him and not the other way around? Could he have been in love with Carol all along?

No. Absolutely not. Bonnie had the memories—the facts, the witnesses!—to prove that Ken had loved her and only her for all the decades of their relationship.

And Ken had *not* lied about the breakup with her sister. Ken did not lie. He couldn't even tell a white lie; there had been times when Bonnie had wished he had been able to be less bluntly honest, like when she had taken that pottery class and Ken had told her that while she was a gifted quilter it would be better if she abandoned the pottery wheel.

Bonnie put her head in her hands. Why had Carol felt it necessary to tell this lie now, after all these years? And why had she felt the need to confront Carol, to reveal that she knew the truth of the breakup?

Anger alone? The need to wound, the need to pay back a hurt? An eye for an eye.

One thing was sure. No matter what, Bonnie would not tell any-one what had transpired between herself and Carol that afternoon. It was all too dreadful and embarrassing. To tell would be a cheap bid for sympathy. She was better than that.

Bonnie got up from the chair and looked at the bag of tomatoes on the table. Nothing good could come of Carol's being back in Yorktide, she thought.

Nothing at all.

Chapter 54

Carol sat at the table on the back deck. She had prepared a salad for her dinner but had no appetite for it. The glass of wine she had poured sat untouched. She felt frustrated. She felt ashamed of herself.

Why had she gone to Bonnie's cottage in the first place? To brag about the article? Certainly, not with the sole intention of bringing a gift of tomatoes!

And why had she lied about the breakup?

As Carol gazed unseeingly at the expanse of lawn that ended in a virtual wall of fir trees, she remembered the day she had received a letter from her mother telling her that Bonnie and Ken were a couple.

Carol was still living at The Atlanta. Mail for the residents was left on a table in the building's foyer. Carol remembered glancing quickly at the table that afternoon, not really expecting anything, but finding a letter from Shirley Ascher. That was odd; Shirley had written only the week before. Still, Carol had no sense of foreboding, no sense that this letter would be in any way significant.

She took the letter to her room. She sat on the bed, aware of the shrill laughter coming from the far end of the hall and the smell of burning soup—someone was using a forbidden hot plate—and opened the letter. She expected to hear more of the same—a mention that her father and her sister were well; a small complaint about Shirley's own sister, Mary; and maybe the fact that Shirley had read a story in the Sunday paper about how dangerous the New York City subways had become. "I don't know if the streets are any safer," Shirley had added in one letter. "So maybe you had better take a cab when you need to go out. But aren't they expensive?" So, what was she supposed to do? Carol had wondered. The answer was obvious. Move back to Yorktide, where she belonged.

But what Carol found this time was a bit of real news. Her sister was dating Ken Elgort and according to Shirley, an engagement was imminent.

I didn't mention this before now, Shirley Ascher went on, *because it's not wise to jump the gun, as my father used to say. But as every instinct tells me that Ken will be part of the family before long, I thought it right you should know. I'm sure you'll want to wish your sister the best.*

The letter was signed, as usual, *Your Loving Mother in Maine*. As if she would be anywhere else.

This news had come at a very bad moment. The bathroom Carol shared with the other girls on the hall was out of order; for the past three days, they had had to use the bathroom on the second or fourth floors. Tempers were short; people were late for work or dates; there was no word about when the third-floor bathroom would be back in use. A customer at the small lingerie shop where Carol was working claimed Carol had been rude to her and Carol was forced to endure a scolding by her boss. To make the day even more of a disaster, a five-dollar bill seemed to have gone missing from Carol's purse. Had it been stolen? Had she been careless? Either way, now she would not be able to put a down payment on a blouse she had seen at a nice shop on Third Avenue.

All in all, it was not a great time to be receiving the news that your little sister was dating your ex-boyfriend, the only guy who had ever said no to Carol Ascher.

Carol balled up her mother's letter and threw it in the direction of the waste paper can. Rather pathetically, it landed on the floor. She got up from the bed and stamped from one end to the other of the tiny room, then back again, until a pounding beneath her feet indicated that the girl in the room below hers had had enough.

So, Carol took her bad temper into the streets and for the next hour and a half she stalked the sidewalks with no aim in mind other than to keep moving. The sights and sounds and smells of the city barely registered as she darted across intersections, and around overflowing trash cans, and dodged rough-looking characters asking for handouts.

Later that night, worn-out, feeling the grime of the city on her skin though she had taken a very hot shower, lying on her hard and narrow bed, Carol suddenly realized that this was the very first time Bonnie had succeeded in getting something Carol had wanted or had possessed first. The revelation made her feel magnanimous. Poor Bonnie. She could have Ken. Carol didn't want him.

In the morning, Carol wrote her sister a note of congratulations. But she couldn't help wonder why Bonnie hadn't herself written with the news of her romance. Maybe Bonnie had planned to tell Carol once things between herself and Ken were more settled. Whatever the case, Bonnie would soon know that her sister was absolutely thrilled for her and sure that Bonnie and Ken Elgort made a lovely couple.

Carol sighed and took a sip of the wine. It was now warm. Maybe she should just go back to New York, give up this naïve scheme of embracing her family before it was too late. Besides, she didn't even like Ferndean House. She was tempted to tear the whole thing down and start afresh, build something contemporary.

Of course, that could only happen if Bonnie relinquished her hold on the house.

And then what? Carol frowned. She would still be stuck in Yorktide, albeit in a sleek new home, with a resurrected stone maze or decorative feature or whatever it once had been. Poor Bonnie. The look on her face when Carol had mentioned incorporating an Eastern influence on the property! Why had she said that? She had no such idea in mind at all.

Carol picked up her fork and speared a bit of avocado from the salad. The avocado was already going brown, but she popped it into her mouth anyway. And she decided that she would stay on in Yorktide, at least until the end of the summer. She was not a quitter. If New York City hadn't beaten her as an innocent nineteen-year-old, then Yorktide and its residents could not beat her as a seasoned sixty-five-year-old.

Sixty-five. She was officially old.

But not as old as Bill Elliott, editor-in-chief of the local rag. Why, oh why had she agreed to do that stupid interview! And Mr. Elliott had been a bit of a flirt; if he persisted in that sort of thing, she would firmly but tactfully shut him down. The very last thing she needed was to be the subject of the paper's next headline: INTERNATIONALLY RENOWNED INTERIOR DESIGNER SET TO MARRY ANCIENT EDITOR-IN-CHIEF OF SMALL-TOWN NEWSPAPER.

It was not to be borne.

Chapter 55

Nicola walked along the corridor that led from the administrative offices of Pine Hill to the wing of the building where those who qualified for Independent Living status made their homes. The walls were lined with colorful prints of flowers and famous landmarks. The floor was kept meticulously clean and free of impediment. The windows were always sparklingly clear.

Automatically, Nicola felt for the card in the back pocket of her chinos. It was still there. A hefty gift certificate to The Bookworm, the independent book shop in town. The gift from her mother was welcome; Nicola loved to read and didn't have a lot of spare income to spend on books.

But why the gift? Why delivered through the mail and not in person? The answer seemed obvious. Her mother was trying to make amends for years of neglect but had been afraid Nicola would refuse to accept the gift if she presented it to her in person. And maybe her mother had a good reason for fearing another face-to-face meeting. Nicola hadn't exactly welcomed her mother with open arms this summer. Truth be told, Nicola routinely displayed more loving behavior to the residents of Pine Hill than she did to Carol Ascher.

Nicola turned a corner and knocked on the door to #33. Hermione Wolcott invited her to enter. Her apartment was furnished with several pieces of art she had brought with her from her previous home; there was a stunning nineteenth-century landscape from a member of the Hudson River School over the couch and an abstract Modernist sculpture on the sideboard. Hermione herself had a definite personal style, one Nicola didn't know how to define, though her mother probably would. Today Hermione was wearing a dark, slim-fitting pantsuit with a white blouse buttoned to the neck, large gold hoop earrings, and three gold rings, one of which was set with a bright green emerald. Her lips were perfectly painted red. Nicola knew only a bit about Hermione's life before her coming to Pine Hill; she often thought she would like to know more. But that was up to Hermione.

"Have a seat," Hermione offered. "I see the *Chronicle* has printed an article about your mother."

Nicola nodded. "Yes, I heard."

"You mean you haven't seen it yet?"

"No," Nicola said. "I'm sure I'll see it around later."

"Here." Hermione leaned forward and took a folded newspaper from the coffee table. "Take my copy. You must be so proud of her."

Nicola accepted the newspaper and smiled noncommittally.

"She's made a great success of her life."

Had she? Nicola wasn't so sure about that. "Yes," she said.

"But you're not close, are you?" Hermione said. "You and your mother."

"How did you know that?" Nicola blurted.

Hermione laughed. "I may be old, but I'm not stupid. If you two were close you'd have read the article and be bragging about her."

Nicola felt her cheeks flame. "It's just that we haven't lived together in a long time. Not since I was fifteen. I was sent to Yorktide to live with my aunt and uncle."

Hermione nodded. "Yes, I heard that. Small-town gossip. Anyway, I'm sure your mother had a good reason for sending you to your relatives."

"How can you be sure?" Nicola asked, more sharply than she had intended.

"People don't usually do that sort of thing for no reason. At the very least, the reason must have seemed good to your mother at the time. And you've flourished. Your mother's choice seems to have been the right one for you."

"I guess," Nicola said after a moment. "Yes, I mean, I'm pretty happy, actually. Mostly."

"No one is ever entirely happy, not if they're honest." Hermione shrugged. "What does it even mean to be happy? Has anyone ever really figured that one out?"

Suddenly, Nicola remembered something she had said to Sophie recently. Something like, life was rarely the way you wanted it to be, but it was often pretty good anyway.

"I had a daughter," Hermione said suddenly.

Nicola startled. "Oh. I didn't know."

Hermione's posture looked exceptionally straight at that moment. When she spoke again, her voice was clear but low. "Not many people here do. Maybe you're the first to know. I can't remember everything I've said since I moved in. She died a very long time ago. When she was only thirty."

"I'm so sorry," Nicola said feelingly. "Had she been ill?"

"Cancer."

"What was her name?" Nicola asked. She realized she felt close to tears.

"Her name was Grace. We were very close. In a way, I suppose we were each other's best friend. Her death was the worst thing that ever happened to me. For a while I really didn't think I'd survive it." Hermione smiled briefly. "But here I am, forty years later."

"Do you . . . How often do you . . . I'm sorry," Nicola said, swallowing hard.

"How often do I think of her? Every day. All the time." Hermione looked at Nicola shrewdly. "You lost your uncle last year, didn't you?"

Nicola nodded. She must not cry on the job.

"Remembering never ends," Hermione went on, "but it does shift forms. Don't worry about the shape it takes at any given moment. Your uncle is always with you. That's a constant."

"Thank you," Nicola said.

"For what?"

"For talking to me about . . . about everything."

"Not at all," Hermione said briskly. "Now, what was it that brought you to see me this morning?"

When Nicola had completed her routine weekly assessment of Ms. Wolcott, she said her farewells and headed back to her shared office. She wondered why Hermione had chosen to tell her about her daughter, today of all days. As Nicola sank into the chair at her desk, it struck her how very often she found herself the recipient of care from the very people she was meant to serve.

She hadn't thanked her mother for the gift certificate to The Bookworm. She would. Soon.

Chapter 56

Scott was sitting across from Julie at the kitchen table. He was mending a tear in one of his flannel work shirts. Julie vaguely remembered the last time she had bought him a new flannel shirt. It had to have been four or five years earlier. For his birthday. Back when her husband had loved her.

Sophie was leaning against the counter, legs and arms crossed. She was wearing a T-shirt that said CUTE AF. Julie hadn't seen it before. She didn't know what the message meant. But she didn't care enough to ask.

"Did you see the cool article about Grandma's sister?" Sophie asked, nodding at the day's paper on the kitchen table.

"What's cool about it?" Julie asked.

Sophie shrugged. "I don't know. All I know is that I want to be rich and famous like Aunt Carol one day."

"Being rich and famous doesn't necessarily mean that you're happy," Scott said mildly.

Sophie laughed. "Like you would know?"

Julie knew she should scold Sophie for talking so rudely to her father, but she said nothing.

"I can use my imagination," Scott said evenly. "And my common sense."

"I didn't think you had any common sense," Sophie retorted with a smirk.

Scott flinched. "Sophie, you can't talk to me that way."

"What way?"

"As if I don't deserve your respect."

Sophie stood away from the counter. "You don't. Not anymore." And then she stomped out of the room. A moment later, a door slammed.

That was getting old, Julie thought. Slamming doors. Been done to death.

Scott shoved his needle into the shirt he was mending and pushed the work away. "What is becoming of this family?" he muttered.

Julie didn't respond.

"Julie?" he said, more loudly. "Do you hear me? Do you even care?"

"Don't talk to me about caring," she said flatly.

"Right. Okay. I'm the one who didn't care, I'm the one responsible for this whole mess. I get it. It's all my fault. I accept that. But now what? You either have to forgive me or . . . or tell me to go. You have to do or to say something. You have to come back from wherever it is you're hiding."

"Hiding?" Julie laughed. She wasn't amused. But still, she laughed.

"From wherever it is you are now. Julie, you've got to help me. You've got to help Sophie."

I've got, Julie thought, *to help myself.*

Scott got up from his seat and stood there, hands hanging at his sides. Julie knew he was expecting a response; at least, he was hoping for one. But she had none to give. After a long moment, he turned and left the room.

Julie pushed the newspaper aside. She knew her mother resented the fact that Carol was being feted by the town she had left behind so long ago. For her part, Julie didn't really care if Carol Ascher made a splash or not. Her aunt's popularity didn't change anything about Julie's life, for better or for worse.

It certainly didn't affect the fact that the second of Sara's summer workshops was coming up. Julie was determined not to embarrass herself again in front of her colleagues. She simply *had* to muster the energy and the focus to read the materials she was supposed to read, to come up with the three discussion questions she was supposed to suggest, and to be ready to smile, chat, and be allaround presentable.

The first step is always the most difficult. Start small. One day at a time. All annoyingly familiar and perhaps overused clichés of socalled wisdom. Nevertheless, Julie got up from the kitchen table and headed for her office, where those materials awaited her attention.

If she had any attention to give them.

Chapter 57

Bonnie sat at the kitchen table with a cup of coffee and the day's edition of the *Yorktide Chronicle* before her. Bill Elliott's article was a puff piece, laudatory but empty. Not like the article about Carol Ascher that had run in the *Chronicle* the year Nicola was seventeen. Bonnie would never forget the opening line.

Everyone in Yorktide knew from day one that Carol Ascher would grow up to be somebody.

It seemed that Carol had been awarded a respected prize by an important architecture firm. Bonnie had forgotten the details. She had wondered how the *Yorktide Chronicle* had learned of this accomplishment. Maybe the story had been picked up from a larger paper and reworked by a local reporter with an emphasis on the pride Yorktide took in its prize-winning former resident.

When Nicola saw the paper that evening she had scanned the article with a frown. "Who did she have to pay to get the award I wonder?" she said, tossing the paper onto the kitchen table.

It had occurred to Bonnie to ask Nicola why, when her life was going so nicely, she still carried so much antipathy toward her mother. But she hadn't. She should have talked to her niece about the importance of being kinder toward Carol. But she never did. It had been in Bonnie's best interest to ensure Nicola's loyalty to her and her alone.

When Ken had finished reading the paper after dinner—"Well, Carol seems to have done it again. Good for her."—Bonnie put it in the recycling bin, along with the junk mail, the empty cans of dog food, and the flattened pasta boxes.

And now there was this latest article. It was enough to make Bonnie want to scream.

"Oh, Ken," she murmured. How she missed him!

It was not long after Carol's departure from Yorktide that Ken began to pay Bonnie small attentions. When he ran into her at the pharmacy in town one afternoon, the one with the old-fashioned soda fountain, he treated her to a dish of ice cream with caramel sauce. When he caught sight of her pushing her bicycle along a steep section of road that ran from the heart of town to Ferndean House, he lifted the bicycle (it had a flat tire) into the bed of his truck and gave her a lift home. At the annual Yorktide Christmas Dance, held at the high school, Ken asked Bonnie three times to dance. And each time, as Ken whirled her around the other couples, Bonnie noticed her parents' expressions of approval.

Not once did Bonnie feel guilty for her friendship with her sister's former boyfriend. And Ken rarely mentioned Carol after telling Bonnie, without fuss or drama, that it had been he who had broken up with Carol and not the other way around. "Just so you know," he had said. "Just so you don't believe what everyone is saying. It was easier for Carol this way. And it doesn't bother me."

It didn't bother Bonnie, either. Much.

When Bonnie turned seventeen, Ken asked her out on a real date. He picked her up at Ferndean House one Saturday evening and they went to a movie in Portsmouth. They shared a tub of popcorn and a box of Raisinets. From that point on, Bonnie Ascher and Ken Elgort were considered an official couple by the good people of Yorktide.

A few months later, Shirley Ascher wrote to her older daughter in New York City, telling her of the relationship and predicting an engagement before long. She was right. Just weeks later, Ken proposed with his grandmother's modest but very pretty engagement ring. Bonnie said yes.

When Bonnie was eighteen, she and Ken married. Ken was twenty-two. For the first six months of their marriage they lived at Ferndean House while Ken and his father and uncle finished the cottage they were building for the next generation of Elgorts. The day she and Ken moved into 329 Rosehip Lane was one of the happiest days of Bonnie's life. To share a home all alone with her husband was a dream come true. If it was a humble dream, no matter.

Bonnie and Ken were two birds of a feather. Homebodies. Ambitious only for a marriage and a family. And content to live out their lives in Yorktide.

Bonnie glanced again at the *Chronicle*. Contentment did not mean cowardice. Bonnie had wanted to stay in the town in which she had been born because she loved everything about Yorktide. She was happy. She always had been. How many people could say that and mean it? Sure, there had been difficult times, but above and beyond the challenges of daily life, Bonnie had felt sure that she was right where she was meant to be.

Tears sprang to Bonnie's eyes and roughly, she wiped them away. She had work to do. Laundry. Return a book to the library. And there were the bags of mulch she needed to drop off at Ferndean.

She didn't want to see Carol, though. Maybe she would just leave the bags on the porch, like she had meant to do with the box of garden gnomes. . . .

Bonnie rose from her seat. Maybe she would ring the bell instead.

Chapter 58

"Darn!"

The glass slipped from Carol's hand and landed with a thud in the kitchen sink. At least it hadn't broken. The way Carol felt at the moment she was sure to accidentally lacerate herself on the shards.

She refilled the glass with cold water and took a deep drink.

Her eczema was flaring. She felt sluggish. Her conscience was bothering her. She had lied to Bonnie about the breakup with Ken. What was wrong with her these days?

Carol turned to leave the kitchen. Her eye was caught by a photograph of Shirley Ascher held to the front of the fridge with a magnet. It had been taken about a year or two after Ronald's death. Shirley had already become ill. Her hair was pathetically thin. Her clothes hung off her bony frame.

Carol looked away. She would never forget the last time she had spoken to her mother face-to-face. Bonnie had begged her to come home. "Mom's dying," she said. "You need to say goodbye."

Carol had come. The visit was emotionally challenging in ways for which she had not been prepared.

Shirley Ascher was lucid; Bonnie had led Carol to expect her mother's mind to be wandering. But maybe being with her older daughter, whom she hadn't seen in almost a year, had somehow, if momentarily, invigorated Shirley. Whatever the case, the story her mother had told her that day had made Carol realize that in many ways her mother was a complete stranger to her and always had been.

Carol was startled by the ringing of the doorbell. She put a hand to her heart, took a deep breath, and went to answer it.

She found Bonnie standing on the doorstep. Her expression was tight as she pointed to two large plastic bags lumped at her feet.

"I'm just here to deliver these bags of mulch for the vegetable garden."

"Thanks," Carol said. She wondered why Bonnie hadn't brought the bags around back. Why even let Carol know she was there?

"Why don't you stay for a bit, have a cup of tea or something?" Carol said, before she could consider the wisdom of her invitation.

Her sister accepted.

"I've got chamomile, peppermint, and Irish Breakfast," Carol said. "I can make it with ice if you want."

Bonnie chose Irish Breakfast, hot. Carol remembered that their mother had always drunk hot tea on even the steamiest of days. That was a habit both of her daughters had inherited.

"The back deck is the coolest place on days like this," she said. "I'll be out in a moment."

Carol went to the kitchen to prepare the tea. She used the microwave, ancient though it was, to heat the water. Did Bonnie have a microwave at the cottage? Carol thought it likely that she didn't.

Carrying a mug in each hand, Carol joined her sister. Carol was expecting Bonnie to mention Bill Elliott's article and when she didn't, she was relieved.

Still, she wished her sister would say something. The silence began to weigh heavily. Carol felt sweat trickling down her chest.

And then she wondered. Shirley hadn't made Carol promise not to tell her sister what she had revealed just before dying. Maybe Bonnie deserved to know about an important moment in their mother's youth, before marriage and motherhood had changed her from girl to woman.

Besides, Carol thought rather desperately, maybe sharing Shirley's story would serve as a sort of roundabout apology for her recent bad behavior.

"When I last saw Mom," she began, "she told me something she'd never told anyone else."

"What?" Bonnie said sharply, looking up from her mug of tea.

"About six months after Mom started to date Dad she met someone. He had just sort of shown up in the area, and no one really knew anything about him, other than that he drove a flashy car and seemed to have cash to spare."

"And?" Bonnie prompted.

"And they had a brief and passionate affair, brief because after about a month he left for California, something about a cousin in Los Angeles with a can't-miss business scheme. He didn't ask Mom to go with him and that was that."

Bonnie's expression darkened. "You're lying."

"No," Carol said evenly. "I'm not."

"Was she dating Dad all along?" Bonnie asked after a moment. "While she was having the affair?"

"That's what she said."

"How in the world did she keep it a secret?" Bonnie cried, setting the mug of tea heavily on the table at her side. "This is Yorktide!"

Carol shrugged. "I don't know. Maybe she didn't. Maybe people just looked the other way for once. Anyway, Mom swore she was in love with Dad, but that she just couldn't help herself with this other man. It was one of those once-in-a-lifetime things."

"Why didn't she tell me?" Bonnie said.

Carol heard the plaintive note in her sister's voice. "I don't know," she admitted. "Maybe she thought I'd be less shocked than you would, though I certainly was surprised."

"An affair is hardly something to brag about," Bonnie said sternly.

"Which is probably why she only spoke of it on her deathbed."

"A guilty conscience?"

"I don't think so. Just a secret that needed to be told." Carol knew all about secrets. And about not telling them.

"She never saw the man again?" Bonnie asked.

"Never. She had no idea if he was alive or dead. If I thought it would have changed anything for her I'd have offered to hunt him down, but I don't think that's what she wanted. She didn't even tell me his name."

"Do you think she was lying?" Bonnie wondered. Her tone sounded more thoughtful now, less strident.

"No, it's not the sort of thing you lie about on your deathbed. If anything, you'd pretend to have been better than you were."

"You're probably right," Bonnie admitted. "Do you think Mom thought about that man all those years she was married to Dad?"

"I don't know," Carol said. "She certainly never forgot him, but that doesn't mean she was pining away."

"I'm sure Dad never knew," Bonnie said stoutly. "If he did he wouldn't have married her."

"I doubt he knew, either, but even if he did know, or suspect, he might still have married her. Shirley and Ronald were different people before we knew them as Mom and Dad."

"I don't like to think about our parents—"

"As people?" Carol smiled. "Bonnie, isn't it about time you recognized your mother and father as full individuals? Life can't be all rosy retrospection."

Bonnie never answered that question. Not long after, she went home, looking distressed.

And Carol was left with a bad feeling that she had made another mistake. Why was she sabotaging her plan to heal old wounds by revealing secrets best kept hidden, by lying, by antagonizing her sister in every way that she could?

Was she losing her mind? She owed Bonnie an apology. Why hadn't she offered it?

Carol's hands began to shake ever so slightly. Her mouth felt dry. She took the last sip of her tea. It helped a bit. But not enough.

Chapter 59

Sophie had persuaded Nicola that an afternoon at Ogunquit Beach was an awesome idea.

"But it's Saturday," Nicola had pointed out. "It'll be a mob scene."

"So what?" was Sophie's reply. "Oh, come on. It'll be fun."

Nicola's idea of an enjoyable visit to the beach involved walking along the shore, collecting the occasional interesting stone, noting the dramatic cloud formations, and watching the seagulls gracefully swoop and dive through the air.

Sophie, on the other hand, was committed to the idea of sunbathing. She had come laden with a chair, a blanket, a sunhat, two tubes of sunblock (one for her face and neck especially), a battery-operated, handheld fan, two giant bottles of flavored water, and a super-size bag of chips.

"Don't you have a bathing suit?" Sophie asked, eyeing Nicola critically.

"Not at the moment," Nicola admitted, glancing down at her T-shirt and cargo shorts. "Usually when I come to the beach I wear, you know, clothes."

"But what about when you go into the water?"

"I guess I haven't gone swimming in a while." Nicola wondered why.

"You should have more fun," Sophie pronounced.

"I have plenty of fun. I really enjoy my job."

That made Sophie prop herself on her elbows. "You like spending every day with a bunch of sick, old people?"

"The point is that they're people," Nicola scolded. "And not all are sick. You can learn a lot from people who've been around longer than you have, both good and bad things. You just have to listen."

Sophie looked dubious. "I wish I didn't have to work," she said, settling back on her blanket. "I'd come here every morning and stay until the lifeguards made me leave."

"Do you ever bring a book?" Nicola asked.

Sophie laughed. "Why? I've got my phone."

Nicola smiled to herself. She and Sophie were so very different in so many ways. But they were family. And that meant something.

Carol Ascher was also her family. Arguably, she was the most important person in Nicola's family. So why was Nicola so awfully grim and unbending where her mother was concerned?

It was a question for another time.

"So, what are your friends doing today?" she asked Sophie. "You could have asked someone along."

Sophie sighed. "Yeah, I guess."

"Is there a boy you like?" Nicola asked. Why? She had hated being asked that question when she was Sophie's age.

"A boy?" Sophie tone was incredulous. "Boys are ridiculous. They're so immature."

"Then, someone older?" Nicola did not say the word *man.*

"Maybe."

"Where do you know him from?" Nicola asked, thinking of that creepy guy she had seen outside Sophie's camp.

Sophie shrugged. "Just around. Anyway, it's not like we're going out or anything. He's just—cool. You know."

"Do your parents know he exists?"

"Are you kidding? Like I would tell my father? After what he did to me, I don't owe him anything. And like my mother would even know I was in the room? She's not interested in anything these days but herself."

"Sorry," Nicola said lamely.

"It's all right. Like I said, their problems aren't mine."

That was true to a certain extent, Nicola thought. But Sophie's problems were certainly of importance to her parents. At least, they should be. Not that she was judging her cousin. How could she really know what Julie was going through?

"So, what about you?" Sophie asked.

"What about me?"

"Why don't you have a boyfriend?"

Nicola laughed. "I don't know. I just don't."

"Isn't there anyone you like?" Sophie pressed.

"Not at the moment." Sophie didn't need to know that her cousin's attitude toward romantic love was less than enthusiastic. Sure, for the last ten years she had had the good example of Bonnie and Ken, but before that she had grown up with a woman who eschewed romance as totally unnecessary for a fulfilling life. Early impressions went deep.

"Well, you never know when you'll fall in love. That's what my grandmother always says." Sophie frowned. "But what does being in love even mean? Supposedly my father loved my mother, but look what he did. What's the big deal about love, anyway, if it can fall apart? I mean, why bother?"

Nicola feared they had wandered into territory about which she was too unfamiliar to be of any help. Her own mother had avoided love to have her child with an anonymous sperm donor, the least romantic way you could go about starting a family. And Nicola had had only one semiserious relationship back in college. At the moment, she couldn't for the life of her remember Harry's last name. Was that normal?

Nicola looked down at Sophie and was about to say something—she wasn't sure what—but realized from the girl's slightly open mouth and even breathing that she had fallen asleep. A wave of fondness for her young cousin coursed through her, followed closely by a surge of annoyance. Why wasn't Julie getting the help she needed to effectively deal with the trouble in her marriage? Sophie was suffering. It wasn't right.

Nicola drew her legs up to her chest and rested her chin on her knees. But you couldn't force someone to take a step she wasn't able or willing to make.

And you couldn't force yourself to take a step you weren't able or willing to make. Like forgive your mother.

Chapter 60

There were floaters in Julie's eyes. They were worrying her. The Internet said they could either be harmless or a sign of something serious. The Millers' medical insurance didn't cover much in terms of eye care, but Julie felt she had no choice but to have her eyes looked at by a professional. Dr. Murphy knew her well and she trusted him.

There was one hitch, though. Her pupils would be dilated; she would need someone to drive her home. Scott had offered. It would be no problem to take the afternoon off, he said. He would talk to the foreman. Bob was a family man, too. He would understand.

But the last thing Julie wanted was to feel beholden to Scott. Anger, sadness, hurt, and resentment had become friends of a sort. Toxic friends but familiar.

Problem was, there wasn't much in way of public transportation in Yorktide. There was only one taxi company and that operated only in the evenings. There were a few Uber and Lyft cars around, but Julie hadn't signed on for either service and. at the moment, she felt utterly incapable of handling a new task, even one so simple.

She could, of course, ask her mother for a ride, but her mother would ask why Scott couldn't drive her, and Julie would have to lie and say that he couldn't get out of work. It would be the same with

Judith, only Judith probably wouldn't believe the lie. Nicola might not ask questions, but Julie didn't want to drag her cousin away from her job. Nicola's work was so important.

Reluctantly, Julie accepted Scott's offer.

Scott was waiting for her in his car; he smiled when she slid into the passenger seat. Julie didn't return the smile. She was very conscious of Scott only inches away. She hoped he didn't try to touch her.

Before the affair, Scott and Julie had often gone on road trips together. Scott drove. They took turns selecting the music. The Beatles. The Rolling Stones. Pearl Jam. Counting Crows. They would pack a picnic lunch and stop somewhere picturesque to eat. Sophie had taken to teasing them about acting like two lovestruck teenagers.

Now, those days of easy friendship seemed so very far away.

Scott was talking.

"She must feel so alone. I'm glad she at least has Nicola."

"What do you mean, at least?" Julie asked. She assumed he was talking about their daughter.

"Because she doesn't really have you or me at the moment." Scott sighed. "She doesn't want either of us."

Was that true? Julie realized she didn't know much of anything about what her daughter wanted or needed at this moment, except for Julie to go back to being the person she had been before the affair.

That was impossible.

Julie was vaguely sorry she couldn't help her daughter, but she didn't feel the deep regret she knew she should feel.

That was wrong.

"Maybe we should take her to a professional." Scott went on. "Maybe a therapist could . . . could make her not hate me so much."

Julie wondered. Was she supposed to comfort Scott, reassure him that his daughter didn't hate him? Maybe Sophie did hate her father.

Hate wasn't good. At all. Ever. But it could be real. Maybe it was real for Sophie.

It wasn't for Julie. She didn't hate Scott. What did that mean? That there was hope for them? That she could forgive him for what he had done to her?

"She has my mother," Julie said as Scott pulled into the parking lot outside Dr. Murphy's office.

"What?"

"Sophie. She can turn to my mother."

Scott shook his head. "Do you want me to come in with you?" he asked quietly.

"Why?"

"I don't know. Just because."

"I'm fine."

"I'll be here then."

Julie got out of the car and walked up to the medical building. It was one of those long, nondescript, one-story buildings, with a big pot of flowering plants on either side of the entrance. Julie stepped inside, out of the summer sun.

And as she walked down the corridor, a small but insistent voice whispered in her head. *Sophie*, it said, *might have her cousin and grandmother looking out for her. But you're her mother. Don't forget that, Julie.*

You are her mother.

Chapter 61

The roar of the old vacuum, loud as it was, was not loud enough to drown out the thoughts racing through Bonnie's head. She had hoped, vainly as it turned out, that a vigorous session of house-cleaning might help her forget, even just a bit, even for just a while, what Carol had told her about their mother.

Shirley had had an affair.

Bonnie remembered Judith pointing out that her parents had been far more liberal than Shirley and Ronald Ascher. How little she knew!

Bonnie turned the vacuum to the worn runner just inside the front door and attacked it as if her life depended on stripping it clean of every particle of dust and grit it possessed. Bonnie wiped a bead of sweat from her forehead. She had always seen her mother as a model of moral rectitude, a genuinely decent person who always did the right thing no matter how it might inconvenience her.

But an affair . . .

She was sure her mother had loved her father. There had been evidence in the way Shirley had taken Ronald's arm whenever they were in public, protective and proudly possessive at the same time; it was obvious in the way Shirley's eyes had lit up when Ronald came home from work at the end of the day.

The vacuum began to whine alarmingly and Bonnie turned it off. It was probably time for a new machine. Ken had been urging her to buy a new one for months before he got sick. Bonnie unplugged the vacuum and hauled it to the closet, where she stored her cleaning supplies.

Suddenly, she felt exhausted. She went back to the living room and fell gratefully into the plaid lounger. It had been her gift to Ken on his fiftieth birthday.

Bonnie rested her head against the back of the chair. The thing that hurt and confused her most about the whole thing was the fact that Shirley Ascher had chosen to share her secret with Carol. Why not with her? Bonnie was the dutiful daughter. The least her mother owed her was her confidence. But perhaps with Carol, the adventurous child, Shirley had trusted she would not be judged.

In spite of her tiredness, Bonnie hauled herself out of the chair and went into the kitchen. She would at least clean the window over the sink. No matter how careful she was when washing the dishes, splashes of soapy water found their way to the window pane. She spritzed Windex onto a sheet of paper towel and began to scrub.

If Carol was telling the truth about their mother's long-ago lover, and for better or worse, Bonnie believed that she was, there might have been other secrets Shirley Elgort had kept from her family. Like another child? Like a second affair? Of course, everyone had a right to her secrets, but . . .

Bonnie shook her head and gave the window one final wipe. She had to let it go. It was in the past, all of it. You could think about the past, obsess over it, reinterpret it, view it from a variety of angles, but you couldn't fundamentally change it. End of story.

Anyway, she had more immediate problems to tackle. Like her own future. How was she to live the rest of her life, with or without possession of Ferndean House? Bonnie just didn't know. Maybe she could talk to Judith now that she no longer had Ken to advise her.

But she was only in this situation of confusion and loneliness because Ken had died! For the very first time since her husband's death, Bonnie felt a flare of anger toward her husband. He had abandoned her. The fact that he hadn't wanted to die meant nothing. He *had* died. And now she was alone.

Bonnie didn't want to be alone.

It was all too much. Bonnie clutched the edge of the sink and sobbed.

Chapter 62

"I thought it was a charming article. Really charming. Bill Elliott is such a charming man."

Carol's smile was about to crack. This woman was not the first to have approached her that evening at the cocktail party being held at the Ogunquit Museum of Art to mark the retirement of the current longest serving docent. Carol was longing to say: "It's just a silly piece in a silly local rag." But she wouldn't say that. The woman meant no harm.

The woman moved off in the direction of the bar. Carol was on her own that evening. She had asked her sister if she planned on attending the party. Bonnie had laughed. Maybe it had been a naïve question. A glance at the well-heeled guests was enough to demonstrate that they were not the sort of people among whom Bonnie Elgort felt most comfortable.

Carol hadn't even considered asking Nicola to join her. She knew that Nicola would reject the invitation. Nicola had thanked her mother for the gift certificate to The Bookworm, but there had been a grudging spirit in her thanks. At least, Carol had thought there was.

Poor Julie was out of the question as a date. She didn't have enough energy to smile at her family, let alone make polite conversation with strangers.

Judith had made other plans. She had promised to help a friend just home from the hospital. "Believe me," Judith had said, "I wish I could join you. Ted is a terrible patient."

But Carol was an old hand at navigating the world on her own. In truth, she preferred it that way. At least, she had for a very long time. Now? Now it would have been nice to have a companion with whom to share remarks about the food, observations about the art on display, and critiques of the guests' attire.

Carol took a sip of her champagne and surveyed the crowd; she estimated the average age of the guests at about fifty-five, or even sixty. The good-looking man in the navy suit, the one with his arm around the waist of his female companion. Carol was sure they all had gone to high school together. She wondered if either of them had read Bill Elliott's article and thought: *I remember her!* But if they did remember Carol Ascher, they had not recognized her in their midst.

"It is Carol Ascher, isn't it?"

Carol smiled at the woman who had joined her. "Yes," she said. "And you're Abigail Collins. You had the nicest boutique in Yorktide when I was growing up."

"You have a good memory, my dear. I closed the shop twenty years ago. Anyway, I heard you were back for the summer and I've been hoping to run into you so I could say hello. You always were so different from the others in your family. Right from the start."

"Yes, well . . ." Carol didn't know what else to say.

"You and your sister were such opposites. She always struck me as one of those people who thrive on a simple life." Abigail Collins smiled a bit roguishly. "Would I be correct in assuming she's never been to visit you in New York?"

Abigail was correct, but Carol didn't much care for her slightly mocking tone. "Bonnie," Carol said, "is very much needed here in Yorktide. She doesn't have the leisure to travel."

Abigail Collins didn't seem to know what to make of Carol's response. With a nod, she moved on to chat with another guest.

Carol left the party soon after this encounter. She had had enough of small talk.

One of those people who thrive on a simple life.

The keyword there, Carol thought as she slid behind the wheel of her car, parked on Shore Road, was thrive.

Bonnie had always thrived in Yorktide. Her sister had not.

And never would?

Carol wished she had stayed home that evening.

If she could call Ferndean—or Yorktide—home.

Chapter 63

Carol Ascher was stubborn and persistent. There was no point in saying no. She would only ask again, and again after that, so Nicola had accepted her mother's invitation to lunch.

But there was another reason for Nicola's having accepted the invitation. She had been thinking a lot about her recent conversation with Hermione Wolcott. No one lived forever. The idea of her mother—or herself—dying before they had made at least a little progress toward a reconciliation suddenly seemed very much to be avoided.

You couldn't force yourself to take a step you weren't able or willing to make.

Like forgive your mother.

Nicola had been thinking about this, too, and the conclusion she had come to was that she *was* in fact able to forgive her mother for whatever wrongs or missteps she might have committed in the past. Of course, Nicola was able. She was strong and intelligent.

Was she willing? The answer to that question was still open.

They arrived at the restaurant moments apart.

The Daffy Duckling was one of Nicola's favorites. It did not serve duck. It was in fact a vegetarian place with a few vegan options. Every inch of it was decorated with duck-related items, from kitschy ceramic statues from the 1950s and '60s, to paintings on a board in a consciously primitive style, to vintage advertising signs for products as various as shoe polish and baby food.

"It's very cute," Carol said when they had taken their seats at a tiny table barely big enough for two.

"You don't find it tacky?" Nicola asked.

Her mother shrugged. "Tacky can be fun. If done the right way."

"Aunt Bonnie told me you went to a party at the Ogunquit Museum," she said.

"I did."

"And?"

Her mother shrugged. "And it was all right. So, tell me what you do for fun?" she asked.

Nicola frowned. "Fun?" It was a strange word for her mother to use. Adults didn't set out to have fun. Not really.

"Yes, social activities, hobbies. That sort of thing."

When the waitress had taken their orders, Nicola replied, "I like to go hiking and camping," she said.

Her mother smiled. "I remember the summer your aunt and I went camping with Judith and her parents. I think I was thirteen, so that means Bonnie was ten and Judith eighteen. Judith brought a friend along with her, but I can't remember her name. It was the first time I'd had to use an outhouse, share cooking and cleanup chores, carry my portion of the equipment into and out of the site. I was not amused."

"I can imagine," Nicola remarked. It was no surprise that her mother had always preferred the easy way of getting through rather than the more arduous, responsible one. Except when it came to her career.

"Your aunt wasn't thrilled, either," Carol said with a laugh. "She was pampered at home. As the older child, I was the one with chores, like doing the dinner dishes three nights a week and sweeping the front porch and dusting the downstairs rooms every Saturday morning. Still, she didn't whine too badly."

Nicola wondered. The idea of her aunt whining didn't fit well with the image she had formed of Bonnie these past ten years. But Bonnie had been only a child at the time of the camping trip, and children whined. And maybe Carol was bending the truth for her own self-serving reasons. Nicola decided to let it go.

"Aunt Bonnie said you encountered a bear one night in the campsite," she said.

"We did and that marked the end of my nascent camping career. Never again."

"What happened?"

"Didn't your aunt tell you the story?"

"Yes," Nicola said. "But I want to hear it from you."

The waitress delivered their meals then, an Asian-inspired salad for Carol and a cold pasta dish for Nicola. When she had gone, Carol resumed her story.

"We four girls were sharing a tent. I remember suddenly waking up in the middle of the night to find Judith and her friend peering out of the tent flap and whispering frantically. I asked what was going on, and Judith told me there was a bear in the campsite. I suppose he was looking for food, but Aunt Mary and Uncle Matthew had hung our supplies in a tree . . ." Carol frowned. "Wait. Can't bears climb trees? Anyway, then Bonnie woke up and when Judith told her about the bear she started to scream. It was ear-shattering. I clapped my hand over her mouth and we both just froze. I was sure we were about to be mauled to death by an angry beast. And then I heard a shot and the next thing I remember, Aunt Mary was poking her head into our tent to tell us everything was okay and that Uncle Matthew had scared the bear away by shooting into the air." Carol shook her head. "The next morning, I asked Bonnie if she'd had enough of camping and she said yes and I announced that we wanted to go home. Uncle Matthew hiked us back to the nearest road, called our parents from a pay phone at a little grocery store, and they were there in about an hour to pick us up."

Nicola pushed a bit of pasta around her plate. "That's not how I heard the story," she said, aware there was a bit of a challenge in her voice. "Aunt Bonnie told me that you were the one who started screaming and that Judith had to slap you to make you stop and that after the bear was gone you refused to stay there for the rest of the night and that your aunt and uncle had to break camp and hike out before dawn."

Nicola's mother put her fork carefully against her plate and dabbed at her mouth with her napkin. "Well, it's probably how she remembers the incident. That's the trouble with memory. It's often grotesquely at odds with reality. But if everyone recalls the reality differently . . ." Carol shrugged. "What's really the truth?"

Whatever you need it to be, Nicola thought. After a moment, she said, "I guess it wouldn't have been safe to set out through the woods in the middle of the night."

"As seasoned campers, Aunt Mary and Uncle Matthew would never have agreed to that. And I wasn't silly enough to suggest it." Carol picked up her fork again. "So, who do you go camping with?"

"Mostly I go with a group of people from a church I sometimes attend," Nicola told her. "Anyone wanting to plan a trip e-mails the others and something gets organized. Sometimes you wind up camping with families with small children, sometimes with older, retired people, sometimes with people your own age."

"And do you see these people at other times?" Carol asked.

"Rarely," Nicola admitted. "Most people are too busy with kids and work and other obligations."

"Yes, I know what that's like, being too busy. But you like your job?"

"I love my job," Nicola said stoutly. "I'm doing what I'm meant to be doing."

"And the Peace Corps?" her mother asked. "How does that fit in?"

Nicola flushed. "Maybe it doesn't right now. I don't know. Don't say anything to anyone," she added hurriedly. "I need to think about my immediate future without a lot of questions. People are well-meaning but . . ."

Carol smiled understandingly. "You've learned a lesson. It's often best to keep an idea or a resolution to yourself until it's fully formed and ready to be put into action. My lips are sealed."

"Thanks," Nicola said. She realized that she trusted her mother to keep her word. She didn't really know why.

They left the restaurant soon after.

"Do you want a ride back to work?" Carol asked when they were outside.

"No, thanks. I've got my car."

"Oh. Right. How else would you have gotten here? Anyway, this was fun."

"Yeah," Nicola said. And it occurred to her that her mother hadn't mentioned Ferndean House and her plans for it. It might mean anything. It might mean nothing.

"Well," her mother said. "Goodbye."

Nicola took a step back before her mother could hug her. If that was what she had intended. "Goodbye," she said. And then she turned and walked purposefully toward her car.

Her mother did not call her back.

Chapter 64

The second workshop of the summer was not a total disaster for Julie. In fact, it wasn't a disaster at all. She had held her own in the guided discussion and had even managed to chat beforehand with a few of her colleagues. Thom had just come back from Provence and was eager to share photos of his pastoral adventures. Shelly asked after Sophie, and Julie had smiled and not let on that she really didn't know how her daughter was faring. She had even caused the clueless Miranda to chuckle when she declared that the highlight of her summer so far had been learning that the floaters in her eyes were not a sign of imminent death.

When the meeting broke up, Sara asked Julie to stay behind. It was only then that Julie felt the hand of doom on her shoulder. At least, the sure sense that she had done something wrong or stupid and was about to be taken to task for it.

"Have you ever heard of the Ackroyd Institute?" Sara asked when they were alone.

Julie hadn't.

"It's relatively new," Sara explained, "but already it's gaining respect for its work promoting religious tolerance and fighting religious prejudice. The Institute has developed courses for all ages of students, starting as early as preschool."

"That sounds admirable," Julie said. She wondered why Sara was telling her this.

"The Institute offers a limited number of scholarships for a week-long intensive course each spring. All educators are welcome to apply."

"Have you won a scholarship?" Julie asked. She wouldn't at all be surprised if Sara had. She was a very intelligent and skilled educator.

Sara smiled. "No, I want *you* to apply for one."

"Me!" Julie laughed. "You must be crazy. Sorry, I don't mean that, but . . ." She shook her head. "I can't."

"Hear me out," Sara went on. "I know you're as passionate about tolerance as I am. This could be an excellent opportunity for our school to make a difference. Look, in the past, towns like Lewiston have been a destination for African immigrants. Portland is currently the big draw, but just because families aren't flocking to Yorktide doesn't mean they won't be. We need to be ready to welcome them when and if they do."

Julie nodded. "I agree," she said. "But I just don't think . . . I don't think I'm the person you should be asking."

Sara leaned forward. "Look," she went on, "I know you're going through a rough patch right now. But I know you'll get through this intact and in my opinion, as someone who respects your devotion to education, you'll regret not having applied for the scholarship. Maybe you'll get it. Maybe you won't. The competition will be stiff. But I wouldn't suggest you go for this opportunity if I didn't believe you stood a good chance of winning."

Julie was silent. She felt a disconcerting mix of emotions. Fear. Gratitude. Excitement. "Where is the course given?" she asked.

"Chicago. At the Ackroyd Institute itself. Our children need this, Julie," Sara said firmly. "The children of immigrant families deserve this."

Julie swallowed. Did *she* need this? Did *she* deserve this opportunity? "All right," she said. "I'll give it some thought."

Sara beamed. "Great. But we don't have much time. Applications are due in a few weeks. You can find the form on the website."

Julie left the building soon after this conversation. On the way to her car she reminded herself of how she had always derived a hefty portion of her self-worth from her work. It was hers and hers alone. Not Scott's. Not Sophie's or her mother's or her father's. She was pretty sure that no one in her family really understood how much thought and preparation went into teaching small children. It wasn't that they were dismissive of her work, just that they were not all that interested in the details. Not like she was.

Julie slid behind the wheel of her car.

Chicago. How cool would it be to visit Chicago?

She realized she was smiling.

Chapter 65

Bonnie woke with a shout. The sheet was wet with sweat. She was wet with sweat.

She reached for the lamp on her bedside table. The light further helped to dispel any remaining shreds of panic and dismay. The details of the nightmare were soon vanished. All that remained now was a terrible sense of loss.

Bonnie struggled to sit up.

Loss.

Why were the most revolutionary moments of a life so often about loss?

The death of her parents had changed so much. Ken's passing had irrevocably altered Bonnie's future. And Carol's leaving Yorktide all those years ago . . .

Bonnie shivered and reached for the lightweight robe she kept at the foot of the bed. She held the robe tightly against her as the fateful day that Carol had announced her intention of going away played out as if before her eyes, as if she were watching a film of the moments in which her young life drastically shifted course.

Bonnie had been watching *The Six Million Dollar Man* on TV when Carol had come striding into the living room of Ferndean House. She was wearing lime-green platforms. Bonnie was annoyed when her sister turned off the TV, and embarrassed when

Carol commented on her sister's crush on Lee Majors. But all was forgiven when Carol announced she had something very important to tell her. Bonnie had always loved being sought out by her older sister for the sharing of a secret or a bit of juicy gossip.

"What is it?" Bonnie asked eagerly, sitting forward on the couch.

Carol perched on the arm of their father's favorite chair. Only Carol ever did that. It was something Bonnie would never do, out of respect. "I'm leaving Yorktide," Carol said.

Later, Bonnie remembered thinking: No one we know leaves Yorktide.

"What do you mean?" she asked.

"I mean that I'm moving to New York City."

"But why?" Bonnie knew she wasn't stupid, but for some reason she couldn't quite take in what her sister had told her.

Carol leaned forward; her look was intense. "Because I'm bored here," she said. "I need something more out of my life than what I can build in Yorktide. An early marriage. A passel of kids. A dead-end job. No thanks."

"But what about Mom and Dad?" Bonnie asked. "They'll never let you go!"

Carol had laughed. "They can hardly stop me. I'm nineteen. Anyway, I've already told them. They're not happy about it but like I said, what can they do?"

"But what about Ken?" Bonnie asked then, her voice trembling just a little. "Is he going with you?"

Carol uncrossed and then recrossed her legs before replying. "I broke up with Ken. He doesn't have what it takes to make it in New York. I'm going alone. On my own," she added defiantly.

A feeling of relief flooded through Bonnie's sixteen-year-old heart. Ken would be staying. At least she wouldn't be losing him, as well. Not that he knew she existed.

"So, what do you think?" Carol prodded. "Are you excited for me?"

"I guess," Bonnie said automatically. "I don't know. Sure." A million thoughts were running through her mind. What would she *do* without Carol sleeping in the room next door to hers, sharing the breakfast table every morning, secretly laughing at the way their mother drank her coffee in a series of tiny little sips?

Ken.

Would Carol take her record player with her or leave it behind for Bonnie? Would her father pay more attention to her once Carol was gone?

Ken was staying.

Would her mother stop making her really delicious chocolate coconut cake, which was Carol's favorite, because it would remind her of Carol and make her too sad?

Ken . . .

"When are you leaving?" Bonnie asked.

"In two weeks."

Bonnie felt the words as a slap. "So soon?" she cried. "But you'll miss the harvest festival! Maybe you could stay until after the festival or maybe—"

"Bonnie," Carol said firmly. "I'm going in two weeks. For good if I can help it."

Bonnie wanted to ask her sister if she would miss her. But she didn't. She was too afraid the answer would be no. And why would Carol miss her little sister? She was a nobody, at least compared to Carol. Worse, Carol might lie, say, of course I'll miss you, and Bonnie would know it was a lie but not have the nerve to admit as much to Carol.

"Okay?" Carol said. There was a smile on her face.

Bonnie nodded. "Okay," she said, but she wasn't sure to what she was agreeing.

Carol got up and left the room with her usual brisk stride. Bonnie sat staring at the ugly gray television screen. Carol was going away. Bonnie put her face in her hands and sobbed.

That night she had tiptoed through the dark second-floor hall to the closed door of her sister's room, where she leaned close, hoping to hear the familiar and reassuring sound of her sister's rhythmic breathing in sleep. In only a few weeks' time there would be no sound at all coming from that bedroom. It would be empty. Carol would be gone. Bonnie's world would be hollowed out.

By the next morning, however, Bonnie's deep sadness had taken a dramatic turn. She realized that she felt an almost overwhelming need to punish her sister for what she was about to do to her family.

When Carol was taking a shower, Bonnie snuck into her sister's room and stole Carol's favorite lipstick. Then she dashed from the house and threw the lipstick—a shade of icy shell pink—into the pond at the end of the road. When Carol stomped through the house that evening on a frantic search for the missing lipstick, Bonnie had sat quietly on her bed, pretending to read a Nancy Drew novel she had read about a million times before and listening with satisfaction to her sister's wails of frustration.

But Carol's plans to abandon her family did not waver, in spite of Bonnie's subsequent small subterfuges meant to undermine her sister's confidence. Desperate times called for desperate measures. Bonnie had heard her father say that often enough. So, two days before Carol's scheduled departure, Bonnie drank an entire bottle of ipecac. If Carol found her little sister terribly sick, there was no way she would leave. Ever. Bonnie was sure of it.

The results were not what she had hoped they would be. There were a few nasty hours of vomiting, during which she was attended to by her worried mother. Carol refused to visit her sister's sickroom. What if she came down with whatever bug had felled Bonnie? There was no way she was going to miss that bus out of town.

As far as the sixty-two-year-old Bonnie knew, Carol never suspected her sister of the sabotage and the subterfuge. She would die before she would ever admit to either.

With a sigh of frustration, Bonnie threw the rumpled sheet from her legs and got out of bed. Sleep, a restful one, was not going to happen now.

Visiting the past was dangerous, she thought as she stuck her feet in her ancient fuzzy slippers. What if you couldn't make your way back to the present?

What then?

Chapter 66

Carol was thinking about her daughter. She was far too realistic to consider Nicola's hesitation to commit to the Peace Corps a reaction to her mother's settling in Yorktide. Stay home to be close to Mom? No.

Still, Carol wondered what was going on. Asking would be futile. She would just have to be patient and accept the possibility that Nicola's thoughts might always be strictly her own. Like whatever had been going through her daughter's mind when they parted company outside the Daffy Duckling. Nicola had stepped aside before hurrying off, almost as if she had expected her mother to reach out for a hug, the one thing she wanted most of all to avoid.

Well, Carol told herself as she parked outside Judith's house, life was never simple. It just never was.

Carol found her cousin in the backyard. Bonnie was with her. Carol was startled; she felt a sort of buzzing in her head. How had she not seen her sister's car out front?

"I didn't know you'd be here," she said.

Bonnie shifted awkwardly in her seat. "I was in the neighborhood and . . ."

"We've just been discussing this year's Fourth of July shindig at

Ferndean." Judith gestured for Carol to take a seat at the table, on which sat a pitcher of iced tea and several glasses.

Carol sat and poured herself a glass of tea. She hoped there wasn't sugar in it. She felt jumpy enough already.

"You haven't been in Yorktide for a holiday in a very long time, have you, Carol?" Bonnie asked in a barely repressed accusatory tone of voice.

"You know I haven't," Carol replied evenly. She would not be baited.

Bonnie sighed. "Holidays in the old days were always so much fun. Remember how everyone contributed a dish, potato and fruit salads in the summer, casseroles and pies in the winter. And except for church on Christmas and Easter, nobody bothered to dress up, except for Mrs. Harrison, who wore those ancient, tattered ball gowns everywhere. She was always leaving a trail of broken sequins and torn lace in her wake."

Judith shuddered. "I used to wonder if the gowns were gruesome reminders of lost loves, like Miss Havisham's decaying wedding dress."

"I asked her about her clothes once," Carol said. "Some of them were actually couture pieces. A few were by Charles James and she even had a Schiaparelli. She wasn't entirely clear on how she'd come by the dresses—I think her mind had been going for some time before that—but she appreciated my interest."

"The point is," Bonnie said in an unnecessarily loud voice, "that parties around here—at least, *our* sort of parties—aren't fancy affairs. This year's Fourth of July party . . ."

Suddenly, Bonnie reached for her napkin and held it to her eyes. Carol squirmed.

"It's okay," Judith said, patting her cousin's hand. "Hosting for the first time without Ken will be a challenge."

"Excuse me." Bonnie got up from her chair.

"Poor thing," Judith said when Bonnie had disappeared into the house. "Being on her own is still so new. And I know the cost of giving the party isn't insignificant. She must be thinking about how she can cut corners without people really noticing."

Carol considered. This might be a chance for her to be of real benefit to her family. "I'd like to contribute something," she said. "Take some of the burden off Bonnie."

"Fantastic," Judith said enthusiastically. "What do you have in mind?"

"Well, I could pay for the food, the drinks, whatever it is Bonnie and Ken used to provide."

Judith shook her head. "Bonnie won't like it. You know how proud she is."

Carol did know. "But I can still offer."

"And I can't stop you. Any other ideas?"

Carol thought for a moment. "We could set up a sort of art studio on the lawn. You know, easels and palettes with a selection of paints and brushes. A friend of mine who lives in the Hamptons did something very similar and it was a huge hit. We could end the day with someone judging whose painting is the best and whose is the worst."

Judith cleared her throat. "Let me get this straight. You want people to paint pictures during the party."

"Exactly. Maine has a long history of artists' colonies. For years, people have journeyed here to make art. I think it will be fun."

"I'll tell you what's fun," Judith said, lowering her voice, though Bonnie still had not returned. "At least, what Bonnie and Ken's circle think is fun. Eating hot dogs. Drinking beer. Playing horseshoes. More eating and drinking. Then heading to one of the evening fireworks displays. Not painting en plein air."

"Mark my words," Carol said. "My idea will be a hit."

"You're not also handing out black berets and Gauloises cigarettes, are you?" Judith asked wryly.

"Very funny."

Out of the corner of her eye, Carol spotted Bonnie walking toward them.

"Sorry," Bonnie said, taking her seat. Carol noticed there was no trace of a tear on her face. "What did I miss?"

"Carol wants to help out with the party," Judith said.

Bonnie frowned. "How?" she asked bluntly.

"I'd like to pay for your contribution to the festivities. Well, it could be considered our contribution, yours and mine. Just tell me how much you think the food and drink will cost."

"No," Bonnie stated. Her face was flushed. "Absolutely not. Ken and I never—Just no."

"But as cohost I have a duty to—"

Judith shot Carol a look that said, Don't push it. Maybe, Carol thought, she shouldn't have used the term *cohost*.

"Well, then," she said, "I have another idea." And she explained. "It was a lot of fun to see who could actually draw and who was still at a kindergarten level."

Bonnie's lips tightened to a very thin line.

"It won't work," she said dismissively. "You'll be wasting your money on all that stuff, paint and easels and whatnot."

Carol took a calming breath and a sip of the iced tea. That buzzing in her head had returned. "I'm not worried about the money," she said after a moment.

"What if it rains?" Judith asked.

"Then we'll move the easels inside and people can paint portraits or still lifes," Carol said.

"Absolutely not," Bonnie stated. "We've never done anything like that and we're not going to start now."

"Why are you so opposed to trying something new?" Carol asked almost desperately.

"If it isn't broken, it doesn't need fixing."

"I'm not saying your party plan is broken," Carol protested. "I'm just offering to help."

"If I may intervene," Judith said loudly. "Bonnie, why don't you do what you do best, and, Carol, you contribute your bit and as long as there's plenty of food and booze, I'm sure everyone will have a good time."

"All right," Bonnie said after a moment. Her tone was begrudging. "And you can help with other things, too, if you really mean it. Like cleanup."

Carol nodded. "Thank you," she said.

She didn't stick around for long after that. She felt worn out by the latest encounter with her sister. Why did Bonnie always have to be so difficult? As Carol maneuvered her car away from the curb in front of her cousin's house, she became aware of a new burning itch on the left side of her neck.

"Damn it," she muttered. Stress always brought on her eczema, and sometimes psoriasis and hives, as well. And people thought she was an expert at being calm as the proverbial cucumber. Well, appearances could be deceiving.

Carol forced her mind to concentrate on driving. She would stop for another tube of cortisone cream on the way back to Ferndean and call her dermatologist when she arrived. Dr. Foss could have a prescription medicine sent on.

And then, Carol would take a nap. After making a call to an art supply house.

Chapter 67

Nicola was seated at a picnic table on the grounds of Pine Hill Residence for the Elderly, a medical journal open before her, a peanut butter and jelly sandwich and an apple next to that. It was a lovely day. The temperature was hovering around eighty, and there was enough of a breeze to cause her hair to flutter against her neck.

But Nicola was not happy.

She didn't know why she had to remember that awful time now. Well, of course, she did. Sophie had asked about her troubled past in New York and Nicola had told her.

But not everything.

Not about what she had done to her mother's assistant.

Though Nicola's encounters with Ana had been few and far between, she had always been acutely jealous of the woman she viewed as a rival for her mother's attention. It had all come to a very ugly head one afternoon about three weeks after Carol's surgery.

The twenty-five-year old Nicola literally squirmed. She was still appalled that she could have been so horrid to another human being.

Ana had come to the apartment to save Carol the trouble of traveling to the office. Carol Ascher hadn't been right since coming home from the hospital. She had little energy; she was in constant pain; she slept badly and had no appetite. Nicola was frightened.

Whatever was *really* going on was being kept a secret. She hadn't even been allowed to visit her mother in the hospital.

Ana was tall and slim. She dressed a lot like her boss in tailored pieces in neutral colors. Her jewelry was simple and expensive, just like Carol Ascher's. Sometimes Ana even sounded like Carol Ascher. Nicola wondered if her mother's right-hand woman ever had a thought of her own. Probably not.

Ana stood in the center of the living room, a large black case in one hand, a small black bag slung over her shoulder. She greeted Nicola with a smile. "It's nice to see you again," Ana said. Sucking up to the boss's daughter, Nicola thought. Nice try.

Nicola did not return the greeting. Instead, she slowly circled Ana, her arms folded across her chest. When she had completed her inspection, she stopped directly in front of her mother's assistant.

"Your nose is huge," she said. "You should get a nose job."

Ana, whose nose was indeed big, but in a way reminiscent of the magnificently elegant Anjelica Houston, didn't even flinch. Instead, she smiled blandly at her employer's daughter. "I'll take your advice into consideration," she replied.

Suddenly, Carol Ascher was in the doorway. "Nicola," she said firmly as she came into the room. "Apologize this minute."

Nicola had shrugged. "Why? It's not like I lied."

"You were rude to my guest. Apologize now."

"I won't apologize for telling the truth," Nicola replied.

With a look of disgust—that was how Nicola had read it—Carol Ascher waved her hand in her daughter's direction. "Go to your room," she said.

Nicola had been absolutely shocked that her mother would take Ana's side over hers. She realized that she was shaking and that she felt like she was going to vomit. "But, Mom—" she began to protest.

Too late. Her mother, followed by her assistant, was leaving the room. A moment later Nicola heard the door to her mother's office close behind them.

Nicola felt humiliated. And angry. Until she hit upon the idea of retaliation. She would force her mother to notice her. She would force her mother to realize just how much she loved her daughter and to feel sorry that she had ever scolded her in front of her precious, big-nosed assistant.

One of the girls at school gave Nicola a few tips on how to tell the story to achieve maximum pity. It was a performance worthy of an Oscar. Until it wasn't.

Nicola arrived home one afternoon a few days after the incident with Ana with her hair a knotted mess, a scrape on her cheek, and a tear in the arm of her jacket. She had never faked tears before but somehow, they came the moment she saw her mother. She claimed to have been attacked on her way home from school. No, she hadn't seen the faces of the two men who had grabbed her; one put a hand over her eyes. They had dragged her into an alley. Where? She didn't remember where. Everything was all muddled. She had tried to scream, but they had stuffed a dirty rag in her mouth. She had kicked out and hit one of them in the leg. Then they had tried to tear her clothes off, but she had struggled.

There was more of the same. But as Nicola talked on she began to flounder. The details she had rehearsed slipped away. Her mother's look of concern slowly morphed to a frown of suspicion. Was the scrape on her cheek too obviously self-inflicted? Were her tears, now forced, losing effect?

Finally, Nicola broke down. Nothing had happened to her. It was all her mother's fault. Why had her mother embarrassed her in front of Ana? What was wrong with her mother? Why didn't she like any of her daughter's friends? She was always punishing her for nothing. Why didn't her mother just leave her alone?

The whole sorry scene ended with Nicola running off to her room. She didn't come out for dinner. No one came to get her. When she crept out to the kitchen the following morning, warily, unsure of what she would encounter, she found a note. Her mother had gone to the office. The housekeeper would be in later. Nicola poured a bowl of cold cereal and congratulated herself for having gotten through the latest debacle unscathed.

But within two weeks' time Nicola was packed off to Yorktide, an inconvenience to a busy parent, an embarrassment to a successful businessperson. No one wanted anyone associated with a juvenile delinquent having access to their homes chock-full of valuable art and antiques. What if Carol Ascher's problematic daughter got her hands on the alarm code to their Fifth Avenue apartment or their estate in the Hamptons? What if she and her equally delinquent cohorts broke in and trashed the place, made off with the jewels, terrorized the staff and tortured the pets?

Nicola's Pine Hill colleagues at the next picnic table suddenly got up and began to gather their empty cartons and paper bags. Nicola looked at her watch. Her lunch hour was over. She hadn't read the article she had meant to and had barely touched her food.

She took a deep breath and began to gather her things. She would never stop feeling ashamed about the way she had behaved. She had never apologized to Ana; she had never really had the chance. Maybe it wasn't too late to seek forgiveness. She could send Ana a letter. But maybe it was better to let the incident rest. Ana had probably forgiven Nicola long ago; she would have known about Nicola's troubles at the time and figured the verbal attack was just another instance of teen angst.

Nicola walked back to the building. Mothers forgave their children anything, she mused; at least, in novels and movies they did. And daughters forgave their mothers almost anything. Or, they were supposed to. The problem was that there were still so many unanswered questions. Like Hermione Wolcott had said, there had to have been a very good reason for Carol Ascher's sending her daughter away above and beyond punishment. There had to have been.

But would she ever learn the full truth? Or would her mother's motives always remain in the realm of the unknown?

Nicola was tired of the unknown.

Chapter 68

Sara Webb had left Julie a voice mail in which she asked if Julie had given any thought to the Ackroyd scholarship, and offered to talk through any questions involving the application process.

Julie felt vaguely guilty for not having even glanced at the Institute's website; after all, Sara was making an effort on her behalf, and the topic of religious and cultural tolerance was one that Julie felt passionately about. Rather than respond to Sara with a call, she had sent a text promising to read the application guidelines that very afternoon.

Once Scott had left for his dental appointment.

Scott had always been afraid of going to the dentist, which meant that he didn't go as often as he should. The last time he had seen Dr. Wilde she had predicted that a back tooth would have to be pulled before long; it had been neglected for too many years to be saved without procedures that would cost the Millers a small fortune.

Now, the tooth was ready to come out. Scott hadn't told Julie about the appointment; she had seen his scrawl on the old-fashioned calendar that hung in the kitchen. Before the summer, Julie would have dropped everything to be with Scott during the ordeal. But things were different now.

Scott had gone out of his way to take her to the eye doctor the week before. He had been pleased to learn that the floaters were harmless. But Julie was not prepared to reciprocate the favor or the support.

Her husband chose that moment to walk into the kitchen.

"Good luck," she said without much expression.

Scott took his car keys off the hook by the landline. "Thanks."

"You'll be fine," Julie went on.

Scott didn't look convinced. Suddenly, Julie *wanted* to drive him to the dentist's office, to sit in the waiting area during the procedure, to bring him home afterward, where she would give him an aspirin and a cold cloth to help ease any pain. It was what a good spouse would do. But she couldn't make the words "Let me help" take shape.

Scott stood there for another moment, as if hoping for something more than his wife's silence. "I'll be late," he finally said, and turned toward the kitchen door.

When he was gone, Julie realized that she felt slightly sick. Why couldn't she figure this out?

She knew for sure that she didn't hate her husband. According to some, she had a right to hate him for what he had done to her. Revenge was popular. Vindictive behavior was allowed in a case like this. Reality television told you so, as did pop music. It was okay for women who had been scorned to fight back. Hell hath no fury.

Everybody believed that.

But fury wasn't going to work for Julie. It just wasn't.

Julie rose from the table and headed for her office. She was going to log in to the Ackroyd Institute's website like she had promised Sara she would do.

Chapter 69

"Hi!"

Bonnie flinched. Running into her sister was something she was going to have to get used to, at least for the moment. Carol, a member of the Yorktide community, strolling along the same sidewalks, chatting with the same shop owners.

"What are you doing in town?" Bonnie asked.

Carol smiled. "I might ask you the same thing. Running errands."

"We're in for rain."

"So the Internet tells me."

"You don't watch the local news?"

"No," Carol said. "Oh, listen to this. I got a call earlier from someone named Clare Wood. She said she's the president of the Women's Benevolent Society."

"I know who Clare is. What does the WBS want with you?" Bonnie asked suspiciously.

"They asked me to march at the head of the Independence Day parade. I suppose I should be honored that they want to include me with the local notables—the mayor, the high school principal, even the police chief."

"Yes," Bonnie said tightly. "You should be honored. Are you going to accept?"

"I don't know," Carol admitted. And then she laughed. "I don't like sashes. I hated having to wear that awful sash when I won the title of Miss Yorktide 1973. I don't know how the royals do it, though maybe the fact of there being important jewels pinned to the sash makes it bearable."

Bonnie, who had never been offered the opportunity of wearing a sash, bejeweled or not, was silent.

"I have to run," Carol said abruptly. "I have an appointment for a facial. Don't get caught in the rain."

With a wave, her sister was dashing off across the street, dodging traffic as she went. A New York thing to do, Bonnie supposed. Crossing the street anywhere at any time, regardless of the rules.

Bonnie was not happy. She was the sister who had lived in Yorktide all her life, paid taxes, voted in every single local election. She was the one who had served seafood casserole and blueberry pie at church suppers and had stuck around to clean up afterward. She was the one who had joined with her neighbors to help the sick and needy of Yorktide both at the food bank and with the town's hot meal delivery service. She was the one who had seen her child— and for a while, Carol's child!—through the local school system. Why hadn't *she* been the subject of an article in the *Yorktide Chronicle*? Why wasn't she the one being honored by the Women's Benevolent Society? More like the Women's Sucking Up Society!

Ken. What would Ken think of this situation? "It's a tradition for a community to honor one of its own who made good in the wide world before coming home," he would have said. "What harm is it doing you?"

No harm, Bonnie admitted, her anger cooling. Just—annoyance. First the lie. Then the article. Now the parade.

A big fat raindrop landed on Bonnie's forehead. It was followed by another and another. By the time Bonnie reached her car, she was soaked.

Chapter 70

That very afternoon Carol declined the Women's Benevolent Society's invitation to march at the head of the Fourth of July parade. She wasn't stupid or insensitive. She had seen that Bonnie was upset about her sister's being chosen as one of the parade's VIPs. Truly, the last thing Carol wanted was to further alienate her sister and daughter, and yet that seemed to be happening without her consent.

"I was very diplomatic," she told her cousin over the phone. "They seemed a bit disappointed but not heartbroken."

"Good," Judith said. "I'd been hearing grumblings from the socially active residents of Yorktide who couldn't see why someone who left town over forty years ago and who never since then contributed to the good of the community should be singled out for such an honor. I can't say I don't see their point."

"You mean you wouldn't have supported me if I had accepted?" Carol asked, feeling slightly stung.

"I always go to the parade," Judith replied carefully. "I would have cheered like I always do."

"Just not for me."

"I wouldn't have shouted your name, no."

"You're quite the diplomat."

Judith had agreed and signed off.

Carol felt chastened. If even Judith, notoriously neutral, was not entirely pleased about the attention being paid to her cousin, then Carol's situation in Yorktide was indeed more complicated than she had expected it to be. She should never have lied to Bonnie about the breakup with Ken. She should not have agreed to that silly article. She should not have considered for even a moment the WBS's proposal. She had failed to imagine the consequences her sudden reappearance in her hometown might have not only for her family but for her neighbors as well.

That little boy's death. The sudden, intense need to assure that someone would genuinely mourn her when she was gone.

Alex. Alex would mourn her.

Wouldn't he?

Carol's purse was in her bedroom. She went upstairs and from her wallet she removed a photograph slightly worn around the edges. It was the only photo she had of her and Alex; it had been taken at a party about two years before she had approached him with her plan.

Her fabulous plan.

Holding the photo gingerly, Carol sank onto the edge of the bed. Her family thought her unsentimental, maybe even cold. What would they say if they knew she had kept this photo in her wallet for the past twenty-eight years? Of course, that would presuppose they knew of the deal she had made with Alex and they must never know. Bonnie, Julie, Judith, Nicola.

Especially Nicola.

But the burden of her greatest secret was weighing more heavily on Carol than ever before. She felt trapped inside the secret, held prisoner by it.

She felt—unmoored. Confused. Unsure.

Abruptly, Carol got up and returned the photo to her wallet. She could not afford to be defeated by doubts and worries. Not now.

Not when the relationship with her family was at stake.

She would just have to listen and learn. Stop misjudging. Stop telling lies. Do her utmost best to be accepted.

Do her utmost best to be remembered and mourned.

Chapter 71

Nicola was miserable.

She was very rarely sick but seemed to have caught a cold in spite of using hand sanitizer several times a day as she moved around Pine Hill. A sore throat and a congested and achy head meant that she was confined to her apartment for the duration. Working with the elderly, many of whom had compromised immune systems, meant she couldn't take a chance on infecting someone in turn.

The worst part about being sick—not so sick that you couldn't think straight, but just sick enough that all you could pretty much do *was* to think—was thinking! She had tried to read but couldn't seem to get past a paragraph. She had begun to watch a movie on her phone but staring at the small screen had hurt her eyes. So, she was left to sit propped in her bed, thinking and dozing and all in all feeling miserable.

And guilty. That awful story she had told her mother all those years ago! How must her mother have felt when her child, disheveled, bleeding, and in tears, had begun to relate a tale of a near kidnapping or rape! Nicola cringed. She was pretty certain she hadn't even noticed her mother's expression before the story fell apart. She had been focused only on her own sorry self. Nicola tried to imagine what her aunt Bonnie would feel if Julie came to her with a similar story, or if Sophie came to Julie with a tale of having been a victim of force and brutality. They would be devastated. Sickened.

Carol Ascher was not a monster. She must have felt as if her world was crashing to the ground. Maybe that was one of the reasons she had sent Nicola away only weeks later. Could she have been so angry with her daughter for telling such an outrageous lie that the very sight of her was impossible to bear?

Nicola sneezed and coughed and squirmed. She would probably never know. What did it matter now, anyway? Nicola was alone and it hurt to swallow and her nose was red and . . .

Poor pity me. Stop it, she told herself.

Her mother was strong. She was tough. She had gotten over that incident. She must have. She was back in Yorktide, wasn't she, supposedly eager for her daughter's friendship? And she was determined to lend a hand hosting the annual Independence Day party at Ferndean. Not that her contribution was going to be appreciated, Nicola thought. Her aunt had laughed in scorn when she told Nicola what Carol had planned. Nicola had laughed, too, though a small part of her had felt bad that she was mindlessly joining in her aunt's mockery. A painting station or whatever you could call it wasn't a terrible idea in and of itself, just not a good idea for a Ferndean gathering.

Nicola squirmed, this time not because of physical discomfort but because her conscience was nagging her more forcefully. In a way, she had betrayed her mother by immediately taking her aunt's side in a conflict that shouldn't even be a conflict. Why couldn't Carol do her thing and Bonnie do hers? Why did the Ascher sisters always have to be at odds, fighting, jabbing at each other? It could be exhausting. It was unfair to Nicola, always being put in a position to take sides. It was . . .

It was up to her to be an adult and step back from the sisters' problematic dynamic. She was twenty-five-years old, not a child. She didn't need to be a favorite or a pawn or—

"Achoo!"

Nicola was miserable.

Chapter 72

Julie was not looking forward to the annual Independence Day festivities. Lately, loud noises were bothering her more than they ever had. She would have to stay away from the various fireworks displays around town; she would have to remember to buy earplugs. Her parents had always forbidden everything but sparklers at their party; neither had wanted the risk of injury or fire. Still, the guests gathered at Ferndean would be a loud lot. Revelers always were.

The microwave alerted Julie to the fact that her lunch was ready. A few days before she had bought a large supply of instant soup. Just add water and pop into the microwave. Couldn't require less effort. She removed the cup with a dishtowel. The soup was a sickly yellow. She blew on it and took a sip. It was like swallowing a spoonful of salt. Julie drank it all anyway.

There had been a scene the night before. Sophie had announced that she wasn't going to her grandmother's Fourth of July shindig; a fellow counselor at camp was having a party that was, according to Sophie, going to be totally awesome.

Julie had said nothing. Scott, however, had insisted that Sophie attend Bonnie's party with her parents. Julie didn't share her husband's intense concern about their daughter's summer friends, but she still had enough respect for Scott's parenting instincts to let him have his way. Sophie had stomped off in a rage.

There was another reason Julie had not fought Scott's decision. Guilt. Scott had been at the dentist's office for about an hour the other day when the receptionist had called to let Julie know that the extraction had been a success but that Scott was extremely woozy from the anesthesia.

"He's welcome to sit here for as long as he needs to," Shari explained. "Unless someone can come to pick him up."

Julie had fought hard with her better instincts. But pride had won out. "I'm sorry," she said finally, staring blindly at the far wall of her office. "I'm not able to get there right now."

If Shari thought Julie Miller heartless, she didn't let on.

Scott was home about an hour after that. He said nothing about not having felt well. Julie wasn't sure he knew that she had been called—and that she had refused to help him. Part of her hoped that he did know. Part of her hoped that he didn't.

So, Julie had backed her husband's decision to keep Sophie from her party. It was a way of making amends.

But there was still the matter of her own attendance. It wasn't in her at the moment to be social, to ask after a person's parents, to admire a person's attire, to answer a person's polite enquiries about how her summer was progressing. Maybe if Aggie was going to be at the party things might be easier, but she wasn't. Julie had not invited her.

Of course, at the last minute, Julie could claim a headache and stay at home. Some people might believe her, but not her sharply intuitive mother. No, for Bonnie's sake, Julie would go to the party, the first one without Ken Elgort as cohost. Julie felt ill-equipped to be of much help to her mother—to anyone; she had proven that— but her gut told her that her presence would be better than her absence.

And she would try to remember what Sara had said to her. That she believed Julie was going to make it through this difficult phase of her life intact.

Not broken.

That didn't mean not damaged. But it did mean whole.

Chapter 73

Bonnie Ascher shook her head at the folly of it all. Expecting the guests to stop having a good time and draw pictures! Ridiculous. And those designer cocktails! Carol had hired a professional bartender to create artisanal spritzers and other such nonsense. She and Ken had never served anything but beer and wine and soft drinks, and nobody had ever complained.

Bonnie watched as Carol made her way through the crowd of guests. Some of them were obviously in awe of her. Others were merely friendly in their greetings. No one ignored Carol or was in the least bit rude. That was Yorktide, Bonnie thought proudly. Sure, there were a few nasty gossips and troublemakers around town, but only a few, and they were not and never had been friends with the Ascher or Elgort families.

A guest waved and began to make her way toward Bonnie. Eleanor Keats was a tall, slim, attractive woman of about fifty. She was the author of a popular series of vampire mysteries. She had never married, though Bonnie remembered hearing through the grapevine that there had once been a man in Eleanor's life. A married man, when Eleanor was in graduate school in Boston. But then Eleanor had come back to Yorktide alone and had continued alone for the past twenty years.

"This must be a bit trying for you," Eleanor said. "The first party without Ken."

"Yes," Bonnie admitted. "It is."

"I think he'd say it was a success. Except, maybe, for the easels . . ."

Bonnie smiled. "Yes, well, my sister is used to a very different sort of party I guess."

"Good for her for trying to introduce something new, though. It doesn't hurt to shake things up once in a while." Eleanor smiled. "You must be thrilled she's here in Yorktide for the summer."

"Yes," Bonnie said flatly. "It's very nice."

"I suppose once she's gone back to New York you'll miss her. And with Nicola going off to a far corner of the world things will be pretty quiet around here, won't they?"

"Nicola hasn't actually committed to the Peace Corps yet," Bonnie blurted, wondering if she was telling tales. She didn't mean to be; she just wanted Eleanor to stop talking. "Will you excuse me?" she asked. "I need to check on the food."

So, word of Carol Ascher's plans to inhabit Ferndean House hadn't gotten around town. That was a bit of a miracle. Maybe, Bonnie thought suddenly, she should find her sister and talk to her. And say what? Lie about the success of her fancy drinks? Ask if she was enjoying the party when it was pretty likely she was not?

Really, Carol offering to pay for the food and beverages as if her sister was a pauper, as if Carol's money came anywhere near equaling the hard, physical work Bonnie and Ken had done for all those years! *They* were the ones who knew about dedication. *They* were the ones who knew about devotion.

Bonnie took a steadying breath and turning away from the crowd, she headed for the house. She needed to be alone before the tears started to flow.

Chapter 74

There were excited shouts from the horseshoe pitch. There was laughter from the corner of the yard where a few of the guests were playing badminton. There were hoots and hollers from a group of men playing a game of bocce ball.

There was silence from the semicircle of easels. Carol thought they looked downright pitiful, standing there on their slender legs, all on their own and neglected.

Judith was making her way toward Carol, a jaunty, wide-brimmed straw hat perched on her head.

"The easels aren't a big draw, are they?" she said as she approached. "Pardon the pun."

"Someone tried her hand," Carol pointed out. "Look. There's a rendering of something or other on the easel on the end. It's not very good. In fact, it's awful, but at least someone had the right spirit."

"That was me," Judith said. "It's supposed to be a lighthouse."

"Oh. Thanks."

"No worries. Maybe I should have doodled something on every canvas. Where did you get this stuff, anyway?"

"I rented it from an art supply place in Portland."

"Must have cost a pretty penny."

Carol didn't reply.

"Why don't you paint something?" Judith suggested. "You know, a city slicker being drawn and quartered."

"I'm not in the mood," Carol said sharply. "Have you seen Nicola?"

"The last time I did she was carrying a case of soda. By the way, I had one of those gin cocktails. Wow. Packed quite a punch. I'm on water for the rest of the afternoon. Look, there's what's-her-name. I told you about her, the girl who used to terrorize me in high school. I think I'll go and say howdy."

Judith traipsed off. Carol wished that she could disappear, get in her car and drive and drive, and only return when this annoying afternoon was over. Before she could give this idea any serious consideration (who would miss her?) she was being accosted by one of the guests.

Carol remembered him. How could she not when his name was Edgar Poe? He was badly bent and a little unsteady on his feet, but his voice was booming and his eyes bright. He wore a threadbare white shirt (well, it had once been white) partly tucked into a pair of very faded blue pants that were held up by red suspenders.

"It's not the same without Ken manning the grill. And what an arm for bocce he had." Edgar eyed Carol keenly. "Weren't the two of you courting once upon a time?"

Carol nodded tersely. The memory of a small town was a formidable thing.

Edgar chuckled. "Well, that was a mismatch if ever there was one! Now the moment Ken turned his attentions to your sister, we all knew that was a pair made in heaven. It's just too bad he's no longer with us. We weren't finished with Ken Elgort here in Yorktide, not by far."

Edgar nodded and made his way across the grass to the food table. Somehow, Carol wasn't surprised when she saw him take a huge bite out of a hot dog. The man had to be near ninety, but she suspected he would be at next year's party, and the one after that.

A burst of shrill female laughter caught her attention. It had come from one of three young women sitting at one of the heavy plastic tables Bonnie and Nicola had found in the depths of Ferndean's garage. People were really enjoying themselves. Carol hadn't been to a party like this in years—casual, raucous, with absolutely no sense of an interest in impressing one's fellow guests.

She felt out of place.

She was out of place.

Unlike Bonnie. Carol had spoken to her briefly as the first of the guests were arriving. After that, her sister had darted off. Three hours later and Bonnie was still buzzing around like a bee, clearly enjoying being the Hostess with a capital H. If Ken's absence was bothering her she wasn't letting on to her guests. Carol admired that kind of fortitude.

Carol glanced again at the forlorn easels. It was rare she judged so badly. Judith had tried to warn her, but Carol's hubris had gotten in the way of common sense. Hubris and a genuine desire to help her sister in her hosting duties.

The desire truly had been genuine.

Chapter 75

Nicola wasn't really one for parties, but her aunt and uncle's Fourth of July celebration had always been an exception. There were several reasons for this, the main one being that because the Elgorts were so well loved by everyone in Yorktide, the mood of their guests was invariably happy and thankful. And the fact that Bonnie always made massive amounts of her famous clam chowder also made the party one Nicola had no trouble enjoying.

But this year, so much was different.

What had happened to her family? Nicola frowned as she caught sight of Sophie sitting by herself at a small table. Her arms were folded tightly across her chest and there was a frown on her face. Earlier, Nicola had tried to engage Sophie in conversation, but Sophie had just grunted and shrugged. So, Nicola had moved on to chat with other guests, many of whom wanted to offer yet again a word of condolence on the loss of her uncle. Even after almost a year it was still difficult to speak about Ken in the past tense; often, Nicola simply gave up trying and spoke of her uncle as if he were still there with his family. And he was. Just not in the flesh.

Nicola scanned the yard until she found her cousin; like her daughter, Julie was on her own and looking miserable. There were times when her cousin's depressed state annoyed Nicola. She knew that Julie had not asked to be cheated on or to fall prey to this state of sadness and self-loathing, but all the same, it could be trying to be around her.

Where was Scott? She had lost track of him for a moment. So far, he had been spreading his attention among the guests, not lingering too long with any of the women, laughing with some of the men. The affair had happened months ago and while no one could have forgotten, no one at the party seemed eager to remind him of what had gone on with Laci Fox. Scott Miller was a local boy; he had always been well-liked; clearly, he had been forgiven his utterly commonplace dalliance.

Still, Nicola thought, Scott should be at his wife's side.

A loud giggle, followed by a low rumble of male laughter, caused Nicola to turn to her left, where she saw a teenaged girl and a guy in his twenties standing by one of the easels her mother had provided. Nicola squinted and the cause of the couple's amusement became clear. The guy—it had to have been him—had scribbled a rude image on the paper. Nicola sighed, knowing she had to remove the offending image, but before she could take a step the young man yanked the paper off the easel, grabbed the girl's hand, and led her away.

What had her mother been thinking? Bonnie and Ken's crowd wasn't an arty one, not that some of the men and women weren't proficient carpenters, quilters, seamstresses, and custom boat builders. They might have creative talents, but they weren't the sort of people to turn their backs on a rousing game of horseshoes to pick up a paintbrush and attempt to capture the beauty and intricacies of nature.

Nicola realized that she was hungry. A bowl of her aunt's clam chowder would really hit the spot. But then, her mother was coming her way, her stride purposeful. Unsurprisingly, Carol Ascher was the best-dressed woman at the party, though she was exposing less skin than the majority of women who were in tank tops, T-shirts, shorts, or low-cut sundresses. Now that Nicola thought of it, she couldn't recall her mother ever wearing revealing clothing. There was a restraint and discipline about her that held through every aspect of her life.

"Are you having a good time?" her mother asked when she had joined Nicola.

"The party is a success," Nicola said carefully. "But this is difficult for Aunt Bonnie. The first annual Fourth of July party without Uncle Ken as her cohost."

"I know. Several people have pointed that out to me. She seems to be holding up well enough."

"Aunt Bonnie wouldn't allow herself to fall apart in public. Besides, these are people she's known all of her life. She feels comfortable with them. They've stuck by her and she's stuck by them."

"Unlike me," her mother said in a weary tone.

"Sorry," Nicola mumbled. There really was no need to keep nagging at her mother about the distance she had put between herself and her family all those years ago. It was a fact. They all knew it. And honestly, hadn't Nicola herself contributed to the dynamic of estrangement?

"I'm going to get something to eat," Nicola said. "Can I bring you anything?"

"No, thank you," her mother replied.

Nicola moved off but couldn't resist one quick glance over her shoulder. What she saw surprised her. Carol Ascher was making her way toward the wooden bench where Julie was sitting on her own. If Carol thought she could get anything more out of her niece than a grunt or grumble, well then good luck to her. Nicola continued on her way to the food tables.

Chapter 76

Even though she had known pretty much everyone at the party since she was born, and knew them to be good, solid people who cared about their neighbors, Julie still felt so terribly obvious. How much of that was down to paranoia and how much was just an acceptance of small-town reality, Julie didn't know.

Scott had left her almost the moment they had arrived at the party. She had told him to go. He was now talking with three men Julie recognized from town, though she wasn't sure of their names. She watched as Scott laughed at something the tallest of the men had said. Had he found the man's words genuinely funny? Or was he just keeping up appearances for the sake of the family?

Julie scanned the yard for Sophie and spotted her leaning against a porch post; she was stripping a flower of its petals. Sophie looked supremely bored, probably because there were only a few other teens at the party. One couple had brought their fourteen-year-old grandson who was paying them a visit from California. He had been taken up by the horseshoe set and seemed to be having the time of his life. Patricia Doolan was there with her mother, but Sophie had never gotten along with Patricia, who was a dedicated athlete with no time to spare for girls whose idea of exercise was waving their wet fingernails in the air until they were dry. There was one other teenaged girl at the party, someone Julie didn't recognize, and she was glued to the side of a guy who looked to be in his early twenties. It took her a moment to realize that the young man was one of her former students. Could she, Julie Miller, really be that old?

Julie frowned and turned away. She wandered over to the food table. No one stopped to speak to her. She had already eaten three hot dogs and wasn't really hungry, but the iced cupcakes caught her attention. One of the Wolf Lane neighbors had brought them; Tara never skimped on the icing. Julie reached for one and retreated to a rather rickety wooden bench that was in the shade of a large old oak. She took a bite of the cupcake and wondered how soon she could leave without causing her mother concern. Scott and Sophie wouldn't notice she was gone, but her mother, a good hostess, would be noting the comings and goings of each of her guests.

She had just swallowed the last of the cupcake when she realized that her aunt was coming toward her. The temperature was well into the eighties, but Carol looked as fresh as the proverbial daisy. Julie was very aware that there were probably sweat marks under her own arms.

Carol smiled when she reached Julie. "You seem to have found a nice, shady spot," she said.

Julie wondered if there was criticism in the comment. There was the paranoia again. "It's so hot in the sun," she said. What a stupid thing to say. Of course, it was hot in the sun!

Carol, however, didn't laugh or roll her eyes. "Thank God for baby powder," she said. "I use so much of it in the hot weather."

There was silence for a moment or two; it was not really an uncomfortable silence.

"I'm sorry no one seems interested in painting," Julie said suddenly. She wasn't sure why she was offering her sympathy to the woman her mother considered an enemy and a usurper. But the words had just come out.

"Yes, well, their loss," Carol said lightly.

"Maybe if there were more children," Julie went on.

Carol turned to Julie and smiled. "I'll try to better gauge the guest list next time."

Silence fell again. Julie couldn't think of anything else to say and was beginning to feel uncomfortable when Carol spoke.

"I hope you don't mind my making this offer," she began, "but my apartment in Manhattan is sitting empty at the moment—I haven't yet put it on the market—so if you feel the need for a little getaway, I'd be happy for you to stay there. You could bring a friend if you like."

Julie was forcibly struck by the kindness of her aunt's offer. For a moment, she felt it difficult to breathe. "Thanks," she finally said. It was an inadequate reply but all she could manage.

"Just let me know," Carol said. Then she walked off in the direction of the other guests.

Julie was grateful for her aunt's having sought her out and if Carol's offer had been genuine, and Julie felt that it had been, it was evidence that maybe Carol Ascher wasn't the entirely self-centered person Bonnie Ascher had made her out to be.

Suddenly, Julie realized that nobody was looking in her direction; at least, she thought the coast was clear, so she got up from the bench and hurried toward the side of the road, where Scott had parked his car. She had a copy of his keys with her. Scott and Sophie could get a ride home from one of the other guests.

Chapter 77

Bonnie was bone tired but sleep just would not come. She had turned the light on. Then she had turned it off again. Then she had propped herself in a sitting position. Then she had stretched out prone again.

By all accounts the party had been a success, but Bonnie felt dispirited. In spite of her earlier mean and critical thoughts, she took no pleasure in the unpopularity of her sister's party efforts. But if Carol had been disappointed, she had not let on. Gamely, she had made good on her promise to help clean up after the guests had gone. She had folded chairs and dumped dirty paper plates into garbage bags; she had gathered cans and bottles for the recycling bin and chased stray napkins as they skittered across the grass in a stiff evening breeze. With Judith's help, she had hauled the easels and other equipment to the back deck from where they would be picked up the following morning. She had paid the bartender and brought endless bottles of locally made gin back into the house to be stored in what had been Ronald Ascher's rarely used liquor cabinet in the den.

Bonnie had been surprised at her sister's industrious behavior but had made no comment. She had offered no thanks. She should have.

Bonnie turned onto her right side and stared blindly into the dark. She had seen her sister talking to Julie for some time. But before she could ask her daughter what they had spoken about, Julie was gone. Scott had become worried. Bonnie advised that he check to see if their car was still parked where he had left it. It was not. Later, Scott and his daughter got a ride home with a neighbor.

Sophie had acted poorly from the moment she arrived with her parents. It was no secret that she had wanted to go to a party given by one of the older counselors from camp, but that was no excuse for her to spend the afternoon moping around, rolling her eyes, and merely nodding when a neighbor said hello.

In fact, from what Bonnie had been able to tell, Judith was the only one of the family who seemed to have truly enjoyed herself.

The lights from a passing car flared through the darkened bedroom. Bonnie turned onto her left side; her back was now to the window and she was facing the pillow on which Ken had once rested his head. One thing Bonnie knew for sure. Ken would have wrangled guests to the easels and people would have had fun drawing badly or playing Hangman; he would have tried a few sips of the various locally made gins and made jolly comments about them; he would have taken the time to speak with Carol and thank her for her contributions. Ken had had the most generous spirit of any person Bonnie had ever known.

What would it really have cost her to show some appreciation for her sister's efforts? Maybe more than she could have afforded. It had been a struggle to play hostess without Ken by her side. At one point, she had even sought refuge in her childhood bedroom and cried as if her heart was freshly broken.

With a rough and impatient gesture, Bonnie threw the covers from her and sat up. Another sleepless night. Well, she thought, as she climbed out of the bed, she might as well not waste time staring at the ceiling when there were floors to be swept and furniture to be polished.

Work, Bonnie had always found, was an excellent antidote to sadness.

Chapter 78

Carol had never found Adirondack chairs in the least bit comfortable, but they seemed to be considered necessary for a house in the country. Carol twisted uncomfortably. As soon as Ferndean was hers she would toss the chairs and buy a set of stylish and comfortable garden furniture. Maybe she would offer the old chairs to her sister. Bonnie probably had an emotional attachment to them, too, like she did to every corner of the house and every fork and knife in it.

Carol was in a glum mood that not even the brightness of the sun and the singing of the birds could alleviate.

It was clear to her now that she had moved insanely far away from the ability to sustain an intimate emotional relationship with a fellow human being. Why had she offered to pay for the party? Only recently her sister had stated that she would never take money from Carol (Nicola's care excepted), and she remembered Nicola saying, in a somewhat superior way, that money could not be equated with time and effort.

Carol Ascher was out of her depth. She needed to rethink what to say, how to act, how to let her family know that she needed them—without coming right out and saying the words.

I need you. I need to know that when I'm gone someone will genuinely mourn me.

The return of the native. The reemergence of the prodigal daughter. The long-anticipated homecoming was a time-honored journey, a commonplace of the human condition, explored in countless books and movies, from Homer's *The Odyssey* to Toni Morrison's *Song of Solomon*, from *The Royal Tenenbaums*, and even, it could be said, to Dante's *Divine Comedy*. How did the opening lines go? Depending on the translation, something like: "In the middle of the journey of our life, I came to myself in a dark wood, where the direct way was lost."

That was the thing about being a reader, Carol thought. No matter what situation in which you found yourself you could easily call up a quote to illustrate or illuminate the matter. Like that famous line by Charles Dickens: "Every traveler has a home of his own, and he learns to appreciate it the more from his wandering."

Carol wasn't sure that was true in her case. First of all, she had not spent her life wandering. She had left Yorktide deliberately and had deliberately put down roots in New York City. She did not appreciate Yorktide more now than she had. Maybe she had hoped to; why come back only to feel as tepid about the place as she always had in the past? Would Dickens's statement make more sense for her if she substituted the word *understand* for *appreciate*? No. She would be kidding herself if she believed she understood Yorktide any better now than she had in the first nineteen years of her life. She had always been a stranger here and she always would, even if she settled back into Ferndean House, even if her sister and her daughter finally welcomed her, even if Julie managed to dig her way out of the depression and learn to consider Carol an ally.

At least Julie hadn't rejected outright Carol's offer of her New York apartment. In truth, the offer had come out of the blue; perhaps it had been spurred by the pathetic figure her niece had cut that afternoon. Maybe the offer had been an attempt at atonement for her earlier harsh words about the dangers of self-pity. Whatever the reason, the offer stood and Carol sincerely hoped that Julie would accept it.

"Hello!"

Carol turned to see her cousin striding across the lawn.

"I never found those things comfortable," Judith declared as she joined Carol. "I'll sit on the ground, thank you."

"What brings you by?" Carol asked. She was not sorry for the company.

Judith shrugged. "I had nothing better to do. Sorry. That came out wrong."

"Doesn't matter."

"No sign of the party. Good job with the cleanup."

"As if it never happened."

"The cocktails weren't a big hit, were they?"

"There's enough gin left to drown the city of London. Oh, well. It will keep."

"Carol?" Judith was looking at her intently. "Are you still committed to the idea of living here in Yorktide?"

Carol spoke carefully. "I have to be here."

"I'm not sure I understand."

"I'm not sure I do, either," Carol quipped. "Not entirely."

Judith frowned. "Now you're just being annoying."

"Sorry. It's just that being back here in Yorktide isn't . . . It isn't great. In fact," she said with an unhappy laugh, "it's kind of awful."

"Don't you think you're exaggerating a bit?"

"Are you saying that things will look better in the morning?"

"They often do. At least long enough for you to take another, more clear-eyed view of the situation."

"But in the morning, I'll still be here in Yorktide," Carol countered.

Judith sighed. "You're not alone in returning to the place where you were born. Even Shakespeare went back to Stratford in the end."

"And he died there. Some think he caught typhoid fever from the river close to his house. Sometimes home can be deadly."

Judith rose from the ground. "Well, be miserable if you want to be," she said. "I'll be on my way."

Carol smiled weakly. "Sorry, Judith. I didn't mean to inflict my grim mood on you."

"No worries. I'm largely made of Teflon. Need help getting out of that thing?"

Carol took the hand her cousin extended.

"Final word of advice?" Judith said. "Give things another try."

Chapter 79

Nicola's mother had invited her to Ferndean for tea. Nicola had accepted, largely because the invitation had brought to light a long-buried memory of the afternoon Carol and Nicola Ascher had enjoyed high tea at The Plaza in New York City. Nicola didn't remember the specific occasion; a birthday, maybe? But she did remember feeling as if she were a princess in a movie, special and pampered. And she remembered all the delicious food.

As Nicola turned onto Wolf Lane, she wondered if her mother also remembered that happy afternoon at The Plaza, and all the others like it, when it was just the two of them on an urban adventure, exploring new neighborhoods in Brooklyn or Queens; window-shopping along Fifth Avenue; sitting side by side on a bench in Central Park while eating hot dogs from a vendor's cart.

She must remember, Nicola thought as she pulled the car to a stop. How could a mother ever forget? Even a mother who had sent her child away.

How dramatically her feelings about Ferndean had changed over the years, Nicola thought as she made her way up to the house. When she was very young she had been frightened of it. It was so big and dark. On rainy days, it looked like a mansion in an old black and white horror movie. Also, it smelled musty, not at all fresh and clean like her home in New York smelled.

When Nicola was eleven or so, Ferndean suddenly morphed into a romantic castle from a classic fairytale. She was eager to explore the many rooms on her own, to sneak up into the attic in hopes of uncovering a hidden treasure or maybe, if she was very lucky, a ghost. Not the scary kind, but the kind who was dashing and handsome, the kind of ghost who would vow to protect her from harm until the day she died and was finally able to join him in eternity as his bride.

When she was fifteen and had come to live full-time in Yorktide, Ferndean soon lost its air of menace and mystery and became simply what it was, the family homestead. Special in its way, but not frightening or especially attractive.

Nicola found her mother on the back deck. The small table was covered with a daisy-print cloth. There was a pitcher of iced tea with mint leaves floating on top. The pastries looked as delicious as those they had shared at The Plaza.

"So, is the whole town still chuckling about my artisanal drinks and paint boxes?" her mother asked when they had taken seats.

Nicola was surprised by her mother's tone. She sounded upset, maybe even embarrassed, by the failure of her efforts to entertain Bonnie and Ken's circle.

"I don't listen to gossip," Nicola said truthfully. "And I don't think anyone is still chuckling. Really. It's not that big a deal."

Her mother laughed. "Oh, I know. I'm just being silly. Look," Carol went on, "I know things between us have been strained for a long time, but I hope you still have happy memories of the first fourteen years of your life, when it was just you and me."

Nicola was taken aback. "I was just thinking about the old days," she admitted. "About all the fun we had. Like the afternoon we had tea at The Plaza. We got all dressed up. We even wore white gloves."

Carol laughed. "I think I gained five pounds that afternoon, but it was worth every calorie." She poured a glass of tea for each of them before going on. "And remember how we traveled almost every school break? Niagara Falls. Boston. Universal Studios in Florida. And remember the birthday party you had at the American

Museum of Natural History? And how we'd spend rainy Saturday afternoons browsing Tiffany's?"

"I remember," Nicola said. She felt—overwhelmed. She felt as if she might cry.

"How about the night we went to the opening of *Seussical* on Broadway?" her mother asked.

Nicola swallowed hard before speaking. "I wore a purple dress."

"We got that dress in a little boutique in SoHo. It was handmade in Denmark."

"What happened to it?" Nicola asked. She had liked that dress.

"When you grew out of it I donated it to a thrift shop," her mother explained. "I used to sell my unwanted things on consignment, but for some reason I couldn't bring myself to sell anything that had belonged to you."

Nicola didn't know what to make of that.

Her mother smiled. "I'll never forget the time we were having dinner in the Village and the lead singer of that British boy band you were mad about came into the restaurant."

"He was pretty short," Nicola said with a smile of her own. "I remember being surprised."

"It was nice of him to give you an autograph."

The entire experience now came flooding back to Nicola. The excitement upon seeing her idol up close. And the mortification she felt when her mother waved him over to their table and asked him to sign a page in her small, leather-bound notebook. "It's for my daughter," Carol Ascher had explained. Nicola had been completely tongue-tied.

"Yes," she said. "It was nice of him." And it had been nice of her mother, too. "What happened to that older couple who lived in our building?" Nicola asked. "Bert and Margot. The last time I saw them—"

"Was the last time you visited me," her mother said quietly, "the summer you were seventeen. The Shapiros died. It was to be expected. They were ninety if they were a day."

Nicola felt real sorrow at this news. "Oh," she managed. "I wish I had known."

"I'm sorry. I should have told you then. Margot passed and Bert followed a month later. Not uncommon for couples who've been together most of their lives."

"I can almost smell the delicious apple pies Margot used to bring us. And I can see Bert all dressed up in a suit and tie, no matter how hot and humid the day. In some ways," she went on, "they were the inspiration for my interest in working with older people."

Carol smiled. "I'm glad they had such a positive impact."

"Me too. So, have you made any big changes to the apartment?" Nicola wasn't sure why she was asking. At times, she could barely recall the layout of the home in which she had spent the first years of her life.

"Not terribly big, no," her mother said. "I had the kitchen and bathrooms upgraded at one point, but the other rooms are pretty much the same as they were, including your room."

Nicola's eyes widened. "You mean you didn't make it into an exercise room or something?" she asked.

"Why would I have done that? I kept it so that you would have a place other than Yorktide to call home. If you ever wanted one."

"Thanks. I mean, I'm surprised." But she wouldn't have been surprised, Nicola realized, if she had slept in her bedroom on those few, long-ago visits back to New York. She had refused even to enter the room, sleeping instead in the library. A silly act of rebellion.

"I've mentioned this before," her mother went on, "but if you want any of your old belongings, well, they're yours to have."

Nicola shrugged. "It doesn't matter."

"There might be some items you want to keep," her mother went on. "Like that brass Art Deco statue of a nymph you picked out in Paris. You loved going to the Les Puces de Clignancourt in Saint-Ouen." Carol smiled. "Sounds so much better than 'flea market,' doesn't it?"

Nicola returned her mother's smile. "I'll think about it," she said. She did like that statue.

"I could have it all sent to Ferndean, if that would be easier for you than coming to New York. I know you're busy with work and all."

Nicola noted that her mother had not mentioned the Peace Corps as a factor in Nicola's busyness. She was thankful for that.

"I'll let you know," she said.

"Let's not let these pastries go to waste." Carol selected a jam tart and Nicola chose a particularly decadent-looking pastry with a crown of whipped chocolate cream.

The conversation turned to less vital topics, like the large number of fireflies to be seen in the vicinity of Ferndean and the outstandingly bad reviews that had been accorded to one of Yorktide's newest restaurants.

"The food critic had to have had a grudge against the chef," Nicola noted.

"More like a vendetta," her mother said dryly.

Nicola left when the pitcher of iced tea was empty; she had an appointment with a plumber; the landlord was finally going to fix the leaky faucet in her tiny kitchen sink. As she pulled away from Ferndean House, she saw that her mother was standing at the front window.

Nicola waved. Her mother waved back.

Afternoon tea at The Plaza was all well and good, Nicola thought as she drove away, but in some ways, it had nothing on afternoon tea at Ferndean.

Imagine that.

Chapter 80

Julie was pretty sure the expression on her face betrayed the extreme shock she felt on finding her aunt on her doorstep.

"I know," Carol said, rolling her eyes. "Everyone tells me it's rude to just show up at someone's house and maybe everyone is right. But here I am."

Julie smiled in spite of herself.

"I thought we could go for a drive," her aunt went on. "You pick the destination. As long as wherever it is isn't too rocky or muddy. These shoes are not made for the great outdoors."

"Let me get my bag," Julie said, surprising herself with the snap decision. "And change my clothes."

"I'll wait by the car."

Julie hurried upstairs. Quickly, she shed the dirty clothes she had been wearing, put on a clean T-shirt and pair of chinos, ran a comb through her hair, and hurried back downstairs.

"So," Carol said, when Julie was buckled in beside her. "Where to?"

"How about the Sarah Orne Jewett House?" Julie said. "Is that okay?"

"Sure," Carol said. "Though I have to admit I know next to nothing about her. She was a writer, yes?"

Julie nodded. "If you want to read her work you might start with the novella called *The Country of the Pointed Firs*. That's probably the most popular."

Neither woman said much on the drive, but that was okay. Julie noted that her aunt was an alert driver and that further helped put her at ease.

"This is a charming little town," Carol said as they parked a block from their destination in downtown South Berwick.

Julie laughed. "Maine is lousy with charming little towns."

Together, they walked to the corner of Portland Street. "This house belonged to Sarah's grandparents and was built in 1774," Julie explained. "Sarah and her older sister, Mary, inherited it in 1887. When Mary died in 1930 she left the house to Historic New England." Julie pointed. "The house next door was built by the sisters' parents. I'll let the tour guide tell you the rest."

Julie and Carol went inside and joined three other people—a couple from New Hampshire and a man from Illinois—on the tour. Their guide was well-informed and well-spoken. As she led the group through the front hall she enthusiastically pointed out the eclectic blend of styles.

"The wallpaper is fantastic," Carol whispered to Julie as they climbed to the second floor. "Such energy. I wish more people these days went bold in their homes. But if their neighbor is going minimal, chances are they will, too."

"You might want to visit the McLellan House," Julie suggested. "It's part of the Portland Museum of Art. Well, you probably know that. The paint and wallpaper and painted floor cloth are exact reproductions of the originals. It's also pretty out-there stuff."

"Thanks," Carol said. "I'll do that. I don't know why I haven't before."

Maybe, Julie thought, they could go together. But at the moment it wasn't in her to make that suggestion.

The group was now gathered in Sarah's bedroom, decidedly less impressive than her sister's room across the hall. When the guide and other visitors moved on, Carol and Julie lingered for a moment.

"So many lives that have come before," Carol mused. "And now here we are. And when we're gone, there will be others. And every single person who has ever lived or who will ever live will experience birth and death, joy and sorrow, pleasure and pain." Carol sighed. "You'd think that with all human beings have in common with one another they'd be better at getting along."

Julie nodded. "History shows us that nothing really changes. Not the core things. Love. Hate. Ambition. Curiosity. Compassion."

"So, do you consider yourself a nostalgic person?" Carol asked.

Julie smiled. "Like my mother? Not really. I mean, there's nothing wrong with nostalgia, but it is a form of selective memory."

"Yes, necessary at times but not always."

Like self-pity, Julie thought.

"Does Sophie enjoy studying history?" Carol asked as they left the room to join the others.

Julie shook her head. "Generally speaking, if it took place more than six months ago, she's not interested. Scott's that way, too," she admitted. "I mean, focused on what's happening right now. Except that he likes some of the classic rock bands."

Carol smiled. "Oldies but goodies. So, who comes along when you explore historic sites? I'm assuming you do explore historic sites?"

"I do, and I go on my own," Julie told her aunt. "I've always enjoyed my own company."

"I'm a bit of a social loner myself," Carol said. "But having someone who shares your passion is also a good thing."

"Yes," Julie admitted. And she thought that if she could get out of this swampy mental place she was in, a goal for her future might be to cultivate more friendships. She might have lost Aggie for good; even if she hadn't, Aggie didn't share Julie's interest in history. Julie would like to know someone who did.

"I'm glad you suggested we come here," Carol said when the tour was over and they had stepped outside the house. "Now, how about we have lunch? Do you know of a nice place in town?"

Julie did. She had heard about a restaurant from one of her colleagues who had eaten there a few times with her mother, one of those notoriously fussy eaters. At least, according to her daughter.

As they crossed the main street, Julie felt what could only be described as a glimmer of pure enjoyment. Carol was engaging with Julie as a person, not as a bundle of issues. She hadn't once mentioned Scott's affair or the plans Julie was supposed to be making to dig herself out of her depression. She hadn't commented on, or in any other way taken notice of, Julie's recent weight gain. They had engaged in real conversation about something other than Ferndean, housekeeping, or who in Yorktide was doing something he or she shouldn't be doing.

"Lunch is on me," Carol said as they entered The Green Apple. "I have to make up for appearing on your doorstep with no notice. Maybe one day I'll learn. But I doubt it."

Julie laughed. She liked her aunt Carol.

Chapter 81

Bonnie was seated at her kitchen table, mending the summer duvet cover; that morning while making the bed she had found a spot worn completely through. She wondered what Carol did when she discovered a tear in an otherwise good bedsheet or a slight nick in an otherwise whole drinking glass. She probably threw out the damaged piece and bought a replacement. That was fine for those with money to burn, but not for a woman like Bonnie Elgort, a woman who had always known the value of a hard-earned dollar.

Bonnie frowned at the spot she was mending. Things looked a little fuzzy through her glasses. She wondered if her prescription had changed. She hoped not. New lenses could be expensive. Not that Bonnie was a pauper or anything. Now someone like Carol wouldn't be inconvenienced by the need for updated glasses. No doubt she would buy herself a few new designer frames to boot.

With a sigh of frustration, Bonnie stuck her needle into the pin cushion, took off her glasses, and rubbed her eyes. She had been out of sorts since that morning when Julie had told her that Carol had shown up at the Millers' doorstep to invite her niece on an excursion.

"We had a really nice afternoon," Julie said. "We talked about all sorts of things."

About Julie's mother? Bonnie had wondered. Well, why not?

Bonnie had tried to co-opt Nicola, even at times to turn her away from her mother; there was no point in denying that. Was Carol now trying to co-opt Julie, get her to switch allegiance from her mother to her aunt?

Roughly, Bonnie pushed her chair away from the table and stood. She was being ridiculous. Most likely Carol's intentions in inviting her niece out for a pleasant afternoon were perfectly harmless. Family harmony was a good thing, something to strive for. Ken would be the first to remind her of that. And if Carol could in any way be of help to Julie—though for the life of her Bonnie couldn't see how!—then that was a good thing.

It was.

Bonnie fetched a glass of water and returned to the task of mending. Maybe she wouldn't dwell so much on Carol and her involvement with Yorktide if her own life were fuller, if, while she waited anxiously for the future of Ferndean to be decided, she had more responsibilities and more enjoyable activities to keep her busy.

For one, she could volunteer like she had done so often in the past. There was no down side to volunteering. She might ask Nicola if there was an opportunity at Pine Hill. The local library might need assistance. There were all sorts of possibilities.

As for hobbies, well, it had been a few years since Bonnie had belonged to a quilting group or to a book group. When Ken got sick, she had retrenched and focused all of her time and energy on caring for him. It might be fun to contact one of her former quilting or reading group buddies and see if there was room for one more at the next gathering.

And as for paying work . . . Something unpleasant had occurred to Bonnie the night before as she lay in bed. What if she applied for a job in town and was given the position out of pity? How could she be sure she was being hired by one of her fellow Yorktide residents for her skills and not for being Ken Elgort's widow?

"Ow! Darn!" Bonnie sucked the tip of the finger she had stabbed with her needle. How could she handle the responsibilities of a job, volunteer or paying, if she couldn't even concentrate on a simple task like mending a hole in a bit of fabric?

Bonnie put down the needle and pushed the duvet away from her. If she was grumpy it was because she was lonely. If she had a job, she would have a place to go and people with whom to interact. So what if she was hired because people felt bad for her? She hadn't asked to be alone. She hadn't wanted her life to look like it did.

With a groan of impatience, Bonnie got up again from her chair and began to pace the kitchen. Carol had gone on about the dangers of self-pity. And loathe though Bonnie had been at the time to admit that her sister was right, now she was prepared to agree. Ultimately, self-pity got you nowhere. But once you started down the dark and slippery slope of self-pity, it could be awfully hard to turn around and climb back up.

Bonnie abandoned her mindless pacing and strode out to the garden. The fresh air, the bright summer blossoms, the smooth green of the lawn, within moments all of these had worked their usual magic on Bonnie Ascher Elgort. Gosh, how she loved it here in Yorktide! How could anyone in her right mind not?

All would be well, Bonnie decided right there and then. She would banish self-pity. She would rebuild her life, with or without her sister a few miles down the road. Yorktide had never let her down before. Why would it let her down now?

Chapter 82

Carol turned away from the idyllic scene outside the kitchen window with an impatient sigh. Verdant fields and swaths of wildflowers were all well and good, but they could be so . . . so dull.

Earlier in the summer Judith had asked her what she planned on doing once she was settled in Yorktide. Carol had pretended a confidence she hadn't really felt. She would lecture. She would mentor. She would travel out of Yorktide on cultural quests. She would be fine.

But the truth was, even with all the family drama whirling around her, Carol was bored. What she wanted was a paying job, a task on which she could focus, the pressure of performing and producing. She wanted the subsequent praise and respect.

Carol reached for her cell phone, surprised she hadn't thought of this before. She would call Ana, ask how things were going with her husband, catch up on a bit of industry gossip, and then she would offer her services on a short-term, contractual basis. There must be some project on which Ana could use help. Carol would set her rates low, a special deal for a colleague. Ana would be thankful.

Carol placed a call to Ascher Interior Design. Ana was in a meeting. She would be given the message that Ms. Ascher had called. Was there any other message? No.

*   *   *

A day had passed. Ana had not called back, nor had she sent Carol an e-mail or a text. The message was clear. Carol had become surplus to requirements as far as Ana was concerned. So be it. Nothing lasted forever and it was right that the young should inherit the earth. Still, the realization that she no longer mattered to the person she had mentored for so long stung a bit. Carol might receive a card at the holidays and maybe even a gift basket, packed with cheese straws, jams, and cookies. And in turn Carol would send a—

What would she send to Ana? Nothing. Ana didn't need anything from Carol Ascher, not any longer.

But what really mattered, Carol realized, was the problem of her boredom. And then it happened, the proverbial lightbulb moment.

She had never been serious about putting in a zen garden at Ferndean, but she *was* truly curious to know more about whatever it was that her ancestor had begun to build behind the house. The logical first step would be to seriously investigate the markings on the stones that remained half embedded in the ground.

Carol located a craft store a few towns away and set off to purchase a kit of tough, water-resistant paper and sticks of solid graphite. In spite of her diligent efforts, what she uncovered was disappointing in the extreme, just a bunch of short curves and broken lines running every which way but seeming in no relation to one another, at least none that Carol could understand. Time had done its best to annihilate whatever images or patterns had been carved into the rocks.

After a light dinner, Carol undertook a second and more detailed search of the house, though she had little hope of finding anything. Surely, if plans had existed, tucked away in an old desk or bureau, someone would have discovered them by now. Under a loose floorboard? Possibly, but why would anyone want to hide what was essentially a public document? The house had no secret safe as far as Carol knew; still, she peered behind paintings that had been hanging on the walls since her childhood, tapped on the back walls of closets in search of a hollow area, and ran her hands along wainscoting that might conceivably be masking a latch to a hidden door.

After a few dusty hours of futile searching—she hadn't even unearthed a tarnished silver button or a faded postcard—Carol abandoned the chore. The next morning, she made a call to the Yorktide Public Library. The librarian on duty knew immediately that there was nothing in the library's archives pertaining to the history and construction of Ferndean House. "I've often thought that odd," she admitted before suggesting that Carol check with the local historical society. "Ask for Terry Brown," she said. "He's been there forever."

Later that morning, Carol arrived at the Yorktide Historical Society. Terry Brown was there as promised. He was a wiry, straight-backed man, probably strong as the proverbial ox, maybe in his late seventies, maybe a decade younger. It was hard to tell with some people. He wore a pair of glasses low on his nose and as they were talking, he rocked slowly back and forth on his heels.

Though Terry Brown was sorry to report that, like the library, the historical society had nothing in its archives relating to the construction of the Ascher homestead, it didn't take him but a moment to recall that one of his ancestors had been the foremen on Ferndean House back in 1848. There might be some old paperwork in the attic of the Brown family homestead. "I'll check if you'd like," Terry offered. Carol gratefully accepted his offer and gave him her phone number.

Carol left the building and got into her car. Before she started the engine, she checked her phone. There was a text from Ana. But Carol didn't need Ana's help now. She had her own mission. She put her phone back in her bag.

Chapter 83

Nicola shut off the engine of her car and looked up at Ferndean House. Just that morning her aunt had told her what Carol intended to do with the remains of the old, mysterious structure on the property. Unlike Bonnie, Nicola wasn't fundamentally opposed to the idea of change, but she shared her aunt's wariness about the nature of some of the so-called improvements Carol might make. It couldn't hurt to sound her mother out on those improvements, especially now that they seemed to be getting along better than they had in some time.

"I was in the neighborhood," Nicola said when her mother answered the door to her knock. Why had she lied?

Carol smiled and ushered her inside. "This is a pleasant surprise."

Nicola extended the flyer she had pulled from her pocket. "I wanted to give you this. We're having our annual summer crafts sale next weekend. A lot of the residents keep up with their sewing and knitting and model building. The sale never brings in much money, but it's a fun event for all of us."

"Thank you." Her mother took the flyer and scanned it. "I'll be sure to make a donation."

"You don't have to," Nicola protested.

"I want to." Carol smiled briefly. "I wouldn't want to be forgotten in my old age."

Suddenly, Nicola felt vaguely guilty. "I shouldn't have just dropped by. I asked you not to do that to me and here I am doing the same."

Carol laughed. "My bad habits are rubbing off on you! Seriously, though, it's not a problem. I'm always glad to see you."

Nicola realized that she believed her mother. Only weeks ago, she probably would not have.

"I was just about to make myself lunch," her mother said, heading for the kitchen. "Are you hungry?"

"Don't go to any trouble," she said.

"It's no trouble. Do you still like tuna salad?"

Nicola felt her empty stomach rumble. "With celery? And fennel?"

Carol smiled. "You remember."

"I haven't had your tuna salad since—"

"Since New York," Carol said quietly, opening the fridge and taking out a Tupperware container.

Nicola perched on a stool at the small kitchen island; her uncle had put it in place not long after Shirley Ascher died and he and Bonnie were preparing the house for occasional renters. "Aunt Bonnie tells me you have plans to rebuild the stonework in the backyard," she said. "Something about making it into a zen garden."

"And she's not happy about it, is she?" Carol asked, putting a sliced loaf of whole wheat bread on a wooden board and bringing it to the island.

"Of course not," Nicola said quickly. "And neither am I, to tell you the truth. What does a zen garden have to do with Ferndean?"

"Well, you can rest easy," her mother told her. "Nothing's set in stone, pardon the pun."

Nicola wondered. Did her mother mean to suggest that she might be open to some form of negotiation regarding the future of Ferndean? Or, Nicola thought, was she being way too naïve?

"Are you coming to Judith's dinner?" she asked.

Carol brought the rest of the makings for sandwiches to the

counter. "I don't think so. To be honest, the PMA is showing a film I've been wanting to see for ages and I'd really like to catch it."

Did a film trump family, Nicola wondered as she piled tuna salad onto a piece of bread? Well, maybe in some cases. Nicola recalled having backed out of attending one of Sophie's birthday parties in order to catch the opening of a popular zombie film.

"You haven't made any big changes to the house yet," she said. "Not that I can see."

"No, I haven't. Would you like coffee? Or iced tea?"

Nicola noted how quickly her mother moved away from the topic of Ferndean—again.

"Iced tea, please," she said.

Her mother brought the drinks to the counter and perched on a stool across from Nicola.

"That's a pretty blouse," Nicola said suddenly. "I could never pull off that intense shade of yellow, though. Not with my complexion."

"Yes, you have your—" Her mother laughed. "I mean, yes, this isn't your color. I remember when you were a little girl you loved to wear bright colors. It was a bit horrifying, actually, all the hot pink and electric blue."

"That was then," Nicola said. "When I came to live in Yorktide I changed. I became more myself. The real me."

"Is that true?" Carol asked. "I've sometimes wondered how much you were influenced by your . . . I mean, by the new environment."

"Yes," Nicola said firmly. "It is true."

"Good. Some people spend a lifetime trying to know who they really are."

Nicola laughed. "Well, I'm not saying I have all the answers!"

"No one ever does. So, will you take some time off work this summer?"

"No, at least, I haven't scheduled any vacation time until autumn."

"Have you been out of the country since the summer before you came to live in Maine?"

"Yes," Nicola said. "I've been to Canada twice during winter break, back in high school. I went skiing with a friend's family."

"I didn't know that." Carol smiled. "I suppose there are lots of things about your life I don't know."

"And there are lots of things about your life I don't know. Is that normal? I mean, for a mother and daughter to be so—estranged?"

"Do you really consider us estranged?" her mother asked.

Nicola thought for a moment. "I suppose I do," she said then. "It was bound to happen, with our living so far apart for the past ten years."

"Maybe if you had come home more often we—"

"Yorktide is my home. It became my home when you sent me away." Nicola did not say this angrily.

Carol nodded. "Then I should have come to Yorktide more often. Frankly, I got the idea you didn't particularly want me around, but maybe I should have forced the issue."

"Maybe you should have." Nicola sighed. "Look, Mom, I don't know. Can we just talk without getting all introspective about the past? What's done is done."

Did she believe that? At the moment, yes.

"Okay. But can I bring up one other memory? Nothing tragic, I promise."

Nicola sighed. "Sure."

"I was thinking the other day about the time we were at the Brooklyn Botanical Gardens to see the cherry blossoms and we came across that little lost boy."

"I haven't thought about that in years," Nicola admitted. "He was so distressed. I wanted to dash all around looking for his parents, but you wouldn't let me."

"Because then there would have been two lost children. And who knew how far the little guy had already wandered before we found him?"

"You knew just what to do," Nicola said. "You sat right down on the grass with him and had him smiling in minutes."

"My heart was in my mouth the whole time," Carol admitted. "I remember thinking that maybe the boy was on his own because his parents were irresponsible types who didn't know how to keep an eye on their child in a public place. And if that were the case, what sort of people would I be returning him to?"

"And I remember the parents running across the lawn the moment they spotted us. The mother was sobbing. The father looked as pale as a ghost. The little boy jumped right up into his mother's arms. I remember being so . . ." Nicola swallowed hard. "I was so proud of you. They thanked us both like crazy even though I hadn't done anything. But you had. You'd made sure he was safe and that he didn't feel scared."

Carol shrugged. "It was instinct. Nothing more than that."

Nicola thought about that. A mother's—a woman's—instinct to protect the young and innocent. Carol Ascher was not immune to that. It was silly to pretend otherwise.

"This tuna really is the best," Nicola said. "Thanks." Then she smiled. "No Devil Dogs for dessert?"

Her mother grimaced. "I tried so hard to keep you away from those things. But somehow, there was always a box at the back of the cabinet."

"Never try to get between a kid and her favorite chocolate treat."

"Do you still like them?"

Nicola shook her head. "Ugh, no. But the memories are good!"

Not long after they had finished lunch, Nicola took her leave. As she drove away from Ferndean House, she found herself again puzzled by her mother's attitude toward the old homestead. She seemed to have lost interest in her plan to buy out her sister, not entirely but to a noticeable degree. Could her mother actually be having second thoughts about occupying Ferndean? Or was Nicola once again indulging in wishful thinking?

Only time would tell, she supposed. For the moment, Nicola had other things to worry about. Like the fact that she was suddenly craving a Devil Dog.

Chapter 84

The front door slammed. Heavy footsteps sounded through the house, growing closer and closer.

Julie sighed. "What's wrong?" she asked when her daughter appeared in the doorway of the office.

"You noticed me?" Sophie snapped. "That's an improvement."

Julie didn't scold. Sophie was clearly distraught. "Tell me," she said, pushing away the magazine she had been absent-mindedly flipping through.

Sophie stomped into the room and propped herself against the old filing cabinet, arms folded across her chest. "What's wrong," she said, "is that I was in the convenience store earlier getting a bag of chips and a soda and there were these two women, I'd never seen them before, and they were gossiping about you. They were, like, Julie Miller's really let herself go since she caught her husband cheating on her with Laci Fox, and Scott Miller always was a horn dog, and if Julie Miller didn't get her act together her husband would be at it again." Sophie stopped to catch her breath. "Then one of them said she thought you should dump the bastard—that would be Dad, in case you didn't know—and that's when I couldn't take it anymore and I went right up to them and told them I was your daughter and that I thought it was totally wrong and horrible that they were talking about someone they didn't even know personally." Sophie laughed harshly. "One of them looked like she was going to faint. She was so embarrassed! The other one told me that eavesdropping was wrong and I said, how could I help but overhear when someone talks so loud, and didn't she ever hear about using her indoor voice?"

"What did the women say then?" Julie asked. Her voice came out as a croak.

"Nothing. They just left the store and I paid for my stuff. I looked around when I got out to the sidewalk, but I couldn't see them anywhere."

And if Sophie had seen the women? What would she have done then? Gone after them?

Sophie pushed herself away from the filing cabinet and began to pace. "Parents are supposed to put their kids first," she said. "Well, Dad didn't think of what it would do to me when he slept with Laci Fox, and you aren't thinking of what you're doing to me by falling apart so that everyone in town is laughing at you."

Julie put her hand to her forehead. Everyone in town probably was laughing at her; at least, some were laughing and others were pitying her, and still others must be taking a stance of moral superiority.

Suddenly, Sophie was at her side, awkwardly patting her mother's shoulder. "Sorry, Mom. I didn't mean that. About everyone laughing. But I . . ."

Julie took her hand from her forehead and looked up at her daughter. "What?" she asked gently.

"I'm scared," Sophie blurted. Her face suddenly looked ashen. "Look, I know about how depressed you got after I was born. You told me yourself. But then you got help. You did something about it. I know this is different but . . ."

"I'm all right," Julie said with an attempt at a reassuring smile.

"No, Mom, you're not. But I guess I can't do anything about that."

Sophie moved away. When she had reached the door to the office, Julie spoke.

"I'm sorry," she said.

Sophie turned back to her mother with a small, sad smile. "I know," she said.

When her daughter was gone, Julie slumped in her chair. At least Sophie had been honest about her feelings. That had to be a good thing. But to know that your child was frightened and to feel helpless to relieve her fear—that was not a good thing.

There had to be *something* Julie could do to get back to a place from which she could help others. There had to be. Suddenly, she remembered something Carol had said to her when they had been at lunch the other day. That courage was most often found when a person was most afraid. Was that true? Why couldn't it be?

And Julie reminded herself that Sara Webb, a woman she admired both personally and professionally, had faith in her. Sara believed Julie would come through this time intact.

Stronger? Wiser?

Maybe.

The most important thing, Julie realized, was to keep moving forward.

Chapter 85

Julie had shared a nice day out with Carol.

Nicola had mentioned that she had gone to Ferndean House twice in the past week. She told Bonnie she felt that she and her mother had connected while talking about old times.

If her daughter and her niece both reported pleasant experiences with Carol, with no discussion of Ferndean's future, maybe there was still a chance for Bonnie to change Carol's mind about the house.

Judith had offered a bit of advice. "Keep making efforts at conversation," she said. "Nothing gets accomplished by sitting around waiting for the other person to act."

So, Bonnie had invited her sister to the cottage for lunch, in spite of still being upset by memories of the last time Carol had been in her home. What a disaster that had been, and Carol had still not offered an apology for her bad behavior. Of course, when and if she did apologize, Bonnie would graciously accept and offer her forgiveness. It was what Ken would have wanted her to do.

Carol arrived at exactly noon. She had always been punctual, even as a child.

"I brought flowers," Carol said, holding out a bouquet of summer blooms. "I passed a little farm stand on the way here."

Bonnie accepted the bouquet. She thought that Carol seemed a bit nervous. Guilty conscience? But maybe Bonnie was imagining things. "I'll put them in water right away," she said, leading the way through the living room.

"This is lovely," Carol said.

Bonnie turned to see her sister running a carefully manicured finger along one of the quilts draped across the back of the couch. "Whoever made this has a fantastic eye for color and design."

"I made it," Bonnie said. "I made all of the quilts in the house, with the exception of a few that were given to me as gifts. Some of them are my own designs, like that one you're holding now. Sometimes I follow traditional patterns."

"Really? Why didn't you ever tell me you were so talented?" Carol asked. "I've had clients who would have paid a fortune for a quilt like this. People going for a cozy look at their beach houses or a retro feel at their ski lodges eat this stuff up."

"You would have shown your clients my work?" Bonnie asked dubiously.

Carol nodded. "Absolutely. If I had known it existed and was this good. When did you learn to quilt?"

The women continued on to the kitchen. Bonnie felt a frisson of pleasure and importance. Her sister's compliments were so very rare. "Not long after you left Yorktide," she said, reaching for a vase in which to put the bouquet. "Ken's mother taught me. She invited me to join her quilting circle once it became clear that, well, that Ken and I were going to be married."

"I never knew Mrs. Elgort quilted," Carol admitted. "Then again, I never made much of an effort to know her, or Mr. Elgort."

"They were lovely people." Bonnie brought the flowers to the table. She had set two places using her best plates. She had sewed the napkins herself and debated telling this to Carol.

"I'm sure they were," Carol said, taking a seat. "Look, what else don't I know about you?"

Bonnie shrugged and began to bring the meal to the table. "There's nothing much to tell," she said.

"Come on, Bonnie. There's always something to tell, especially after all the years we've lived apart."

"Okay," Bonnie said, taking her own seat and offering the salad tongs to her sister. "For a number of years, I served on the PTA of the grammar school. For ten years, I was a crossing guard during the school terms. I did the books for Ken's business when his aunt who had been doing them for years got too old and ill to work."

"But you also had a job at the grocery store, didn't you?" Carol asked.

"Yes, but when Ken got sick and I needed to be home to care for him I quit my job at Hannaford's and Ken's nephew took over for me at the garage."

"You've certainly kept busy," Carol noted.

"What did you think I was doing," Bonnie asked sharply. "Sitting here twiddling my thumbs? Life goes on in Yorktide as well as in New York City."

"Of course," Carol said quickly. "I didn't mean anything by my comment. Just that I never knew—"

"You never asked."

"And you never offered to tell me about your personal life," Carol pointed out.

Bonnie realized she couldn't argue that point. She took a deep breath and willed her sudden defensive posture to go away.

"This pasta salad is delicious," Carol said.

"I got the recipe out of a magazine."

"I don't cook much," Carol admitted. "When Nicola was little I made dinner almost every night. It's more fun when there's someone else around to feed."

Bonnie nodded. "I know."

"I'm sorry," her sister said. "With Ken gone . . . Everything must still feel so new, so raw."

"Nicola comes by for dinner one or two times a week," Bonnie said.

"That's good."

"And Julie and her family. Well, not lately, but . . ."

"I'm sure everything will work out there," Carol said.

Bonnie shook her head. "How can you be sure?" She got up to clear the plates. "I know you're not much for dessert," she said, "so I have fresh peaches. But if you do want something more, I made these cookies this morning."

"Your famous shortbread cookies!" Carol exclaimed. "Oh, I can't say no to those."

"I didn't know you were such a fan."

"You first made them back when we were kids." Carol took a bite of a cookie, chewed, and swallowed. "Wow. Still delicious. Same recipe?"

"Same recipe. Why mess with success?"

"If it ain't broke, don't fix it. Not an idea I've always adhered to, as you know."

Bonnie wondered if her sister had *ever* adhered to the idea of leaving well enough alone. Did it matter?

"Are you thinking of going back to work?" Carol asked.

Bonnie hesitated. She still didn't know the answer to that question. Ken was gone. She was getting bored and lonely. She could use the money; she might own the cottage and half of Ferndean but that didn't mean she wasn't cash poor. She had envisioned herself as the mistress of Ferndean House, but Judith was right. How would she afford the house all on her own? Now, with Carol in the way, that dream seemed shattered . . . But what if she could make it come true after all? Would it bankrupt her unless she had a good-paying job?

"I don't know," she said. "Probably. One day."

"What will you do?"

"There are always jobs if you're willing to take them." That much was true. But at sixty-two, there were several jobs Bonnie would not be willing to take, like the babysitting of energetic toddlers.

Suddenly, Carol smiled. "I don't know why this popped into my head," she said. "But I just had a memory of you sitting under the white pine out behind Ferndean, reading a Nancy Drew hardcover mystery. I can almost see the cover illustration. A girl in a tunnel. She's holding a flashlight."

"I was addicted to Nancy Drew stories," Bonnie admitted. "The library couldn't keep them coming fast enough. The Judy Bolton and Cherry Ames series, too."

"You spent a lot of time under that tree if I remember correctly."

"It was like my own private castle. I used to pretend that no one could see me through the heavy boughs. And I loved the scent of crushed pine needles. It was always cool, too, even on the hottest days of summer." Bonnie patted her mouth with her napkin. She was surprised she had said as much as she had.

"Every child needs a sanctuary," her sister said quietly.

"What was yours?" Bonnie asked.

"My room," Carol said promptly. "I was never really into the great outdoors like you were. I guess I was meant for city life all along."

"But you used to enjoy our family beach walks," Bonnie pointed out. "I know you did. Those summer evenings when the four of us would pile in the car and head to Ogunquit Beach. We'd walk along the shore even at the highest tide. Dad would look for a shell to add to his collection, and Mom would look for a sand dollar. I don't think she ever found one. Sometimes we stayed until the sun was set. Then, on the way home, we'd stop for ice cream at that little place on Stella Lane. Mom and Dad and I always got exactly the same thing. A small vanilla cup for Mom, a chocolate cone for Dad, and a vanilla cone with chocolate sprinkles for me." Bonnie smiled. "But you would always get something different. I remember being excited to see what flavor you would try next."

"I did enjoy those excursions," Carol said musingly. "Thanks for reminding me. By the way, what happened to Dad's shell collection?"

"After he died Mom boxed it all up and asked Ken to haul it to the attic at Ferndean. I'm sure it's still there. I haven't been in the attic in years." Bonnie smiled. "And no, I'm not still afraid of Emily the ghost."

Carol grimaced. "I'm really sorry about that. I shouldn't have made up that silly story."

"It's okay. Water under the bridge."

"What's done is done."

Not long after this, Bonnie walked her sister to the front door.

"Thanks for having me over," Carol said.

"It was my pleasure," Bonnie replied. She had spoken the truth. Even if nothing had been settled about Ferndean.

Bonnie stood at the window and watched as her sister got into her car. Only when she could no longer see the taillights did she look away.

Chapter 86

Carol Ascher was growing frustrated by the lack of news from Terry Brown. It wasn't that Terry had been unduly long in his quest; she had only approached him days earlier. No, Carol's impatience was oddly wrapped up in the idea that she might actually be hoping to restore the maze or whatever it was as a token of peace to her sister who was so invested in the family's past.

And what if she was? Carol had enjoyed the latest visit with her sister. She had felt more at ease with Bonnie than she had all summer. And while it was true Carol still hadn't apologized for lying about the breakup with Ken, at least she had apologized for the long-ago ghost story that had caused her sister nightmares. Maybe there was hope after all that the two sisters could reestablish the close relationship they had shared as children.

Her cell phone rang. As if in response to her impatience, it was Terry Brown. He had found something. Could he come to Ferndean right away? Carol said that he could.

Fifteen minutes later, Terry was handing Carol a large, dusty, and slightly crumbling brown envelope.

"I didn't go through it all," he told her. "Just took enough of a peek to be sure this is what you're looking for."

"I'd like to pay you for your pains," Carol said, gently setting the old envelope on a side table.

"Oh, no," he replied hastily. "This rightly belongs to you and your sister."

Carol didn't press the point. "Why do you think there are no surviving photos of the part of whatever it is that got made?" she asked as she walked him to the door.

Terry shrugged. "Probably lost along the way, as such things often are. People cleaning out after someone dies don't always look through the person's memorabilia, do they? Too much effort. Just chuck it all in the bin."

When Terry had gone, Carol went back to look at the envelope he had delivered. *Just chuck it all in the bin.* Earlier that summer Bonnie had accused her of treating the past with a cavalier attitude.

That wasn't quite right. Or maybe it had been, but it wasn't any longer.

That evening, Carol settled in the den with her ancestor's papers spread out on the coffee table. Pretty quickly she realized it was a good thing she knew about the Victorian passion for cryptic messages. She herself owned a poesy ring from about 1870, a band set with stones the first letter of which spelled out REGARD. She also knew of what was sometimes called floriography, the practice of assigning to flowers a meaning that would be known to the giver and recognized by the receiver. Countless books had been published detailing such meanings. Even the manner and style of giving a bouquet to someone could hold a message. Given with the right hand. Received with the left. Tied with a pink ribbon or a white. Romance or friendship. Apology or question.

This knowledge was going to stand her in good stead. Marcus's papers were not only crammed with not very good sketches, they seemed totally disorganized. Add to that the fact that his handwriting was difficult to read, spidery and badly slanted, and Carol was going to need all of her knowledge and then some.

After almost an hour of hard work, Carol had been able to identify the following symbols from her ancestor's notes: a daisy for innocence and purity; a violet for faithfulness; a peony for romance or possibly for prosperity; an orchid for admiration; and a rose for passionate love.

There was more on another page. A sprig of rosemary, which Carol assumed represented remembrance, as well as being a direct reference to the woman for whom this entire project might have been conceived. An anchor, probably for steadfastness, security, or reliability. A bird—Carol guessed it was meant to be a dove—for peace? A sheep? Carol squinted. No, maybe a lamb, representing purity?

Carol worked on. An oak tree. That was meant to represent strength. A snake with its tail in its mouth. That was easy enough. The uroboros represented eternity. Queen Victoria and her beloved husband had been drawn to the symbolism of the snake. An arrow meant . . . time? Clasped hands had to mean marriage or friendship.

There were literally pages of symbols that Marcus supposedly wanted incorporated in his massive project. Though there seemed to be no master plan or final written description of this project, there were notes suggesting the inclusion of an obelisk, a fountain, and a wishing well.

No doubt about it, Carol thought. What her great-grandfather Marcus Ascher had designed was a folly, a fundamentally useless structure—or, in Marcus's case, a series of structures—existing primarily for decoration, usually extravagant, and often looking purposely out of place. The term *folly* held connotations both of madness and of delight.

Very little of Marcus Ascher's exuberant vision had seen the light of day, and Carol could hazard a few guesses why. Still, she was greatly touched by what she had found. At the start of the summer she wouldn't have thought the discovery of her great-grandfather's project would have meant much of anything to her. But things were different now. She hadn't intended them to be different, but they were. She had thought she would change Yorktide, or at least her corner of it. But Yorktide had begun to change her.

Carol realized she was tired. Carefully, she gathered the papers in a large, clean cardboard box and went up to her bedroom. On the way, she decided that she would keep the discovery of Marcus Ascher's plans a secret, and only reveal them to her sister and the rest of the family once restoration work had begun.

A token of peace.

Chapter 87

It was a humid evening following an even more humid day, but Judith explained that it was even worse inside the house. "Plus," she said, "there's a breeze coming up. I'm sure of it. We're better out here."

Nicola, seated at the table with Bonnie and Sophie, always appreciated an invitation to a meal, bad or good weather.

"Where is Julie tonight?" she asked

"Mom said she didn't feel well." Sophie frowned as she said this.

"Maybe what she needs is a quiet night at home," Bonnie suggested.

"And why isn't Scott here?" Nicola asked.

"He told Julie he was working overtime," Bonnie said.

Sophie smirked. "Maybe he's seeing his girlfriend."

"She's not his girlfriend," her grandmother replied sternly, "and never was. Besides, he promised your mother that the—affair—was over."

Before Sophie could reply, Judith came in sight bearing a platter on which sat several cooked lobsters. "Well, look who's joined the party," she said as she laid the platter on the table.

"Dad?" Sophie whirled around in her chair. "Oh. Aunt Carol."

"I thought you had other plans," Bonnie said.

Carol shrugged and set a bottle of sparkling wine on the table. Nicola thought her mother looked a bit tired. Maybe it was the heat.

"It was just a movie," Carol said. "I thought it would be nicer to have dinner with my family."

Nicola smiled at her mother. "You can have my seat," she said. "I'll grab another one." She rose and hurried off to the garage, where Judith kept a few folding chairs.

"The dogs are out and about." Judith nodded in the direction of the two canines. They were stretched out under a large maple tree. "When they get the scent of the food . . ."

"That's okay," Carol assured her. "I'll be fine. It's not as if I'm allergic."

"When you told me that you weren't coming, I only bought four lobsters."

Carol waved her hand dismissively. "No worries. I should have called ahead of time."

Nicola smiled at her mother. "One of your bad habits. Like just showing up."

Carol laughed.

"You can share my lobster," Sophie offered.

"That's very generous of you, but no. You enjoy it. I will, however, have some of that coleslaw."

Judith grinned. "It's spicy," she warned.

Carol put a spoonful on her plate and then a forkful into her mouth. No sooner had she chewed and swallowed did she begin to cough.

Nicola and the others laughed, but not meanly.

"I think I'll stick to the corn on the cob," Carol said, her voice raspy. "My teeth are still strong. I think. And I'll have a glass of that wine if you're pouring."

Suddenly, Cocoa and Puff rose from their prone positions and came loping toward the table, where they stopped and sat quietly.

"They're well behaved," Carol noted. "I thought they'd be jumping all over us."

"A dog needs a loving but firm parent," Judith explained.

So, Nicola thought, did a human child. And in effect, she had

had three loving but firm parents. Her mother, her aunt, and her uncle. That wasn't such a bad thing.

"Are you enjoying work this summer?" Carol asked Sophie.

Sophie suddenly became animated. "Yeah, there's this one senior counselor, he's so funny. He plays these awesome pranks on some of the junior counselors. Mostly the guys. One guy even quit after he was pranked, but nobody really liked him, anyway. He was a total nerd."

Nicola glanced around the table. Was she the only one who thought the antics of the senior counselor problematic?

"I hope the administration doesn't tolerate bullying," she said.

"Oh, it's nothing like that," Sophie said with a laugh.

"Do you remember your first summer job here in Yorktide?" Bonnie asked Nicola.

Nicola smiled. "How could I forget?" She turned to her mother. "I was a server at a clam shack. It was hot and smelly and paid terribly, but I loved every minute of it."

"I didn't know that you worked summers while you were in high school," her mother said. "I gave you an allowance."

Nicola shrugged. "Everyone I knew was getting a job for summer. Why wouldn't I want to as well?" She turned to Sophie. "I'd never had a job before coming here."

"Lucky you," Sophie mumbled.

"You were just a child," Carol pointed out. "And I wanted you to use your vacations to continue your studies in a hands-on way." Carol looked to Sophie. "That's why we traveled a lot and why Nicola went to specialty camps, like the Shakespeare drama camp in the Catskills and the camp in the Everglades that focused on wildlife conservation."

Sophie frowned dramatically. "All I ever get to do is hang around boring old Yorktide."

"With your boring old relatives?" Judith asked, eyebrow raised.

Sophie colored. "I didn't mean that."

"Just teasing," Judith assured her.

Nicola managed to catch her cousin's eye and gave her a brief but reassuring smile.

"I remember my first job," Judith announced. "I was fifteen and it was making deliveries on my bike for the old pharmacy in town. Remember Norton's All and Sundries?"

Carol nodded. "I bought my first lipstick there. I think it cost fifty cents, which for an eleven-year-old was a hefty sum."

"I remember the penny candy counter," Bonnie added. "Root beer barrels, peppermint swirls, those chewy mint leaves. No wonder I had so many cavities as a kid."

"Didn't your parents tell you not to eat candy?" Sophie queried.

"They didn't know what I was up to," Bonnie explained. "Parents in those days didn't watch their children's every movement the way they do now."

"Anyway," Judith went on, "everything was going fine. I loved being out on my bike for hours every day, all on my own, riding down beautiful country lanes and singing at the top of my lungs."

"And then?" Sophie asked. "It sounds like there's something bad coming."

"And then, one super-hot and sticky day, I had to deliver a prescription to someone on the far east side of town and another prescription to someone on the far west side of town. I was soaked with sweat and could feel my neck burning. All I wanted was to deliver the stupid packages and go home."

"And?" Nicola prompted.

"And I got the packages mixed up and took off before anyone realized the mistake I'd made. I got all the way back to Norton's, ready to pass out, dying for a soda, only to find Mr. Norton in a rage. Both patients had called to complain they'd got the wrong prescription, so I had to go back out in the stifling weather and make it right."

"It could have been worse," Carol noted. "One or both of the patients might not have noticed the mistake and taken the wrong medicine and something dreadful might have happened."

"Don't I know it! One of the scrips was for a heart condition and the other was for a bowel disorder."

"Were you fired?" Sophie asked.

"No," Judith said. "But I got an earful from Mr. Norton and I deserved it. I never made a delivery mistake again."

"What was your first job, Aunt Bonnie?" Nicola asked.

"Let me see, was it babysitting for one of the neighbors or was it doing light housekeeping for one of Mom's older friends from church? I think they might have overlapped the summer I was fourteen."

"Housekeeping?" Sophie shuddered. "Ugh."

"I remember dying to get a job long before I was old enough to be of real use to anyone," Carol said.

"Why did you want to work when you could hang out?" Sophie said with a laugh. "I'd never work if I didn't have to."

"I wanted money," Carol said. "And I was a restless kid. So, when I was twelve, I took it upon myself to go around to the shopkeepers in town and ask if they had any jobs I could do. One let me sweep the sidewalk for a quarter. Most of them just smiled and sent me on my way. It was only when I was fifteen that I was able to get steady work after school and in the summers."

"You used to give me money."

Nicola turned to her aunt in surprise.

"What do you mean?" Carol asked.

"When you got paid," Bonnie said, "you would always give me a bit of money to do with whatever I wanted. I never told Mom or Dad. I thought they might make you stop. You were so nice to me." Bonnie laughed a bit. "I can't believe I just said all that out loud. It must be the wine."

Judith picked up the wine bottle and held it out to Bonnie. "Then have more."

"That's what big sisters are for, I guess," Carol said with what seemed to Nicola an elaborate attempt at a casual tone. Her mother was embarrassed by Bonnie's having shared the memory. Why?

"I'm glad you came tonight, Carol," Judith said. "The more the merrier."

"Yes," Nicola added. "Thanks for joining us, Mom." Then, she smiled. "I hope you don't hold the coleslaw against your host."

Judith laughed. "Hey, I gave her fair warning!"

"If I had known you were coming," Bonnie said, turning to Carol, "I would have brought some of those shortbread cookies you love so much."

Carol raised her glass. "Next time."

The evening wound down quickly after that. Carol was the first to leave. Nicola initiated a brief hug. It was the first time she and her mother had touched in years. Nicola was pleased that her mother hadn't pulled away. Had she really thought that she would?

Sophie and Bonnie left moments after Carol. Nicola stayed to help clean up. As she carried dirty plates and glasses into the house she realized that the evening had felt—normal. A bunch of women, related by blood and affection, if not always by similar interests or beliefs, sharing a meal and conversation on a summer evening.

In fact, the evening had been so pleasant Nicola had almost forgotten that her mother was intent on taking full ownership of Ferndean House. Even though it had been some time now since Carol had mentioned her plan to either her daughter or her sister.

"I think I'll ask Julie to lunch," Judith said, turning from the sink, where she was rinsing dishes. "Just the two of us."

"That's a nice idea," Nicola said. "Well, I'm off. Thanks again for the lobsters."

It was only when she was parking outside her building on Gilbert Way that she recalled Sophie's tale about the troublemaking senior counselor. Should she say something to Julie? But maybe Julie and Scott knew about this person. Besides, Nicola thought as she climbed the stairs to her apartment, she was probably just being overly cautious. A worrywart.

If Sophie wasn't troubled by this counselor, why should Nicola be?

Chapter 88

Julie had accepted her cousin's invitation to lunch, though she suspected Judith's real intention was not to have a casual meal and a friendly chat, but to give her a pep talk and then report back to Bonnie. Just because her mother hadn't spoken to her in a while about "the situation" didn't mean that she wasn't concerned.

Well, of course Bonnie was concerned. She was Julie's mother.

Carol, too, was concerned. But somehow her concern no longer felt oppressive.

Julie dashed up to the front door of Judith's house. Rain was falling heavily and in spite of an umbrella, she was wet by the time Judith let her in.

"Lovely weather we're having," Judith said, leading her guest to the dining nook off her kitchen.

Judith always set a nice table, with cotton napkins, artfully mismatched plates, cups and saucers, and milk in a whimsical pitcher. Today, the vintage pitcher was in the shape of an elephant. The milk poured out of its trunk. A bundle of wild flowers sprouted from a small glass vase.

"I'm sorry you weren't able to join us the other night," Judith said, gesturing for Julie to take a seat.

Julie flushed. She had not been sick, just feeling incapable of socializing. With Scott needing to work a special shift, she had the opportunity to stay home on her own. "Yes," she said. "I heard it was nice."

"I remembered you like curried chicken salad," Judith went on, setting a large bowl in the center of the table. "It's one of my favorites, too."

Julie folded her hands on her lap. "I should only have a little bit. I've put on a lot of weight lately." She was immediately aware that she had stated the obvious and opened the door for a conversation she did not want to have.

But Judith didn't comment, only heaped chicken salad on her own plate and reached for a piece of baguette.

"Did my mother ask you to invite me over?" Julie asked. Judith wouldn't lie.

"Absolutely not," Judith said promptly. "I act only for myself, if sometimes in the interests of others."

"Sorry. It's just that—"

"No need to apologize," Judith said, lifting the water pitcher and filling Julie's glass.

Julie took a bite of the salad. It was delicious. She should ask Judith for the recipe. For whenever her interest in cooking returned.

"I've been thinking a lot about forgiveness," she said quietly. "Not everyone thinks it's such a great idea."

"Forgiveness is a choice," Judith said. "It doesn't just happen over time, much as we might like it to. You have to want to forgive."

Julie nodded.

"Forgiveness is not a lazy person's option," Judith went on. "It takes courage and hard work. But once it's achieved, it's forever."

"Even if the person commits the same crime again?" Julie asked.

Judith laughed. "Forgiveness isn't a free pass for future bad behavior!"

"Scott thinks he needs to be forgiven. I mean, he knows he's guilty."

"He is guilty," Judith said firmly. "End of story."

"But don't you think—"

"No," Judith interrupted. "I don't think that the wife or the other woman is to blame for the man's decision to cheat. Ever. Look, the guy doesn't have to be a total shit to cheat on his wife. Maybe he's genuinely miserable with her and maybe she really is a harridan. But there are better ways of dealing with a bad relationship than committing adultery." Judith reached across the table and patted Julie's hand. "And you, my dear, are no harridan."

Julie smiled. "I think I'll have some more," she said, taking hold of the serving spoon in the bowl of curried chicken salad.

"You're not being scrutinized while under my roof. It's against my policy."

"Thanks. You know, my father would have been so disappointed in Scott. But I can't imagine Dad confronting him about the affair. He was so protective of me, but . . . Would he have wanted me to get a divorce? Would he have understood if I didn't want that? Would he have forgiven Scott?"

"Ken is gone, Julie," Judith said firmly. "It doesn't matter what he would or would not have done about Scott's infidelity. All that matters is what you feel, what you want to salvage or preserve, and what you want to let go of."

"What I feel is overwhelmed," Julie admitted. "I don't know what to do five minutes from now, let alone tomorrow or the day after that." Suddenly, Julie made a decision. "Don't tell anyone, because I'm not sure I'll be able to go through with it, but my principal is urging me to apply for a scholarship awarded by the Ackroyd Institute. There's a week-long intensive course next spring for early childhood educators. The focus is on religious tolerance and understanding."

"That's fantastic," Judith said with genuine enthusiasm. "But I can understand why you don't want people to know. You don't need the pressure."

Julie wondered. Maybe pressure was exactly what she needed. But pressure from within.

"What would be the downside of applying?" Judith asked.

"Not being chosen."

"That doesn't have anything to do with the process of applying, though," Judith pointed out. "Just doing the work of completing the application can only be a positive. A challenge. That's how I see it. But it's your call."

"Yes," Julie said. "It is." And that, she realized, felt empowering.

"Coffee?" Judith offered.

Julie accepted. She was in no rush to leave.

Chapter 89

Bonnie was sitting at the kitchen table, going through the want ads in the *Yorktide Chronicle*. It was a disheartening enterprise.

Such and such a skill required.

Knowledge of so and so necessary.

Familiarity with blah blah a plus.

College diploma a must.

Bonnie sighed and pushed the newspaper away. Well, she hadn't *gone* to college; she hadn't even considered it, though she had liked school well enough. Maybe it wasn't too late for her to enroll in a course or two at the community college, but to what end?

Maybe, Bonnie thought, instead of reading the want ads she should be looking for a class designed for people reentering the workforce after the age of sixty. What would such a class teach you? How to dress so that you didn't look your age? How to speak so that you didn't sound your age? Interview protocol in the world of e-mail and text and FaceTime and drones, whatever they were?

Bonnie took a sip of her tea. Experience had taught her that one didn't necessarily need a college education to succeed in life. Carol had gone to college for only a year and look at all she had achieved. But Carol was different. She had ambition. She was restless and could be, Bonnie assumed, ruthless. She was all the things Bonnie was not.

Ken, too, had been a successful man and there had been no question of his ever going to college. From the day he was born, he was destined to inherit the family's auto repair business. As a little boy, he spent endless hours at the garage with his father and uncle, absorbing the atmosphere, becoming familiar with the smells of paint and grease, learning how to perform an oil change and identify every bit of an engine. At the age of twelve, he began to work part-time as an apprentice. After high school, he took on a full-time position and by the age of twenty-six, he had taken over a great many of his father's responsibilities and a few of his uncle's as well. Ken's father, Ken Elgort, Sr., didn't officially retire for another ten years, and his uncle for twelve, but everyone knew that increasingly Ken was in charge.

And though Ken had brought his family's business to new heights of financial soundness, he and Bonnie had still had to scrimp and save so that Julie could continue her education after high school. It was clear from early on that she wanted to work with small children in a capacity that required a college education and Bonnie and Ken had done all they were capable of doing to make that degree possible for their daughter.

It had been well worth their every effort.

Bonnie finished her tea and brought the cup to the sink to rinse. Nicola's schooling hadn't been a hardship for Carol, she remembered, but on her own initiative, Nicola had insisted on working through each semester to help defray costs. If Nicola had been born with a silver spoon in her mouth, no one meeting the humble and hardworking twenty-five-year-old would know it. Bonnie would be lying to herself if she said that she had had nothing to do with her niece's good character.

She would also be lying to herself if she failed to admit that Nicola was already a fundamentally decent human being when she arrived in Maine. Yes, she had fallen in with a bad crowd in New York and caused her fair share of trouble, but both Bonnie and Ken had seen right from the start that the *real* Nicola was kind and loving—and wanting to be loved.

Carol Ascher had not done a bad job at parenting. She had probably made mistakes. All parents did. But she had not ruined her daughter's chances for a happy, healthy life—in spite of what Bonnie had pretended for so long. In spite of what she had needed to believe, that Carol's success was somehow unearned, mere luck.

Bonnie squirmed. Had her need for attention been so rabid? Had she really let jealousy have an unregulated upper hand? What would it have cost her to give credit where credit was due? Carol *had* earned her success. And showing appropriate respect for Carol's accomplishments in Nicola's hearing would have been the right thing to do. Nicola *should* admire her mother.

She should.

The landline rang, startling Bonnie. Caller ID told her it was Nicola. Bonnie had seen her niece hug her mother after dinner at Judith's house. She had felt ever so slightly jealous, not enough to feel guilty about. Not really. It was good for a mother and child to be close.

It was.

"Nicola," Bonnie said into the receiver. "I'm so glad you called. I was just thinking about you and your mother."

Chapter 90

The tenderness Carol had felt in Nicola's brief hug after dinner at Judith's had left her feeling rather melancholy. Nicola's touch had emphasized the fact that for so long Carol had been a stranger to the love and affection of her family, isolated from the day-to-day interactions that allowed people to be truly close and forgiving of each other.

But there had been no other path open to Carol all those summers ago. She had been compelled to leave Yorktide. And she would do the same again.

Carol settled in her father's armchair—was she imagining that it now felt more comfortable than it had at the start of the summer?—and within moments she was transported to that fateful summer of 1974.

Stepping off the bus at Port Authority had been like stepping into an alien universe. She had been immediately overwhelmed but as equally determined not to dash across the station to a bus that would take her back to Yorktide. Her neighbors would see her return as proof of failure. Failure was not an option.

For the first years of her new life, Carol lived in a women's hotel on Third Avenue in midtown called The Atlanta. It was at best a descendant of a nineteenth-century boardinghouse, or a faded version of the Barbizon residential hotel for women in which so many famous and infamous women had lived—Lauren Bacall, Joan Didion, Grace Kelly, Sylvia Plath . . .

Rent was cheap. There was one meal provided per day, in the evening. It was usually tasteless though filling; only occasionally was it inedible for all but the least discriminating of the girls. Men were not allowed beyond the lobby. Alcohol was not permitted. Carol's room was barely larger than a closet. The heat either worked or it didn't. She shared a bathroom in the hall with five other girls, none of whom were in the habit of tidying up after herself.

New York City in the seventies was not a nice place. There were frequent sanitation strikes. The subways were filthy. Drugs were rampant. Times Square was not the Disney-fied family playground it eventually became. Muggings were common. Racial tensions were high.

The first job Carol landed was as a waitress in a diner. Tips were generally bad, but she was allowed one meal per seven-hour shift (the food was much better than what was served at The Atlanta) and the other waitresses were all right, mostly leaving one another alone, occasionally lending one another a hand when the lunch rush was on. It was the owner who became a problem, with his wandering hands and habit of leering with his watery pale-blue eyes. After three weeks of dodging his disgusting attempts at seduction Carol lost her temper, loudly told him never to come near her again, and was promptly fired. There was no one to whom Carol felt she could complain and be heard.

Next, she worked at a five-and-dime. That was bearable if boring, and she only left when the store closed its doors due to lack of business. One of the girls at The Atlanta suggested Carol look for work as a nanny. Carol ignored the suggestion; she had no interest in children.

Office work was not a possibility at first. She had no suitable clothes and few secretarial skills; she didn't even bother to sign up with a temp agency, not until she could afford something smart to wear and until she had practiced on the typewriter one of the staff at The Atlanta rented out for such purposes.

Within a few weeks of her arrival at The Atlanta, Carol found herself chums with three other girls who had come to New York

City with the dream of a life nothing like the one they had left behind. Years later, Carol was to realize that each of these girls had been very much a "type"; no doubt she had appeared to them as another "type."

Annie hailed from a small town in Colorado. She was a self-proclaimed wild child, a dope smoker, a dabbler in hard drugs, into the downtown music and art scene, a believer in free love. She was also sweet, and Carol liked Annie enough to go with her one night to a club on the Lower East Side. The club wasn't Carol's scene. The music was too loud and half of the revelers were zoned out. Carol didn't like to be out of control, or to be around people who were.

Annie died of a drug overdose about four months later. Her body, lying crumpled in an alley between two buildings, had not been found for several days after her death.

Betty, who had the room to the right of Carol's, had been in the city for about eight months when she became engaged to a very rich, older man. Betty was smug about her success; it was what she had come to New York from a small town in Ohio to achieve. She wasn't naïve. She knew—or claimed she knew—just what sort of situation she was signing on for. The day she moved out of The Atlanta, fetched by one of her fiancé's staff in a big black limousine, she was wearing a fur wrap and a large diamond and emerald ring, both gifts from her soon-to-be husband.

For several years after, Carol noted her former housemate in the society pages, smiling and magnificently decked out, until one day she realized she hadn't seen any tidbit about Mrs. Giles Treehorn for some time. A little asking around unearthed the information that Mr. Treehorn had divorced her for wife number four, an ingénue originally from Kansas City. Carol never knew what happened to the former Mrs. Giles Treehorn, nee Betty Murphy, but she had a pretty good idea of what might have become of her.

Andrea, the third girl Carol had gotten to know at The Atlanta, had moved on about the time Carol had done. Carol had not seen or heard from Andrea for twenty-five years when she ran into her one evening in the ladies' room of a swanky hotel bar. Andrea was a partner in a law firm that specialized in corporate real-estate deals. She had come to New York City to pursue a career in the art gallery scene; that had not worked out, so she had cut her losses and gone to law school. Carol admired her old chum's practicality. She told Andrea that she had her own interior design firm. "You were one of the lucky ones," Andrea commented. "You found what you came to the city to find." They exchanged business cards. One said something about getting together for a drink one evening. It might have been Carol. They never did.

Back in those early years, Carol remembered, she had lied to her family in her letters, told them her life was just fine, and had actively discouraged them from visiting. She couldn't stand them to be witness to her tiny room at The Atlanta or, later, to the crappy little hovel on the Lower East Side to which she retired each evening; she didn't want them to know that she cleaned toilets for a living, when she wasn't waiting tables in a shabby diner.

And she hadn't wanted to give Bonnie the chance to smirk at what was so obviously not the glamourous life her big sister had left home to find.

But maybe Bonnie wouldn't have smirked. Maybe she would have offered a genuine word of comfort.

It was too late to know.

Carol sighed. What a true success Bonnie had made of her life. She was loved and admired by family, friends, and the community. If that wasn't a triumph, then nothing was.

Suddenly, Carol was struck by a frightening thought. Maybe all those years in New York, fighting to survive on her own, had ruined her for a simple life with her family. Maybe she was no longer capable of learning how to truly connect with them in a way that would prove beneficial to them all.

The thought was heartbreaking.

Abruptly, Carol stood from her father's armchair and strode toward the front door. She would go for a drive. She needed to get away from Ferndean.

Chapter 91

"I love this view," Nicola said. "That big, old white pine is just magical."

"Your aunt used to spend hours under that tree reading," Carol replied. "She was at the library almost every day of summer break. I imagine she belongs to a book group today."

"Actually," Nicola told her mother, "when Uncle Ken got sick he needed an awful lot of care and Aunt Bonnie quit everything, her book group, her quilting circle. She even had to stop doing the accounting for the garage. Luckily, she had been training one of the Elgort cousins to take over one day."

"I'm sorry to hear that," Carol said. "Poor Bonnie. Always sacrificing herself for others."

"I don't think she'd want our pity," Nicola said. "She made her choices freely." Still, Nicola thought, gazing out over the expanse of green behind Ferndean House. Who had ever taken care of Bonnie? Besides Ken, that is. But now he was gone. . . .

Suddenly, Nicola remembered what Judith had told her, that Bonnie had never made peace with the fact that Carol and Ken had dated. If that was true, and Judith didn't lie, then her aunt had in some ways been her own worst enemy all these years.

Sitting side by side with her mother this mid-summer afternoon, Nicola believed they had reached enough of a state of détente for her to mention this interesting bit of the family's past without causing a blowup.

"I only recently found out that you and Ken dated before you left for New York," she said evenly. "I was at Julie's and I came across on old picture. Ken's arm was around your waist. Julie explained. And then I talked to Bonnie."

Her mother's eyes widened. "It never occurred to me that you might not know. I figured that living in Yorktide these past ten years you would have heard the gossip. I'm rather amazed that you didn't."

"Would people have tried to keep it a secret from me?" Nicola asked.

"I don't know why. Ken and I were totally unsuited, as I'm sure you can believe."

"So, what attracted you to him?" Nicola asked.

Her mother smiled. "He was very handsome."

"Just physical attraction?" Nicola pressed.

"No, Ken was a good guy, one of the best. I don't have to tell you that."

"He was. He . . ." Nicola took a steadying breath. "He really became a father to me. I didn't understand until I came here to live with Bonnie and Ken just what I had been missing."

"I'm very glad you had Ken in your life," her mother replied softly. "And I'm so very sorry I didn't visit Yorktide when I got back from India. I should have."

Nicola felt a wave of gratitude. "Thank you," she said. "Your apology means a lot."

"And thank you for talking to me about your uncle. About it all. The past is always with us. We can't ever outrun it." Her mother smiled. "Your aunt would be shocked to hear me say that. She thinks I have no respect for what's gone before. But I do."

Nicola knew that her mother had respect for the past; why else would she have kept Nicola's childhood bedroom exactly as it had been the last day Nicola had slept there?

"Do you miss New York?" Nicola asked. The question hadn't occurred to her before now. It was an important one.

"Yes," her mother said promptly. "It's been—it was—my home for the majority of my life."

Nicola waited a moment before asking another, even more important question. "Are you sure this is what you really want, Mom? A life in Yorktide?'"

"I want to be close to you and to my sister," her mother said carefully.

It was an answer, if a slightly evasive or opaque answer.

Yes. Something had changed for Carol Ascher, or it was beginning to. Nicola wanted to know what it was.

"All right," she said.

What she couldn't quite bring herself to add was: And I want to be close to you.

Soon, Nicola thought, glancing at her mother's regal profile. Soon.

Chapter 92

It hadn't been difficult to learn where Lacy Fox lived—she was listed in the local phone book—or to learn that Laci worked mostly evening shifts as a bartender at an Irish pub on Route 1 in Wells.

What was difficult was gathering the nerve to show up at her house, uninvited and unexpected.

Julie was not a confrontational person; she was by nature generally content to remain in the background, happy to let others take the spotlight. But there were rare moments when every instinct urged Julie to speak out. This was one of those moments.

The idea had first come to her while driving home from Judith's the other day. They had been talking about Julie's applying for the Ackroyd scholarship, and Judith had pointed out that it was Julie's choice to make. Julie had realized the power she possessed in that situation. Why not exercise the power of choice in another?

Still, she was unsure of what she hoped to achieve by confronting the woman with whom Scott had had an affair. An apology? An explanation? Whatever her goal, Julie had no doubt that Scott would be mortified if he knew what she was planning to do. How her daughter would feel she could only guess; Sophie might be embarrassed or proud. As for what her mother, aunt, or cousins would think . . .

For this momentous venture, Julie dismissed any concern regarding her clothing. She knew she was not looking her best. What was the point in donning what would essentially be a disguise? She was who she was.

Scott had gone off to work and Sophie to camp when Julie left her house. She had lived all of her life in Yorktide and yet had never been to the part of the town in which Laci Fox made her home. It only went to show that neighbors could be strangers and that there were social dividing lines in even the most hospitable of small communities.

After taking two wrong turns, Julie finally arrived at Pebble Way. There were only three houses on this stretch of road; the first house, on Julie's right, was Number One. Julie continued on until she reached the one house on the left side of the road. Number Two. There was no curb or sidewalk.

The house was very small and fairly run-down. The tiny bit of yard out front hadn't been mowed in months and a broken road bike lay on its side in the tall grass. Given the state of general disrepair and the air of disregard, Julie was surprised to see a pair of bright yellow curtains in the windows of the front room and a flourishing green plant on the windowsill.

With a steadying breath, Julie got out of her car and, clutching the strap of her bag, walked up the narrow, broken concrete path to the front door of the house. There didn't seem to be a bell so after a moment's hesitation, Julie knocked on the door. She waited for a response, heart pounding. There was no going back now.

When at least thirty or forty seconds had gone by, Julie raised her fist to knock again, but the door suddenly opened and for the first time Julie was face-to-face with her nemesis.

Laci Fox was not as young as Julie had assumed her to be, maybe in her mid-thirties rather than mid-twenties. She was wearing a Boston Red Sox T-shirt and jeans torn at the knee. Her hair, dark at the roots, dull blond thereafter, was scraped back into a messy ponytail. She wore no makeup; her skin was a bit rough. Her eyes, though, were bright and blue. Otherwise she was fairly average all around, Julie thought. Middling height, not thin nor fat. Just a woman. Just a person. What then had been her appeal for Scott?

That she was not his wife.

"Yes?" Laci Fox said. Her tone was neutral though not particularly friendly. Well, why should it be?

Julie cleared her throat. "Laci Fox?" she asked, just to be sure.

The woman frowned. "Who wants to know?"

"I'm Julie Miller."

For a moment, the woman's face registered nothing, not surprise or fear or recognition. Then, she abruptly folded her arms across her chest. "Oh," she said.

"Can I come in?" Julie asked.

"No," Laci said quickly. She unfolded her arms, stepped outside, and closed the door behind her.

Julie looked over her shoulder, half expecting a crowd to have gathered.

"No one comes by here," Laci said. "If you're afraid of someone seeing you."

Julie decided not to respond to the comment. "I want to talk to you."

Laci shrugged. "Go ahead then."

"I . . . You slept with my husband."

"Yeah." Her reply was ready; her tone was flat. "It was just a bit of fun."

Julie, having half expected a denial, was overcome by surprise and confusion. She felt tears spring to her eyes. A bit of fun. A bit of fun was dancing on top of a table at the local watering hole on a Saturday night because your BFF dared you to. A bit of fun was not sleeping with a married man.

"I swore I wouldn't cry," she blurted.

Laci reached into the back pocket of her jeans and removed a folded tissue. "Here," she said, offering it to Julie. "It's clean."

Julie took the tissue and wiped at her eyes. "Thanks," she murmured.

"Look," Laci said abruptly, "don't let it get to you. All men are rats. The difference between you and me is that you still give men the benefit of the doubt while I don't waste my time."

Julie hesitated to ask her next question, but she needed to know the answer. "Didn't you think of me?" she said. "Didn't you wonder what I would feel?"

Laci shrugged. "Sorry. Not really. I mean, a guy who cheats on his wife, with no big persuasion on my part, I figure his wife knows what he's like and puts up with it for whatever reason she's got. For the money. Security. The sake of the kids. Some outdated religious belief. Whatever."

Julie thought about that. Putting up with infidelity. It wasn't quite the same as putting up with messy eating habits or a nervous tic like the one her father had of drumming his fingers on the arm of his chair while watching television.

"I don't put up with infidelity," she said stoutly. "I won't."

"Good for you," Laci Fox said. And then she looked slightly embarrassed. At least, Julie thought that she did. "I'm sorry you feel bad, really," Laci went on. "I mean, you're not the one who should. If anyone should be feeling miserable it should be Scott."

Julie nodded. "I know. He does."

"But it's not enough for you." It was a statement. "Will it ever be enough?"

"I don't know." And then: "What makes you the way you are, cold and unfeeling?"

Laci laughed. She didn't seem offended. "Cold? Unfeeling? I'm not either. Just practical about certain things. I learned long ago that happiness has a lot to do with managing your expectations. Don't expect much, don't get disappointed much."

"I never want to be that way," Julie said. "It sounds so sad."

Laci laughed again. "To each her own."

"I don't know why I came here."

"You hoped for some answers. You hoped to find that I was an evil bitch who forced your husband into an affair against his will. Or something like that." Laci turned and opened the door of her home. "I'm busy now," she said.

Julie nodded. "Goodbye." She turned to walk away and then stopped and looked over her shoulder. "I'm sorry," she said. She wasn't sure why she had.

"You don't have to be sorry," Laci replied.

Julie got back in her car. For a while she drove without a destination in mind; eventually, she found herself at Ogunquit Beach and pulled into the crowded parking lot. Even after all these years it still felt strange to live in a community that was virtually taken over by strangers for a few months every year.

She wasn't sure what exactly she had accomplished by confronting Laci, but she felt okay. Proud of herself for having remained—largely—in control of her emotions and for maintaining her dignity.

Yes. Her dignity.

And she had realized something. Distance made it easy to demonize a person, and she had demonized Laci Fox. But Laci was not a demon, nor was she a harridan, bitch, whore, or any of the other terms used to condemn a woman who flouted societal conventions. She was simply a person, flawed, disappointed, not happy but not necessarily unhappy, trying her best to make her way through life.

Sitting there in that crowded parking lot, hearing the cries of seagulls, the conversation of adults, the happy squeals of children, Julie realized that she forgave Laci Fox for her part in the affair. She did not want to become Laci's friend and confidant, but she also did not need to have her as an enemy.

The question remained: Could she learn to forgive herself as easily as she had forgiven the Other Woman?

If there was anything for which to forgive herself.

There was still so much work to be done. But Julie felt she had taken the first step.

Chapter 93

How things had changed since that disastrous dinner party weeks ago, Bonnie thought, when every member of the family had been at each other's throats or mired in personal misery.

Here she was, once again at Ferndean House, having been invited for a meal by her sister. And this time, Bonnie was glad to be there. At least, she wasn't bristling with anger and that was an improvement. And it made her feel good to see that Ferndean was being cared for. It looked as clean and tidy as it had been the day Carol had arrived at the start of the summer. The grounds, too, were in good shape. The grass was being mowed and the flower beds regularly watered. She herself had been keeping an eye on the vegetable and herb gardens.

Still, Bonnie was curious to know why Carol hadn't made any significant changes yet; Nicola and Judith had noticed this as well. And it had been some time since Carol had last brought up the subject of Ferndean's future. Of the family's future. Maybe that meant something. Maybe it meant nothing. Bonnie's policy for the afternoon was to remain silent on the topic of Ferndean.

"Do you find Nicola a bit reserved?" Carol asked her sister.

The two women were in the kitchen. Carol was wearing a pair of floaty linen pants with a matching linen top. Bonnie was in cotton shorts and a T-shirt.

"I suppose I do," Bonnie said after a moment.

"She wasn't that way as a little girl," her sister said, taking things out of the fridge for their lunch. "She was full of high spirits. One of her teachers suggested she be on an ADHD drug. I was appalled by the suggestion, but I took her to see a child psychiatrist anyway, and thankfully, she dismissed the idea as ridiculous. Nicola, she said, was simply an energetic, bright, and curious child. In short, normal."

"And she's still normal. There's nothing wrong with being reserved," Bonnie pointed out. Briefly, she wondered if Carol blamed her for the change in Nicola's behavior. But Carol's tone had not been angry or accusatory. "I'd say it's something that often comes with maturing."

"You're right, as long as it's a conscious choice and not the result of repressed emotions." Carol waved her hand. "Ignore me. Yes, even Carol Ascher worries too much at times."

"You're a mother," Bonnie stated. "Worry is what mothers do. I lie awake nights thinking about Julie. And I scold myself for not being able to help her."

"I think that Julie's journey home has begun," her sister said. "Beginnings are always rocky, of course, one step forward, two steps back, but at least there's motion."

"I'm not sure I've seen what you have," Bonnie said with a sigh. "But I hope you're right."

Carol put out the final component of their lunch. There was ham and cheese for sandwiches; a plate of sliced tomatoes, red onions, and shredded bits of Romaine lettuce; a bowl of bread and butter pickles; a selection of condiments; and a fruit salad drizzled with balsamic vinegar. Bonnie thought that strange.

"Taste it," Carol urged.

Bonnie did. "This is delicious," she said. "I never would have thought to add balsamic vinegar to fruit."

Carol smiled. "You know me, always a fan of new adventures."

"On the subject of new adventures," Bonnie said after a moment's hesitation, "you asked me not long ago if I was thinking about going back to work. Well, I have been. But I have to admit I find the idea very daunting. Acquiring new skills. Going on interviews. Competing with younger people, and probably even having to work for them. I don't know where to begin."

"Let me help," Carol said. "Sometimes two heads are better than one."

Like when they were small, Bonnie thought. Carol was always the leader and Bonnie the follower, but that didn't mean they hadn't been together in their adventures.

"We could practice interviewing," Carol went on. "I could help you craft a résumé. Or maybe none of that is necessary. You might be able to make good money selling your quilts. You could set up an online presence, maybe open a shop on Etsy or hire someone to build a website."

"I'm not sure about online," Bonnie said quickly. She was not a big fan of the computer and wasn't even on Facebook, unlike pretty much everyone else she knew. "But there is a wonderful quilt shop in town. I know the owners pretty well, actually, but I've never attempted to place anything on commission with them. The truth is, I never thought in terms of a career."

"You don't necessarily have to now," Carol pointed out. "What I mean is, try not to separate life into job versus home, career versus family. In any case, it can't hurt to talk to the owners of the shop. What's it called?"

"The Busy Bee. It's owned by Adelaide Kane and Cindy Bauer. Now that I think about it, it's only one of several of local businesses owned by women."

"Obviously, I've always been a fan of women owning their own businesses. I—" Carol's next sentence was interrupted by a yawn. "Excuse me," she said. "I shouldn't be tired. I slept for eight hours last night and ten the night before that but somehow, I can't seem to wake up."

"Maybe you're just feeling relaxed for the first time in years," Bonnie suggested. Ferndean House working its magic on Carol Ascher? Maybe.

The doorbell rang before Carol could comment.

"That must be Nicola," she said, hurrying from the kitchen.

A moment later, Carol returned with Nicola at her side.

"I was passing that farm stand that sells the sour cherry pies you're mad about, Aunt Bonnie," she said, settling two cardboard boxes on the counter. "So, I bought you one to take home. And the other one is for you, Mom. Oh, good, lunch is ready. I'm starved!"

Nicola began to put together a sandwich piled high with pickles, tomato, onion, and lettuce.

"I didn't know you liked Dijon mustard," Bonnie noted as Nicola reached for the jar of Grey Poupon.

"It's what we had at home when I was growing up," Nicola told her. She took a bite of her sandwich and rolled her eyes heavenward. "I forgot how much I liked it," she said when she had swallowed.

Bonnie smiled, but the truth was that she felt a bit left out. Nicola had never asked her aunt to buy Dijon mustard; she had used the yellow mustard the Elgorts preferred without complaint. The memory of Nicola's giving Carol a hug after dinner at Judith's house flashed across Bonnie's mind and suddenly, for the first time in a very long time, Bonnie realized just how little she knew of Nicola's early years with Carol. Her mother. The two must have been so close. Mother and daughter against the world.

"Are you okay, Aunt Bonnie?" Nicola asked. "You've hardly touched your sandwich."

Bonnie smiled. "Just wool-gathering," she said. "It happens a lot at my age."

Chapter 94

"I'm going to have another sandwich."

Carol smiled. A mother always liked to see her child eat. Now she could only pray that Nicola wouldn't mention the fact of her mother having dated Ken once upon a time. It might create an awkward moment, especially given that Carol still hadn't apologized for lying to her sister about the breakup. Some topics were better left to the Ascher sisters alone to hammer out.

"Ah, to be young again," Bonnie said, patting her stomach. "I remember eating an entire half gallon of ice cream at one sitting! These days, I'd have to fast for a month afterward."

"And I'd have to take an entire bottle of Lactaid beforehand," Carol added. "Ice cream in limited quantities is definitely the way to go once you're over the age of thirty."

"So, what were you guys talking about when I came in?" Nicola asked. "Not ice cream, I bet."

"I was telling your mother that I've been thinking about getting a job," Bonnie said.

"Really?" Nicola said, her hand hovering over the plate of sliced cheese. "I think that's a great idea. You've a lot more to give than what you give to your family."

That, Carol realized, was probably very true.

Bonnie laughed. "Me?"

"Don't be self-effacing," Carol scolded. "Better to acknowledge your talents honestly. And by that I don't mean bragging, just accepting that you have certain skills and strengths."

"What was your big career break, Mom?" Nicola asked. "Doesn't every successful person have a big break moment?"

"I don't know about that," Carol said honestly. "All I know is what happened in my case. Do you really want to hear this?"

Both her sister and daughter said, "Yes."

"Okay. Well," Carol began, "I'd been in New York close to two years, earning next to no money, working ridiculous jobs, and beginning to feel I'd made a colossal mistake in coming to New York."

"I had no idea you second-guessed your decision," Bonnie said, eyes wide.

For a moment, Carol didn't know how to respond. Had Bonnie really thought anyone who did something as crazy as move from a sleepy little town to a major metropolis at the age of nineteen would *not* have second thoughts?

"Well, my doubts weren't something I was proud of," Carol said finally, "and certainly not something I was going to admit to the people back home in Yorktide."

"Even your family?" Bonnie said.

"Telling family would have made the shame worse." Nicola shrugged. "At least, that's what I would have felt."

Carol nodded. "Exactly. Anyway," she went on, "one day I was roaming the home furnishings department in Bloomingdale's. Bloomingdale's was pretty important back then; even Queen Elizabeth visited and designers like Ralph Lauren got their first really big opportunities there. It was a regular stop in my week, off the dirty, crime-ridden streets and into the cool and relative quiet of an important retail experience. I'd spend hours taking note of colors and fabrics, observing what piece of furniture worked next to another and what pieces didn't. Sometimes, I'd even subtly rearrange displays of table trinkets. The salespeople knew me and as soon as they'd seen I wasn't there to make trouble they mostly left me alone to . . . well, to dream I suppose."

Nicola laughed. "You were lucky they didn't call the police on you!"

"I wouldn't have had the nerve to hang around without having the money to buy something," Bonnie admitted.

"That's me," Carol said with a laugh. "Always pushing boundaries. Or maybe it was the reckless bravery of youth. Anyway, that particular day I was wearing a Mary Quant dress I had found in a resale shop in the Village. I'd been poking around among the lamps and side tables for about a half hour when this exceedingly well-dressed man approached me, thinking I was a salesperson, and asked if I could show him the new line of sofas. I wasn't even flustered. In that moment, I believed I was an employee of Bloomingdale's and I immediately began to act like one. It was only after he asked for detailed information on the pieces, like what other fabrics and colors were available, that I realized I was in trouble. Suddenly, the manager of the department was hurrying over, wringing his hands, apologizing effusively to Mr. Spencer—that was my customer's name it seemed—for any inconvenience. Then he turned to me with a look that could have killed and said, "Do you know who this is you have been bothering? This is Mr. Spencer, the celebrated interior designer."

"How embarrassing!" Bonnie cried.

"I was shaking in my shoes," Carol admitted. "I'd never seen a picture of the famed Mr. Spencer, so how was I supposed to know who he was? Mr. Spencer spoke up then and soothed the manager, and then asked me to accompany him to the store's restaurant— there was one for the wealthier customers, white linen tablecloths and ladies who lunched dressed in the heavy-hitter designers, Givenchy and Chanel—and though I was in a bit of a daze, I went along and over tea and scones he asked about me. Where I was from. Why I had come to New York. Did I have a job? At the end of our meal he offered me a place in his studio."

"You didn't wonder if he was just a guy on the make?" Nicola asked.

"Not for a moment," Carol said. "He was a gentleman. He just wasn't the type to use and abuse people, you could see that right away. And the deference in which he was regarded by the embarrassed manager and the way he was greeted by so many of those wealthy, elegant ladies at lunch—he was Somebody. The very next morning I showed up for work at his studio on Seventh Avenue. And that's where my real education and career began."

"You've had a charmed life," Nicola said with a smile.

How little Nicola knew! Then again, Carol thought, whose fault was that? "In some ways, yes," she said. "In other ways, I paid my dues and then some."

"We all do." Bonnie looked at Carol with an expression of—what? Conciliation? "You never know someone until you've walked a mile in their shoes."

"No one is only what she appears to be," Carol said with a smile for her sister.

"Why didn't you ever tell us this story before?" Nicola asked.

"I don't know," Carol admitted. It was the truth. Could she have remained silent because she didn't think her family would be interested? Or had she thought that sharing the story of her good fortune would be seen as bragging about her connections to the rich and famous?

"Where is this Mr. Spencer now?" Bonnie asked.

"He died in 1991. He was a victim of the AIDS crisis." Carol shook her head. "That was a horrible time in New York. So many sick and dying. Such talented lives cut short. I likely would have been chewed up and spit out of the city like countless other young dreamers if not for Mr. Spencer. Luck plays a part in life, or fate or chance, call it what you will. Maybe charm is the term, like Nicola said."

"This is kind of off the subject," Nicola began, "but maybe not really. We had this speaker at Pine Hill the other day and she was talking about women and their relationship to work. She said what's important about working is not only the financial reimbursement for services rendered, but also the real fulfillment we get from whatever it is we do. At one point, she used this great phrase, 'kin keeping,' to describe what women—well, mostly women—do so well, keeping the family close and in touch, whether it's by sending birthday cards or calling the grandparents on a regular basis or organizing family reunions." Nicola shrugged. "I guess I'm only now beginning to realize how important that job is."

Carol was silent. Kin keeping was not something she had known how to do or, to be truthful, had wanted to do. Maybe it wasn't too late to learn from Bonnie, clearly a master.

"The speaker also said this really fantastic thing," Nicola went on. "She said, 'A successful woman is one who can build a firm foundation with bricks others have thrown at her.'"

Carol felt her heart leap. "That's one of my favorite quotes," she said. "I've used it a thousand times when talking to other women, old and young, about crafting a meaningful life."

"Maybe," Bonnie put in, looking from Carol to Nicola, "the apple hasn't fallen that far from the tree after all."

Nicola nodded. "We do share DNA. All three of us."

At that moment, Carol felt closer to her sister and daughter than she had felt all summer. As tears threatened, she reached quickly for the pie server. "We do, indeed," she said. "Now, who wants a piece of this gorgeous cherry pie?"

The party broke up not long after. When her guests had gone, Carol put away the rest of the food and loaded the new, energy-efficient dishwasher. She believed that the afternoon had been a great success. She had sensed no underlying tensions; perhaps they had been there but were simply being kept under control. That was all right.

Carol glanced around the kitchen. She remembered her mother saying grace before each meal. She remembered her father having a glass of milk with his lunch and a glass of ginger ale with his dinner every day of every week. She remembered her sister scarfing her food in order to get to dessert sooner rather than later. She remembered them all laughing.

And Carol? What had she been doing?

She had been counting the minutes until she was free to be somewhere else.

Chapter 95

Nicola was stretched out on her bed, the fan aimed at her neck and chest, several books tumbled around her. She always slept with books in the bed. They were excellent companions, day or night.

It was about nine o'clock. Her mother had sent her home earlier with half of a cherry pie and Nicola had eaten a slice for her dinner. She hadn't been all that hungry, not after eating two big sandwiches for lunch. Followed by that scrumptious pie.

But the best part of the afternoon had been listening to her mother's story of meeting Mr. Spencer, her guardian angel. Envisioning her mother as a twenty-one-year-old pretending to be someone she was not but hoped one day to be . . . The image made her smile. Carol Ascher had always had pluck, guts, drive, call it what you will. It was admirable.

No doubt about it, Nicola thought. Her relationship with her mother was improving, and she was glad for it. Her mother, the woman who had given her life—along with that anonymous sperm donor, whoever and wherever he was. Did men like her father ever regret not knowing their own flesh and blood? And if they didn't— why? How did you casually contribute to the making of a new life and then walk away?

Nicola didn't want to judge or condemn. She did want to understand, but that might never happen. What she did know—and was maybe coming to understand, just a bit—was her mother. And she felt more hopeful than ever that Carol and Bonnie could mend fences and come to an amicable agreement about Ferndean House and, more importantly, about their future as sisters.

Suddenly, Nicola recalled her mother reminding her of all the things she had left behind in their New York City home. That statue from Paris. Toys. Books. Photographs. Maybe, Nicola thought, she would use her upcoming vacation days to visit the place of her birth. It felt important somehow to focus on what was in front of her in the present—her family—rather than on a future in a far-off place like Eastern Europe.

To keep her kin.

She remembered, however, what her mother had said about keeping her intentions to herself until she was one hundred percent sure of her commitment. So, she would say nothing but continue to imagine walking into the apartment where she had spent many happy years watching scary movies with her mother on the big-screen television in the library; decorating the Christmas tree in the living room while her mother hung wreaths on doors and draped greenery across mantelpieces; hanging out in the kitchen while her mother prepared dinner, regaling her with tales of what had happened at school that day.

For a very long time it had all been very good. It was important to remember that.

Nicola reached for a book—it almost didn't matter which one—adjusted the fan, and scooted down in the bed to read.

And to dream.

Chapter 96

People. Real Simple. Vogue. Julie chose the current issue of *O*. The waiting rooms in which she usually found herself had awful options. But this waiting room was different. There was a refreshment station offering herbal teas, enhanced water, and refreshing spritzers. The music playing was low and melodic. The temperature was perfect.

Julie was treating herself to a massage at a salon in a town ten miles from Yorktide. A professional wouldn't make (or think?) disparaging remarks about her body. And Julie very much needed a healing touch, especially after the emotionally fraught scene that had taken place a few nights earlier.

Sophie had gone to a party given by one of the junior counselors. Ten o'clock, Sophie's curfew, came and went. Julie had sent her a text, asking if she was okay. Sophie's response had been brief and vague.

Waiting for my ride.

Be home soon.

It's cool.

For the first time in months, Scott and Julie, husband and wife, father and mother, had stood together in parenting. They were worried. They were annoyed. Scott blamed himself.

"I shouldn't have allowed her to go," he said, shaking his head as he paced the living room. "It's that crowd. They're trouble. She's never ignored her curfew before."

"It isn't your fault," Julie had told him, half surprised that she was reassuring her errant husband. "Besides, we don't know for sure that anything is wrong." But her stomach had been in knots.

Sophie had tiptoed in near midnight. She was surprised to find her parents waiting for her.

"I thought you'd be in bed," she said, nervously tucking her hair behind her ear.

Scott had frowned. "You thought wrong."

"We trusted you to act responsibly," Julie added. "You betrayed that trust. If your ride went missing, you should have called us and we would have come to get you."

Sophie had turned to Scott. "Dad," she said, with a whine she often used when she wanted something from her father, "you know how it is when you're having a good time and—"

But Scott was having none of it. "I'm one hundred percent with your mother on this," he said firmly. "You're grounded for one week. You can go to work and you'll come right home."

There had been tears. There had been words to the effect that Julie and Scott were the most unfair parents in the world.

When Sophie was safely in her room, Scott had turned to Julie with a small smile. "Well, she hates us. Again."

"But we did the right thing," Julie said. For a passing moment, she was filled with tenderness and was tempted to ask him to sleep with her in their bed that night. But she had remained silent.

"Julie?"

Julie stood, dropping the magazine and clutching her bag to her chest. "Yes," she said. "That's me."

She followed the young woman who had come to fetch her down a corridor painted a pretty pale blue. She had felt guilty about spending the money on herself, but something her aunt had said helped to assuage that guilt. "What used to be called pampering is now called self-care," Carol had told her over lunch at The Green Apple. "I think the term is more accurate. Learning how to take proper care of yourself can be a very hard lesson to learn. Start small. Treat yourself to a pedicure or a facial. Let the feeling good happen from there."

Julie was left in the dressing room to change into a plush white terrycloth robe and store her belongings in a locker. When she had done so she took a deep breath.

She was ready for an adventure.

Scott's car was in the drive when Julie returned home. As she walked through the front door he came hurrying from the kitchen.

"Where were you?" he asked. "I was worried. You're always here and—Wait. Your hair. It looks good. It looks great."

Julie smiled. "Thanks for noticing," she said. So, it had been worth the last-minute decision to stop for a haircut and blowout after the massage.

"I always notice you, Julie," he said. "Always."

Julie knew this was true. It was why he had been so worried about her. He had been witness to her anguish. He hadn't turned his back. In that moment, Julie felt a shiver of longing for her husband, her friend, her companion in life.

Scott followed her into the kitchen.

"I thought I'd make that Mexican dish you like," Julie said. She didn't look directly at Scott as she spoke. But her back wasn't to him, either.

"Are you sure it's not too much trouble?" His voice betrayed an excitement that had nothing to do with food.

"No trouble. I do need some things from the store, though."

"Make a list. I'll run out right now."

Julie reached for the notepad she kept on the counter by the toaster oven. She thought about what Carol had said about self-care. The same message could hold for the care of a relationship.

Start small. Let the feeling good happen from there.

Chapter 97

Bonnie had just finished cleaning the bedroom she had shared with Ken for so many years. His clothes still hung in the closet and sat in the bottom two drawers of the dresser. One day she would bring the best of the clothing to the charity shop in town. But not quite yet. She went across the hall to the bedroom that had once been Julie's and then Nicola's. It hadn't been used since the last time Sophie had come for a sleepover. That must have been at least three years before, Bonnie thought sadly as she stood looking around at the yellow walls; at the narrow bed neatly made, with one of Bonnie's own quilts folded across the foot; at the small desk one of Ken's carpenter friends had made as a gift for Julie on her twelfth birthday. That was what she had wanted from her parents. A desk.

Nicola had used the desk in her turn. Bonnie could almost see her niece there now, head bent over her homework. The vision was too bittersweet and Bonnie turned from the room and went downstairs to the kitchen to make a cup of tea.

She had enjoyed the time she had spent with Carol and Nicola at Ferndean the other day, in spite of her usual misgivings. What had been particularly moving to witness was the relative ease with which Carol and her daughter had interacted. Things had changed since the start of summer, when Nicola had adamantly refused even to see her mother, let alone to share a meal and conversation with her.

There was no denying it, Bonnie thought, as she put water on to boil. Carol and Nicola were alike, maybe in more ways than they currently realized. Most obviously, they each had a passion and had committed to it. And that funny quote about women building something good from the bricks people had thrown at them. Both Carol and Nicola had responded to that so enthusiastically. It wasn't impossible that over time they might grow closer, learn to accept their differences and celebrate their similarities.

Bonnie truly hoped this would be the case.

She did.

Nicola was no longer a child. And she never had been Bonnie's child. Sometimes, too often, Bonnie had forgotten that. She would force herself to remember this fact going forward. After all, she had her own child, and a grandchild. Her life had been a good one. She had no major regrets. She had never felt that she had been held back. She had lived a contented life. If she was given the chance she would do it all again—marry Ken, raise a child, care for her mother, and yes, even take in her niece.

Kin keeping. That was valid work.

Still, Bonnie thought, as she poured boiling water into a cup, maybe now was a good time for her to pay attention to herself.

All of the other women in her family showed respect for their passions. Judith had her gardening. Carol was a talented designer. Nicola's passion was for service. Julie's vocation was teaching.

And Bonnie's passion was twofold, quilting and caregiving. They each brought joy and challenges. The question was, could she parlay either of those passions into a job that would earn her income, without losing the component of joy that was so essential?

Yes, Bonnie thought. She could. Not caregiving; she had no desire to do that work on a professional level. But she wouldn't mind selling her quilts, even, as Carol had mentioned, taking on custom projects, and maybe also teaching basic and advanced needlework.

But to come face-to-face with a client or student or customer probably meant a makeover. Bonnie put down her half-empty cup of tea and considered her faded blue T-shirt and shorts. Maybe she would ask Judith to go shopping with her for some new, more tai-lored clothes. Judith had a good fashion sense.

Would she need to do something with her hair? Wear makeup? She hadn't worn makeup in at least twenty years! Bonnie's stom-ach began to flutter. And then she heard Ken. He was laughing. "Look at you getting all worked up over nothing," he was saying. "Bonnie, you're perfect the way you are. Everything's going to be all right. Now, get moving!"

And Bonnie did. Within moments she was in her car and headed for The Busy Bee. It had been too long since she had talked with her fellow craftswomen, with others who shared her passion, skills, and talents. She would have a friendly conversation with Adelaide and Cindy and see what developed from there.

All would be well. Ken had said so.

Chapter 98

Since she had sold her business, Carol rarely checked her e-mail. There was never anything of real importance these days—a note from a colleague suggesting a lunch date; the announcement of a sale from a store in which she had never shopped; a photo from a former client showing how they had added various personal touches to the interior Carol had created for them.

But this evening, curled up in Ferndean's den, she found an e-mail from Alex. Carol immediately opened the message. *I need to speak to you as soon as convenient*, it said. *I've something very important to discuss.*

Carol frowned; she couldn't remember how long it had been since she had heard Alex's voice. The last time they had communicated was when Carol had sent Alex a text telling him that she was headed off to Maine for the summer. She hadn't mentioned her plans regarding Ferndean.

For a moment, she wondered if Alex needed money. It seemed unlikely, but if he had fallen on hard times she would do what she could for him. No questions asked.

Carol looked at the time at the top right of her computer screen and compared it to the time at which Alex's e-mail had been sent. Just a few moments ago. Buenos Aires was only an hour ahead of New England. It was not too late to call.

Carol reached for her phone.

Alex answered almost immediately.

"You got my e-mail," he said.

"Just now. So, what is it you wanted to talk about?" Carol asked. She realized her body was tensing.

"I'm dying, Carol."

In spite of her shoulders feeling rigid, Carol laughed. She couldn't have said why. "What do you mean dying? We're all dying, from the moment we're born. Are you saying—"

"Yes, I have stage four pancreatic cancer. I have six to nine months to live. It's likely I won't make it to my seventy-sixth birthday."

Carol put her hand to her head. She felt odd. Cold. A bit dizzy. "Have you had a second and third opinion?" she asked.

"Of course. There's no doubt."

No doubt. No doubt that the father of her child was dying. "I'm so very sorry," she said, surprised at the steadiness of her voice. She did not feel steady. "I . . . I don't know what else to say. I don't know what to do."

"There is something very specific you can do for me, Carol," Alex went on. "I'd like to be introduced to our daughter. I know what I promised and if you think it would damage her too badly to learn the truth at this point, then I'll drop the whole thing. I'm not threatening exposure. Honestly. But I would very much like to speak with her before I die."

Carol felt a wave of panic surge through her. What would happen if Nicola learned the truth of her paternity? Would it drive her further away from her mother or bring her closer? Carol took a deep breath. This could not be about her, not any longer. She had to think only of her daughter. And of Alex.

"I don't know how Nicola would feel," she admitted. "I'm not her favorite person. I haven't been for a long time."

"But you're with her now in Maine?"

"Yes, but . . . Alex, I need to think about this. I won't delay, I promise. I want to do the right thing for the both of you. I'll call you with an answer before the end of the week. Is that all right?"

"Yes," Alex said. The relief in his voice was clear. "Carol? Thank you."

"Goodbye." Carol realized that she had whispered the word.

They had been on the phone for less than ten minutes, but in those ten minutes her entire world had turned upside down.

Carol put her hand over her heart. Alex had thanked her. But what did he have to thank her for? She had in effect denied him the experience of fatherhood and withheld the chance of his having a proper wife.

Still, this was the last thing she had expected to hear from Alex, that he wanted contact with their daughter, though why the possibility hadn't occurred to her before now she couldn't say. It was a reasonable request from a dying man. From any man who had been kept away from his child, because although Alex had agreed to Carol's terms regarding Nicola, he hadn't been in his right mind when he did so. He had been in love.

And Carol had always loved him for the gift he had given her. She imagined him all alone in Buenos Aires . . . although a man like Alex Peters could never be entirely alone; he was a talented friend and was sure to have a support system after all these years. For all she knew, Alex might even have a girlfriend.

Whatever the case, the father of her child was facing the final months of his life.

Carol felt too devastated to cry.

Chapter 99

"What's going on in that head?" Hermione asked. "You're a million miles away."

Nicola startled. She had been staring out the window of Hermione's living room, seeing nothing. Her mind, if not a million miles away, had been at least in another neighborhood of Yorktide. "I'm sorry," she said. "Really. Please, go on with your story."

Hermione, dressed impeccably as always, smiled and waved her hand. "It can wait. Tell me what's on your mind."

It might, Nicola thought, be unprofessional to confide in one of Pine Hill's residents, even one who had previously confided in her, but at the moment she felt she had little choice but to speak.

"It's kind of silly, really," she began, embarrassed. "Maybe it's a sort of existential crisis, if I'm not too young to be having one. It's just that for the past months I've been feeling there's something *else* I'm needed for in this life, but I don't know what it is. For a while I thought that maybe I was being called to join the Peace Corps, but now I think that maybe I'm needed closer to home."

Kin keeping, Nicola thought. But how?

Hermione leaned closer to Nicola. "Wait," she advised. "Listen. Breathe. The answer will come to you when you're ready to hear it. The universe will speak to you when it's ready to speak."

"I'm not very good at being patient," Nicola admitted. "I mean, with myself."

"Just give it a try." Hermione smiled again. "Trust me. I'm old enough to know these things."

Nicola felt the proverbial butterflies take flight in her stomach. "There's something else," she went on. "I mean, it's part of the same thing but . . . In the past few days, I've had the strangest sense that something is drawing near, that something big is going to happen. The thing is, I've never been particularly in touch with instinct or whatever you want to call it. It's all so odd."

"Life is odd," Hermione said. Her tone was kind. "And that's what makes it so interesting. Infuriating sometimes, almost unbearable at others, and at other times, heartbreakingly beautiful. You'll be all right, Nicola. All will be well."

Nicola reached for her friend's hand. And Hermione *was* a friend. "Thank you," she said feelingly. "Thank you."

Chapter 100

"I really like your new haircut. I think Dad really likes it, too."

Julie smiled up at her daughter. She was in her office and had been scribbling notes for the essay that was the major focus of the Ackroyd Institute's scholarship application when Sophie appeared. No stomping of feet this time or slamming of doors.

"Thanks," she said. "I like it, too."

Sophie perched on the windowsill. "I didn't mean it when I suggested you have an affair," she blurted. "I don't want you to get a divorce. I don't want to have to choose who I'm going to spend Thanksgiving and Christmas with for the rest of my life, tiptoeing around so that neither you or Dad feels left out. And I want my wedding to be happy. I want to take pictures with my mom and dad, not with a stepmother and a stepfather I hardly even know and don't want to know. And what if I have kids one day?" Sophie went on. "There'll be like a million grandparents fighting over who gets to see the baby on his birthday! And what if you or Dad don't get remarried and are all alone? Do you know how awful that will make me feel? Maybe even worse than if you got married to someone totally annoying."

Julie resisted a smile. Sophie was so young, unabashedly concerned with her own comfort. But could she be blamed for that?

"Most of all," Sophie went on, "I really do want you guys to be happy. I don't know what that means, exactly. You probably have to figure that out yourselves."

Julie's heart swelled. For a moment, she couldn't speak.

"You will figure it out, won't you, Mom?" Sophie went on. "What it will take for you and Dad to be happy?"

"I promise to try my very best," she said. That much was true.

"Thanks. I'll be in my room."

Sophie left the office as quietly as she had entered. A moment later, the doorbell rang and Julie got up to answer it. Her mother had asked if she could come by to return a book she had borrowed.

Julie realized she would be glad to see her.

Chapter 101

"Something's different," Bonnie noted as she stood in her daughter's kitchen. "But I can't put my finger on it."

Julie smiled. "New kitchen towels," she said, pointing to two bright floral printed towels hanging from the oven door. "It's amazing what a little color can bring to a room."

A little color, Bonnie thought, and a refreshed attitude. Julie had lost a few pounds. And she looked neater than she had in some time. And her hair was styled a bit differently.

Carol was right. Something was subtly better. Maybe Carol was in some small degree responsible for this change. All things were possible.

"Tea?" Julie asked.

Bonnie nodded. "Carol hasn't mentioned her plans to buy Ferndean from me in weeks," she said as her daughter filled the tea kettle. "I wonder what's going on."

"You could just ask her," Julie suggested.

"I'm afraid to," Bonnie admitted. "Things between us have been better, not perfect but better. I guess I want to enjoy that for a while." Bonnie laughed. "How crazy is that?"

Julie put two cups on the table. "You love your sister."

"Of course, I do. I always have and I always will."

"And I believe she loves you, Mom, and all of her family. Why else would she have come back to Yorktide? I mean, what's here for her other than you and me and Nicola and Judith? She's not exactly a nature lover or a beach bum."

"She came back for Ferndean," Bonnie said, but almost as if she was testing the truth of the statement.

Julie quirked an eyebrow. "If you believe that . . ."

Bonnie shook her head. "Oh, I don't know what I believe anymore. But I'm glad Carol came back. In spite of everything I'm glad. But don't tell her that."

"Mom," Julie laughed, "you're incorrigible!"

Chapter 102

Carol didn't know why she had told Alex she needed time to think about her decision. She *had* to tell Nicola about her father. Didn't she? Would it really be for the best?

Once again, Carol sat in Ferndean's cave-like den. Once again, the gloom fitted her mood. Melancholic. Regretful. Frightened.

The emerald necklace her parents had given her on her sixteenth birthday. It was probably her fault that it had gone missing. If she had been in the habit of taking it off before bed the tiny clasp might not have worn out and she would still have that tangible link to her childhood and to Yorktide.

How careless she had been with the things and worse, with the people most important to her!

Shirley and Ronald Ascher.

And dear Bonnie. Carol had never properly expressed her deep gratitude for the care she had given Nicola.

Carol put her hands over her eyes.

Little Jonathan's death.

The need for someone to genuinely mourn her, like she would mourn Alex when he was gone.

The realization of just how fragile and fleeting life was had been a prime motive for her coming home to Yorktide.

So yes. The answer was now clear.

First, she would tell Bonnie and Judith the whole story, every last unsavory bit of it. And she would ask for their advice about approaching Nicola. That was unprecedented. For better or worse, Carol had always done things her own way, even when that way involved upsetting or inconveniencing others. But in the past weeks she had come to realize that she was not in control of the dynamics in Yorktide, as she had not always been in control of other aspects of her life.

Ferndean and Yorktide had finally gotten the best of its famous daughter.

Chapter 103

Nicola felt restless. If there was room in her apartment to pace she would have paced. Hermione had said she needed to allow her path to reveal itself. She was supposed to relax and be patient. She was supposed to listen. To what? To the still, small voice within her?

But what if her hearing wasn't acute enough to hear a still, small voice, her own or anyone else's?

Nicola considered going out somewhere. Maybe for a walk. Maybe for a beer at one of the craft breweries that were so popular. Maybe to a movie. For the first time in a very long time, Nicola wished she had a friend to call, someone to hang out with, someone with whom she could laugh about silly things.

But she didn't.

Once, she had had her mother. But that was when she was a child. And her mother had had her.

A memory. Something she and her mother had talked about earlier that summer.

She had a memento of that night . . .

Suddenly, it was vital that Nicola find that old photograph. She was pretty certain she had stuck it between the pages of a book not long after she had moved in with her aunt and uncle. And as Nicola never got rid of a book, ever, the photo had to be there somewhere.

Not in the hardcover copy of *A Tale of Two Cities*. Not in the paperback edition of Jung's collected writings. Not in any of the mass market mysteries Nicola consumed like some people consumed potato chips.

Finally, the treasure revealed itself between the pages of a sociology textbook. Nicola sighed with relief. It showed mother and daughter the night they had gone to the Broadway premiere of *Seussical*. Nicola was wearing the purple dress she had liked so much. Her mother was wearing a casual suit; it might have been silk. She looked like a model.

It was a nice picture. She and her mother were smiling and holding hands. And yet . . .

Nicola frowned. Something was . . . wrong. Or missing. She shook her head. The image itself hadn't changed. It had always just been the two of them, mother and daughter. But now, something . . .

Nicola propped the photo against the nearest milk carton and continued to stare at it. Again, she was swamped with that strange feeling that something important was about to happen. She felt nervous and scared and excited, both apprehensive and eager to greet whatever it was that awaited her.

For a half a moment, Nicola considered calling her mother at Ferndean. Just to say hello. Maybe her mother would invite her over.

But she didn't reach for her phone.

Chapter 104

Julie pressed the start button on the dishwasher and closed the door to the machine. The daily kitchen cleanup had been done. A load of laundry was in the machine. There were a few items that needed ironing; Julie would get to them later. She would.

Things were changing.

Julie and Scott had acted in concert the night Sophie ignored her curfew.

Scott had noticed his wife's new haircut.

He had helped make the Mexican meal she had suggested.

The evening before, Julie had asked if he wanted to watch one of their favorite television shows with her.

Scott had sat on the couch with his wife but at the other end. Still, they were side by side and had shared a few comments on the plot and had laughed at the antics of the goofy character. Things had felt almost normal.

Julie found Scott in the garage repairing their ancient lawn-mower. It had been a gift from her father and mother when the Millers had bought the house. Though for the past three seasons it had been breaking down every few weeks, Scott refused to let it go.

"Still breathing life into that machine?" Julie asked with a smile.

Scott looked up and wiped his brow with the back of his hand.

"It's got a good two or three years in it," he said. "That's my story and I'm sticking to it."

"Can we talk?" she asked.

"Yes, of course. Do you want to go into the house?"

"No," Julie said. "Here's fine. I just want to know, if I hadn't confronted you, would you have gone on with the affair? I know you told me you'd decided to end it, but was that a lie?"

"No," Scott said immediately. "It was not a lie. I was sick about it. Sick of her and sick about hurting you and Sophie."

"I'd like to believe you."

Scott nodded. "You can. It's the truth."

"What else have you lied about?" Julie asked, not angrily.

"Nothing. I haven't lied to you about anything else, I swear."

Julie thought for a moment. She could continue to punish him, snap back with a reply on the order of: "And I'm supposed to believe that?" and then the cycle of blame and shame would continue. Or, she could let the comment go. She could choose to believe it or not, but either way she could keep her remarks to herself and listen.

"All right," she said. She turned to go.

"Thank you for talking to me, Julie. Anything is better than your silence."

Julie looked back at her husband. "Even my anger?" she asked.

"Yes," Scott said, and there was a catch in his throat.

Julie smiled and went back to the house. She wondered what Scott would think of her applying for the Ackroyd Institute's scholarship. She thought he would be proud of her.

And at that very moment Julie decided to finish the essay she had begun and reach for the prize. But not for Scott. Or for Sara.

For herself.

Chapter 105

Carol had asked her sister to come to Ferndean as there was something important she had to say.

Bonnie wondered. Could Carol be abandoning her plans to settle at Ferndean House? Judith would be there this afternoon as well; maybe Carol wanted to open negotiations again and hoped that Judith would act as mediator.

Bonnie got into her car. Things were different now than they had been when Carol first came back to Yorktide weeks earlier. Not perfect but better. And she meant what she had said to Julie, that she was glad Carol had come home.

In spite of everything, she meant it.

Chapter 106

Carol sat in her father's armchair. Bonnie and Judith sat on the couch directly facing Carol. Bonnie looked decidedly nervous. Well, Carol thought, she wasn't the only one. Judith's expression betrayed nothing but her usual attitude of calm acceptance.

"Thank you both for coming," Carol began, aware she sounded as if she was opening a corporate meeting rather than a family discussion. But she was doing the best she could.

Bonnie nodded.

"What is it, Carol?" Judith said. "What's been on your mind?"

For a moment, Carol, who had rehearsed her story repeatedly, didn't know how to begin.

"From the beginning," Judith said gently. "That's your answer."

Carol smiled. She had been right to include her cousin in this moment.

"I was in love once, a long time ago," she began. "His name was Martin. He was a year older than me, had never been married, had no kids. He had just been made a partner in his law firm when I met him." Carol shook her head. "I'm not making him sound particularly special, but he was, to me. I'd never felt about anyone the way I felt about Martin. It was love. At least, I believed that what I felt for him was love. And he loved me. That I'm sure of. We were together for about eight months when one evening over dinner at our favorite little Italian place in the Village he broke things off."

"Whoever thought that a public breakup was acceptable?" Judith asked. "I think it's cruel."

"Cruel or not," Carol said, "it took me utterly by surprise. I had no idea he was unhappy. He said I was incapable of really knowing another person, or of letting myself be known."

Judith frowned. "He might have been just a tad judgmental. Most men are."

Bonnie said nothing. Carol thought her sister looked puzzled.

"He said he sensed that I wouldn't make him a good wife," she went on.

Judith sniffed. "A bit presumptuous."

"Maybe. But then he listed several incidents as proof." Carol smiled ruefully. "Like, the time he asked me to accompany him to an important dinner with his partners and their spouses. I really wanted to watch the latest episode of *Law & Order*, so I said I couldn't make it."

"Did you tell him why?" Judith asked.

"Yes, he didn't understand why I couldn't just have taped the show and watched it when I got home."

Bonnie shifted in her seat. "He had a point," she said, but not unkindly. "If you cared enough about him, that's what you would have done."

"Probably," Carol said. "Not long after our relationship ended he got married and the last I heard, he and his wife and children were blissfully happy. And I'm happy for him. Now. Back then, I wasn't really capable of a generous spirit."

"Not many people would have been," Judith said. "I've been through my fair share of breakups. The one left behind is rarely pleased to hear about her ex's newfound happiness."

Bonnie folded her hands in her lap and leaned forward. "I don't understand," she said. "What does all this have to do with today?"

Carol took the requisite deep breath and began to tell her family about Alex Peters, Nicola's conception via IVF, and finally, about Alex's recent phone call.

"Everything is unraveling," she said finally, exhaustedly. "The structure I put into place twenty-five years ago is crumbling."

"All along you've known Nicola's father?" Bonnie shook her head slowly.

"Yes. Why I thought I'd ever make a good mother I'll never know. I was angry about Martin leaving me. I wanted to prove to Martin, to everyone, that I was capable of love and sacrifice."

"You weren't a bad mother. You weren't," Bonnie said firmly. "And I'm sorry if I ever made you feel that you were. Which might have been my intention at times."

"Bonnie is right," Judith said firmly. "You're a good mother, Carol. No one is a perfect mother. No one."

Carol was moved by her sister's honesty and comforted by her cousin's support. "Thank you both," she said, her voice wobbly.

"Would your friend Alex have married you if you wanted him to?" Bonnie asked.

"Yes, I think he would have and it would have been a disaster. I made him unhappy enough in the end by asking what I did of him. I knew he would never refuse me."

Judith suddenly eyed Carol closely. "There's something else, isn't there?" she asked. "There's something else you want to tell us."

Carol managed a small smile. "Yes," she said. "There is. Fast forward to Nicola's becoming an adolescent and starting to get into trouble. Things deteriorated rapidly. I was at my wit's end. Nothing seemed to be helping, not therapy, not punishment. And then I had the surgery, the radical hysterectomy. The recovery was long and painful. I was completely unprepared for the harsh reality of healing. I was prescribed an opioid by my doctor. I took the pills I was given, as I was instructed to do. And I was hooked. It was that sudden. When my prescription had run out, I turned to someone I knew who could get hold of the pills illegally. I never asked for details."

Bonnie had put one hand to her heart, the other over her mouth. Her eyes were wide. Judith's mouth was set in a grim line.

"So, you see," Carol went on, "one of the reasons I wanted Nicola to live with you all in Yorktide was that I knew she would then be safe from anything nasty that might happen as a result of my need for the drug."

There was a long silence during which Carol honestly didn't know if she had managed to alienate her sister and her cousin forever.

"But you're all right now?" Bonnie asked finally, her voice low.

"I haven't touched opioids in over six years and I never will again."

"You must have been so lonely," Judith said gently.

I still am, Carol said to herself. To her cousin, she merely nodded. "So," she asked, "do I tell Nicola the truth about her father?"

Judith spoke first. "I'd encourage you to tell Nicola everything. She might freak out at first, but I believe she'll come around and be grateful for the knowledge."

Carol turned to her sister. "Bonnie," she said. "What do you think?"

"I think Nicola needs to know the truth," she said promptly. "It will be a shock. But she's a strong young woman. She'll be all right."

"Largely thanks to the good care you and Ken gave her," Carol said feelingly. "Look, please don't tell Julie any of this until I've worked things out with Nicola, assuming I can work things out. Julie is under so much strain at the moment I'm afraid she'll let slip the news to Nicola and that would be a disaster."

"Agreed," Judith said firmly.

Bonnie nodded. "Agreed."

All three women stood and moved closer to one another. "Thank you. Thank you both," Carol said. She took the hand of each woman. As if compelled to complete the circle, Bonnie and Judith reached for one another's hand.

United we stand, Carol thought, tears in her eyes.

Chapter 107

Nicola grinned and waved as her cousin drove past the crowd of people waiting at the crosswalk in the center of town. Judith didn't see her. She was looking straight ahead, as she probably should have been, Nicola thought. But there had been a pained look on her face.

The light turned green and Nicola joined the other pedestrians in stepping into the street. Very little got to her cousin. She hoped Judith hadn't had bad news, like a friend's illness or sudden death. When you got to Judith's age, that kind of depressing thing seemed always to be happening.

Nicola reached the sidewalk and headed toward the bookshop, her mother's gift certificate tucked into her wallet. Maybe, she thought, she could find a good book on learning how to better access your intuition or, like Hermione had talked about, how to listen to the universe so that its messages were clear and instructive.

Nicola opened the door to the bookshop. Or maybe she would just buy a big stack of mystery novels.

Chapter 108

"Keys, keys, wherefore art thou keys!"

Julie dashed from the kitchen, glancing at every surface on her way through the living room. And there they were, for some reason on the mantel above the fireplace. Funny place for car keys to be hiding.

With more speed than she had been able to muster for months, Julie hurried from the house and into her car. She didn't want to be late for her appointment with Sara. Julie had completed the scholarship application; Sara would read it and make suggestions for improvement. A part of Julie dreaded to hear her principal's criticisms. A larger part of her was eager for the feedback.

Only when Julie was nearing Sara's house did she remember her mother mentioning that she and Judith had been invited to Ferndean that day. Carol had something important to say to them. Julie wondered what it was.

Oh, well, she thought as she pulled into Sara's driveway. She would find out soon enough. Frankly, she had more important things on her mind. Like reviving her vocation.

Chapter 109

The moment Bonnie got back to her cottage she fairly collapsed into Ken's lounger. She felt exhausted by what Carol had told her. Exhausted and overwhelmed and sad and thoroughly surprised.

The pain her sister must have endured through the long years of her addiction! Bonnie had never known anyone addicted to drugs; she had known plenty of heavy drinkers but very few alcoholics. How sheltered she had been from the harsh realities so many others faced. And how fortunate that Ken had convinced her to take in their niece all those years ago. Carol had been right in not wanting her child to live in the vicinity of an addiction, especially to something that had to be acquired through illegal means.

As for Nicola's parentage, well, Bonnie had always been uncomfortable with the idea of anonymous sperm donation. Now that she knew the truth about Nicola's father, she felt only slightly less troubled by the way in which Carol had chosen to bring a baby into the world. It seemed so cold to make a legal agreement with someone you considered a friend over such an emotionally charged event as having a baby.

But a man with a name was better than a man with no name. Or something like that. It was all so confusing. But at least now Nicola would have the opportunity to know her father.

And Bonnie firmly believed that was a good thing.

Now, to remember not to let slip to Julie that the dynamics of the family were about to change drastically yet again!

With a groan, Bonnie got up from the lounger and went into the kitchen to make a cup of tea. As she passed through the tiny living room, she was overcome by a wave of fondness for her lovely little house. Life would be just fine if she were to spend the next phase of it here in the home she and Ken had shared. Maybe, if it meant so much to Carol, she should relinquish her hold on Ferndean House. . . .

But that was easier said than done. Bonnie wasn't sure it was in her to make a sacrifice that large, not for anyone but Ken. And he was gone.

Bonnie put the kettle on the stove and yawned. Tea and a nap. That sounded good.

Chapter 110

"I'm going to tell Nicola the truth about you and me. She's coming to the house in about an hour."

"Thank you, Carol," Alex said. "I'm so relieved."

"I told my sister and my cousin the whole story," Carol went on. "They were both more accepting than I'd imagined they might be."

"We did nothing wrong, Carol."

"You might be innocent, but . . ." Carol swallowed hard. "I'm not at all sorry that Nicola was born," she went on, "but I am so very sorry that I asked you to be her father in the way that I did. It was unfair of me to expect such an enormous sacrifice for so little in return."

"I made the decision, Carol. You didn't force me to agree. But thank you for acknowledging that it was a difficult decision for me to make and to honor. Staying out of our daughter's life."

Both Alex and Carol were silent for a moment.

"Have you considered the possibility that Nicola might not want to talk with you?" Carol asked gently then.

"Of course."

"What will you do if that's the case?"

Alex laughed softly. "I'll deal with it. There's not much choice, is there?"

"No, I guess there isn't. Though she might come around in time."

The moment the words were out of her mouth, Carol cringed. Only there wasn't time. Alex was dying.

"You'll let me know either way?" Alex asked.

"Of course. Goodbye, Alex."

Carol put her phone down. The biggest challenge of her life lay before her. She truly had no idea how Nicola would take the news that her father was known to her mother, that he always had been, that if her mother had allowed it, her father might have been a part of her life for the past twenty-five years.

But she was about to find out.

For one terrible moment, Carol thought that Nicola, her face flushed almost purple, was going to pick up one of the knickknacks on the closest side table and throw it against a wall. But Nicola didn't have a temper like she had had in those bad times. Or maybe she did. What did Carol really know of her daughter?

"Alex and I talked about all the possibilities at the beginning," Carol went on quietly. She was sitting rigidly, her hands flat on each arm of her father's chair. "About all that might possibly happen should one of us get too sick to care for you or even should one of us die. Our lawyers made sure of that."

"Is it really possible to talk about every imaginable possibility?" Nicola countered. "When a *life* is concerned?"

"We did our best," Carol said. "At least, we did what we thought was the best for you."

"And no one tried to talk you out of it?" Nicola asked, her tone incredulous.

"No one knew." Carol sighed. "Nicola, there was nothing unusual in choosing to have a child in the way I did. Nothing illegal or dangerous or immoral. How many of your schoolmates had donor fathers?"

"A few," Nicola admitted.

"And how did those kids seem to you? Normal? Well adjusted?"

"I don't know," Nicola said with a shrug. "They were just like everyone else."

"You see?"

"What I see is a lie," Nicola snapped. She walked over to the couch facing her mother and sat on the very edge of the cushion, her hands on her knees. "Those other kids with donor fathers really *did* have donor fathers! I had a man with a name, someone who wanted a child enough to go ahead with a crazy idea . . ." Nicola shook her head. "No, he *didn't* want a child. He wanted to give you what you wanted. It could have been a diamond necklace or a fur coat, but no, you wanted a baby so he gave you a baby."

Carol could say nothing. Her heart was beating painfully.

"What would you have done if the IVF didn't work?" Nicola went on. Her tone was challenging. "Would you have adopted a baby?"

"No," Carol answered. "I wanted a child I'd given birth to."

"That's selfish. There are so many innocent little kids in need of good homes."

"I know that. And I also know that adoption was not what I was prepared to undertake. Would it have been better for me to lie to myself and let the child pay the price of my unhappiness?"

Nicola was silent for a moment. Then, she said, "No, of course not. Still, you denied me the gift of knowing my own father."

Carol nodded. "I suppose I did. But now I'm trying to make up for that."

"When he's dying!" Nicola cried. "When he has less than a year to live. You weren't going to tell me any of this, were you? It was my father's contacting you now, telling you he's sick, that forced you to come clean."

"Yes," Carol admitted. "That's true."

"Does he know anything at all about me?"

"Yes, from the beginning I've sent regular updates on your progress. School photos. Drawings you made as a little girl. Copies of awards you won at graduation. That sort of thing."

Nicola shuddered. "So, he's been watching me. This is beyond creepy."

"It's not creepy at all," Carol said forcefully. "Alex cares. He always has."

Nicola got up from her seat again and began to stalk around the living room. "And he wants to talk to me? Why would I want anything to do with a guy who gave up his child for money?" she asked.

"Our agreement wasn't like that," Carol said. "No money changed hands."

Nicola came to a halt and turned to her mother. "I can't . . . I can't get my head around this. If you two were such good friends, why didn't you just get married?"

"Our relationship wasn't romantic," Carol said. "At least, not on my part. How could I have married your father and withheld physical love?"

"But why couldn't he have stuck around?" Nicola asked. "Stayed in New York? Said he was my godfather or something, though that, too, would have been a lie. Why go off to South America? Did you tell him he wasn't allowed to have a part in my life?"

"He had already accepted the transfer when I approached him with my request for . . ." Carol rubbed her forehead. She felt sick with regret. "How can I possibly make you understand what seemed right all those years ago when now it seems even to me to be so very wrong?"

"You can't." Once again, Nicola returned to the couch. Carol thought she suddenly looked terribly weary. "If you wanted a child so badly that you went through with that absurd agreement, how could you have sent me away when things got tough?"

This was the moment, more than any, that Carol had been dreading. "It wasn't like that," she said softly.

"Really?" Nicola laughed harshly. "Then what was it like? Help me to understand."

"I was . . . This is very difficult to tell you, Nicola. Until now I haven't spoken of it to anyone."

Something in Carol's tone of voice or expression must have demonstrated to Nicola that her mother was about to impart a very sensitive and personal piece of information. In a gentler voice, Nicola said, "Mom, what do you mean?"

Carol told Nicola about the addiction to opioids. She admitted to obtaining the pills illegally once her own prescription had run out. She admitted to the terrible shame she felt and the fear that her secret would out and that she would be ruined, the respect with which she was regarded in the design community shattered, the people who held her in personal esteem sickened by her weakness. She admitted she never expected she would find anyone sympathetic to her plight.

When Carol had finished talking she felt hollowed out, as if something heavy and viscous had been scraped from the inside of her bones. Nicola's face was ashen.

"No one knew?" she asked finally. "Not even Aunt Bonnie?"

"No one. There were times when I thought Ana might have suspected something. But she never said so I chose to believe she was ignorant."

"How are you now? I mean . . ."

"I've been healthy for a long time. But . . ." Carol swallowed hard. "But by the time I was free, things between us seemed so broken down. I felt I couldn't ask you to . . . to come home again."

Nicola sighed tremblingly. "I wish you had asked. I probably would have said no, but I wish you had asked."

"I'm so sorry, Nicola. I truly am. And you need to believe that the primary reason I came back to Yorktide was to rediscover my family before it's too late for any of us to make amends." *And now*, Carol thought, *I'm losing Alex. Nicola is losing the father I never let her have. What have I done?*

"Then why the fight for Ferndean?" Nicola asked. "Why not be conciliatory?"

Carol smiled ruefully. "Don't worry about that. I have no intention of making my sister miserable."

"Do you mean you've changed your mind?"

"We'll talk about it some other time," Carol said. "Now I need to ask if you can ever forgive me for what I've done. For what I deprived you of."

"Yes," Nicola said readily. "I can forgive you and I do, though I'll probably never understand the choices you made. But none of that matters now. What matters is that you've finally told me the truth. The truth about my family. Our family."

Carol smiled. "You'll let me know what you decide about your father? If you're okay with his contacting you?"

"I'm okay with it," Nicola said. "But maybe he could write to me first. E-mail is fine. From there . . . we'll see."

"Thank you, Nicola. I'll tell him right away." But first, Carol thought, as she sank wearily against the back of the armchair, she needed to rest.

Chapter 111

"Mom? Are you okay? Your hands are shaking."

"Are they?" her mother asked. Carol Ascher looked pale and small, sunk into the big, old armchair. "I'm sorry."

"There's nothing for which to be sorry," Nicola replied briskly. "You need something to eat. Sit here. I'll be right back."

Nicola dashed to the kitchen and after a few minutes returned to the living room with a tray on which sat the rudiments of a meal: fruit, a chunk of good cheddar cheese, thick slices of whole wheat bread, and two cups of strong tea.

Carol smiled. "Thank you," she said, sitting forward again and accepting the tea from Nicola. "You should know that I met with Bonnie and Judith yesterday and told them everything. I wanted their advice. I wanted to be sure I was doing the right thing in telling you the truth."

"So that's what was distracting Judith," Nicola said. "I saw her drive by yesterday afternoon. I waved, but she didn't see me. I'd never seen her look so far away."

"I'm afraid it was a lot for both Bonnie and Judith to take in. But they were wonderful. They both urged that I tell you everything."

Nicola smiled. "They must be a nervous wreck, wondering what's happening right now."

"We don't have to say anything to them other than . . ." Carol shook her head. "Well, that's your decision, what to tell them and what to keep to ourselves. I'll be guided by you."

"Thanks, Mom," Nicola said feelingly. This afternoon with her mother had been—and continued to be—monumental. Life changing. It didn't feel like an experience to be chatted about, even to other loved ones. "You can simply tell them that I've agreed to hear from my father."

Carol nodded and reached for a bit of cheese and bread.

"Why wouldn't you let me visit you in the hospital?" Nicola asked after a moment.

"I thought it might be too upsetting for you," her mother replied. "You were already going through such a difficult time."

Nicola shook her head. "I thought you were keeping me away because you were even sicker than you had let on, maybe even that you were dying. Or that you were keeping me from seeing you because you didn't love me."

"How stupid I was," Carol said. "I'm so sorry, Nicola. I guess my maternal instincts weren't always very good."

"That's all right," Nicola said. "I believe you meant well."

For a while mother and daughter sat in a silence that was surprisingly comfortable, nibbling on slices of apple and pear, and drinking the strong tea Nicola had prepared. Finally, after Nicola had brought the remains of the meal to the kitchen, she felt it was time she left. She needed to retreat to her own home—humble as it was—and think about what had taken place that afternoon at Ferndean.

"Are you sure you'll be all right, Mom?" she asked, just before going.

Her mother smiled. "Yes, I'm sure. I'm going to let your father know that we've spoken and that he can write to you."

Nicola leaned down and kissed her mother on the cheek. "Call me if you need anything," she said.

Her mother promised that she would.

Nicola felt strangely at peace. She wondered if she could be in shock. Shouldn't she be feeling angry and cheated, furious that she had been duped by the two people who had given her life? Well, she had felt those emotions when her mother had first begun her story. But they had soon been replaced by . . . by tenderness.

As she steered her car toward Gilbert Way, Nicola recalled Hermione Wilcott assuring her that answers to the big questions came when you were ready to receive them. And she thought about her recent premonitions of something momentous about to happen, of something important hovering just out of reach.

She had never, ever imagined it would be the emergence of her father.

Kin keeping.

Suddenly, Nicola remembered a moment earlier in the summer when she had complimented her mother's vibrant yellow blouse, and had commented that the bright shade would not suit her. "Yes," her mother had said. "You have your . . ."

What she had been about to say was: "You have your father's coloring."

Nicola had a father and his name was Alex Peters.

Chapter 112

Julie was sitting at the round redwood table on the patio. Not once this summer had the family shared a meal there. Scott had never fired up the grill; Julie had never set the table with the colorful plastic plates they used for outdoor dining; Sophie had never gathered a bouquet from the wildflowers that grew by the garage. What a terrible waste, Julie thought now. And most of it was her fault. Or, if not her fault, then her doing.

The sliding door that led to the kitchen opened and Sophie stepped onto the patio. So many encounters between mother and daughter this summer had devolved into a fight or angry silence. But not all of them.

Julie smiled. "Hi."

"It's nice out here," Sophie said, taking a seat at the table.

"Yes," Julie agreed. "It is."

Sophie was silent, frowning down at her hands. Her nails were painted a shimmery pink. There were four woven bracelets on her left wrist.

"I feel terrible for saying all those things I said to you this summer," Sophie suddenly blurted. "I love you, Mom, really."

Julie's heart expanded. "I know you do."

"The thing is I didn't want to feel so bad for you because you were already feeling so bad for yourself and not paying any attention to me and what I was going through. Maybe I'm just not a very nice person."

Julie shook her head. "Don't say that. You were—you are—experiencing a situation that's entirely new and unexpected. There's no script for how to feel or what to do. We're all just making it up as we go along."

"Is this what life is always going to be like?" Sophie asked. Her voice shook, just a little. "I mean, never knowing what weird stuff is going to happen when, and what you're going to have to do to get through it?"

Julie wanted to reach for her daughter's hand but expected Sophie to pull away. So, she didn't. "The best way to prepare yourself for the craziness that's life," she said carefully, thinking about the lessons she had learned that summer, "is to cultivate your inner resources and to know when to reach out to others for help."

"What does Agnes have to say about what's been going on?" Sophie asked.

It couldn't hurt to be honest, Julie thought. Not now. "A few days before I confronted your father," she began, "Aggie told me she'd heard a rumor that he was seeing someone. But she didn't tell me until I'd developed my own suspicions and had gone to her for advice."

"That's so wrong," Sophie declared. "She's your friend. She's supposed to have your back."

"She said she didn't want to believe that your father was cheating on me. Besides, the person who told her is known for telling tall tales." Julie shrugged. "She apologized over and over, but I couldn't forgive her."

"So, you're not friends anymore?" Sophie asked.

"I don't know," Julie admitted. "She wants to be. And I have finally forgiven her for holding her tongue. I believe she had no intention of hurting me."

"I'd definitely tell my friend if someone was cheating on her," Sophie stated.

Julie refrained from smiling. Everything was black and white for the young and in a way, that was lovely, that certainty about moral issues, that absolute conviction of rightness when it came to delicate situations, a blithe ignorance of the negative consequences that might follow upon a well-meaning action.

"Well," Julie said after a moment, "I hope you never find yourself in such an uncomfortable situation."

"Too bad we haven't had dinner out here in a while," Sophie said abruptly.

"Would you like to?" Julie asked.

Sophie shifted in her seat. When she spoke, she looked out over the yard, not at her mother. "We'd have to ask Dad."

"I'm sure he would be happy to grill us some burgers."

"Maybe." Suddenly, Sophie got up from her chair. "I gotta go."

"Are you meeting friends?"

Sophie shrugged. "Some people from camp."

"Okay," Julie said. "Have a nice time."

Sophie was considering doing something together as a family. That was progress. Julie felt a tiny glimmer of . . . Maybe not something as big as hope. But what she felt was also not despair.

I should have taken her hand, Julie thought. *Next time, I will.*

Chapter 113

The small cemetery where Ken had been laid to rest alongside the Elgorts who had gone before was always beautifully kept. Even the oldest graves, those dating from the seventeenth century, were nicely groomed. If those oldest headstones were largely broken, tilted, or even lying flat on the ground, and if the carvings were virtually illegible, smoothed over by time and dotted with lichen, there were still *there*, tangible reminders of the people who were now at eternal rest.

"You can imagine how I felt," Bonnie said. She was sitting on a collapsible traveling stool she had bought for just such visits to her husband's grave. "Poor Carol. If only I had known."

Bonnie knew that Ken had heard her. She leaned down and readjusted the fresh flowers she had brought with her. KENNETH ALBERT ELGORT. BELOVED SON, HUSBAND, AND FATHER. If only . . .

No, Bonnie told herself. It was time to stop wishing for what could never be. Ken was gone, at least from this physical world, and she would have to accept that and keep of him what she could. Memories. A presence. Love.

"I don't know what's going to happen now," she said to her husband. "I mean, with Nicola. Will she ever forgive Carol for keeping

her father a secret all these years? Will she want to meet her father?" Bonnie sighed. "I just pray it all goes well."

Bonnie leaned over again and laid her hand on the grass that
covered Ken's grave. She thought that she could feel his heart beating through the all the layers that separated them. A heart never
really stopped beating.

Chapter 114

The big, old white pine. Bonnie's special tree.

Until today, Carol had done nothing more than observe it from a distance. It was majestic and beautiful, as all monumental trees were. But this afternoon, Carol found herself compelled to duck beneath its lowest branches and seat herself against the trunk, the bark thick, dark, and fissured with age. Almost immediately, Carol felt the tree's magic. She felt protected by the endless bluish-green needles that allowed only dancing flickers of sunlight to penetrate, as well as by the sheer bulk of the tree that might very well have witnessed Ferndean House rising from its foundations.

Permanence.

Carol recalled the feel of Bonnie's hand in hers the other day. Her sister's touch had been tender, loving.

This tree had been her sister's sanctuary as a child.

Carol wished she could rest under her sister's tree forever.

Under her sister's care.

That was a strange thought.

Carol put her hand to her head. She felt a bit dizzy. So much had been happening, changing, speeding along . . .

She must have dozed off because suddenly, Carol was aware

that the air felt markedly cooler; she was aware of a vague, wishful hint of autumn, her favorite time of the year.

She looked at her watch. She had been under the white pine for almost an hour. Using the trunk for support, Carol slowly got to her feet and made her way back to the house.

She was so very tired.

Chapter 115

Nicola sighed deeply before releasing the seat belt and climbing out from behind the wheel. It had been a particularly trying day at Pine Hill. A favorite resident was near death, and his son had been resisting the staff's professional opinion that he be moved to the hospice care unit. Mr. Richardson had made peace with his dying, but his child had not. Nicola had spent over an hour with father and son. In the end, the younger man had finally, tearfully, agreed that in this case his father did indeed know best, and papers were signed to that effect.

Now, Nicola was looking forward to watching for the third time an episode of the first season of *Game of Thrones* and eating the leftover pizza in the fridge.

The front door creaked its usual creak and Nicola stepped into the dreary front hall. Mail had been tossed on a small, wooden table under a badly faded tour poster of The Rolling Stones. Nicola sorted through the stack for anything addressed to her. A bill. A packet of coupons.

A letter.

Nicola knew immediately from whom the letter had come. She didn't need to notice the foreign postmark.

All thoughts of television and pizza vanished as Nicola raced up the stairs to her apartment, intensely eager to read her father's letter. She had not expected to feel this way, almost desperate to make a connection.

Once inside, her bag and keys went flying in the general direction of the kitchen while she dropped onto the couch. Carefully, she slit open the envelope and withdrew the pages inside. It was unusual to receive a handwritten letter; in fact, Nicola didn't think she ever had received one until now. Cards, yes, but not a genuine letter.

The paper was cream colored and thick. The ink was black; the pen must have been a fine-tipped one. With a deep breath, Nicola began to read.

> *Dearest Nicola,*
>
> *First, I must thank you from the bottom of my heart for consenting to read this letter.*
>
> *I'm aware that I have no right to your kindness or generosity, which makes your gift of both that much more meaningful to me.*
>
> *To the point – At the time when Carol came to me with her idea of my being a parent in absentia, I didn't give the idea a fraction of the thought I should have given it. Now, near the end of my life, I know it was crazy of me to think I could live without one day knowing my own flesh and blood. Carol's daughter. My daughter. Our child. I was a fool for love, Nicola. Men have done stupider things for love, but not much stupider. And I don't in any way blame your mother for my poor decision. You must believe that.*
>
> *Below you will find a phone number that you can call if you would like to talk via FaceTime. You can text me to arrange a time.*
>
> *Again, I thank you from the bottom of my heart for accepting my request that we communicate.*
>
> *Your father, Alex Peters*

Nicola took a deep breath.

She had a father.

She reached for her phone and immediately sent him a text. There was no time like the present.

Even given the jerking, shifting perspective that was part of the FaceTime experience, Nicola could see that Alex Peters was a handsome man. She reached out with a trembling finger and touched the screen.

"I look like you. I mean, I knew I must look like my father in the ways I didn't look like my mother, but . . ."

Alex smiled. "Carol always told me that you had my eyes. She said that at moments she would almost feel it was me looking back at her. Something in your expression."

"I tried once or twice to imagine your face. But I couldn't."

"I was luckier. I had the photos your mother sent me." Alex cleared his throat. "So, tell me about yourself."

"All right," Nicola said. "I'm a junior gerontological social worker at the local nursing home. I guess my mother told you that. Recently I was thinking about going into the Peace Corps. I was hoping to serve in Ukraine."

Alex looked puzzled. "Did your mother tell you that my family is from Ukraine?" he asked.

"No!" Nicola was stunned. "She never said a word!"

"Carol named you Nicola Kathryn after two of my grandparents, Nikolas and Kateryna. And I still have family—you still have family—in Ukraine. I've kept in touch with them, though I haven't been to visit in more than ten years. I'd be so happy to bring you all together." Alex smiled a wobbly smile. "Of course, first I'll have to explain why I've never told them I have a daughter. But tell me more about yourself. Tell me five things I might not know."

"Okay," Nicola said. "Well, my favorite color is sky blue. I don't really like to drive, but I'm a good driver. I read two or three mystery novels a week. My favorite pizza topping is mushroom. And my favorite old song is 'As Time Goes By.' Now, you tell me five things about yourself."

Alex told her that he used to love playing tennis until he shattered his right knee in a motor scooter accident. That he spoke Spanish and French fluently. That his favorite books were biographies. That he was a pretty good cook and enjoyed giving dinner parties. "And my favorite color is also blue," he said, "though something darker than sky blue. Cadet blue? Is that a color?"

"I think it used to be the name of a crayon!" Nicola laughed. And then, more soberly, she said, "How do you feel? I mean, are you in pain?" Nicola wasn't sure she had the right to ask that sort of question, but if a daughter didn't have the right to ask her father about his health, who did?

"Not yet," he said readily, "though I probably will be. But there will be pain control. I try not to think too much about what's to come."

"Don't anticipate disaster. That's something I always try to keep in mind, though there are times when you do need to prepare . . ." Nicola shook her head. "Sorry. I'm being glum."

Alex smiled kindly. "That's all right."

Nicola hesitated a moment before asking her next question. "Didn't you have any reservations about having a child with my mother?"

Alex smiled. "No reservations. I trusted Carol and I loved her. I believed she would always do the right thing by you."

"Why didn't you ever break your promise to my mother and come for me?"

"I'm a man of my word," he said simply. "I made what I came to know was a ridiculously wrong promise, but it was a promise nonetheless."

"You didn't ever ask her to change her mind about the arrangements? Before now, I mean. Before you got sick."

Alex smiled faintly. "I was pretty certain I'd be rebuffed. And I was afraid that if Carol felt she could no longer trust me she would end our relations entirely and then I would lose you all over again."

"You were afraid of her."

"No," Alex replied. "I had respect for her strength and determination."

"And if she had refused to let us speak now, you would have been okay with that decision?"

Alex sighed. "I would have been unhappy, but I would have accepted it. I had no intention of forcing her hand."

"Do you have any other children?" Nicola asked. Somehow, she knew what the answer would be.

"No, and I never married. I was never in love with anyone but your mother."

To know that degree of devotion . . .

"Is there someone special in your life?" Alex asked when she had not spoken.

"No," Nicola said. "There never really has been. Maybe I'm not cut out for romance."

"Or maybe you're just waiting to be swept off your feet by true love."

"Like you were?"

Alex's expression tightened.

"Sorry," Nicola said hurriedly. "But you can see why I might not entirely believe in love and all that's supposed to go with it."

"And what is supposed to go with it?" Alex asked softly.

Nicola shrugged. "I don't know. Flowers and diamond rings and cheesy songs."

"Not friendship and appreciation and laughter? And yes, sacrifice."

Nicola felt chastened. In some ways, she was so very innocent, even naïve. She had suspected as much but now she knew for sure.

"We can talk again," Nicola said. "If you want."

"I very much want to," Alex said.

"I thought this would be weird. Painful. But it isn't."

"No," Alex said. "It isn't at all."

Chapter 116

"I'm so very sorry, Julie. I can't say it often enough."

Julie reached across the small café table and took her friend Aggie's hand. "I'm the one who should be sorry. I know you were only doing what you thought was best. But it all came as such a shock."

"I can't imagine. Thank you for suggesting we meet. I was starting to think you would never forgive me."

Julie smiled. Only weeks earlier she had been thinking the same sorry thought.

"By the way," Aggie said now, "Prescott says he saw Scott last week at the hardware store."

Julie released her friend's hand. "He did? Scott didn't mention it."

"That's because Prescott didn't know what to do—say hello, ignore Scott—so he just hurried out of the store!"

The thought of big, burly Prescott scurrying away from a chance encounter with her husband caused Julie to grin. "Well, you can tell Prescott that the next time he runs into Scott he should feel free to say hello."

"So, you've forgiven Scott?" Aggie asked.

"No," Julie admitted. "Not yet, but I'm getting there. Interestingly, my aunt Carol has been a help to me. I've spent more time with her this summer than ever before. A few things she's said to me hit home, things about self-care and starting small."

"But I know how your mother feels about her," Aggie said. "She never made it a secret that she—sorry, but I'm going to say it—that she resented Carol. Is she upset that you two are getting close?"

"Honestly, I don't think so. Things between them are a bit better than they had been at the start of the summer."

"Well, that's good to hear! What about Sophie? How is she faring in all this?"

"All right, I think," Julie said. "At least, she doesn't seem to loathe and despise her parents quite as much as she did earlier this summer."

"Thank God for that!" Aggie shook her head. "I figured that Sophie had to be unhappy and I worried she might do as so many teens do when things at home are rocky. Go wild or worse."

Julie took a sip of her coffee. It was a steadying tactic. Then she said, "I'm afraid I've been ignoring Sophie's distress this summer. Not purposely, of course. Scott has been more actively worried. He's convinced that the kids she's been hanging out with—the other camp counselors—are a bad lot. Mostly I've dismissed the idea, but . . ." Julie shook her head. "I've never known Scott to overreact or to worry without good reason."

"But there's no evidence for his concern?"

"Sophie did ignore her curfew one night not long ago." Julie smiled. "The thing is, nothing is the same as it used to be. If my instincts are off-kilter, then Scott's might be, too."

"Don't anticipate disaster." Aggie nodded. "So, you and Scott are communicating?"

"Yes," Julie said. "Some. The other day he thanked me for talking to him. He said that anything was better than my silence."

Aggie smiled ruefully. "Silence is painful."

"Sorry. I'm still not feeling great, but I think the dark cloud is lifting."

"Go at your own pace. Nobody is hurrying you."

Looking into her friend's open and loving face, Julie flirted with the idea of telling her about her confrontation with Laci Fox. But they had spent enough time discussing the Miller family.

"Tell me what's been going on with you and Prescott and the children," Julie said. "Leave nothing out. I've missed so much."

Chapter 117

Bonnie had been weeding the herb and vegetable garden in the rain for about fifteen minutes before she heard a distant voice. It was her sister, shouting for Bonnie to get inside.

"You're soaked!" Carol exclaimed, when Bonnie stood next to her on the back deck. "Why didn't you come in earlier?"

"A little rain never hurt anyone," Bonnie said cheerfully.

"Well, let me get you a towel and a cup of tea."

Bonnie was touched by her sister's solicitous concern. The sisters settled in the den, which looked oddly brighter than it had the last time Bonnie had been at Ferndean.

"That's because I put higher-watt bulbs in the standing lamps," Carol explained. "The gloom was getting to me."

"It makes a nice change," Bonnie said, nodding toward a small table on which sat a framed portrait of her and Ken on their wedding day. "Now I can actually see that photo. Boy, were we young!"

"I completely understand why you didn't ask me to be your maid of honor," Carol said. "It would have been very awkward for both of us, and for Ken. Still, I was a bit hurt, though I didn't realize it until I watched you standing at the altar with Marianne Wallace at your side." Carol shrugged. "Then again, I'd set the stage for my being the outcast."

"You were never an outcast," Bonnie argued. "You were . . ."

She smiled. "You were an exotic and colorful bird in a nest full of ordinary brown sparrows."

"That's a kind way of putting it."

"Maybe. But it doesn't erase the fact that we sparrows admired you for your difference at the same time we were resentful of the attention you attracted. People pay a price for standing out."

"An astute observation. Are you still friends with Marianne?" Carol asked.

"She moved away with her second husband when we were all about forty," Bonnie told her. "I suppose we're still friends, but we don't communicate all that often. I guess that's to be expected. I mean, Marianne and her first husband were Ken and my closest friends in Yorktide. Once Nat died and Marianne remarried, well, nothing was really the same."

"I suppose you told her about Ken's passing."

"Of course," Bonnie said. "She sent a sympathy card." But there had been no personal note in addition to the printed message of condolence. That had depressed Bonnie until it hadn't.

"Do you miss her?" Carola asked.

"Not really," Bonnie admitted. "It used to make me sad that we grew apart. But life goes on, doesn't it?"

"It does," Carol said. "You lose one thing and you gain another. You know, once or twice over the years I wanted to tell you the truth about Nicola's father. I knew you probably wouldn't approve but all the same, there were times when I wanted you to know."

Bonnie's heart swelled. "Because we shared so much when we were little."

"As sisters do. And that's important."

"It is," Bonnie said. "Which is why I wanted you by my side at Ken's funeral. But that's forgiven now."

"Thank you," Carol said. "It means a lot that you're able to forgive me."

"About what we were saying earlier," Bonnie went on, "sparrows and colorful birds. For a long time after you left Yorktide, I missed your vitality. Life seemed so dull without you around to spice things up."

"I always felt bored growing up," Carol admitted. "I'm not bragging. It's nothing to brag about. Nothing in Yorktide was ever exciting enough for me. I mean, I tried. You remember how I was involved in clubs at school and went with everyone to the community potluck suppers and sang for a time in our church's choir. But inside I was unhappy." Carol smiled. "You always seemed so contented. And everyone liked you."

"Everybody liked you, too," Bonnie said.

Carol shook her head. "No, people were impressed by me. But not many people actually liked me. I didn't make it easy for them to. And I didn't entirely care."

"Dad was certainly impressed. His preference for you over me was pretty obvious."

"I'm sorry about that," Carol said feelingly. "But I'm sure he loved us both equally." Carol rose from her seat. "I'm going to make more tea."

When Carol had gone to the kitchen, Bonnie thought about their father. It had been abundantly clear that Ronald Ascher was hurt by Carol's leaving home. And a small, not very admirable part of Bonnie had felt glad about that. Maybe now he realized that he had made a mistake lavishing the majority of his attention on the bright and shining sister, the one who proved to be shallow and unreliable, the one who proved not to care.

After about a year, when it became clear that Carol would not be making frequent visits home, Bonnie and her father started to spend more time together. They rarely spoke about Carol and when they did it was always in reference to the past. What a hit she had been in her fifth-grade play. How lovely she had looked receiving the Miss Yorktide Award in 1973. How clever she was with a needle and thread.

If Bonnie and Ronald Ascher hadn't shared hopes and dreams, they had grown closer in a comfortable sort of way and Bonnie had appreciated this development in their relationship. And the development had only come about because Carol had gone away.

Life, Bonnie thought, worked in mysterious ways to give you what you needed.

Chapter 118

Carol gripped the counter and took a deep breath. Her knuckles were white. Her head was tingling.

And then, the moment of panic was gone. If that's what it had been, panic.

Maybe it had been sheer emotion. After all, she and Bonnie had never spoken as honestly with each other as adults as they had been speaking in the past few days. An experience like that was enough to rattle anyone.

Even Carol Ascher.

"Remember the summer you were in a production of *Oklahoma!* at the little theater out by the Shandy's farm?" Carol asked when she had rejoined her sister with more hot tea.

"Of course, I remember. It occupied every waking moment of my life from the day I got out of school in June 'til the last performance in August." Bonnie frowned. "I seem to remember both of us at that first open call."

"I was there, but I could see how much being in the play meant to you and I knew you'd have a better time if I wasn't stealing the limelight. So, I decided not to audition."

Bonnie smiled. "I suppose I should thank you. Remember how I had a crush on one of the older boys in the play? You encouraged me to flirt. You offered to lend me those knee-high boots, the ones with the stacked heel."

"I was trying to boost your ego as well as your height!"

"My feet were too small for them," Bonnie said. "But it was the thought that counted."

Carol shrugged. "Maybe I shouldn't have encouraged you to act as someone other than who you were."

"An awkward fourteen-year-old. The boy—what was his name?—never noticed me, of course. I wouldn't have known what to do if he had," Bonnie said with a wry laugh. "Girls that age don't want a boy to reciprocate a crush, not really. Too scary."

"I was never scared of boys," Carol admitted. "Or of sex for that matter. I guess in a way none of it seemed important enough to be concerned about." None of what, she asked herself? Love?

Bonnie leaned forward a bit. "Has Nicola told you anything about her conversation with her father?" she asked.

"Nothing other than she was glad they had spoken and that they plan to speak again."

"That's wonderful," Bonnie said. "Ken would be so pleased."

"I know. You two were . . . You and Ken were like guardian angels to my daughter. I can't ever thank you enough, I can't ever express my gratitude for—"

Carol pressed her linen napkin to her eyes.

Bonnie's voice was soft and low. "You already have," she said. "You already have."

Chapter 119

"My father and I talked again on FaceTime. We get along so well. I guess on some level we've always known each other. Does that make sense?"

Nicola was sitting at one end of the uncomfortable couch in Ferndean's living room. Her mother was sitting at the other end. Every other moment, one or the other of them would grimace and shift.

"Yes," her mother said in answer to Nicola's question. "I believe it does."

"You don't happen to have a picture of the two of you together, do you?" Nicola asked. "No, that would be unlikely."

"As a matter of fact," Carol said, "I do." She got up and went to the small table just inside the front door on which sat her bag and keys. She returned with a photo that she handed to Nicola as she sat down next to her.

"Sorry it's a bit wrinkled. I remember that dress," she went on, nervously, Nicola thought. "It was a classic wrap dress from one of Diane von Furstenburg's early collections."

Nicola gazed silently at the photo for some time. Finally, she looked up at her mother. Her eyes were brimming with tears. "This is the first time I'm seeing my parents together," she said. "You look—happy."

"It was a good party."

"I don't mean that you look like you're having fun. I mean . . ."

"I know what you mean." Carol smiled and wiped at her eyes with her fingertips. "I've always claimed not to be a sentimental person. And yet, I've kept this photo in my wallet for over a quarter of a century. What does that say about me?"

"There's nothing wrong with being sentimental."

"Your father was very handsome."

"He still is," Nicola said. "He's dignified."

"Yes, he's a gentleman of the sort you don't find very often these days." Carol sighed. "I've been very lucky having Alex in my life. I don't deserve him. I never have."

"Don't say that, Mom. He really loves you. I totally believe him when he says he did what he did willingly, for your sake. Look, could I have a copy of this?"

"Of course. I probably have more photos at home. I mean, in New York. You could look through them at any time."

Nicola smiled to herself. It was another reason to pay a visit to her old home. "When you told me about my father, why didn't you also tell me about his Ukrainian background?"

"I suppose I thought it would be a treat if he heard about your interest in that part of the world from you. Maybe that was silly."

Nicola smiled. "It was sweet. Mom, I have a request. I'm asking you not to tell my father about your addiction. I think it would only hurt him to know. He'll wish he could have helped you. I want his last months to be as happy as they can be."

Carol nodded. "Agreed. I don't want to add to his burdens in any way. I've done enough damage to the people I love."

"Mom, stop saying things like that. What's done is done and no decision you made was made with evil intentions. I believe that. And remember I told you that something was holding me back from making a commitment to the Peace Corps? Now I know what it was. My parents need me. I'm going to Buenos Aires to visit my father. And, Mom, we'd like you to come, too."

Nicola had not expected her words to produce the reaction they did. Her mother put her hands over her eyes. Without hesitation, Nicola put her arm around her mother's shoulders.

"I've never seen you cry," she said softly.

"It's the couch," her mother mumbled. Suddenly, she dropped her hands and gently shrugged out of Nicola's embrace. "Children shouldn't have to see their parents in a moment of crisis," she said with a sniff and a dab at her eyes with a tissue she took from her pants pocket.

"That's silly. Besides, I'm an adult." Nicola smiled kindly. "It's about time I understood that my parents are people with full emotional lives of their own. Sorry it took me so long to get that."

"Sometimes I wonder if anyone ever fully gets that, or wants to. Well, what do I know? Honestly, it wasn't long after being on my own in New York that I stopped missing my mother and father. Maybe there's a flaw in my emotional makeup."

"I don't think so," Nicola said. "Everyone is unique. There's no detailed blueprint for a human life."

"Since when did you get so wise?" her mother asked with a smile.

"Since you came back to Yorktide. Now, Mom!" Nicola cried in alarm. "Don't start crying again!"

Chapter 120

"That was a great point you made, Julie." Thom Hunt smiled. "We should always be rethinking our approach to inclusivity in our classrooms. Tolerance is all well and good, but full acceptance is better."

Julie thanked her colleague. Sara Webb's third summer workshop had been a success for Julie. She knew that she looked better than she had in months. It was because she felt better, more capable of focus, less prone to waves of despair and the bombardment of self-abusive thoughts.

And her friendship with Aggie had been restored, and that was a very good thing. In the past week, they had gone for a hike, seen a popular movie, and Julie had visited the farm to play with Colleen and her younger brother, Jason.

Miranda, this time clad in a pair of neon green capri pants, had not apologized for her careless behavior earlier in the summer; Julie suspected that Miranda wasn't the sort to apologize.

It didn't matter.

Sara now approached Julie and for a few minutes they spoke about Julie's essay. Sara had only a few suggestions for improvement and clarity—all excellent—and Julie promised she would work on the revisions that evening, when she got home after having dinner with a few of her colleagues.

She was rejoining the world.

Slowly.

But surely.

"Julie, you ready?" Tessa called.

"Yes," Julie responded. "I am."

Chapter 121

"You really have a green thumb," Carol noted admiringly.

"It comes naturally," Bonnie admitted, taking a seat next to her sister at the table that had been situated to provide an unobstructed view of the Elgort garden. "Ken had one, too."

"I have a few plants in my apartment. All plastic." Carol shrugged. "I tried to keep live plants, but they never stayed live for long."

Bonnie laughed. Since Carol's revelation about Nicola's father, the sisters had moved into their own little bubble apart from the other members of the family, apart from the other residents of Yorktide, apart from the world. Bonnie was experiencing the excitement of getting to know someone new, along with the thrill of reconnecting with someone she had once known so well. It was a unique moment in Bonnie's life, the joining of these two journeys.

"Remember when you ran for Miss Yorktide of 1973?" she asked.

Carol laughed. "How could I forget? What possessed me? You know how I feel about sashes."

"Dad encouraged you. He was sure you'd be a shoo-in. The contestants not only had to be beautiful but also have a spotless reputation."

"I remember I had to write an essay about why I thought I should be chosen Miss Yorktide. What a strange thing to ask, when you think about it. I suppose Miss Yorktide didn't need to be humble."

Bonnie hesitated. Did she really want to admit to this bit of bad behavior? And then she plunged ahead. "The thing is," she said, "I didn't want you to win the contest, so I sent an anonymous letter to the judges saying that you had cheated on a test back in high school. But I guess they figured out the letter was a hoax. There wasn't even an investigation and you won the title."

Carol's expression was difficult for Bonnie to read. She didn't look angry. Maybe surprised. "It's strange," Carol said after a moment, "I knew that someone had sent a letter to the judges slandering me—nothing is ever a secret in Yorktide—but I never suspected that you were the one who wrote it. I assumed it was one of the other contestants who hadn't made it to the finals."

"It was me. I can't believe I'm actually telling you this after all these years. I guess I still feel guilty for acting so childishly."

"We've come a long way this summer, admitting our weaknesses." Carol shook her head. "What made you try to sabotage my chances of winning?"

"You embarrassed me in front of Ken," Bonnie said. In for a penny, in for a pound.

"Why would you be embarrassed?" Carol's eyes widened. "Oh, you had a crush on him when I was dating him!"

"Yes, I did. And this one afternoon when he was at the house you teased me about what I was wearing."

"I'm sorry," Carol said feelingly. "If I'd known you had a crush on Ken, I wouldn't have teased you, really. I don't know why I did it in the first place. Maybe I was just being a stupid teenager."

Bonnie believed her sister. And she wondered if she should also admit to the acts of sabotage she had committed in the weeks leading up to Carol's departure from Yorktide for New York. But no. She had been honest enough for one day.

The sisters were silent for a long moment. The sun was pleasantly warm. The garden truly was looking its seasonal best. Just how bad would it be, Bonnie thought again, if Carol lived on her own at Ferndean? Bonnie would still have her beloved cottage, as well as the freedom to visit Ferndean—and her sister—as she pleased.

It really wouldn't be that bad at all.

Chapter 122

Carol turned to her sister. "I'm sorry I lied to you earlier this summer," she said. "About Ken and me. It was despicable and I should have apologized earlier."

"Better late than never," Bonnie said matter-of-factly.

"Is it?" Carol very much hoped that was true. "Anyway," she went on, "I don't know how much Ken told you of what happened between us at the end, so I'm sorry if I'm repeating what you already know. The truth is that I asked Ken to leave Yorktide with me because in spite of my bravado, I was afraid of undertaking such a big adventure on my own. I thought having a strong man by my side would make the transition easier. Honestly, I never stopped to imagine what Ken would do with himself in New York while I was pursuing a bright and shiny career. My motives for asking him to come along were entirely selfish."

Bonnie looked genuinely surprised, though not angry. "He never told me you had asked him to leave Yorktide with you!"

"Really?" Carol smiled wryly. "Well, not only did he refuse, he also broke up with me there and then."

"But you went to New York, anyway, in spite of being afraid."

"Terrified is more like it. And I can't tell you how many times during those first two years I wanted to come home. But I didn't allow myself to lose courage. I'm sure there were people here in

Yorktide just waiting for that too-big-for-her-britches Carol Ascher to fall flat on her face. It's human nature to want people who stick their heads above the crowd to be shot down."

"I don't think you should have been afraid to come home," Bonnie said. "This is a good community. You wouldn't have been judged."

Carol shrugged. Her sister would always be far more trusting a person than she was. "Well," she said, "that's all in the past. And I should get going." She wanted to do more work on interpreting Marcus Ascher's elaborate plans. But first she would need a nap. She felt unaccountably tired, as if something giant was sitting on her and preparing to settle for a good, long stay.

"Thanks for coming by," Bonnie said, rising to accompany her sister out to her car.

"It was my pleasure," Carol told her truthfully.

By the time Carol reached Ferndean, she could barely keep her eyes open. No sooner had her head touched the pillow than she was soundly asleep.

Chapter 123

Nicola pulled her car along the curb outside the Millers' house. She was hoping Julie was free for a walk along one of the local nature trails. She knew she should have called first, but for some reason she hadn't. Maybe she *was* becoming more like her mother!

She rang the bell, but no one answered. She turned the doorknob and the door opened. "Hello?" she called, stepping inside. There was no reply. Nicola made a quick search of the first floor; no Julie. Sophie didn't seem to be home, either. Scott was in the garage; Nicola could hear him using an electric tool of some sort.

Nicola headed back to the front door. Bad luck. But maybe it was better Julie wasn't around. Carol and Bonnie wanted Alex's presence to be kept from Julie for a while longer, until she had gotten a handle on her own emotional crisis. Nicola wasn't entirely sure she could keep from blurting out the astounding news.

As she passed through the living room, something caught Nicola's eyes. That was Sophie's phone on the mantel. The hot-pink case was unmistakable. She must have left it behind. That was odd. Sophie was addicted to her phone. To forget it she must have been in a state of excitement or tension or . . .

Nicola picked up the phone and began to scroll through the recent text messages.

What she found made her stomach drop. There was an exchange between Sophie and some guy named Tim. She was meet-ing him by the abandoned barn on Ferny Lane at three o'clock; he would drive them to a party in New Hampshire; there would be booze and pot. There was no attempt at hiding any of this, no code words, no sly references.

My parents won't even notice I'm gone, Sophie's last text said.

Nicola's hand tightened on the phone. An image of that nasty-looking guy she had seen the day she had picked Sophie up at the camp came to her mind. Tim?

This was bad.

Nicola raced out of the house, across the yard, and into the garage. She shouted and waved at Scott; after a moment, he be-came aware of her through the shrill noise of the drill he was using. He turned off the machine, took the plugs from his ears, and wiped his forehead with the back of his hand.

"What's up?" he asked.

"I think Sophie's in trouble," Nicola panted. "I didn't mean to snoop, but . . . Look at this. She must have left it behind acciden-tally." Or, Nicola wondered suddenly, had Sophie unconsciously wanted rescuing?

Nicola handed him Sophie's cell phone. She watched as Scott read the text exchange. The color drained from his face. When he looked up at Nicola, his eyes were dark with emotion.

"My car's out front," he said. He stuffed his daughter's phone in his pocket and tore out of the garage.

"I'm coming with you," Nicola said, running after Scott.

He didn't protest; Nicola wasn't sure he was fully aware that she was sliding into the seat next to him.

"What time is it?" he asked when they had gone a few miles in the direction of the meeting place Sophie had mentioned.

Nicola swallowed hard. "Ten minutes after three."

Scott stepped on the gas and Nicola gripped the seat beneath her. What was the chance they could stop a disaster from happen-ing? What if Sophie had indeed used a code of sorts in her text, or what if she had mistyped, and she was meeting Tim at two o'clock, not at three . . .

And then, miraculously, just up ahead . . . "That's them!" she cried.

"How can you be sure?" Scott demanded.

"Sophie told me once about the red sports car one of the older counselors drove. That has to be it."

Scott increased speed again until the car was within spitting distance of Tim's.

"He's pulling over!" Nicola cried.

The red car had barely come to a full stop when the front passenger side door opened and Sophie came tumbling out. Her face was distorted with panic; tears were flooding her eyes.

"He's not driving away," Nicola said, stunned.

"That would be an admission of guilt," Scott said, unbuckling his seat belt. "He's going to deny everything."

Scott leapt from the car just in time to catch his daughter, who threw herself into his arms.

"Daddy!" Sophie sobbed. "I was so scared. I tried to open the door, but he'd locked it and I thought . . ."

"It's okay, Sophie," Scott murmured. His grip on his daughter was tender but fierce. "You're safe now. Nicola," he commanded, "take care of her."

Scott released his daughter and Nicola embraced her as Scott strode toward Tim's showy vehicle. Sophie buried her head in Nicola's shoulder; Nicola kept her eyes riveted on the men. So far, Scott was in control of his temper. He was the larger of the two, taller and heftier. But Tim had that look of a sneak about him; he would fight dirty and feel no guilt about it.

Nicola could hear every word the men said.

"You do know it's illegal to take a minor across state lines." Scott's hands clenched into fists at his side.

Tim's hands were shoved in the front pockets of his slouchy jeans. He wore a baseball cap backward; there was a thick gold chain around his neck. "She said she wanted to come with me," he said with a shrug. "Nobody forced her."

"She's fifteen. A child. You're an adult. That makes you guilty."

Tim grinned. "Of what, dude? We're still in Maine."

Nicola shuddered. Of course, his intention had been to rape Sophie once at the so-called party in New Hampshire. Of course, it had.

"Only because I stopped you," Scott said coldly. "I'll be notifying your employer. And I'll be going to the police."

Tim laughed. "Go ahead. I'm not scared of you."

"You should be. Get out of here before I do something I'll regret."

Tim slouched his way back into his car, started the engine, and tore back onto the road, sending loose gravel flying.

"Oh, Daddy, I'm so sorry!" Sophie cried, breaking away from Nicola and running to her father.

Nicola watched the father and daughter embrace. A parent's love for his child knew no bounds and stopped short at no sacrifice. Suddenly, Nicola saw her mother's sending her away to her family in Maine as a supreme gesture of love. It must have been so difficult for Carol Ascher to admit to herself that she might not be able to properly care for her child. And it must have been wrenchingly hard to actually let her child go.

Nicola wiped the tears from her cheeks and joined Scott and Sophie as they climbed into the car to go home.

Chapter 124

Sophie sat between her parents on the living room couch; each held one of her hands. She had fallen asleep there almost as soon as Scott had brought her home. Julie had stood watch over her. When she woke, Julie had made her cinnamon sugar toast and scrambled eggs. Sophie ate with gusto.

Though her daughter was safe now, Julie's heart still beat painfully. Sophie had come so close to a violence that might well have destroyed her soul. A violence that might even have resulted in the loss of her life. Julie knew she could never have recovered from being—however inadvertent—the cause of something so disastrous to her child. Never.

Suddenly, Sophie let go of her parents' hands and got up from the couch. "I'm going to bed," she said. "I'm so tired, I feel like I could sleep for days."

"Do you want me to stay with you for a while?" Julie asked.

Sophie smiled a bit. "That's okay. But thanks."

When she had gone, Scott turned to his wife.

"She's not going back to the camp," he declared.

"Of course. Do you want to report him or—"

"I'll do it."

Julie reached out and gently touched Scott's hand. "Thank you."

Scott took Julie's hand in his. "We almost lost our daughter today," he said quietly, "and maybe it's not entirely our fault, but we're to blame in some way and we can't deny that. We've got to do something to make this situation better."

"You're right." Julie moved closer to her husband. "You're a hero," she said softly. "You saved our daughter's life."

"I'm not a hero," Scott said gruffly. He let go of Julie's hand and stood. "I'm going to make those calls now."

Julie watched as her husband left the room.

The affair with Laci Fox had happened. It had ended. Fact. Maybe there was a level on which Julie could never trust Scott again. But Scott's lack of stability did not reflect on her character, her personality, her career, her being a mother. Scott was who he was. Julie was who she was. And never the twain shall meet?

Maybe. But maybe not. Julie was emerging from this summer wiser. She loved Scott, but if at some point he chose to destroy their marriage, she would not die. She would be sad and disappointed—in Scott, not in herself—but she would not give up.

Most importantly, Julie wanted Scott and Sophie to make peace. Scott was a good father. He had done something stupid and callous, but what person didn't do something stupid and callous at some ugly point in his life? Sophie needed to learn the messy truth about human nature—that it was endlessly varied—and to realize that her parents were human beings, simultaneously glorious and flawed.

Julie rose from the couch. She would make dinner for herself and her husband. Just the two of them.

Chapter 125

When Carol had gone home the other afternoon, Bonnie had spent a fair amount of time wondering why Ken had never told her that Carol had asked him to accompany her to New York. She would never really know the answer to that question, but she might hazard a guess. Ken had been further protecting Carol from ridicule or judgment. He might even have sensed that Bonnie would take a bit of mean-spirited pleasure in knowing that her big sister wasn't so perfect after all, that she had expressed a need, even if it had been couched as an invitation to an adventure, and that she had been turned down.

Bonnie felt a bit ashamed. She couldn't be mad at Ken for keeping part of the story to himself. He had always been a better, kinder person than she could ever be.

Now, Bonnie reached out to lift the anchor-shaped knocker of Ferndean's front door but before she could, a voice called, "Come in, it's open!"

With a smile, Bonnie stepped inside.

"I saw you drive up," Carol explained. Bonnie thought her sister looked tired.

"Let me take that from you," Bonnie said, stepping forward to relieve Carol of the tray she was holding. "You didn't have to go to all this trouble."

"It was no trouble," Carol said, leading them into the living room.

"Scones with butter and jam, tea, coffee, milk, sugar, honey! I'll spoil my dinner." Bonnie set the tray onto the coffee table. The table really was ugly, she thought. Carol had a point about so much in the house being ready for retirement.

"Look at it this way," Carol said with a smile. "You won't have to bother to cook dinner."

"True! I have a bit of family news to share," Bonnie said, pouring a cup of tea for her sister. She related the tale of Sophie's terrifying ordeal, highlighting Nicola's part in Sophie's rescue. Carol reacted with a particularly colorful expletive and a threat of severe bodily harm should she ever come upon the guilty party.

"Thank goodness Nicola didn't stand on ceremony when she saw Sophie's phone on the mantel," Bonnie added.

"Thank goodness, indeed," Carol agreed. "Respecting a minor's privacy is all well and good, but there are times when, well, when instinct tells you to interfere."

"You're thinking of those difficult times before Nicola came to Maine, aren't you?" Bonnie asked gently.

"I am. I'm sure Nicola hated me for snooping, but I felt I had no choice." Carol settled back in their father's chair. "There's something else I probably should have told you before," she said. "Ken and I never had sex. He said he wanted to wait for the person he was going to marry."

Bonnie smiled. Deep down she had known all along that Ken was a virgin—as was she—on their wedding night, but she hadn't wanted to embarrass him by asking for confirmation. Men were notoriously sensitive about those things. "Thank you," she said. "For telling me."

"Believe me," Carol went on with a smile. "I tried to get him to change his mind, but all along I think he knew we weren't meant to be. You were Ken's one and only, Bonnie, the love of his life."

"I was lucky to have found that kind of love," Bonnie said. "Now, Carol, have something to eat. You look a little worn-out."

Carol passed a hand across her forehead and didn't reply.

Bonnie leaned forward. "Carol? Are you all right?"

Carol dropped her hand into her lap. "No," she said faintly. "I don't feel well."

"What's wrong?" Bonnie asked, now at her sister's side. "My God, you're drowned in sweat!"

"My chest hurts. I feel dizzy. Bonnie, I don't want to die," Carol murmured.

Bonnie had already reached for her phone and had dialed 911. "You won't," she said fiercely. "I won't let you. Hello? Yes."

Bonnie gave the dispatcher the address and a brief description of her sister's distress.

"Help will be here in a moment," she said, grasping her sister's hand.

"There's something I need to tell you," Carol said, her voice low and weak. "About Ferndean. Important . . ."

"The paramedics are here!"

Bonnie ran to the door and flung it open.

It was only when Carol had been safely settled in the ambulance and Bonnie was behind the wheel of her car that she realized she was trembling violently.

"Please, God," she prayed, starting the engine. "Please, let my sister live."

Chapter 126

Carol felt groggy. She was vaguely aware of where she was but not sure why she was there.

She had other questions, too.

Had she told Bonnie that she was releasing her hold on Ferndean? No. She didn't think that she had. Well, she would tell her soon. As soon as . . .

Carol woke. She looked up at the clock on the far wall. An hour had passed. Or maybe she was reading the clock wrong. . . .

People in white or green came and went. Bonnie might have been there at one point.

The next time she woke she was alone. This time, her brain felt clearer. Her heart was beating normally.

Carol turned her face into the pillow.

She could have worked out a better arrangement with Alex, one in which he would have had access not only to his daughter but to the mother of his child.

Why hadn't she been able to choose a life more accommodating of her family's needs?

Because age comes too soon and wisdom comes too late. Who had said that?

Before Carol could ponder that question, she was again asleep.

Chapter 127

Nicola glanced at the speedometer. The last thing she needed was to be stopped by the police when time could be of the essence. Her mother had been taken ill. Nicola did not know what had happened. She had assumed the worst.

An hour earlier, Bonnie had called Nicola on her cell, but Nicola had had her phone turned off, her habit when working at Pine Hill. Her aunt had then called the administrative office and someone had come looking for Nicola. He had no more information other than that Carol Ascher had been taken to Yorktide Community Hospital.

Nicola fought a wave of panic and tightened her hands on the wheel. She could not be losing her mother, not now when she had just found her father and he, too, would be gone before long.

"Please," she whispered aloud, "whoever is listening, don't let my mother die. Please."

Chapter 128

"Mom said that we should wait until she had more news about Carol's condition before we visit."

Scott nodded. "Okay. Whatever she thinks is best."

Julie and Scott were seated at the kitchen table with two cups of tea. Sophie was at a friend's house. There was a sense of quiet and calm in the Miller home, a sense that had been absent for so long that at first, Julie had trouble recognizing it. It made her feel safe enough to ask a question she had asked once before. The answer had been unsatisfactory.

"Scott," she said. "Why did you have the affair?"

"Because I'm weak," he replied immediately. His eyes were sad. "I'm vain. Laci flattered me. The whole thing was all about my ego. And I deserve to be punished. But not this way, Julie. Not by having to witness you falling apart. Scream at me. Throw me out. But stop punishing the wrong person."

"What if it happens again?" she asked.

"What if it doesn't?" Scott's reply was not said challengingly.

"I can't live my life waiting for disaster to strike."

"Then don't live it that way," he said. "Choose to believe in me."

"Can you promise not to betray me again?" Julie asked.

"I can promise," Scott said forcefully. "I do promise. Sincerely.

And I feel confident that I'll never mess up a second time because there's no way I want to see you this miserable ever again."

Julie looked closely at her husband, at the bluish-green eyes she had always found so compelling, at the strong, well-shaped hands that had cradled their daughter so lovingly, at the lock of his hair that flopped above his left eye no matter how many times he pushed it back into place. She believed him. "I did this to myself," she said. "I allowed myself to suffer."

"Don't blame yourself for suffering," Scott said urgently. "Just don't."

"Maybe we shouldn't talk of blame," Julie said.

"Yes, we should. Don't let me off the hook. But forgive me if you can. Because if you can't, we won't be able to go on being married. Not decently married."

Decently married. That meant living together in a home they had built, not cohabitating in a detention center.

Julie considered. She and Scott had already done enough damage to Sophie. For that reason—and for others—she would try her best to mend her marriage. "I can forgive you," she said to Scott. She had always been able, and now she was also willing.

Julie's phone alerted her to a text from her mother. They could visit Carol now. She had been admitted and was in a semiprivate room.

"I'll drive," Scott said, and the two were on their way.

Chapter 129

Bonnie had been with Carol when Julie and Scott arrived at the hospital. In spite of the stressful situation, Bonnie had noticed that the Millers had seemed more like a genuine couple than they had in months. She didn't think she was imagining things.

With assurances that Carol had not suffered a cardiac event or a stroke, but rather a particularly spectacular anxiety episode, Bonnie and the others had finally left her to rest.

Now, comfortably seated in her cozy living room, Bonnie decided once and for all that she would let Carol have Ferndean House if that was what she really wanted. Life was just too short to spend it fighting over what amounted to a pile of wood, glass, and nails.

She loved her sister. She had nothing for which to forgive her. Neither had mistreated the other, as children or as adults, at least not consciously. And they were no longer rivals for their parents' affection and attention. They hadn't been in years, in spite of what Bonnie had told herself to believe. What possible reason, other than stubbornness, could there be at this autumnal stage of their lives not to come together?

Bonnie drew one of her handmade quilts over her lap. She vaguely recalled that Carol had wanted to tell her something just as the paramedics were arriving. But maybe she had imagined that. She had been so frightened, she was surprised she could remember anything that had taken place or been said from the moment Carol fell ill until the moment she was in a doctor's care.

Well, if it was important, Carol would tell her eventually.

Bonnie yawned. It was time for a nap.

Chapter 130

"You really don't need to fuss," Carol said. Since Nicola had arrived twenty minutes earlier she hadn't stopped adjusting blinds, straightening sheets, refreshing water, and generally, well, fussing.

"I like being busy," Nicola told her mother. "I like being needed."

Kin keeping in its most basic form. Carol gestured Nicola closer and spoke softly; the patient on the other side of the curtain didn't need to hear the details of Carol's life. "I've been thinking. There's no need for your father to know about my little scare."

"Nonsense," Nicola said roundly. "I'm calling Alex when I get home and telling him what happened. He has the right to know."

Did he? Carol sighed. She supposed that he did.

"Why did this anxiety event happen now, when all your secrets are told, when everything is so much better between you and me and Bonnie?" Nicola wondered.

"I don't know," Carol said. "But I intend to find out. I'll ask my doctor if she can recommend a therapist." Carol plucked at the neck of her johnny. "There's no way to look stylish while wearing this thing, is there?"

Nicola smiled. "Afraid not. At least they let you put your jewelry back on. Are you cold? I could drape a blanket around your shoulders."

"Nicola, I'm fine. I don't plan to be caught wearing a blanket in public until I'm at least ninety. If then."

"I'm glad to see you looking ahead. I've finally just found my family and I'm not letting them go."

"Stop worrying," Carol said.

Nicola put her hands on her hips. "Right, like I can possibly not worry when my mother is in the hospital. At least you're allowing me to visit, not like the last time."

"That was different."

"I know, Mom. Are you hungry?"

"Actually," Carol said, "I'm famished. But they won't let me order from the regular menu, not that it's particularly enticing. I'm stuck with the heart-healthy nonsense."

"It's not nonsense, Mom. But it probably is unappetizing. How about I run out and get you something edible?"

"That would be lovely, Nicola," Carol said earnestly. "And make it something involving avocado, will you? Nobody can object to avocado."

Nicola hurried off and Carol got out of bed to use the tiny bathroom. She hadn't told Nicola yet that she was relinquishing Ferndean House, though she hadn't been able to resist dropping a hint days earlier. Bonnie deserved to be the first one to know for sure that her future as keeper of Ferndean was assured.

Carol looked into the mirror above the minuscule sink and smiled.

Chapter 131

"Hello, Nicola."

The moment Nicola heard her father's voice, a sob broke from her heart.

"What is it?" Alex said quietly. "Take a deep breath. Tell me."

Nicola wiped her eyes with the back of her hand. "Carol," she began, "Mom, she . . . she's going to be okay, but she's in the hospital. She had a bad anxiety attack. I thought she was dying. I'm sorry," she said as a fresh flood of tears overwhelmed her.

"Don't be sorry," her father said softly. "Don't ever be sorry for loving someone."

And Nicola did love her mother. She always had.

"Dad? Thank you for being my father."

"Thank you for being my child, Nicola." Alex's voice was now almost a whisper.

Only when the call had ended and Nicola was sipping a comforting cup of tea with honey did she realize that she had called her father Dad for the very first time.

That was cool.

Chapter 132

Upon returning from the hospital, assured that Carol was doing well, Julie and Scott had put together a meal of soup, sandwiches, and salad.

Sophie was still at her friend Anabel's house. She had decided to keep what had happened with Tim from her friends not involved with the camp. As for the other counselors, some of them must have known what Tim was up to, targeting an underage girl; Sophie was considering confronting them about their silence. But not quite yet.

"None of this is your fault," Julie had assured her daughter repeatedly. "Tim is the wrongdoer here, not you. It's Tim who deserves to be punished."

Still, Sophie felt deeply embarrassed. She confessed to having had second and third thoughts about meeting Tim up until the very moment she had gotten into his car. She knew she had been wrong when she told him her parents wouldn't notice she was gone. But she felt she had gone too far to tell Tim she had changed her mind without angering him.

And she was still scared. "I don't know why," she had said to Julie just that morning. "I mean, nothing happened. Dad and Nicola found me, but . . ."

It would take Sophie time to work through the emotional damage that had been done to her. And the threat of physical violence could be as damaging as the actual infliction of physical violence. Of that Julie had no doubt.

But at this particular moment, Julie wanted very much to focus on the person sitting across from her.

Now was the time for Julie and Scott to resume the conversation about their marriage.

"My self-esteem issues this summer were triggered by your having the affair," Julie told her husband. "But they're my issues to deal with. I know that."

Scott nodded. "I was an idiot."

"You were."

"I acted badly."

"You did."

"I almost destroyed this family."

Destroyed . . .

A strange and overwhelming urge descended on Julie Miller. In one swift move, she reached for the half-empty bottle of salad dressing and flung it against the wall.

There was a moment of stunned silence. Scott's eyes were wide. Julie's heart was racing. But she didn't feel bad. She felt— powerful.

Suddenly, husband and wife burst out laughing.

"I'm sorry," Julie gasped. "I don't know what came over me."

"Don't be sorry," Scott said when he had recovered his breath. "Actually, that was pretty awesome."

"Yeah," Julie added, "but why couldn't it have been ranch dressing? Why did it have to be Catalina? I hope the color comes out of my curtains."

"If it doesn't, then we'll get new curtains."

Scott got up from the table. He opened his arms and waited.

Julie got up from her seat. She allowed him to hug her. It felt strange, after so many months of physical distance, to be touched in this way. But not so strange that it didn't also feel good.

She tightened her arms around him.

Chapter 133

"Do you think you could teach me how to quilt?" Sophie asked. She had come to visit Bonnie unannounced. Bonnie was pleased. The older Sophie got, the less often she opted to spend time with her grandmother. "Is it hard?"

"Yes, I can teach you, and no, it isn't hard. The important thing is that you enjoy the work. If you don't, there's no point in learning."

Sophie shrugged and ran a finger along a graphic design on the quilt she had heaped on her lap. The house was warm; Bonnie supposed Sophie was holding the quilt for comfort. "I'll think about it," she said.

Bonnie fought back a tear. Her granddaughter—her little Sophie!—had come so close to a dreadful danger. How had that been allowed to happen? How had such a degenerate been hired by the camp in the first place? Hadn't anyone seen that he was bad news? And Sophie's own parents . . .

Well, the miserable tension between Julie and Scott this summer had prevented both from fully embracing their parental responsibilities. It was a sorry situation all around.

But Sophie was safe now and she was talking about her frightening experience. Telling one's story, Bonnie had learned, was an effective way to dispel or neutralize demons. Carol, too, knew that now.

"Grandma," Sophie said now, "why are there evil people in the world? I know that's a rhetorical question. Or do I mean hypothetical? Anyway, why do you think there are?"

"I don't know," Bonnie admitted. "Evil, or whatever you want to call it, is just part of human nature, I guess. In some people, it's stronger than it is in others." She knew that was an inadequate answer, but it was all she knew how to offer.

Sophie sighed. "I miss Grandpa. He was so fun. Why did he have to die? I know. That's another one of those questions no one really expects a good answer to but it would be really nice if you could get one."

"Yes," Bonnie agreed. "It most certainly would."

"I think Mom still loves Dad. I know he still loves her. It's so obvious. Anyway, at least they're talking. Yesterday I actually heard Mom laugh for, like, the first time in forever."

"I'm very glad things seem to be improving," Bonnie said carefully. She had lived too long to assume a happy conclusion to a damaged relationship. Happy endings did happen. Just not always.

Sophie twisted to face her grandmother, the quilt still clutched in her lap. "Will your sister be okay?"

Bonnie nodded. "Yes, it was only an anxiety attack, although a scary one. She's going to have to address what might have caused it and learn how to keep it from happening again. To the extent that a person can control that sort of thing."

"Good," Sophie said. "Aunt Carol is cool. I guess it's Great-Aunt Carol. But I'm not sure she'd like that title. It makes her sound ancient."

Bonnie laughed. "She'd focus on the 'great' as in magnificent and be happy."

"What's this?"

Before Bonnie could stop her, Sophie reached for the notepad on the coffee table and began to read aloud what was written on the top page. "Two-week class on reentering the workforce after age fifty. Basic computer skills. Register?" Sophie looked up. "Are you looking for a job, Grandma?"

"Thinking about it, yes."

"But do you have to work?" she asked with a frown.

"It's not only a matter of having to or not having to," Bonnie explained. "It's also a matter of wanting to do something meaningful with the rest of my life. I know you think of me as old, but I'm not. Okay, I'm not young, but I'm not old."

Sophie quirked an eyebrow. "If you say so, Grandma."

Bonnie laughed. "How about I make us something to eat?"

Sophie sprang from the couch, quilt abandoned. "I thought you'd never ask!"

Chapter 134

Carol adjusted the pillows behind her back. No matter how many positions the bed offered—feet up; knees up; head and shoulders up—Carol was uncomfortable. That seemed about the right response to hospital life.

There was another thing about hospitals. Being stuck in one made you think hard about the important issues. Like the fact that life was not only brief but also terrifyingly unknowable. Anything could happen at any time and it was best not to forget that—or, she supposed, to dwell on it. As with most things in life, finding the middle road was the healthiest way to proceed. Maybe not the easiest, in spite of what pop psychologists would have people believe.

Carol's roommate began to snore. She was not a particularly pleasant woman (at least, she hadn't been to Carol), but in the last twenty-four hours she had been visited by her husband, her son, her daughter-in-law, and a friend. The husband had brought an enormous bouquet of carnations and he had cried openly at the sight of his wife. Before taking his leave, he had professed his love, had promised to return, and had sworn that when she came home she would find the house spotless.

That, Carol supposed, was true love.

Love was one of those big, important issues Carol had been thinking about since being admitted to the Yorktide hospital. The love she had. The love she had rejected.

What was it really like to be loved, to *allow* oneself to be loved, like Bonnie had loved Ken and Ken had loved Bonnie? She might have known with Alex.

Carol thought of Martin. Had she really loved him? Or had it merely been infatuation? Would she have lost interest like she had with all the others who had come before him? It was too late to know. Better to focus on what she could and did know, which was that Alex loved her—to the extent that she had let him—that Bonnie and Nicola loved her, that she had a family she cherished. If she had come to that important realization later than most, so be it.

Carol's roommate switched on the television and the mind-numbing opening music of a midday game show filled the small, sterile room. Carol took a slow, deep breath. The woman had a right to watch a television program. It was not the end of the world. Still, Carol felt she would go mad if she were stuck in this place for much longer. She wanted to be home. And home was . . .

Carol knew the answer to that question. She had known it for some time.

She hadn't really wanted Ferndean in the first place. She had wanted something else, something less tangible but also more real. She had wanted the love of her sister and daughter, and she had found that. Add to that the fact that she would be face-to-face with her dear Alex again before long and her life could be counted as very fortunate indeed.

Besides, as charming as Yorktide was, there was no way she could ever live there year-round. She had only been gone from New York for a little over two months and yet she already missed the sound of heels on pavement. She missed the presence of very tall buildings. She missed bagels. Real ones. She missed the onion soup at her favorite French-style bistro, and the way her favorite waiter, an ancient gentleman, served it with such seriousness and dignity. She even missed the honking of car horns. Sort of.

Once back in New York she would create a game plan for the coming years. She would go back to work in whatever capacity seemed right. She would—

"*Wheel of Fortune!*" the roommate cried.

Carol winced.

Chapter 135

"Why does it take forever to be discharged from the hospital?" Nicola wondered aloud.

"Bureaucracy," her mother said dryly. "Have patience."

Nicola turned from the room's large window and perched next to her mother on the edge of the bed. Earlier, Carol had changed into the fresh clothes Nicola had brought from Ferndean. Bonnie had cleaned, pressed, and put away the clothing she had been wearing when she had fallen ill.

"I've been thinking about what you told me when I asked about your social life," Nicola said. "About spending a lot of time on your own. About how I do the same."

"Just don't isolate yourself too much," her mother said kindly. "Friends are important."

"Do as I say, not as I do?" Nicola asked with a small smile.

"Something like that. Still, no woman is an island."

Nicola laughed. "I just remembered an old rhyme our housekeeper told me. 'Make new friends but keep the old. One is silver, the other is gold.'"

"Matilda had an apt phrase for every occasion."

"You did the right thing by sending me here to Yorktide," Nicola said suddenly. "I was miserable in that school, with those kids, and I needed to be away from it all. Thank you for knowing that."

Carol shook her head. "I didn't know for sure that I was doing the right thing. I just hoped that I was. For the both of us. We were lucky, that's all."

"I'm not sure lucky is the right word. Blessed? Maybe that's not right, either. I guess it doesn't matter now."

"That day you drove away with Scott and Julie . . . Honestly, it was one of the worst days of my life."

Nicola gently squeezed her mother's hand. "Mine too. I was so angry but more than that, I was scared. For the entire drive north, I fought not to burst into tears. When we got to Aunt Bonnie's house and she met me at the door with this sympathetic smile, I pretty much collapsed into her arms." Nicola smiled. "I think I scared her."

An aide appeared at the door with a wheelchair.

"Ready to go home, Ms. Ascher?" she asked.

"Yes," Carol said firmly.

"Aunt Bonnie should be out front with the car," Nicola told her.

Carol eased into the wheelchair. "My sister," she said, "is a good person."

Nicola patted her mother's shoulder. "I know," she said. "And so are you."

Chapter 136

"In the trash," Julie said aloud with some satisfaction. All those articles she would never return to—and if she did want to reread one or two, no doubt she could find them online.

Four large trash and recycling bags stood—or slumped—on the floor of Julie's office. Already the space looked larger and most definitely cleaner. A new start.

And not only for Julie Miller. Carol was going home today. Well, back to Ferndean House at least. As far as Julie knew, her aunt was still intent upon staying in Yorktide, but she wouldn't be totally surprised if Carol had changed her mind.

Whatever Carol decided to do, her presence in Yorktide this summer had helped Julie return to herself. Was that the best way to put it? Maybe she could say instead that Carol had inspired her to remember that she had value as an individual, apart from her role as wife and mother and daughter.

And she had been thinking about her aunt's offer of her apartment. It would be a dream come true in some ways, three or four days on her own in New York City, able to come and go as she pleased, an anonymous observer, independent of her identity as one of Yorktide's own. Yes, Julie thought as she tossed an ancient, inkless pen into a trash bag, once Carol was settled she would approach her about using the apartment.

She might also tell her aunt that she had applied for the Ackroyd Institute's scholarship. She had never thought she might one day visit the Windy City. Who knew what other destinations she might one day explore?

Julie eyed the framed image of a bunch of tulips that had hung on the wall next to the old filing cabinet for as long as she could remember. It was dingy and yellowed. Within a moment, the frame was off the wall, the image ripped out, crumpled, and thrown into a bag of recycling.

Maybe it was this last gesture that called Julie's attention to the fact that her wedding ring was no longer embedded in her finger. In fact, it turned easily now and with only a slight tug, Julie slipped the ring past her knuckle.

She wasn't aware that she had lost weight, but she must have. She had been more physically active in the last two weeks than she had been for months. She hadn't felt the awful need to overeat until she was senseless.

She wanted her wits about her. She had missed them.

Julie pushed the ring back to the bottom of her finger. She didn't need the ring to come off, not any longer. It didn't feel like the shackle it had only weeks ago; it didn't feel like a mocking reminder of the ruin that was her marriage. Her marriage was not a ruin.

Julie heard Scott's car pulling up the drive. She realized she was smiling.

Chapter 137

Bonnie was waiting just outside the main entrance to the hospital. When Nicola emerged from the building on her own, her heart leapt to her mouth. "Where's your mother?" she asked. "Is everything all right?"

Nicola smiled. "Fine. Mom decided she needed to pee before the ride home. The aide will bring her down in a few minutes."

"Good. For a moment..." Bonnie shook her head. "Never mind."

Nicola put her arm through her aunt's. "While we're waiting," she said, "I might as well tell you I've come to an important decision. I've decided not to apply to the Peace Corps, and I took a leave of absence from Pine Hill. I'm going to spend the next months with my parents. Mom and I are going to Buenos Aires to see my father."

"I think that's a wonderful idea!" Bonnie looked with misty eyes at her niece. "I'll miss you, we all will, but what you're doing is very generous."

Nicola shrugged. "I don't know about that. I mean, Mom and Alex did give me my life. And this summer I realized that I've always loved my mother, I mean really loved her, even when I felt hurt and rejected and angry. She was there for me those first important years of my life. She took good care of me and honestly, for a long time I was very happy."

Bonnie felt a twinge of jealousy. But that was normal.

"Please don't think I'm not grateful for what you and Ken did for me," Nicola went on. "I am. More than you'll ever know. But my parents need me right now and I'm going to do whatever I can for them. It's going to be a very bittersweet time for Mom and Alex."

For a moment, Bonnie couldn't speak. Her niece was such a fine young woman. Finally, she said, "You'll take good care of yourself, won't you? It will be hard on you, too, in ways neither of us can probably imagine."

Nicola smiled. "I'll be fine. I'm tough."

"You're your mother's daughter."

"And your niece."

"But no one gets through the tough times all on her own."

"Mom said something like that to me. About the importance of friends. She warned me not to isolate myself, like she has in her own life."

"Speak of the devil!" Bonnie grinned.

A small crowd had begun to gather in the wake of Carol Ascher's wheelchair, old-timers and young staff, all saying farewell to Yorktide's Golden Girl.

"Always the center of attention," Bonnie said fondly.

Nicola laughed. "She's a natural."

Chapter 138

"I'll leave you two alone now," Judith said, reaching for her canvas bag. She had been waiting for the sisters at Ferndean. Once Carol was safely inside, Judith had bustled about fetching her cousin a cold drink and a bowl of fruit salad she had whipped up and a stack of paperback novels to the point where Carol had begun to feel exhausted just watching her.

Finally, Judith was gone, leaving Carol enthroned in her father's armchair and watching Bonnie, now also in Florence Nightingale mode, fetching more things that Carol didn't need, like a box of tissues, and more things Carol didn't want, like a cup of tea with two sugars, and generally being sweetly annoying with her solicitations.

"Are you sure you're warm enough?" Bonnie asked for about the fourth time in the past fifteen minutes.

Carol sighed. "Bonnie, I'm fine. Stop fussing and sit down."

Bonnie did, taking the armchair that had been their mother's and folding her hands on her lap.

"Look," Carol said, before her sister could leap up on another mission of mercy, "there's something I need to tell you. I've given it a lot of thought and I'm one hundred percent sure about this decision, so you have no choice but to accept it."

"You're bossy." Bonnie said this with a smile.

"And that's news? I'm turning over my half of Ferndean House to you, Bonnie. And along with it I'm giving you a financial gift to help make the necessary repairs that will keep this old pile going for another hundred years."

Bonnie's expression changed from one of surprise to one of confusion to one of disbelief. "I can't . . ." she said faintly. "You can't . . ."

"Yes," Carol said firmly, "I can. There's something else. I can't believe I'm admitting this, but I actually decided to give you my share of Ferndean some weeks ago. I didn't tell you then because . . . because I thought that you and Nicola would want . . . would expect me to leave Yorktide immediately and I wanted to stay on. I wanted to spend more time with you both."

"Why would I have sent you away?" Bonnie asked, her eyes wide.

"Well, earlier this summer you told me I wasn't wanted here."

Bonnie blushed. "Oh, right. I'm sorry about that. It wasn't true. Really, it wasn't."

"Be that as it may, the house is yours or soon will be and I'm not changing my mind, so deal with it. I'll be moving back to New York, but things are going to be different with you and me. I'm going to visit you. You're going to visit me. Often. But I just can't live here in Yorktide."

Bonnie was now grinning. "I never thought Yorktide was right for you."

"It isn't. I know that now, but my family *is* right for me, you and Nicola and the whole lot of them."

"And Alex?" Bonnie asked.

Carol smiled sadly. "Poor Alex. I hope I can be of help to him in the time he has left. I hope I can make up for at least a little of the pain I've caused him."

"He made his decision," Bonnie pointed out. "But I think it's wonderful that you two are, well, are finally acting as a family."

"The family we always should have been? It's what I've been thinking, too. Anyway, all I ask is permission to bunk down in my old bedroom when I come to Yorktide."

"No more staying in one of the fancy resorts?"

"No, though I will need an air conditioner."

"Deal. And I promise that in addition to repairs and maintenance, I'll make some much-needed updates to the furnishings."

"I'd love to bring my expertise to bear," Carol admitted, "but I promise to respect your need for continuity and tradition."

"Thanks. But you were right when you said that the past is over. We don't have to forget it entirely, but we do need to acknowledge the present and the future."

"Amen to that."

"Can you believe I've never been to New York?" Bonnie said suddenly.

"We'll do the whole tourist thing when you come, Rockefeller Center, the Staten Island Ferry, the Empire State Building, all the museums."

"And can we actually have breakfast at Tiffany's?"

"We can, at The Blue Box Cafe. Or we could have afternoon tea if you'd prefer."

"No! Oh, what will I wear?"

"We'll see to that, don't worry." Carol would buy her sister a wardrobe appropriate for New York. Bonnie might even enjoy the experience.

"Maybe I'll leave Ferndean House equally to Nicola and Julie in my will," Bonnie said a bit mischievously. "Let them battle out the sole ownership the way we did!"

"They'll be fine. They're not sisters." Carol thought for a moment before going on. "But before you go ahead with that idea," she said, "keep in mind that sometimes a gift can be a burden. I'd talk to Nicola and Julie before making any changes to your will. If neither wants the property, it could be held in trust for Sophie. If she doesn't want Ferndean when the time comes, well, then, it can be sold. Time moves on. Things have to change."

"I know. You're right. I'll be careful with the disposition of Ferndean House. But for now, I'm going to enjoy every moment of its being mine!"

"I know you will, especially when I show you something very special I found this summer. You'll scold me if I try to get up, so would you go into the den and bring me the large box file on the coffee table?"

Bonnie hurried off and was soon back. "I'm dying to see what's inside!"

"Open it," Carol instructed. She watched as her sister carefully pulled a large sheaf of papers from the box.

"I don't understand," Bonnie said, looking up to her sister. "What is all this?"

"Evidence of a rather ambitious plan Marcus Ascher imagined for a folly on the property. You know those half-buried stones we've always wondered about? Well, a few weeks back I got curious and long story short, Terry Brown from the historical society was able to uncover Marcus's long-lost plans. I thought it would be a good idea to finally bring to life what we can of our ancestor's dream."

Bonnie's eyes filled with tears. "I don't know what to say. This is . . . this is wonderful, Carol!"

"It was thoroughly impractical, useless, and no doubt too expensive to build, but the idea behind it was beautiful."

"What does it all mean?" Bonnie asked, paging through the notes and drawings. "All the symbols."

"It means that Marcus Ascher was a whacky Victorian. I'm not sure he had a thoroughly coherent message in mind. I'm guessing the images all somehow express his devotion to his wife. I don't think we need to know more than that."

Bonnie carefully returned the papers to the box and placed her hands flat upon it. "I wonder what Rosemary thought of the scheme," she said, "if she scolded him for extravagance, or if she was as enthusiastic as he was. Without letters or diaries, we'll never know. Do you know I haven't visited their graves in years? Do you want to go with me one day soon?"

"Sure," Carol said. She was curious to see what images Marcus might have had inscribed on his headstone.

"We'll bring some flowers," Bonnie went on. "And we'll tell them what we've found."

Carol winced. "You're going to actually talk to our great-grandparents? They're dead."

"And? Don't worry. You don't have to say anything."

"Good." Carol hesitated. "While we're at the cemetery, would you mind if I paid my respects to Ken?"

Bonnie's eyes began to swim with tears again. "That would make me very happy."

Carol cleared her throat and shifted in her father's old, lumpy chair. "I'll tell you what would make *me* happy," she grumbled. "A new set of living room furniture!"

Chapter 139

Nicola and Carol were seated comfortably in Julie's backyard, sipping icy lemonade.

"Mom told me that you've given her Ferndean," Julie said. "Thank you, Carol."

Nicola beamed. She felt hugely grateful to her mother for having relinquished her claim on Ferndean House, and very proud of her as well.

Carol waved her hand dismissively. "No need to thank me. It was the right thing to do and I should have seen that earlier. And your mother probably told you that I'll be going back to New York in the fall. It's my home. It's where I belong."

"Yes, but I hope we'll see more of you than we have in the past."

"We'll make sure of that," Nicola said. "Anyway, Mom and I came here to tell you something. It's nothing bad," she added hastily. "But we . . . we've been keeping this from you for a few weeks. What with all that was going on with Scott and Sophie and . . ."

"I get it," Julie said. "I wasn't in a good place. So, what is it?"

Nicola gave her mother a look of encouragement. Succinctly and powerfully, Carol told Julie about Nicola's father, and about how a period of addiction to prescription opioids had contributed to her decision to send Nicola to live with her family in Maine.

"This is monumental," Julie said after a moment of stunned silence. "Like something that would happen in a soap opera! Nicola, I'm so very happy for you. And I'm so sorry that your father is ill." Julie turned from daughter to mother. "Your struggle with that drug must have been awful, Carol."

Carol nodded. "It was. And I don't think that my addiction is something that Sophie needs to know about, at least not at this point in her life."

"But you wanted me to know," Julie said.

"Yes, I want you to know that you're not the only one in the family who's fought the good fight. There's a physical component to depression as well as to addiction, we know that. The mind/body connection is real. If one of them is ailing, so is the other."

"Indeed. And I agree that Sophie doesn't need to know, not now."

"Speaking of my great-niece," Carol whispered.

Sophie was rounding the corner of the house. Once again, she was wearing those impossible short shorts she and her friends were so fond of. But she was also wearing something Nicola hadn't seen on the young woman in a long time. A genuinely open smile.

"What's up?" she said, giving her mother's shoulder a squeeze. "Did I miss anything fun?"

So, Carol told her, briefly, about Nicola's father.

"That is so seriously cool," Sophie cried when Carol was finished. "And you're gonna get to go to Buenos Aires! Wait, where is that exactly?"

Nicola smiled. "It's the capital of Argentina."

"Wow." Sophie suddenly frowned. "But I'm sorry your father is sick. That part sucks."

"Yeah," Nicola said, "it does."

Sophie frowned. "I remember things I said to you earlier this summer, Nicola. About not wanting anything to do with my father. And about how you were lucky you didn't have a dad. I'm sorry I said those things. It was stupid. I don't know what I'd do if Dad wasn't here. Or if . . ." Sophie shuddered dramatically. "I don't want to think about it."

Julie reached for her daughter's hand. "Then don't," she said. "Just be glad that we have each other right now."

Nicola and her mother left shortly after. When Nicola had

dropped Carol at Ferndean, she headed for her apartment. And while she drove along the quiet back roads of Yorktide, past green fields and old farmhouses, Nicola smiled remembering how happy her friend Hermione had been when she told her about all that had happened in the past week. A father discovered. A mother restored. A family reunited.

The summer had been a transformational time for Nicola, that was for sure. She wished her uncle Ken was there to share her joy, but she was certain that he was watching over her, feeling proud and pleased.

Nicola's path had become clear, at least the path she was meant to travel at this moment in her life.

She was the keeper of her kin.

Chapter 140

Julie couldn't seem to stop smiling. Rather, grinning. Like the infamous Cheshire cat.

She and Scott had had sex the night before. It had been surprisingly good. Scott was more attentive to her needs than he had ever been and that was nothing to dismiss lightly. And not once—truly—had she thought of Laci Fox.

Julie wasn't naïve enough to believe that everything in her marriage was suddenly back to normal—not that she wanted the old normal, not all of it anyway. But change was happening, and she knew for sure that she had a say in the shape of that change.

Ferndean House. Julie pulled into the drive and turned off the engine. It really was a grand old place. She was glad that her mother would be taking up residence in her childhood home. She was glad that all had worked out so amicably between the sisters.

Carol opened the door on the first knock. There was a dust rag thrown over one shoulder.

"Hi," she said. "What brings you around? I'm afraid you've caught me doing some cleaning."

Julie followed her aunt into the house. "Let's go out to the back deck," Carol suggested. "There's a lovely breeze out there."

"I wanted to talk to you about something," Julie said when the women had taken seats in the new wicker armchairs Carol had bought. "If the offer of a short stay in your apartment in the city is still open," Julie went on, "I'd like to take you up on it."

Carol smiled. "The offer is still open. I won't be going back to New York until after the anniversary of Ken's death in mid-September."

"Mom is happy you'll be with her for that," Julie said earnestly. "As am I."

"So, what does Scott think about your venture?" her aunt asked.

"I think he's a bit nervous I'll decide not to come back!" Julie laughed. "He's being totally supportive, but it surprised him that I want to spend time on my own so far from home."

"Good. He needs to realize that you're not just his predictably comfortable wife but your own person as well."

Julie agreed. "And I've applied for a scholarship from the Ackroyd Institute in Chicago," Julie went on. "It's for a week-long intensive course next spring on teaching religious tolerance. If I get it, the Windy City is in my future, too."

"That's fantastic," Carol said. "I haven't been to Chicago in years. Try to stay a few extra days after the course if you can. There's just so much to see."

"You're assuming I'll get the scholarship," Julie noted.

"Why not? It doesn't hurt to think ahead with confidence."

That was a new notion for Julie. To think ahead with confidence. She liked it. "There's something else," she began. "I'd appreciate it if you kept it to yourself, but I really need to tell someone. I approached Laci Fox this summer, the woman Scott had the affair with."

Carol raised an eyebrow. "You did? Well, I must say that was either very brave or very foolhardy. How did it turn out?"

"Not bad really," Julie told her aunt. "I went to her house when I thought it likely she'd be there. She was. She said I shouldn't be the one to feel guilty for anything."

"Smart woman. So, you got a bit of closure from the encounter?"

"I'm not sure closure is the right word," Julie admitted, "but I don't regret confronting her. In a way, it was the turning point for me."

"Good." Carol nodded. "Back to your New York plans. As soon as you give me your dates I'll let the concierge know that my niece will be staying."

"I'll need to go very soon if I'm to be back for the first day of the semester." Julie smiled. "I can't believe I'm actually doing this. I haven't gone anywhere on my own, not even overnight, since before Sophie was born. I absolutely have to visit the Metropolitan Museum of Art," Julie went on. "All my life I've wanted to see the Impressionist collection in person. And the Temple of Dendur. And all the medieval art! And I want to take the train to New York. There's something so romantic about train travel as opposed to air travel. At least in my mind there is."

"Visions of the Orient Express?" Carol said with a smile.

Julie laughed.

"Well, you're letting me get you a first-class ticket and that's the end of that," her aunt declared. "Consider it making up for all the birthdays and graduations I missed."

"You never missed anything," Julie argued. "You always sent a card."

"But I was never here, was I? Please let me do this."

Julie smiled. "All right. Thank you. Mom always said you were the most stubborn person she ever knew."

"She was right about that. Though I'm going to try to be less stubborn and more flexible going forward. We'll see how it goes. An old dog and new tricks."

"You know, I don't think we're ever too old to learn." Julie smiled. "That is, if we want to. Thanks again, Carol, for all the encouragement you gave me this summer."

Julie couldn't be sure, but she thought she saw the glimmer of a tear in her aunt's eye.

"Don't mention it," Carol said, standing abruptly. "Now, how about something to drink?"

Chapter 141

"All the wonderful summers we spent as children in this house." Bonnie shook her head.

"All our summers together add up to an awful lot of memories," her sister noted. "By the way, have you chosen a Realtor yet?"

"No," Bonnie admitted. "There's some work that needs to be done to the cottage before I can put it on the market. There's a chance it might be ready this fall but if not, then I'll wait until spring to list it."

"There's no rush," Carol said. "Ferndean isn't going anywhere."

"But there is something that needs to happen quickly," Bonnie said. "Replacing Dad's and Mom's armchairs!"

"My back," Carol said, "thanks you. By the way, I noticed the garden gnomes have found a home in the herb garden."

"I know you don't like them but—" Bonnie began.

"But the house is yours. Actually, the more I think about it the more I . . ." Carol laughed. "Okay, I still don't like them. But take a look at this. I hunted down Dad's shell collection." Carol lifted the flaps of a dusty cardboard box that sat on the maroon-colored couch to reveal hundreds of shells piled haphazardly one on top of another.

"I often wondered why Mom put them away after Dad died," Bonnie said, peering into the jumble. "Maybe the shells were too painful a reminder of him. Or maybe she just didn't like them. But what's not to like about seashells?"

"It's a pretty eclectic mix," Carol noted. "Anyway, I thought you might want to make something out of the smaller ones, like a mirror frame or a collage."

"I thought you didn't like crafty art," Bonnie said, examining a particularly delicate shell with a pale-pink interior.

"It doesn't really matter what I like or don't like," Carol said. "I just thought that Dad's collection might deserve to be seen and enjoyed."

"I agree. I'll think about what I can do with these."

Carol reached for her bag. "Well, I'm off. Judith and I are going to a gallery opening in Portland. The artist is one of her friends."

"Will you be back for dinner?" Bonnie asked.

Carol shrugged. "Depends on Judith," she said. "She might want to hang around in Portland for a while after the show. How about I call and let you know?"

"Don't feel pressured," Bonnie said hastily.

Her sister smiled. "I won't."

When Carol had gone, Bonnie surveyed the living room she knew so well and realized she felt every inch a true caretaker of the old house and its property, proud and protective. But if she was the Caretaker, Carol was the Hero of this chapter of their lives, and Bonnie was fine with that. She had decided not to tell anyone that before Carol had handed over the ownership of Ferndean House, Bonnie had already decided to relinquish her share of the homestead.

Let Carol enjoy the limelight and the accolades that went with it. The limelight was her home.

Bonnie left the house and went to look once again at the scanty remains of Marcus Ascher's unfinished project. She was eager to see it come to life. Carol had suggested that once the project was complete they donate the plans to the Yorktide Historical Society. Bonnie thought it was a wonderful idea. She could imagine Terry Brown giving a lively lecture on the subject of architectural follies or Victorian visual symbolism.

Carol had had another good idea. She had offered to act as Bonnie's agent, reaching out to her client base for custom quilt projects. And, thanks to Cindy and Adelaide's enthusiasm, starting after Labor Day Bonnie would be giving advanced sewing lessons at The Busy Bee and manning the shop ten hours a week. She would be too busy to dwell on what might have been if Ken had lived.

But never too busy to *miss* Ken. That was okay. Ken should not be forgotten.

No one should be forgotten.

Bonnie knelt on the grass and touched one of the old stones Marcus had laid all those years ago.

Life was good. Her life was good.

Please turn the page for a very special Q&A
with Holly Chamberlin!

Q. The first and most obvious question to ask is, do you have a sister?

A. No! I have a brother who is exactly two years younger than me. I have to say I've never missed having a sister and maybe that's because Joey and I are so close. Of course, I know lots and lots of sister pairs and groups, so I've had ample opportunity to watch and learn.

Q. Though you've featured characters over the age of fifty in other books, why did you choose to focus primarily on characters the age of sixty-two and sixty-five in *All Our Summers?*

A. For lots of reasons. One, I'm fifty-seven, closing in on sixty, and I'm here to say our lives are valid and interesting! And let's be real. Mature women are major readers. Well, all women are; we rock. Novels should feature characters that readers can relate to. At least, that's how it seems to me.

Q. The second obvious question to ask is, do you have a family homestead on the order of Ferndean House?

A. That's another no. I'm not particularly sad about that, though once I might have been. At this point in my life, I think first of the huge cost of keeping an old place up and running, and I'm glad I was spared that responsibility. Still, the idea is undoubtedly a romantic one. And I'd welcome a ghost or two! I'm far more frightened of the living than of the dead.

Q. The intergenerational family dynamic is a theme you've explored in several novels. Can you tell us why this attracts you?

A. I think I'm drawn to depicting several generations of a family interacting because I was raised in a family where grandparents and great-aunts and uncles were integral figures at any gathering, whether it was a casual Sunday dinner or a holiday celebration. In fact, I remember my great-aunt Kate telling me when I was very young that I would one day be a poet. (I did write poetry for many years.) Socializing with people of all ages was the norm and continues to be for me. It's good to have a strong sense of who has come before and who is coming after. Life doesn't feel so lonely that way.

Q. Can you tell us anything about your next book?
A. The next project will be a bit of a departure for me, as I'll be telling a story that has its roots in an earlier time. Flashbacks and/or a split narrative will happen. As will a crime! I'm afraid that's all I can say for now. Wish me luck!

ALL OUR SUMMERS

Holly Chamberlin

ABOUT THIS GUIDE

The suggested questions are included to enhance your group's reading of Holly Chamberlin's *All Our Summers*!

DISCUSSION QUESTIONS

1. Much time in *All Our Summers* is spent discussing (and arguing about!) the notions of sentimentality and nostalgia. Talk about how the Ascher sisters differ in their response to the past. For example, Bonnie seems to revere it as a time of perfection and Carol to reject it as of little or no value to the present. How are their attitudes shown to be far more complicated and nuanced?

2. How much of a hardship do you think it was for Bonnie and Ken to raise Nicola from the age of fifteen? What sacrifices might have been required of them they might have resented? We learn that Carol paid a sum of money to Bonnie and Ken over and above Nicola's expenses, so financial woes would not have figured into the mix. In the end, do you think there was a significant downside to the arrangement? After all, it's one that many families through the ages have adopted in one form or another.

3. Do you think that Nicola will find a sense of grounding now that she knows her biological father? Do you think she will continue to struggle with the fact of her parents' (perhaps) unusual arrangement? Nicola tells us she's not very in touch with her instincts, but by the end of the story she realizes she's not so out of touch with them after all. How might this better self-knowledge help her going forward? In what ways is Nicola like her aunt Bonnie?

4. Talk about the primary nature of the sibling bond and how a good or bad relationship with a sibling can affect the health of later friendships and romantic relationships. Some studies have shown that childless people foster stronger bonds with their siblings than people with children. Is this true in your experience?

5. Carol tells us that for several years she struggled with an addiction to opioids after a major surgery. So many people in this country are currently battling similar addictions to prescription painkillers. For Carol, though the addiction is behind her, the habits of secrecy and shame linger. What are other ways in which the power of an addiction might linger in a person's life?

6. Talk about Judith's role as cousin to the Ascher sisters. At times, she acts as confidant; at others, as critic; and at others, as mediator. Do you see her as the true matriarch of the family? Clearly, the family considered Ken Elgort the patriarch and are still adjusting to the changes wrought by his death. Do you think that Scott Miller might one day rise to this position? Does the family necessarily need a new patriarch? Do you think families suffer from the lack of an older generation at the helm?

7. "The golden age is before us, not behind us."—*William Shakespeare*. Talk about our culture's views on aging in terms of discrimination versus respectful acknowledgment; in terms of the pressure put on women to try to reverse the natural process of aging; in terms of increased longevity and what that means for one's emotional and financial future. What do you foresee for Carol, Bonnie, and Judith as they grow older?

8. What do you make of Julie not seeking professional help for her depression? Can you understand her family's mixed feelings of concern and annoyance? How much did Sara Webb's support of Julie's professional abilities contribute to her healing? Do you think Julie was brave or foolhardy in approaching Laci Fox? Do you think that her choosing to forgive Scott for the affair was wise? In what ways is Julie like her aunt Carol? What do you foresee for Julie Miller going forward?

9. Consider Sophie and what she experiences through the course of the novel. Do you think that the love and support of her extended family will be enough to help her heal from the upheaval caused by her father's affair and her mother's subsequent depression, as well as from the trauma of her abduction by the older counselor? Do you foresee a difficult road for Sophie as she moves on through high school?

10. Who are your favorite sisters in literature? For example, is it the March sisters in *Little Women*; the Bennett sisters in *Pride and Prejudice*; or Merricat and Constance Blackwood in Shirley Jackson's *We Have Always Lived at the Castle*?